## WITH S

"I prefer the n... ...ally managed to utter.

Joan nodded. "The loss of blood w... ...e feel light headed. Ye need to put something in yer belly besides whiskey."

She broke off a piece of bread, spread it with honey, then handed it to him. He stared at the offering, watching a drop of the golden nectar run onto her thumb. Unable to resist, Malcolm grabbed her wrist and licked the honey with the tip of his tongue.

Joan squealed and snatched her hand away. "Whatever are ye doing?"

"'Tis a sin to waste such fine food," he muttered innocently.

She narrowed her brows and stared at him in disbelief. Malcolm schooled his expression into angelic innocence, doubting he could fool her, but needing to try.

"If I dinnae know any better, I would swear that ye were trying to seduce me, Malcolm McKenna," she said, her expression taut.

"And if I were?"

**Books by Adrienne Basso**

HIS WICKED EMBRACE

HIS NOBLE PROMISE

TO WED A VISCOUNT

TO PROTECT AN HEIRESS

TO TEMPT A ROGUE

THE WEDDING DECEPTION

THE CHRISTMAS HEIRESS

HIGHLAND VAMPIRE

HOW TO ENJOY A SCANDAL

NATURE OF THE BEAST

THE CHRISTMAS COUNTESS

HOW TO SEDUCE A SINNER

A LITTLE BIT SINFUL

'TIS THE SEASON TO BE SINFUL

INTIMATE BETRAYAL

NOTORIOUS DECEPTION

SWEET SENSATIONS

A NIGHT TO REMEMBER

HOW TO BE A SCOTTISH MISTRESS

BRIDE OF A SCOTTISH WARRIOR

THE HIGHLANDER WHO LOVED ME

NO OTHER HIGHLANDER

**Published by Kensington Publishing Corporation**

# No Other
# HIGHLANDER

## ADRIENNE BASSO

## ZEBRA BOOKS
### KENSINGTON PUBLISHING CORP.
http://www.kensingtonbooks.com

ZEBRA BOOKS are published by

Kensington Publishing Corp.
119 West 40th Street
New York, NY 10018

All Kensington titles, imprints, and distributed lines are available at special quantity discounts for bulk purchases for sales promotion, premiums, fund-raising, educational, or institutional use.

Special book excerpts or customized printings can also be created to fit specific needs. For details, write or phone the office of the Kensington Sales Manager: Attn.: Sales Department. Kensington Publishing Corp., 119 West 40th Street, New York, NY 10018. Phone: 1-800-221-2647.

Zebra and the Z logo Reg. U.S. Pat. & TM Off.

First Printing: March 2017
ISBN-13: 978-1-4201-3769-9
ISBN-10: 1-4201-3769-7

eISBN-13: 978-1-4201-3770-5
eISBN-10: 1-4201-3770-0

10 9 8 7 6 5 4 3 2 1

Printed in the United States of America

*For my husband, Rudy*
*With much love and thanks for your constant support,*
*encouragement, and belief in me,*
*for proofreading every manuscript,*
*and for being my first—and still—number-one fan!*

DISCARDED

# Chapter One

*Highlands of Scotland, 1334*

"What is that god-awful smell?" Sir Malcolm McKenna wrinkled his nose and glanced down at his five-year-old daughter, Lileas, who stood at his side in the bailey of McKenna Castle.

The child sniffed loudly, then turned toward the faithful hound that was her constant companion. "It must be Prince. I think he needs a bath."

Hearing his name, the motley beast lifted his ears and cocked his head. Malcolm studied the large dog, yet saw no muck on his fur or paws. However, the hem of his daughter's gown was dark with filth and he suspected her shoes were even worse. She had clearly been in the stables, a place forbidden to her without permission.

Malcolm raised a brow. "Prince?"

"Aye." Lileas nodded her head enthusiastically. "Cook calls him a mangy, dirty cur when she chases him from the kitchens. But we love him anyway, don't we, Papa?"

The little girl smiled broadly at him, looking so like her mother that Malcolm felt a pang of melancholy. His arranged marriage to Margaret Douglas had been brief, and while not unhappy, had hardly been the relationship he sought.

He had wanted a wife who would challenge and excite him. Who had opinions of her own, was blessed with a sharp mind and high spirits. He wanted the close comradery of love and devotion his parents shared. And passion. Aye, he wanted a woman in his bed who would fire his blood and answer his kisses and caresses with bold ones of her own.

When they first married, Margaret had been sweet and kind and so eager to please at times it made him feel guilty for not returning her blind devotion. Over time, his lack of overt affection toward her brought on a clinging, almost desperate behavior that further distanced him from his wife.

She became quick to cry and even quicker to complain. Truth be told, he found his demanding wife exhausting. Perhaps they had wed too young. Perhaps in time he would have found a way to make her happy and in turn learned to give Margaret the love she so desperately craved.

Alas, he would never know for certain. Margaret had died of a sudden fever when their daughter was barely two years old. He mourned her passing with true emotion, knowing he owed his young wife an unimaginable debt of gratitude, for she had given him the most precious gift of all—a child.

It was not the son and heir that so many in the clan had hoped and prayed would arrive. In truth, many believed that Margaret had failed in her duty by birthing a daughter. But Malcolm knew they were wrong.

From the first moment he'd held Lileas's small, squirming body in his arms, Malcolm felt a rush of emotion so strong it had weakened his knees. To this day, every time he looked into the mischievous face of his daughter, his heart swelled with love.

He could not imagine his life without her—impish lass that she was—full of life and laughter and most assuredly the boldest child in all the Highlands. At least that's what his parents, and most of their clan, always told him. He knew that he spoiled and indulged her more than he should, but these early years of carefree childhood disappeared so quickly and he wanted to enjoy them as much as his daughter did.

Malcolm and Lileas made their way across the bailey, stopping in front of the heavy oak door that led to the great hall. Prince followed cheerfully behind them, his large tongue lolling out of the side of his mouth.

"Nay, Lileas, Prince cannae enter the hall smelling the way he does," Malcolm said. "Yer grandmother will have fits."

Malcolm folded his arms over his chest and waited for his daughter to confess that it wasn't the dog who smelled so foul, 'twas her.

Lileas turned to her pet, then gazed beseechingly at her father. "I can help draw the water from the well fer Prince's bath."

Malcolm shook his head. "I dinnae have time to bathe him now. Nor does anyone else," he added, anticipating her response. "He'll have to stay outside."

His parents were nearly as indulgent as he was when it came to Lileas, but even their generosity did not extend to bathing a dog that they insisted should be kept in the kennels and not allowed to sleep in Lileas's bedchamber beneath her bed. Besides, for once it was not the dog who smelled so rank, but the child.

Lileas frowned and pulled her bottom lip back and forth between her teeth. "Prince will feel very sad if he has to stay outside."

"Aye."

"He will probably start barking. Very loudly. He might even start to whimper and cry."

"More than likely."

Lileas's lips began to quiver. "I'll cry, too."

Malcolm's heart lurched at the sight of her watery eyes and he nearly relented. *Nay!* She had to learn to obey, if only for her own safety. She had been warned about the dangers of the stables, but had deliberately ignored the rule.

Thankfully, nothing tragic had befallen her, but what about the next time? Would she be so fortunate? His heart nearly ceased beating at the possibility.

"It will take more than a few tears to take the stench off Prince," Malcolm said casually.

Lileas rubbed her eyes with the back of her hand. "He doesn't smell *that* bad," she insisted stubbornly.

"But ye do." Malcolm leaned down, his broad nose nearly touching his daughter's. "How do ye suppose that happened?"

Lileas lowered her eyes and looked away. "Ye shouldn't say that I smell. Grandmother says it isn't polite to insult a lady."

"Aye, and a true lady doesn't lie. Especially to her papa," Malcolm said reprovingly.

Lileas chewed anxiously on her lower lip. "I'm sorry that I smell, Papa. May I have a bath?"

"Not until ye tell me how ye got this way."

The child took a deep breath. Then looking uncharacteristically serious, she declared, "I stepped in some horse muck."

"In the bailey?" Malcolm questioned, deciding to test her honesty.

Lileas's eyes lit with excitement. She opened her mouth to agree, then paused and lowered her chin. "Nay, Papa. The muck was in the stables. I brought carrots and apples for the horses."

Malcolm slowly exhaled with relief, then gave his daughter an understanding smile. "I know how much ye love being around the horses, but I've told ye many times that ye cannae feed them unless someone is with ye."

"Duncan was there!" Lileas protested.

"An adult," Malcolm clarified. "A lad of ten is hardly a proper escort around such fierce animals. Those horses are bred fer battle. A wee lass like ye can so easily be hurt."

"I'm always careful," Lileas insisted. "And the horses like me. They never hurt me. I feed them treats and sometimes weave flowers in their manes. They always look so pretty when I'm done."

Malcolm tried to mask his amusement as he pictured his father, the warrior laird Brian McKenna, riding into battle on a horse with delicate purple heather in its mane. "Nevertheless, ye must do as ye are told, Lileas."

"I'm sorry." Lileas heaved a long sigh. "'Tis not easy for a poor motherless child to always behave as she should. If I had a proper mother—"

"Lileas," Malcolm warned. "The lack of a mother is no excuse fer yer behavior, as ye well know."

Lileas hung her head and slowly drew her foot across the hard dirt. Malcolm could see the muck clumping around the edges of her halfboots and worried the leather would stiffen after it was thoroughly cleaned. Rigid boots meant blisters, and while not a severe condition, they could fester if not treated properly. He made a mental note to speak with the cobbler about having a new pair of boots made.

"Are ye very mad at me, Papa?"

Malcolm took a deep breath. Aye, he was angry. But that fierce emotion was quickly leaving him. No matter what her behavior, he simply found it impossible to stay mad at his daughter.

"Well, not as mad as I would have been if ye had continued to lie to me," he said, smoothing the hair on the top of her head.

The sudden sound of thundering hoofbeats coming hard and fast from beyond the castle walls pulled Malcolm's attention away from Lileas. No alarm had been sounded, but he saw several of the soldiers on the battlements rush forward. Concerned, Malcolm turned his gaze toward the heavy gate, waiting to see if it would be closed.

He reached automatically for his sword, dismayed to find it was not in its usual place at his side. Having just come from the practice field, he had given the weapon to his squire to clean and oil.

The dirk in his belt was a comfort; he was confident he could defend himself and protect his child, if needed. Yet realistically, Malcolm knew there was no cause for fear.

McKenna Castle was one of the best-fortified structures in the Highlands, boasting a high square watchtower, wide battlements, and a gray stone curtain wall that was nearly fifteen feet thick. Even in the unlikely event that an enemy was able to breach these impressive defenses, they would then be facing an army of McKenna soldiers, arguably the fiercest fighting men in all of Scotland.

A sizable contingent of men rode through the open

gates. Instinctively, Malcolm thrust Lileas behind him, but his rigid stance slowly relaxed when he recognized the man leading the riders.

"Uncle James!" Lileas screeched excitedly and took off at a run.

Malcolm grinned as he watched his younger brother dismount, then capture Lileas in his arms and swing her high in the air, before pulling her to his chest and hugging her tightly. Malcolm followed his daughter at a more dignified pace, unable to hold back his chuckle when he saw his brother wiggle his nose as he sniffed, obviously trying to decide from where a most unpleasant odor was emanating.

James quickly surmised it was Lileas, but to his credit, he still held her close. The lass giggled, twining her arms tightly around his neck as he swung her back and forth.

"What sort of mischief have ye been getting yerself into since I last saw ye, lass?" James asked, as he gently set her on her feet.

"None," she replied, lowering her chin. "I'm a very good girl and I always listen and do what I'm told." Malcolm cleared his throat loudly. His daughter turned to him with a mulish expression. "I try *very hard* to do what I'm told."

"That's all anyone can ask of ye." James reached over to grasp Malcolm's hand in greeting, but Lileas stepped between them.

"Where is Aunt Davina? Is she coming, too? And where is her baby? Is it here? I want to hold it. I promise to be very, very careful. Grandmother told me that I must pray fer them both, and I do, every night. I pray fer ye, too, Uncle James." The words spilled out of the child's mouth faster than she could speak them.

James put his hand on his niece's shoulder. "Aunt Davina is back at Torridon Keep, waiting fer the bairn to arrive. But it will still be many months before it comes."

"I hope it's a lass," Lileas declared. "Like me."

"Och, Lileas, there's none like ye," James said with a laugh, as he ruffled the child's hair.

"And fer that we all give thanks," the McKenna declared, interrupting the reunion.

Their father, laird of the McKenna clan, stepped forward and slapped James on the shoulder affectionately. James barely had time to greet his father before their mother came rushing over. She launched herself forward, hugging her son tightly.

"Why did ye not send word that ye were coming?" Lady Aileen scolded, as she patted James's cheek. "Is Davina with ye?"

"Nay, Mother, she is safely resting at home."

"'Tis best, I suppose, but I would have longed to see her." Lady Aileen's face darkened. "Why dinnae ye send word of yer arrival? If I had known, I would have instructed Cook to prepare all yer favorite dishes."

"Enough of yer fussing, Aileen," the McKenna grumbled. "James will simply have to make do with the swill ye were going to serve the rest of us."

Malcolm exchanged an amused glance with the McKenna, as their mother's jaw dropped in indignation.

"Ye had best be minding yer manners, Brian McKenna," Lady Aileen answered tartly. "Or else I'll make certain that tonight yer trencher is filled with a meal fit only fer the hogs."

There was an instant of tense silence in the busy courtyard. The McKenna glared at his wife. Lady Aileen glared back.

The McKenna broke first, his broad, sun-kissed face

widening into a deep grin. Lady Aileen answered that grin with one of her own, then lifted her cheek for her husband's gentle kiss.

Malcolm watched them with a mixture of confusion and awe. All his life he had witnessed the intense passion between his parents—in nearly every interaction. They fought and made up with equal fervor and yet through it all somehow maintained a level of respect and regard.

Having been married himself, Malcolm honestly did not understand how this was possible. Perhaps it was love that held them so solidly together. Yet he knew it took more than mere affection and emotion. His parents were bound together by a thread so strong that no matter how hard it was pulled, it never seemed to break.

'Twas precisely the type of marriage that Malcolm had dared to hope he could create. Judging by the expression of devotion on James's face whenever his wife's name was mentioned, he believed that his younger brother was well on his way to achieving that kind of relationship.

Clearly, it was not so very rare. It was possible to find. With a melancholy sigh, Malcolm realized that he simply had to keep searching.

James gestured for one of the knights in his party to come forward. "I would like to introduce Sir Gideon Croft. Gideon, this is my father, Laird McKenna, my mother, Lady Aileen, and my older brother, Malcolm."

"'Tis an honor to meet you all," Sir Gideon said as he executed a deep, formal bow.

Lileas poked James sharply in his side with her elbow. "What about me?"

"Och, forgive me, lass." James laughed. "Though I believe that Sir Gideon already knows yer name."

"He does?" Clearly delighted at the notion, Lileas craned her neck and gazed at the tall, handsome knight.

"Does he also know I like horses and dogs and more than anything in the whole wide world, I want a new mother?"

"I do now." Sir Gideon bent his knee and twirled his hand dramatically in the air. "'Tis a great honor to make yer acquaintance, Lady Lileas."

Lileas dipped her chin and favored him with a flirty smile. "No one ever calls me Lady Lileas. I like it!"

Everyone laughed. Well, everyone except Malcolm. He was not amused by his daughter's coy, flirty attitude. Only five years old and already practicing her feminine wiles! Perhaps she did need a mother to take her in hand.

"I bid ye welcome to McKenna Castle, Sir Gideon," Lady Aileen said.

"Ye're not a Highlander," the McKenna observed, his eyes narrowing.

Sir Gideon rose slowly from his bow. "No, Laird. My mother was French. I'm only half Scots."

"The better half," James quipped.

There was a tense bit of laughter. "I fought in the Crusade beside your son, Laird McKenna," Sir Gideon said.

"Aye, and saved my arse a time or two," James added.

He smiled warmly at his friend and the tension slowly eased. Highlanders were naturally suspicious of any that were not their own, but James's approval assured Sir Gideon's acceptance. At least for now.

"Come inside and warm yerselves by the fire," Lady Aileen said, as she entwined her arm with James's.

Malcolm felt an unexpected twinge of jealousy at her obvious favoritism, yet could understand her need to hold her second son close. For five years James had been away from them, fighting in the Crusades. He had returned last year, married soon after, then moved to take command of his wife's keep.

Though happy to have him back on Scottish soil, Lady Aileen often lamented the journey to see James and Davina took a fortnight—if the weather was fair. But the usual Highland rains and muddy roads that were so much a part of daily life added days of discomfort to the trip.

Given her choice, Lady Aileen would be content to have all her adult children—and grandchildren—living within their solid castle walls. Yet she understood James's need for independence, often remarking on how proud she was of the success he had achieved in making his wife's formerly neglected estate thrive.

Once inside the great hall, Malcolm signaled for one of the maids. "Make certain Lileas is thoroughly washed and changes into clean garments," Malcolm instructed. "And clean shoes."

The maid scrunched her nose at the offensive odor wafting off the child, yet offered Lileas her hand. His daughter gave him a pleading glance, but Malcolm stood firm, crossing his arms to show her he meant business.

Lileas's small hands curled into defiant fists as her pleading turned to a glare. Malcolm never blinked. Lileas's face began to turn red, but the maid intervened before the child's fit of temper could be aired.

A small grin escaped Malcolm's lips as he watched his silent, pouting, rank-smelling daughter being led away.

James took a seat on the dais and gestured for Sir Gideon to do the same. Their mother sat beside James, her hand resting possessively on his arm, as though she feared he would vanish if she wasn't touching him.

The McKenna seated himself on the large chair, then waved his hand, and the few men gathered in the hall moved away to allow the laird privacy.

"Is all well? How does Davina fare?" Lady Aileen inquired.

"Getting bigger every day," James answered with a grin. "And bossier."

"A pregnant wife is both a joy and a challenge," Malcolm agreed, proud that his voice remained deep and steady.

The sharp jab of emotion he had experienced when he learned that Davina carried a child had surprised Malcolm, and he was relieved that given time, he was able to successfully bury it.

Yet feeling his mother's keen eyes upon him, Malcolm averted his gaze. There were times when she made him feel as though she could read his thoughts and he certainly didn't want to share them now. He was glad of his brother's happiness—truly. But the occasional pangs of disappointment that Davina had chosen James over him still lingered.

"Sir Gideon has journeyed here from the far north," James said. "He brings troubling news concerning our family."

James lowered his head, then cast a quick, sidelong glance at his brother. Their eyes met for an instant and a sudden sense of foreboding crept down Malcolm's spine. He shook it off, yet traces remained. This had to be something very important to drag his brother away from his pregnant wife's side.

"Tell us this news, Sir Gideon," the McKenna commanded.

Sir Gideon turned to the laird, his handsome face lined with concern. "As James has said, I was in the north these last few months and heard a most distressing tale about your family."

Sir Gideon grew silent as several servants approached,

bearing trays of food, wine, ale, and whiskey. The moment they placed the bounty on the table, the McKenna hastily shooed them away.

"Ye were saying," the McKenna prompted.

Sir Gideon drew in a troubled breath. "The MacPhearson laird has placed a bounty on Sir Malcolm's head."

Malcolm slammed down his tankard of ale so hard half the contents spilled onto the table. "What?"

"'Tis true," Sir Gideon insisted solemnly. "I heard it from several different men, including one who serves in the MacPhearson guard."

"A bounty? Fer what reason? I've never done anything to the MacPhearsons to warrant such treatment!" Malcolm cried indignantly.

"He claims it is retribution for the dishonor that you have placed upon his clan. Specifically, his youngest daughter, Brienne." Squirming slightly, Sir Gideon pushed the hair away from his face. "A few months ago, she gave birth to a bastard child. They say that you are the father."

Malcolm sat back in his chair, too stunned to reply. *A bastard child? My bastard child?*

The McKenna's eyes drifted over Sir Gideon. "Are ye certain that ye heard this right?"

"I am. The bounty is set at a princely sum and word is spreading," Sir Gideon replied. "It won't be long until men hoping to collect it will arrive on your lands."

"Is that why ye are here?" the McKenna inquired smoothly. "To collect the bounty on my son?"

"Father! James pushed back his chair and rose to his feet. "Gideon is a trusted friend. He comes here today as a favor to me."

"And we are grateful fer it, aren't we, Brian?" Lady Aileen placed her hand on James's arm and gently guided him back into his seat.

"I take no offense at your suspicions, Laird McKenna," Sir Gideon said. "It is a reasonable assumption. But I give you my word of honor that I will never take up arms against a McKenna. I owe James my loyalty and I take that oath most seriously."

"Thank ye, Sir Gideon," Lady Aileen said with a gracious smile. "We are indeed indebted to ye."

The McKenna nodded warily, then raising an inquiring eyebrow, turned toward his eldest son. "What do ye have to say fer yerself, Malcolm? Is this tale untrue? Or could the bairn be yers?"

Malcolm was too shocked to be insulted by the question. Frowning, he scratched his head, searching his mind for a memory. "I dinnae recall ever meeting any of the MacPhearson lasses."

"What about last year's spring fete?" James asked. "Members of all the clans were in attendance. Could ye have met the lass then?"

"'Tis possible, but I certainly would have remembered," Malcolm replied strongly, his voice reverberating off the high stone walls.

Yet, in all honesty, he couldn't be certain. Spending several weeks prior to the fete at his brother's keep had left Malcolm in a peculiar mood. It had been difficult continually witnessing the love and affection James shared with his new wife, a woman whom Malcolm had once hoped to claim as his own.

The initial relief he had experienced when finally escaping their company had caused some rather uncharacteristic behavior. He had forgone the tournaments and mock battles at the fete—events he generally enjoyed—and instead spent far too much of his time indulging in the fine whiskey that flowed so freely. And flirting with all the pretty lasses.

Was it possible that he had bedded the MacPhearson lass when he was too drunk to remember? That shameful prospect left a bitter taste on Malcolm's tongue.

"Malcolm? What can ye tell us of the fete and the Lady Brienne?"

His mother's questioning voice pulled Malcolm from his musing. He felt the heat of a blush rise to his cheeks as he glanced at her. She narrowed her brow, making him feel like a green lad of fifteen. Swallowing hard, he looked away.

"Ye can speak honestly in front of yer mother," the McKenna declared. "'Tis better if she hears the words directly from ye, fer it will spare me the burden of trying to remember all that ye said. She badgers me endlessly if I leave out anything."

"Aye, there are no secrets when it comes to my children," Lady Aileen said, leveling an open look at her son. "I want the whole truth, Malcolm. Dinnae think ye need to spare my sensibilities. I'm familiar with the particulars of a man's needs and desires."

All eyes turned expectantly toward Malcolm. The heat in his face rose higher, yet seeing there would be no reprieve, Malcolm cleared his throat. "I do recall that there were a few women that captured my . . . hmm . . . interest."

"Ye bedded them?" Lady Aileen asked bluntly.

Feeling thoroughly uncomfortable, Malcolm nodded his head.

"They were willing?" his mother questioned.

"Of course!" Malcolm replied hotly.

Lady Aileen raised one eyebrow. "Experienced?"

Malcolm barely stifled a groan, then turned a desperate eye toward his father.

"Och, Aileen, ye dinnae think that any sons of mine

have to pay a woman fer companionship?" the McKenna bellowed.

"That's not what I meant," Lady Aileen challenged. "I assume these females were widows, not virgins."

"God's teeth, Aileen," the McKenna shouted even louder. "Malcolm's got enough sense in his head not to be getting himself involved with maidens! Don't ye, Malcolm?"

Malcolm rubbed the stubble on his jaw and wondered if it were possible for the floor to open, just a wee crack, so that he might slip down into it and never be seen again.

"The MacPhearson laird is not only claiming that his daughter was seduced, but that she was promised marriage," Sir Gideon interjected. "That's why the bounty will only be paid if Sir Malcolm is delivered alive."

Malcolm's head snapped up, jerking sharply, as though someone had struck him. "I might have been in my cups during the celebration, and spent a few of my nights sharing my bed with a woman, but I most certainly would have recalled proposing to one," Malcolm declared.

"Hmm, I wonder," Lady Aileen said wryly.

Vexed, Malcolm ran his fingers anxiously through his hair while muttering under his breath.

"If they claim there were promises of marriage, the MacPhearsons are searching fer more than justice," the McKenna remarked, his voice hard.

"Why would the laird lie so publicly?" James asked. "These words bring dishonor to his daughter and his clan."

The McKenna's eyes flashed with confusion. "Laird MacPhearson has approached me in the past about forming an alliance. He wanted to broker a betrothal between his son and yer sister, Katherine."

"Ye were opposed to the idea?" James asked.

The corners of the McKenna's lips twitched slightly. "Not entirely. But yer mother wouldn't hear of it."

"Katherine was four years old at the time," Lady Aileen replied tartly. "I'll not have any of my children married off without having a say in the matter. Especially my only daughter."

"Well, if he wants to form an alliance now, he's going about it in a most peculiar fashion," Malcolm grumbled. "I'll not be forced to wed a woman I dinnae know, nor claim a child as my heir unless I know that it is truly mine."

"Perhaps he is acting in good faith," Sir Gideon suggested. "Perhaps it is the daughter who is lying and Laird MacPhearson is merely trying to protect his child."

"Perhaps." Malcolm took a long sip of his ale, searching for an elusive inner calm. "Or perhaps he is looking for a reason to attack us."

"If it's a fight they want, then we can easily accommodate them," James declared passionately. "Let them see fer themselves how truly formidable the McKennas are when they are falsely accused."

"Calm down, James," Lady Aileen admonished. "I'll not be sending my sons into a bloody battle over something this foolish."

"With respect, Lady Aileen, the MacPhearson laird is not taking this lightly," Sir Gideon said. "He has named a sum that will entice many men to try and capture Sir Malcolm."

"We cannae let this accusation go unanswered, but we also cannae allow these feelings of injustice and vengeance to fester and spread among the other clans." The McKenna stroked his chin thoughtfully. "Especially now that the English king, Edward III, has crowned a pretender, Edward Balliol, to the Scottish throne. Our loyalties must remain with our young King David II, even as he seeks refuge in France. He shall return one day and he willnae be able to rule a country divided by clan war."

"Mayhap that is part of the MacPhearson's plan," Sir Gideon suggested.

"Whatever the reason, 'tis an insult to Malcolm and a slight to our honor," James argued.

"If it's untrue," Lady Aileen said softly.

Malcolm clenched his jaw as a surge of mortification rose on his neck. Though his mother insisted she wasn't shocked by these events, he had grown steadily uncomfortable under her sharp perusal.

"I believe that it is a false claim. Yet I'll need to see the lass to be completely certain," he admitted.

The McKenna leaned back in his chair and stared up at the rafters. "We need someone to broker the peace, to gather both sides together and resolve this matter amicably."

"You'll need someone impartial, yet they must be trusted by both sides," Sir Gideon added.

The McKenna nodded in agreement. "I want a clan that is allied with us who also has ties with the MacPhearsons."

"What about the Armstrong clan?" Lady Aileen suggested. "Their alliance with the MacPhearsons has held fer generations."

The McKenna cocked his head. "An astute choice, my dearest. We are related to the Armstrongs through James's marriage to Davina, but best of all, Laird Armstrong owes us a debt. It appears the time to collect it has arrived."

# Chapter Two

Lady Joan Armstrong gazed out the long, narrow, stone window and sighed. The blue sky was edged with dark, ominous, gray clouds, the wind howling with growing intensity. The spring storm that her maid, Gertrude, had predicted by her aching bones appeared ready to arrive at any moment.

For once, Joan welcomed the stormy weather, as it perfectly matched her stormy mood. What a dismal week! It felt as though nothing had gone smoothly, except that her young son was finally recovering from his cough and fever.

She felt tired down to her bones, but she had duties to attend to that would not wait. She was responsible for running the Armstrong Castle household and could ill afford to give her father cause for complaint. He had begrudgingly taken her and her child under his roof when Joan left her husband over a year ago and made no secret of the fact that he would relish any reason to send her packing.

Joan knew that she must never give him any cause. At least not until she had somewhere else to go. That thought brought a rare ironic smile to her lips. She might find sanctuary in a convent, but that idea was thoroughly unsuitable, given her character. Yet more importantly, if she locked herself away behind abbey walls, she would be unable to bring her two-year-old son, Callum, with her.

He would have to be left behind. Somewhere. She leaned against the cold stone wall, suddenly dizzy at the very thought. Her child was unquestionably the only bright spot in her life; without him there would be little reason to rise in the morning.

What she craved was a household of her own, but that would only happen if she married again. A shiver of disgust and fear ran down her back. Nay, never again would she give a man such power over her person, would she render herself so vulnerable.

She had entered into her marriage to Laird Archibald Fraser with blind naïveté, unaware of his true character. Four years later, she had barely escaped with her life and knew the odds of being so lucky a second time were slim.

Of course, not all men were monsters. Just the majority of them.

Her cousin Davina was married to James McKenna. The second son of the powerful McKenna clan, he seemed to be an honorable man, yet one could never be certain.

James was clearly besotted with Davina and she with him, but the glow of passion would eventually fade, leaving Davina vulnerable. Lord only knew what would happen then.

"Ah, there ye are, Joan," a female voice declared. "Are ye hiding? I've had several pages looking all over the castle fer ye."

*Och, not now! I've a pounding headache and too little sleep fer four nights running. The last thing I need is this annoying hussy.*

"Good afternoon, Agnes." Joan turned slowly and

regarded the woman who stood before her with a critical eye. "Why such a fuss finding me? Has something happened?"

At twenty-six, Agnes was but a year older than Joan, but her face and figure looked much younger. She was short and slender, with a pale complexion, deep blue eyes, and bright red hair. Her features were pleasant, but her voice possessed a natural shrillness that grated on the nerves.

The three weeks that she had been in residence at Armstrong Castle had been a trial for Joan. Lady Agnes had come here with the hope of making a match with Joan's father, Laird Armstrong. Nothing had formally been decided, but the possibility that her widowed sire might in truth take this woman as his new wife was a dilemma Joan preferred not to consider, as the result would have dire consequences for her.

If he had a wife to run his household, what need would he have for Joan? Even more distressing—if he sired a son off this woman, what chance would Joan's lad have of one day becoming laird of the Armstrong clan?

"Yer father has received a letter from Laird McKenna," Agnes said. "There appears to be some sort of dispute between the McKennas and the MacPhearsons and yer father has been called upon to negotiate a peaceful end. We need to prepare to host a large gathering of several clans. They arrive in a fortnight."

*We? Damnation! Agnes must be far more confident in her ability to secure a marriage proposal from my father than I thought.*

"There is much to be done to prepare fer a visit of that magnitude," Joan conceded. "But there is plenty of time to see that all is in order."

A hint of delight rose in Agnes's eyes. "I have already taken things well in hand," she declared importantly. "As I knew that was what Laird Armstrong would have expected of me. He was very pleased when I told him."

"Then why do ye need me?"

Agnes nervously twirled a stray lock of her red hair. "Cook was rather distraught at what he declares is far too little notice to feed such a large number of men. He claims the stores are low and there is scant time to fill them. Ye'll need to speak with him right away."

Joan regarded Agnes with mock surprise. "But ye said that ye already have everything well in hand."

Agnes gave Joan a pained look. "I do. The serving wenches are airing the beds, sweeping the rooms, and washing the linens, so that we can house the lairds and the more important members of their entourage in the castle.

"New chairs are being built fer the dais, so that all who are entitled will have a proper seat at the high table. The garderobes are being cleaned, barrels of wine are being brought up from the cellars, and ale has been ordered from the alehouse."

"Whiskey?" Joan asked.

Agnes flushed. "We shall require more, along with fresh meat, vegetables, and bread. Cook feared that would prove difficult. Ye'll need to reassure him 'tis possible."

*Reassure him?* Joan smiled inwardly at that absurd notion. Cook was a large, burly man, with enormous biceps and a fondness for drink. No doubt he was well into his cups by this time of day and hardly in the mood to listen to Agnes's demands.

"Did he chase ye from the kitchen with a cleaving knife?" Joan asked casually. "Or a hot poker?"

"Nay! He wouldn't dare to treat me with such disrespect." Though she denied it most vehemently, Agnes's forehead creased with unease, revealing the truth of the matter.

Joan turned away, resisting the temptation to laugh. To keep the peace she would go to the kitchen, but she was not about to challenge Cook when he was in a drunken state. Instead, she would listen to him grumble and complain and then tell him to do his best.

When he sobered, the pride he took in his work, along with his desire to please the laird, and the clan, would get the job accomplished.

Of course, there was no need to share that bit of information with the overbearing Agnes.

Joan turned away from the window, then carefully made her way down the stone steps. She moved gracefully through the great hall with Agnes following close on her heels.

The kitchen was hot and filled with hazy smoke. Joan took in a deep breath, relishing the delectable smell of roasting venison that permeated the air. Under Cook's jaundiced eyes, two young lads struggled to turn the spit, which held the large haunch of meat, their faces red and sweating from their efforts.

There were baskets of spring vegetables resting on the stone floor, bits of damp, fragrant soil clinging stubbornly to their roots. Stacks of dirty bowls and a cluster of buckets were strewn next to the vegetables, resting precariously close to the blistering hearth.

Shirtless, Cook stood at a long wooden worktable, cleaver in hand, butchering a pile of rabbits. He glanced up when they entered the kitchen, then lowered his head and continued working. Mindful of the fresh blood dripping from his knife—and the bottle of whiskey at Cook's elbow—Joan kept a safe distance.

"I regret disturbing yer work, but Lady Agnes seems

to think ye cannae manage to feed the McKenna and MacPhearson clans when they arrive," Joan said, feeling a wicked gleam of satisfaction when she heard Agnes's gasp of horror.

Cook's upper lip curled. He hacked the head off another hare, then lifted his chin and stared hard over Joan's shoulder. She could almost feel Agnes's knees trembling. "Are ye saying that I cannae do my job, Lady Agnes?"

"Nay! I was merely concerned because ye seemed distressed when I told ye," Agnes answered.

"Did I?" Cook poured himself a large dram of whiskey, took a long sip, then rested the cup against his hip. "Ye were mistaken."

The words hung in the smoky air. Out of the corner of her eye, Joan could see Agnes's lips compress into a thin, tight line. She doubted Agnes had ever encountered a servant like Cook and clearly the woman had no idea how to manage him.

"Perhaps Lady Agnes should take an inventory of the larder?" Joan suggested, knowing full well how possessive Cook was about all aspects of his kitchen.

"She's welcome to try," Cook replied. He drained his cup, picked up his cleaver, and resumed his butchering.

Joan turned. "Agnes?"

She could clearly see Agnes's jaw move as she ground her teeth. "As ye are more familiar with the stores, I think that task should fall to ye," Agnes muttered.

Joan's brow lifted. "Truly? Well, if ye insist, then I shall take over from here. Oh, and do be sure to let my father know. As it is what he expects of me, I'm sure he'll be very pleased."

Agnes's back stiffened at hearing her own words being flung back at her. "I was hoping that we could work together. That, above all else, would please the laird."

"I'll do the work and ye'll take the credit?" Joan asked, with a knowing scowl. "Is that what ye had in mind?"

Agnes tossed a fierce glare back at her. "Ye would be wise to show me some respect and deference."

"Really? Why?"

Agnes drew herself up to her full height, yet the gesture was almost comical, as she was nearly a full head shorter than Joan. "Soon, I shall be chatelaine here and all will be obeying my orders, including ye."

Joan's shoulders tensed and she could feel her eye begin to twitch. She shot a dark look over her shoulder at Cook, who shrugged with disinterest.

"Och, have I missed the reading of the banns?" Joan asked, her steady voice reverberating through the thick stone kitchen walls.

There was a muted gasp from one of the kitchen lads, who must have let go of his end of the spit, for it was quickly followed by a yelp of distress from the second lad. Their reaction sent a trickle of triumph through Joan, pleased to confirm that her barb had hit the mark if these young lads understood her.

Agnes's eyes widened and her mouth formed a circle of astonishment. Joan smiled inwardly. *God's blood, 'tis almost too easy to intimidate her.*

"Make no mistake, Agnes," Joan continued. "Ye aren't the first female to catch my father's eye, nor will ye be the last."

"I'm to be his wife," Agnes insisted, but her voice lacked its usual conviction.

"That remains to be seen."

Agnes's jaw lowered in shock. She started to speak, stuttered, then started shaking with rage. "I've tried to befriend ye. To be kind, considerate. But ye make it impossible. Ye're just as cold and haughty as they say. 'Tis no wonder Laird Fraser rid himself of ye."

Heat flew up Joan's cheeks. She hadn't liked Agnes from the first and her dislike grew stronger every moment she spent in her company. "Ye know nothing of my relationship with Archibald Fraser."

Agnes blanched, but stood firm. "I know enough."

Joan favored Agnes with a humorless smile. It seemed ever since Agnes had arrived—invaded, actually—there was precious little peace to be found. The woman needed gossip and intrigue to sustain her and she delighted in searching for both.

Unfortunately, Joan's unsavory past made her an ideal target. Few could understand why she had run from a young, handsome, accomplished laird like Archibald Fraser, though none questioned *his* decision to dissolve their marriage.

After Joan had returned home it had taken almost a year for the ugly speculation that had spread through Armstrong Castle like wildfire to die out. Yet with just a few pointed inquiries from Agnes, it had all been easily resurrected.

That alone was cause enough to resent her. But this self-important, all-knowing attitude was the final straw. Joan knew her wisest course of action would be to turn her back and ignore these comments, but she had always had difficulty walking away from an argument. That defiance had cost her dearly in her marriage, resulting in beatings administered by her husband that were so savage she couldn't walk for days.

"Ye are a small-minded, petty female lacking even the brains God gave a goose," Joan stated emphatically. "Yer so-called knowledge of my marriage is nothing but idle gossip, lies, and falsehoods. If I thought ye were a person of value or importance in my life, then I'd share the truth with ye, but I'll not waste my time or breath."

Agnes's face turned three shades of red. "I'll not stand here and be insulted by the likes of ye! Ye'll regret making an enemy of me," she promised. "When I am mistress here—and I will be—I shall take great delight in having ye thrown out—along with yer mangy brat."

Reflexively, Joan's arm raised to slap the foolish woman, but instead of striking her, Joan clenched her fist tightly and slowly counted to ten. She would not raise a hand against anyone, no matter how much they deserved it.

Agnes spun on her heel and hurried out of the kitchen, nearly tripping over a basket of vegetables on her way. The ensuing silence was broken only by the sound of Cook's chopping and the hiss of fat and drippings hitting the fire as the venison haunch was once again turned.

"'Tis ill advised to make an enemy out of her," Cook observed.

Still feeling agitated, Joan wheeled on him. "I know, but the woman would drive a saint to sin."

"Aye, Lady Agnes is a shrill one." Still clutching the bloody cleaver tightly in his fist, Cook lifted his arm and gestured expressively. "Her threats dinnae sound like idle ones. Ye'd best have a care."

Surprised at this rare show of support, Joan nodded gratefully. "Do ye think he will marry her?"

Cook shrugged. "Mayhap. The laird makes no effort to hide his desire fer a son and heir, and fer that, he'll need a young wife."

The truth of the words stung. "What about his grandson?" Joan asked. "He would make a fine laird."

"He's not an Armstrong; he's a Fraser," Cook answered bluntly. "Well, he was until his father disowned him. I dinnae rightly know what the lad is now."

"He has Armstrong blood," Joan insisted.

"Aye. Among others. Tainted blood most would say."

Joan's hopes fell. Sweet Virgin, there truly was no escaping her mother's legacy—for herself or her child! Isobel Armstrong had hidden her madness for years, but when it finally emerged, all were shocked and stunned at her actions. Joan, too, was sickened by her mother's deeds, though she had let no one see her true feelings.

Aye, Isobel had lost her wits and now the clan watched and waited to see if Joan would do the same. She saw how they looked at her, heard what they said about her. Sideways glances of curiosity and pity, mingled with a healthy dose of fear. Remarks made beneath their breath wondering if she carried the same madness as her mother and speculation on the possibility that she was as clever as her mother in hiding it.

They all appeared to be waiting, with an odd mix of anticipation and fear, to witness Joan taking leave of her senses. In order to survive, Joan had hardened herself against the unfairness of it, refusing to be defined by it. She prayed long and hard that her son would be spared the same fate.

'Twas heartbreaking to learn that he might not.

Of course, it hadn't helped her cause that in order to secure the annulment from her marriage, she had allowed her husband to vilify her. As neither she nor Archibald were too young, too closely related to each other, or already married to someone else, the only way to secure the annulment was by declaring that she was insane at the time of their marriage.

The outrageous lie hurt her pride, but 'twas a small price to escape the horror of being Archibald's wife. Or so she believed. She had been too desperate at the time to realize this action would have such severe consequences for her son.

Shame-faced, Joan admitted to herself that if it were the only path open to her to escape from Archibald, she would do it again.

"But Callum will be raised here, among the clan," Joan said, hearing the desperation seeping into her voice. "Surely in time, if he proves himself worthy to lead, they will accept him."

Cook slowly shook his head. "The clan makes no secret of their wish fer the laird to take another wife and produce a male heir. If he does, they will follow that lad, a true son of their laird."

Joan sighed with frustration. She always knew it would be an uphill climb to make Callum the Armstrong laird. But she believed that time was on her side. Callum was a young lad, barely two years old. She believed that as he grew, the clan would see that it was Armstrong blood ruling his head and strengthening his heart.

Apparently, this would prove to be harder than she thought. Yet Joan refused to believe it was impossible. There had to be a way to turn the opinion of the clan, to make them realize that Callum would be a capable, skilled leader. A man who could be trusted to act in their best interests.

If not, what would become of her son? The possibilities were almost too frightening to consider.

Turning her mind away from these fearful thoughts, Joan changed the subject, bringing herself back to the more pressing matters at hand. "Shall I take an inventory of the larder and make a list of what will be needed when the clans visit?" she asked.

"The laird willnae be pleased if we let them starve," Cook said. "Ye'd best take a look."

Joan straightened her skirt and stepped into the storeroom. With a practiced eye she quickly saw that Cook did indeed have cause for concern. There were barely enough provisions to adequately feed the current inhabitants of the castle for the rest of the week, let alone a large contingent of men.

The barrels of oats and wheat flour were only half full as were the wooden boxes of dried, salted fish. The pots of honey were nearly empty; the few cabbages nestled in a dirty basket looked old and wilted. The only items they seemed to possess in abundance were onions and turnips, two things her father despised.

Joan poked her head out. "I thought the men went hunting yesterday."

"Aye." Cook snorted. "Ye see before ye what they brought me."

Joan clucked her tongue. "A pitiful showing."

"I'll not argue that point with ye, milady." Finished with the hares, Cook wiped his bloody hands on a none-too-clean cloth. "They said they would go again this morning, but they brought back nothing else."

Joan frowned. While caring for Callum, she had been forced to neglect some of her regular duties. But it had only been a few days. The storeroom shelves should not be so barren. She would need to discover why. But first, she needed to solve the immediate food problem.

Joan returned to the larder. She removed a small key from the chain on her belt and unlocked the spice chest. The pungent scent stung her nostrils, but she was relieved to see a good selection. A deft hand with the right spice could elevate the most humble dish. Thankfully, Cook possessed one.

"We've plenty of rich spices to flavor the food," Joan said. "That should help. Now let's decide what we'll need to get done before the clans arrive."

Cook nodded. He poured himself another dram of whiskey, reached for a second goblet, poured a generous portion, then handed it to Joan. She hesitated, then accepted it. The liquor went down smoothly, burning her throat and warming her stomach. It made her a bit light headed, but also calmed her agitation.

'Twas only the second time she had drunk such a large amount of the potent liquor, but she suddenly understood why Cook—and other men—could become so fond of it.

Her mood much improved, Joan left the kitchen, confident that they would be prepared to feed everyone. Now all she needed to do was find more kitchen help. Cook disliked having the castle maids working in his kitchen. He claimed they were slow and clumsy, scurrying around him like frightened mice.

Truth be told, the wenches were terrified of his temper. Nay, it would be best to bring in women from the village. Older, confident females who would not be so easily intimidated by a bellowing, half-drunk man, even when he held a bloody cleaver in his hand.

Joan chuckled as she imagined the scene, deciding she would make herself unavailable to play the peacemaker and instead allow Agnes to sort out such matters. That would certainly provide some entertainment.

As she entered the great hall, Joan's mind turned to the reason for this gathering and she realized that Agnes had not told her. Most likely because she did not know.

The one thing Joan did know was that the McKenna clan was coming—which meant she would probably see Malcolm McKenna again. Her nose wrinkled at the thought. It had been over a year since she had last been in his company; they had both been staying at Torridon Keep. She with her cousin Davina; Malcolm was there because of his younger brother, James.

Both men had been suspicious and distrustful, doing little to hide their disapproval of her. Yet Joan hadn't cared. She had finally escaped Archibald and the nightmare of her marriage; the negative opinion and clear distaste she felt from the two knights was hardly something to concern her.

There was no denying that Malcolm was a handsome man, yet after living with Archibald, Joan had an inherent distrust of handsome men—well, any man, really. She did concede that Malcolm appeared more open and direct than others, but that meant little. During her stay, she had tried to avoid being in his company whenever possible and was usually successful.

Hopefully, she would be able to do the same during this visit. And hopefully, whatever business the clans were here to conduct would be resolved quickly and they would depart.

Then she would be able to turn her full attention toward getting rid of the incorrigible Lady Agnes.

# Chapter Three

Two weeks later, Joan stood concealed behind the stone at the far edge of the battlement wall, anxiously waiting for the guests to come through the gates of Armstrong Castle. She was exhausted from all the last minute preparations and annoyed that her father had been so close-mouthed with the details of this impending meeting.

Even at this late hour, she had no idea how many men each clan would bring or how long they would be staying. Frustrated at the lack of information, Joan had taken matters into her own hands, deciding she would simply count them as they arrived.

She had sent one of the pages as a lookout, instructing the lad to call her the moment the alarm bell was sounded and the first clan was spotted. He had done her bidding, but the gray skies and murky weather made it difficult to distinguish the number of riders in the distance.

Hence, she was forced to wait, tapping her foot impatiently as a steady, light rain fell, dampening her clothes. After what felt like an eternity, the riders drew closer. Squinting, she could see the McKenna banner cutting through the thick, misty rain like a blade, flying proudly.

Riding three abreast, the long column of mounted men behind it made an impressive sight.

With little effort, Joan spied Malcolm McKenna in the lead. Surrounded by an aura of untamed energy, he sat tall and proud on his large stallion, his dark hair gleaming in the rain. It had been over a year since Joan had last seen him, but he appeared much the same—lean, fit, and dangerous.

She appraised him with a detached air, conceding that most women would find him handsome. There was something about a square jaw, deep-set blue eyes, strong cheekbones, and a straight nose that females seemed to find irresistible.

Except for her.

Closing her eyes—and mind—to Malcolm McKenna, Joan began counting the men who rode behind him. She had just reached fifty when a commotion beyond the tree line pulled her attention away. Farther in the distance she could see another clan was fast approaching, gaining ground on the McKenna.

'Twas most likely the MacPhearsons, Joan assumed, though their numbers were considerably smaller.

Suddenly, the second group halted. Joan leaned forward, wondering if they were preparing for an attack. Her breath came hard as she imagined a battle in the open field. She glanced down the battlements at the Armstrong guards standing on the wall. The tension in their stance told her that they, too, had observed the scene and were thinking the same.

Joan's nostrils flared as she watched, but the McKennas kept riding at a fast pace and the other clan never moved. 'Twas clear that they were deliberately keeping their distance.

Sighing with relief, Joan tried to resume her counting, then cursed softly under her breath when she realized she didn't know where she had left off. Determined to do better with the next clan, she planted her feet firmly and leaned forward.

Finally, the second group advanced. Their banner also fluttered in the wind, but it was not the black and green of the MacPhearson colors. Nay, it was . . .

Joan's hands shook and a cold, deep fear seized her gut. *It cannae be!*

She blinked hard, refusing to accept what her eyes were seeing. Sweat beaded on her forehead. She leaned far over the battlements, staring hard at the plaid banner this group carried, straining to confirm what she feared the most.

She was so caught up in the intensity of the moment that she didn't hear the footfalls as a female figure stepped out of the shadows.

"Ah, I see that the Frasers have arrived," Agnes said in a syrupy tone. "Splendid! They weren't initially included, but I pointed out to yer father that it would be a grave insult not to extend them an invitation. Lord knows, with all the unpleasantness from yer marriage to Laird Fraser, the Armstrongs have already subjected them to enough humiliations. 'Tis past time to start building a truce between the clans. Don't ye agree?"

The dampness on Joan's brow turned into a cold sweat. *A truce?* She had never been so foolish as to expect her father to seek retribution for the harm done to her by her former husband, even though other men, better men, would never have tolerated such mistreatment of their daughters. But to welcome the monster who had abused her so cruelly into his home—aye, that betrayal cut deep.

"Is Archibald among them?" Joan croaked.

"I believe so," Agnes answered smugly. "He is, after all, their laird."

"Nay." The denial whispered past Joan's lips at the same moment her stomach knotted in a terror that thundered through her body. In her mind's eye she saw the life she had so carefully built for herself and Callum being slowly torn to shreds.

Agnes pressed her hand on Joan's shoulders. "Why, Joan, I believe that ye secretly pine fer yer husband. Isn't that sweet. Will ye not be pleased to see him?"

A shiver of nerves flashing like a thousand knife pricks ran over Joan's skin. Gasping, she pulled away. "Ye bitch!"

"Och, there's no need fer ye to be so vulgar," Agnes gloated. "I do agree that it might be awkward between the two of ye at first, but hopefully Archibald has forgiven ye fer being such a wretched wife. I'm sure it will be a most tender reunion. Why, he might even welcome ye back into his bed."

Pain clogged Joan's throat. Archibald wasn't capable of tenderness. Hell, he didn't understand the meaning of tenderness. Or gentleness. Or caring. He was a monster, a brute, and a tyrant.

Laird Armstrong was well aware of the extent of Archibald's violence toward her. The beatings Joan endured had come close to killing her. Yet her father had done naught to aid her. She shut her eyes against the painful edge of memory, refusing to let herself experience it all over again.

Returning to the present, Joan snapped open her eyes only to find herself under unwelcomed scrutiny. Agnes's gaze swept her face, taking in the distress etched on her features, clearly delighting in it. "In any case, I'm sure that Laird Fraser will be happy to see his son," Agnes concluded.

Joan lowered her eyes. The words infuriated her. Inwardly, she cringed at the thought of what Archibald might do to Callum. Yet she refused to give Agnes the satisfaction of seeing her anguish. Instead, she clamped her fingers on Agnes's arm, hoping she was digging into the flesh hard enough to leave a bruise.

"Ye are an evil, vile woman," Joan said, her voice low with fury. "One day soon, I shall take great delight in sending ye away from this castle and back to the demon that spawned ye."

The barb hit the mark. Agnes's eyes widened and her brows rose with indignation. Shaking off Joan's viselike grip, she pulled away and absently began rubbing her arm.

"Ye cannae speak to me that way!" Agnes cried.

But Joan had no time to spare. Callum was in danger; she had to protect her child. Gathering her scattered wits, Joan scurried away from the wall, knowing she needed to find Gertrude as soon as possible.

Callum had to be taken from the castle immediately and hidden somewhere in the village. Somewhere close. Somewhere the lad would be safe from Archibald's vicious eyes and cruel vengeance.

The clean smell of a gentle rain filled Malcolm's nose as he guided his horse along the muddy path. With a weary sigh, he brushed away the misting rain dripping down his forehead, hardly believing this was an improvement in the weather. The McKennas had been riding hard for nearly a week and this was the first day they were not slogging through a downpour.

His father had decided to bring a sizable contingent of men, no doubt as a show of strength. Malcolm appreciated the gesture, but was uncertain if so many men were truly needed. The ground shook from the pounding of their horses; the mud flew in all directions. None complained, but all were hopeful this wretched journey would end soon.

As they crested a small hill, Malcolm squinted through the drifting layers of thickening fog, straining for a glimpse of the stone walls of Armstrong Castle. He had only been here once prior and had a vague memory of it. James had described it as a rather bleak place, but he had suffered a great tragedy while at the castle, so Malcolm reasoned his brother's opinion was biased.

They rode down the hill and up a second one and Malcolm's heart skipped a beat when an austere, fortified stronghold came into view. Two squat towers surrounded by a thick curtain wall blended into the mist. There were no signs of life; no men to be seen on the battlements, no people milling about the gatehouse.

A banner hung limply in the wind, looking dejected. Gray walls that matched the gray of the fog gave the structure an almost dour appearance.

Startled, Malcolm heard the clanging sound of alarm bells and realized they had been spotted. Apparently, there was some life behind those thick walls. A part of him was hardly anxious to arrive and face the Mac-Phearsons, but a far stronger part wanted to confront the woman who had falsely accused him, deal with the matter, and then forget it. He fervently hoped things wouldn't turn violent, since the MacPhearsons were known to be tough, vicious fighters.

Then again, the McKennas gave as good as they got.

The wrong words, a real or perceived insult, a dishonorable gesture or slight, and swords would be drawn. This peaceful meeting could quickly turn into a series of sword fights, or even one messy battle, if Laird Armstrong couldn't keep the peace.

That was what Malcolm feared most of all.

He couldn't fully understand why his father had asked the Armstrongs to intervene in this matter. Laird Armstrong was not an especially strong leader nor had he demonstrated any particular diplomatic skills. Hell, the man hadn't been able to keep his own wife under control, and the willfulness of his daughter, Joan, was well known.

Yet for some reason, his father insisted this would be the best way to handle the matter. Malcolm was not nearly as certain, but he knew the wisest course of action was to trust his father's judgment. Laird McKenna had a sharp mind, along with an innate instinct for survival, and he was seldom wrong.

And yet, Malcolm still felt grim, burdened by a heavy weight on his shoulders. If any harm came to his family or his clan, it would be his fault.

"Ye look troubled, Malcolm."

Malcolm turned and found James riding beside him. His brother stared, concern crinkling the corners of his eyes.

"Wouldn't ye be, if ye were in my boots?" Malcolm asked.

"Aye." James grunted. "'Tis all a grand misunderstanding that will soon be set to rights."

Malcolm grunted. "From yer lips to God's ears."

James's eyes considered him thoughtfully for a long moment. "Is there any possibility that the lass speaks the truth?"

Malcolm stirred uneasily in his saddle. "I dinnae think the babe could be mine, but I'll not be certain until I set eyes on the mother." He leaned toward his brother and lowered his voice. "I did spend a good amount of my time at the fete drunk as a lord and my memories of all the events aren't particularly clear."

James's eyes darkened. "I dinnae care how far in yer

cups ye were—I know that ye'd never take advantage of a woman. If ye bedded the lass, then she was willing."

"Which means the child could be mine."

James shrugged. "A female who beds a man in that condition deserves little respect or consideration. Who knows, she might have set out to trap ye."

Malcolm rubbed his rain-soaked brow. "It doesn't matter. The result still leaves a bastard child. An innocent life caught in a mess that was none of his making."

James's mouth pulled into a grim line. "He'll not be the first."

"'Tis a hard, sorry life. We both know how difficult it was fer Uncle Ewan when he was a lad," Malcolm added, mentioning their aunt's husband.

The bastard son of an earl who refused to acknowledge the blood tie, Ewan had suffered physical and mental torment. To survive, he became an outlaw, raiding on his half brother's lands. He was eventually caught—and would have been killed—but thankfully his skillful sword was needed by Robert the Bruce.

"Aye, Uncle Ewan did suffer as a lad," James agreed. "I believe that makes him appreciate all the more the love he found with Aunt Grace."

"Ewan was lucky and he knows it." Malcolm could feel the lines deepen on his forehead as he furrowed his brow. "He was knighted by the king fer his service and given a small estate. Few bastards are granted such a rare privilege; many live a frustrating life of mockery and humiliation. I'll not allow any son of mine to endure such a bleak fate. I swear to ye, if there's even a small chance that the babe is mine, then I'll claim it."

"And the mother?"

Malcolm shook his head slowly. "I honestly dinnae know what to do about her. 'Tis true that I want to marry again, yet not under these circumstances. If we declare the babe is a McKenna, Father will want me to take him, so we can raise him properly. But a child needs a mother, as Lileas continues to tell me."

"Och, I cannae imagine her reaction if instead of bringing home the new mother she craves, ye return with a wee squalling babe in yer arms," James said with a smile.

Malcolm rolled his eyes. "My ears hurt just thinking of Lileas's dramatic wails."

"If it comes to that, I'll count myself lucky to be safe at home when Lileas hears the news," James replied.

"Ye should be home now," Malcolm said, guilt invading his heart at his brother's sacrifice. "Yer place is with yer wife."

James shook his head. "My place is at yer side."

"What of Davina? And yer child?"

James smiled. "Davina would have my head if I abandoned ye. Anyway, our babe willnae be born fer several months. I'll be home in plenty of time."

"We've got company," one of the men shouted. "A good-sized contingent of men are forming behind us."

"The MacPhersons?" Malcolm asked, twisting his head around for a better look.

"Nay," James replied. "I dinnae recognize the banner, but it isn't the MacPhersons."

"Father?" Both men called out to the McKenna at the same time, awaiting his command.

"They fly the Fraser banner," the McKenna answered. "Magnus and Duncan have dropped back to keep an eye on them. If they want a fight, we'll be happy to oblige. But fer now, we'll assume Laird Armstrong invited them, though I cannae understand why."

Malcolm grimaced. He had hoped this meeting would be a relatively private negotiation between the two clans, but alas, that did not appear to be the case. Mood souring even further, he turned his full attention toward the castle. The sooner they arrived and settled the matter, the sooner they could leave.

Under the watchful eye of the Armstrong men-at-arms, the McKenna men and their soldiers rode beneath the steel-tipped spikes of the raised portcullis. When they entered the bailey, they were greeted by a line of Armstrong men. Malcolm could feel their curious eyes upon him as he slowly dismounted.

None met his gaze directly; he wondered if they knew the reason for this gathering. Well, if they didn't know yet, they soon would; secrets were nigh impossible to keep in a castle, and a tidbit of gossip this salacious would be repeated over and over until there was no one new left to tell.

Malcolm straightened his shoulders and stood tall, determined to appear unaffected by their stares. Leaving their men to see to the horses, Malcolm, James, and their father followed the servant, who nodded respectfully, then opened the door to the great hall.

The rushes rustled beneath their feet as they entered. Laird Armstrong stood at the ready to greet them, a short, red-haired woman at his side. Malcolm briefly wondered why his daughter, Lady Joan, was not there, too. He had been under the impression that since her annulment, she ran the household.

"Welcome to Armstrong Castle," the laird said. "I hope that yer journey was a pleasant one."

His inane comments made Malcolm wonder how much his father had revealed about their feud with the MacPhearsons. Or perhaps Laird Armstrong was trying to appear impartial, as requested. Yet Malcolm had no doubt that the MacPhearsons had delighted in stating their side of the story. They were, after all, the aggrieved party in this instance.

Or so they believed.

"There was rain and mud," the McKenna answered. "As expected when spring comes to the Highlands."

Laird Armstrong's answering laugh was loud and forced. The McKenna's glare was sharp. Malcolm felt a wee bit of the tension in his neck and shoulders ease. His father had never been a man who suffered fools gladly. It was an amusing distraction to watch him struggle to remain cordial and keep a tight rein on his famous temper under these circumstances.

"Goodness, where are my manners?" the red-haired woman tittered. "Ye must be tired from yer long journey. The steward will show ye to yer chambers."

The McKenna turned his critical eye upon the female who had spoken, his assessing gaze wandering over her lush form. "Who are ye?" the McKenna asked bluntly.

So much for manners. As he tried to hold back his own gaffe, Malcolm heard James snicker beneath his breath.

The woman cringed at the McKenna's booming tone, yet still managed a weak smile. "I am Lady Agnes Stewart. A distant cousin."

"A cousin?" The McKenna stepped forward. His assessing gaze raked the woman from head to toe a second time. "Truly?"

Though the smile remained on her face, Lady Agnes moved back a few steps. Laird Armstrong frowned. "A cousin, though someday she might be more to me. Agnes has been a tremendous help preparing fer this meeting. The castle benefits greatly from a woman's touch."

"Aye, Lady Agnes has made her presence known in nearly every chamber," a female voice intoned. "Especially those above stairs."

Malcolm turned his head, recognizing the voice. *Lady Joan.* She sauntered into the great hall like a queen, head high, nose in the air. "Forgive my tardiness, Laird McKenna," Joan continued, walking boldly forward until she stood toe to toe with the warrior. "I was attending to my son."

She dipped a graceful curtsy, then rose. Malcolm resisted the urge to reach out and clamp his father's jaw shut. Their mother was a lovely woman, but few on earth could compete with the physical perfection of Lady Joan.

Though it seemed impossible, Malcolm conceded that Joan grew more beautiful every time he set eyes upon her.

"Davina sends her regards," James said, filling in the silence.

"I trust my cousin is in good health," Joan replied.

"Aye," James answered.

"Please let her know that I was asking fer her." Joan added with the barest of smiles, "Good day to ye, Sir Malcolm."

"Lady Joan."

As he bowed in greeting, Malcolm was struck anew at her effortless beauty. Her shining golden hair hung in a thick braid down the center of her back. Pulled away from her face, it showcased her perfectly formed, delicate features and emphasized the deep blue of her eyes.

Perched atop her head was an elegant gold circlet that held a short, gauzy, silk veil in place. It floated around her like a cloud, adding to the ethereal aura of her beauty.

Her skin was the color of fresh cream, smooth and radiant. Though he assumed that she was near to his own age of twenty-eight, Malcolm decided that she looked as young, fresh, and pure as a maiden.

If only her heart were as unblemished as her face.

As was the fashion, she wore a velvet gown of deep blue that molded her body snugly, accentuating an impressive bosom, small waist, and lush hips. Around her waist was a thick gold chain, studded with small red gems and a ring of keys, signaling that she was the chatelaine.

That, too, caught Malcolm's interest. Lady Agnes had clearly set her sights on taking on that role, yet apparently in the battle of female supremacy, Joan still held sway over the pretty, plump Agnes. He wondered idly if Joan would be able to retain control if her father married Agnes.

"Now that ye are finally here, Joan, ye may escort Laird McKenna and his sons to their chambers," Agnes commanded.

Malcolm quirked his brow at the order and the smug voice with which it was given, interested to see how Joan would react at being ordered to perform a task usually assigned to a servant.

"I would be honored," Joan answered smoothly, a slight edge of sarcasm in her tone. "However, while I'm doing that, ye'll need to attend to matters in the kitchen, Agnes. Cook has many questions about this evening's meal ye'll need to answer."

Lady Agnes blanched. She looked helplessly toward Laird Armstrong, but he ignored her. For whatever reason, Lady Agnes was fearful of performing this particular task.

And Joan's smug expression made it clear that she was well aware of it. Malcolm chuckled beneath his breath, admitting that he had been foolish to even consider that Joan would be defeated. *Ah, now that's the Joan I remember.* Though she was a prickly and often disagreeable female, he had long admired her courage and tenacity.

Malcolm watched Joan intently as she led them up

the narrow, winding stairs, his eyes taking pleasure in the tantalizing sight of her lovely, rounded backside. With a small grin, he noticed his father and brother doing the same.

"Here is the chamber fer ye and yer sons," Joan announced when they reached the top landing, stepping aside to allow the men to enter.

The McKenna walked in first. The room they entered was large, boasting a wide bed. To avoid the drafts, it was set on a raised platform and tucked neatly away in an alcove. An intricate tapestry hung on the stone wall behind it, keeping out the chill. A fire burned in the large hearth, yet the room still felt damp.

Wavy panes of glass covered the two windows. There was an arched doorway leading to a second chamber that was nearly as large as the first. Pallets and blankets were neatly set atop a carved chest that was pushed against the wall. Instead of rushes, there was a finely woven rug on the floor.

"Are these the laird's chambers?" the McKenna asked.

Joan paled. "Nay, milord. These were my mother's rooms."

Malcolm exchanged a glance with first James and then his father, not certain if being placed in these chambers was an insult or an honor. They were obviously the best rooms in the castle, after the laird's. But the deceased Lady Isobel had been revealed to be a madwoman.

So which was it—an honor or an insult?

Did the essence of her madness still remain within these walls? James's wry expression told Malcolm that his brother shared a similar thought.

"There's plenty of room fer all of us," Malcolm ventured, deciding he was not going to be offended.

"And the chamber is appointed with every comfort," James added, but they both knew it would be their father's decision if they stayed or asked for different accommodations.

The McKenna's lips twisted as he once again looked around the chamber. "We'll sleep well here," he declared. "Though if my sons' snoring keeps me awake, ye'll have to find somewhere else to put them."

Malcolm could see the tension in Joan's shoulders ease. He smiled. His father possessed an amazing ability to intimidate anyone at any time over anything. Well, except for his wife. In matters involving Lady Aileen, the McKenna wisely consulted, listened, and if necessary, capitulated. 'Twas the only way to keep peace in their household.

"Will ye take some refreshments in the great hall or would ye like me to have them brought to ye here?" Joan asked.

"We'll avail ourselves of the Armstrongs' hospitality in the great hall," the McKenna declared, fixing her with a cold stare. "I am anxious to speak with Laird Armstrong alone. Be sure to inform him."

Joan slowly lifted her brows, her displeasure at the order obvious. Yet she did not protest, instead dipping a low, graceful curtsy. "I will relay the message," she said, rising once again to her full height.

Her exit was efficient, unhurried. Malcolm was surprised to see that once in the hall, she leaned against the wall and took several long, deep breaths. Curiously he noted that the arrogant Joan was apparently not as tenacious as she wanted everyone to believe.

# Chapter Four

Joan peered cautiously into the great hall, needing to make certain that none of the Fraser clan—specifically Archibald—were present. It took longer than she'd anticipated to steal a glimpse of every face, as the hall was alive with activity; it seemed as though every servant in the castle was helping to set up for the evening meal.

A meal Joan dreaded attending.

Her father and Lady Agnes were nowhere to be seen, which suited Joan. The McKenna would no doubt be annoyed with her for not delivering his message personally, but she could now truthfully report there had been no opportunity. Instead, she would assign one of the pages to relay the request and then retreat to her bedchamber.

Joan kept her expression calm as she crossed through the chamber toward the staircase on the opposite side that led to her private quarters. Yet her heart sank when she caught several wary glances from the servants directed her way. Word must have spread that Archibald Fraser and his men were within the castle walls and all were curious to witness her reaction.

Fortunately, she had learned well how to hide her emotions. There was no trace of the turmoil she felt on her face; nay, to one and all she appeared serene and distant. Yet her thoughts were consumed by an almost crippling fear for her son.

*Dear God, I pray that Gertrude has hidden Callum somewhere safe.*

Prayerful thoughts of her maid seemed to conjure the woman to life; suddenly Joan spied Gertrude at the far end of the hall. Wasting no time, she hurried to her side. As she drew closer, Joan felt a sudden draft of cold wind and noticed Gertrude shivering.

The older woman was bone thin and frail, yet beneath her fragile exterior was a Highland spirit as strong as it was proud. The maid had risked much to help Joan escape from her marriage. If not for Gertrude, Joan knew she would still be an abused, neglected wife.

Joan grabbed the wool blanket that hung near the hearth, then drew it carefully around Gertrude's shoulders.

"Ye shouldn't be serving me, milady," Gertrude whispered, but she pulled the blanket tighter across her chest. "The others will see yer kind heart as a weakness."

Joan could barely contain her laughter. "I highly doubt anyone will call me kind. Ever. Besides, I dinnae care what they think," she added truthfully.

"Ye should," Gertrude insisted. "Ye must. Who knows what notions Laird Fraser will get into his head once he sees ye? Ye might need a champion to defend ye."

Joan shook her head sadly. "There's none here that would interfere. I must rely on my wits and sharp tongue to keep us safe."

"Thank the Lord that ye're clever," Gertrude said. "But he is dangerous."

Joan flinched. "I remember all too well."

The maid patted her hand soothingly. "At least Callum is far from his reach. That should put yer mind at ease."

Joan's heart instantly lifted at the mention of her son. "Where is he?"

"Mistress Claire has agreed to keep him."

The answer surprised Joan. "But she has six bairns of her own. How will she manage with another?" Joan asked, visions of an unattended Callum wandering off and injuring himself dancing through her mind.

"Her eldest lass is twelve now," Gertrude said. "She keeps a sharp eye on the wee ones."

"Was there no one else?" Joan inquired, still feeling uneasy at the notion. Callum was an active, curious lad; he would need constant supervision to keep him out of mischief. "I would have preferred to shelter him with a childless woman, one who could give him her complete attention."

"That was my first thought, too. But then I saw all the bairns playing in Mistress Claire's front yard and I knew it was the answer to our prayers." Gertrude sniffed and tugged the blanket closer to her chin. "'Tis better to hide him in plain sight. I daresay, few will notice or recognize the lad when he's part of Mistress Claire's parcel of brats."

Though still uncomfortable with the choice, Joan could see the logic of the argument. Yet her heart ached at being separated from her child. "Let's hope it willnae be fer too long. Have ye heard any gossip about the reason fer this meeting of the clans?"

"Aye. They say one of the McKennas fathered a bastard child on MacPhearson's daughter and Laird MacPhearson seeks retribution fer the insult to his honor."

Joan's brow rose in shock. "Which McKenna?"

"The eldest. Sir Malcolm."

"Well, at least it wasn't James. I would not have wanted my cousin Davina to have to endure the humiliation of a faithless husband," Joan replied, realizing she meant every word.

Raised together since they were young lasses, Joan and Davina had never been close. Yet Davina had sheltered Joan when she first escaped from Archibald, and that act of compassion was one Joan would never forget.

"Do ye know why the Frasers have come, too?" Joan asked. "This has naught to do with them."

"I've heard no specific reason, though I see Lady Agnes's manipulating hand in it," Gertrude replied. "'Tis no secret that she takes great joy in angering ye."

Joan nodded. "She has proven herself to be far more of a nuisance than I anticipated."

Gertrude's lips curled in concern. "I recognize that look in yer eyes, milady. Ye aren't going to do anything rash, are ye? This is not the time to be tangling with Lady Agnes."

"Nay, that fight will have to wait fer another day," Joan agreed. "Though I confess, I dinnae know what I shall do if my father actually marries her."

"One battle at a time," Gertrude clucked. "Come, ye must rest and regain yer strength before the evening meal."

Rest? With her mind and heart in such turmoil? 'Twould be nigh impossible, yet the privacy of her chambers was a lure Joan couldn't resist. "There's still a great deal to be done to make certain all will be ready fer tonight."

"Aye," Gertrude agreed, rising to her feet. "Best to let Lady Agnes worry about it."

Joan smiled. The thought of Agnes scurrying about the castle in a panic was a decidedly cheerful notion. "An excellent idea. I'm quite sure she'll make a muddle of things."

Gertrude nodded. "She seems to have a talent fer it."

Joan followed her maid through the great hall and up the winding stone staircase in a considerably better state of mind. However, her attempts at a short nap failed, for each time she closed her eyes, her mind was filled with the image of her former husband.

She tried to bolster her courage as she prepared for the evening meal, knowing she would have to face Archibald, but by the time she was properly dressed, her nerves were getting the better of her.

"There, all done," Gertrude announced as she adjusted Joan's gauzy white veil. "Ye look like a queen."

Joan turned to the looking glass. She had donned her best gown, of deep red velvet, adding a thick gold circlet on her head and a matching brooch, hoping the finery would give her courage. But the woman who stared back from the wavy glass looked anxious and trembling. "The Frasers?"

Gertrude nodded grimly. "Archibald is seated at the high table with the rest of the lairds."

Joan felt a tight squeeze around her chest as the exhaustion and strain of the last few hours suddenly washed over her. Her breathing grew more rapid; the pounding of her heart increased.

"I'm not certain that I can face him," she whispered, allowing her trusted maid a rare glimpse of her vulnerability.

"Ye must," Gertrude replied, squeezing her comfortingly on the shoulder. "If ye hide from him, then he'll believe that ye still fear him, and that will please him to no end."

"But I do fear him," Joan admitted brokenly, trying— and failing—to compose herself.

"He willnae dare to lay a finger on ye with so many

people around," Gertrude insisted, meeting Joan's eyes with a reassuring look. "Besides, he no longer has the right. He's not yer husband anymore."

*As if that mattered!* "Tormenting me is Archibald's favorite sport," Joan said quietly, the words quivering in her throat. Her hand shook as she tugged on the sleeves of her gown, remembering how often it had been necessary to cover her arms to hide the bruises. "He will no doubt be delighted at the prospect of indulging in it once again."

Gertrude's eyes filled with sympathy. "Then ye must take care not to give him the chance."

Joan turned, pacing the chamber restlessly. "We both know the only way to prevent that from happening is to avoid him."

"Aye. And we both also know that isn't possible." Gertrude stepped in front of Joan and grasped her hands tightly. "Ye must stay calm."

Joan bit into her lower lip, fighting for control. It came slowly as she repeated over and over in her head that Gertrude was right. She had faced far more difficult obstacles and overcome them. That knowledge steadied Joan's nerves and strengthened her determination.

Gradually her breathing calmed and her heart returned to its normal rhythm. Then knowing that she had little choice, Joan pushed back at the memories of her past, lifted her heavy skirt, and left the chamber. When she reached the great hall, she stood in the shadows for a moment, her gaze darting nervously around the room.

The meal had already begun; the noise in the great hall rose to a level that nearly assaulted the ears, but few seated at the tables seemed to mind. All were too engrossed in their drink and conversations, though Joan noted that clan lines were distinctly drawn—none of the men sat beside any one other than members of their own clan.

She smiled grimly. Her father's great sense of importance in his role as the chosen negotiator had certainly fallen flat. Heavens, he couldn't even get the clans to sit together and break bread. How did he expect to resolve this important issue?

Oh, well. 'Twas hardly something to concern her.

Nay, this lack of unity would aid her in keeping away from Archibald. There was only enough room to seat the lairds at the table on the dais, though somehow Agnes had managed to make certain that she occupied the chair at Laird Armstrong's left. The chair that rightfully belonged to Joan.

Not that she cared. Tonight, and every night until the clans left, Agnes could play lady of the manor to her heart's content so long as it would save Joan from having to take a seat near Archibald.

But she had to sit somewhere in the hall and there was no room at any of the Armstrong tables. She knew none of the MacPhearsons or Kennedys in attendance and would not be so foolish as to go near the Frasers.

That left the McKennas. Since they were related through her cousin Davina's marriage to James, it was an acceptable choice that should raise few eyebrows.

Joan's eyes anxiously scanned the faces of the McKenna warriors. Drat! James was sitting at a table far too close to the dais for her peace of mind. Ah, but Malcolm had chosen a table that was set off to the side, barely in view of the dais. Perfect!

Boldly, she approached. "May I join ye?"

For an instant the table was silent with surprise. Then Malcolm rose to his feet and gestured to the man sitting on his right. Reluctantly, the warrior left the bench, taking his trencher of food with him. Joan stared pointedly at the now vacant spot, her brow narrowing.

Malcolm followed her gaze. His face broke into a slight grin as he brushed the crumbs and greasy bits of food off the bench with his palm. "Better?"

Joan nodded, then slowly sank onto the clean wood, wiggling into a position that she hoped kept her shielded from Archibald's view.

"Is he looking this way?" she asked, nervously tearing a thick crust of bread into small pieces.

"Who?"

"Laird Fraser," she hissed, her voice rising.

The sound drew the attention of the men seated across from her. Glaring at them, she lifted a single brow. They stared a moment longer, then hastily turned their attention to their food.

"He's glanced over once or twice," Malcolm replied. "But now he's got a buxom lass sitting on his lap and his eyes are fastened squarely on her ti . . . hmm, bosom."

"Good." Joan pressed her palm tightly against her chest, trying to regain her composure.

"Are ye fearful of him?" Malcolm inquired.

"Nay," she lied calmly. "Though I confess a strong desire to avoid him. Ours was a loathsome marriage."

"Then ending it should have pleased ye both."

Joan let out an ironic grunt. "The only thing that I could have done to please Archibald Fraser was to fling myself from the highest tower of his castle and bash my head on the stones beneath it."

She felt Malcolm's surprise at her comment and cursed her wayward tongue. Her dismal marriage was a private pain that she shared with no one—least of all a man. Thankfully, Malcolm made no further inquiries. Instead, he somehow procured a clean goblet, filled it with wine from the pitcher on the table, and handed it to her. He also moved his trencher between them, so she could partake of the meal.

Joan's stomach churned, yet she removed her eating knife from her pocket and stabbed at the smallest piece of carrot. She chewed it slowly and methodically, washing it down with a long sip of wine.

"Aren't ye hungry?" Malcolm inquired.

"Nay. I've already eaten," she lied.

He gazed at her curiously. "Yer growling stomach tells a different tale."

Joan pursed her lips. "Ye are mistaken, though 'tis understandable given the noise in the hall." She pressed her hand against her midsection, willing it to stay silent.

Malcolm shrugged. "Suit yerself."

To Joan's relief, he dropped the matter, though she noted he moved several choice pieces of meat and vegetables to her side of the trencher. The food did look appetizing, yet she worried anything she put into her stomach might not stay down.

Faint from hunger and confused by the gallant gesture, Joan turned away, but the discomforting feeling of close observation left her jittery. She lifted her gaze to discover the McKenna men were once again regarding her far too closely.

"Please order yer men not to stare at me so openly," she said sharply.

"What? Oh, aye." He glared at the trio across the table. "Ye heard the lady. Attend to yer food."

One of the soldiers let out a wet belch. The other two grinned, but they all obeyed the command and turned their attention to their meal. And tankards of ale.

"If ye wanted to avoid the scrutiny of men, ye should

have worn something plain and dull," Malcolm commented, as he tore a piece of meat in half.

Joan absently noted that the meat fell easily from the bone, indicating that it was cooked properly. She must remember to compliment Cook on the meal.

"I dinnae own any garments that are dull or plain," she muttered.

"Only those that enhance yer beauty?" Malcolm said with a wry grin. "Why doesn't that surprise me?"

Joan felt her back stiffen, taking umbrage at his censuring tone. "I am as the good Lord made me. I take no credit fer my looks, be they fair or foul."

"But they aren't foul, are they?" His eyes drifted over her, slowly, assessingly. "Ye are extraordinarily beautiful."

"Am I?" she asked, instantly regretting the question. After all she had suffered, she still had difficulty controlling the impulse to garner male attention, concluding it must be bred into her bones. But flirting with Malcolm McKenna was a waste of breath; doing it in front of Archibald was both foolish and dangerous. "Dinnae answer," Joan added hastily. "It's been a long, tiring day, after an even longer tiring week. I'm speaking nonsense."

Malcolm leaned back and narrowed his eyes. "Have my wits gone missing? Can it be that ye just refused to hear a compliment, Lady Joan?"

"Indeed. I've no use fer flowery words. Now, I'd strongly advise ye to eat yer supper, Sir Malcolm, before it lands in yer lap."

Joan lifted her goblet and glowered with stern disapproval. But instead of turning him away, the expression brought a grin to Malcolm's handsome face. "As ye wish, my fair lady." He took a large bite of meat and began chewing heartily.

A smile came unbidden to her lips. She hid it with another sip of wine. A page stopped at the table, his arms buckling under the weight of the tray of food he carried. Chuckling, the men immediately refilled their trenchers, nearly emptying the tray.

Joan caught the lad gazing longingly at the generous portions. Malcolm must have also noticed the page's hunger. He picked up a lamb shank and offered it to the lad. The boy's eyes widened with gratitude as he accepted the prize.

The men began talking among themselves. Joan listened with half an ear, content to stay in the background. A shy, unnoticed little mouse. She kept her face down, her expression demure, yet wondered if anyone was fooled. Probably not.

One of the soldiers tossed a bone onto the floor and two large hounds leapt for it. They growled and snarled, fighting for their prize. A few of the men shouted encouragements, while others took wagers as to which dog would be victorious. Yet a stern, quelling look from Malcolm ended any involvement from the McKenna men.

Needing a distraction, Joan turned toward Malcolm. "I've heard the most shocking rumors about the reason the clans have gathered here today. And they all center around ye and one of Laird MacPhearson's daughters."

"Really?" Malcolm lifted his goblet, staring at her as he took a long swallow, his deep blue eyes glinting with caution. "Perchance, have ye seen her? Spoken with her?"

"Who?"

"The laird's daughter."

Joan's mood lightened with mischief. "Ye'll have to be more specific. Three of his daughters made the journey."

"Dinnae be coy, Joan. Ye know full well of whom I speak."

The look in his eyes took away the small delight of teasing him. "I believe the lass ye are referring to is called Brienne."

He nodded sharply.

"She brought a babe with her. They say ye are the lad's father." Joan leaned forward. "Is that true?"

Faint color deepened his tanned face. "Nay."

"Then why have ye come?"

"To clear my name."

"Judging by the scowl on Laird MacPhearson's face, ye might have to do that with yer sword."

He sighed. "Let's hope not." The corners of Malcolm's mouth twitched. "So, did ye speak with Brienne?"

"Nay." Seeing such a powerful, self-assured knight squirm should have brought Joan pleasure, but for some odd reason it didn't. "All the MacPhearson lasses are sequestered in their chamber, with orders that they take their meals within that room. I dinnae think they will be allowed to leave."

"Though I realize 'tis near impossible, I had hoped to have the chance to speak with the lass alone," Malcolm said with a cynical smile.

"'Twould be madness to try," Joan replied. "The MacPhearsons expect ye to seek absolution fer yer disgraceful behavior, not repeat it."

"I only want to speak with the lass," Malcolm exclaimed.

"Why? Ye say the babe isn't yers."

Malcolm glanced guiltily down at the table. "I dinnae believe that I sired Brienne's child. Yet I need to talk to her to make certain. I also need to discover why she has named me as the father."

"I'm sure she has been ordered to stay as far away from ye as possible."

"No doubt." He cocked his head slightly, his expression oddly imploring.

The question hung silently in the air. *He must be truly desperate to turn to me.* Shockingly, she considered it for the briefest moment, but then swiftly came to her senses. "I cannae help ye."

His hopeful expression shuttered closed and Joan felt a surprising stab of regret at disappointing him. But then a female screech drew her attention. She glanced up and saw Archibald push away from the table. He shoved aside the buxom maid he had been fondling, pinning Joan with his full attention, his eyes hot and possessive.

The clear challenge she saw in Archibald's expression left her momentarily terrified, but anger soon replaced her fear. She could feel her cheeks heat with color, knew that her eyes were starting to blaze with anger.

Swiftly, Joan turned away, disheartened at her loss of control. There was nothing that Archibald enjoyed more than getting a rise out of her. 'Twas the fight he liked best, along with the chance to be spiteful and malicious. Well, she was not about to give him that sick pleasure and provide the entertainment he craved.

If for one moment she believed she would be granted justice, she would rise to her feet and reveal to all who sat in the great hall the truth about the monster who sat among them. Yet such a foolish whim could prove her undoing. She kept reminding herself how difficult it had been to escape him, how long she had toiled to carve a safe haven for herself and her son. One misstep and it would vanish in an instant.

Bitterness curdled her tongue, yet Joan's survival

instinct rose to protect her. 'Twas hard to bow her head and appear meek and docile, but she did it, all the while cursing Archibald to hell. She counted slowly to twenty and when she lifted her chin, he was gone.

But not forgotten.

Malcolm leaned back and openly studied Joan. There was a faint sheen glistening on her brow, yet she smelled pleasantly of flowers and soap. Her face was expressionless, eerily calm, yet he knew that she was rattled. She had barely eaten, her complexion was pale, her eyes haunted with undeniable distress.

He had the most ridiculous urge to reach over and brush the stray wisps of blond hair that had escaped from her circlet—a gesture of kindness and comfort. But he restrained himself.

He had heard from his brother, James, what a cold, selfish soul Joan possessed; years ago he had witnessed for himself her self-important attitude and haughty manner. 'Twas said by many that she had a heart of ice and he had seen the evidence of it. She was a woman to be avoided at all costs. He knew that, accepted that, embraced that, and yet . . .

Her vulnerability moved him; her regal bearing intrigued him. Her physical beauty was undeniable, but he was a man who valued far more than a pretty face. Truth be told, given all that he knew of her, there was no logical reason for his fascination with Joan Armstrong.

Yet Malcolm couldn't deny that it existed.

"I bid ye good evening, Sir Malcolm," she announced suddenly.

"Lady Joan." He stood and bowed elegantly.

Malcolm watched Joan as she turned to leave. Her

shoulders were squared, her head held high. He had seen the true fright in her eyes when she caught sight of her former husband, had heard the trembling in her voice when she spoke of him. Yet she did not run; instead she walked, gracefully and slowly, with a confidence few women could boast.

Malcolm tore his gaze from her fading figure. He had far more important things to concern himself with than Lady Joan. Regretfully, she had been unable to impart any information about the reclusive Brienne MacPhearson. Anything he could learn about the lass before he had to confront her father would be useful.

He shoved his trencher away and reached for his goblet. A few men had left the hall, but most were still eating and drinking, including his father and Laird Mac-Phearson. One could almost feel the air of challenge between the two powerful lairds, but to their credit, they had remained civil.

On the surface. Malcolm knew it would take very little for tempers to flare, putting the clans at each other's throats. Malcolm grimaced and wondered how Laird MacPhearson would react when he faced the man he believed fathered his daughter's child, then swiftly decided tomorrow was soon enough to get the answer to that question.

# Chapter Five

Preoccupied with thoughts of her child, Joan tamped down her fear and slipped outside. The night was cloudless and cold, the sky filled with twinkling stars and a full, bright moon. Normally, she would have paused to admire nature's beauty, but there was no time to indulge such whims this evening. Her need to hold Callum close to her breast, to assess his safety with her own eyes, was all consuming. She could wait no longer.

Oh, how she wished she could use one of the hidden passages that ran beneath the castle to sneak beyond the curtain wall. But she dare not risk revealing its location with so many strangers lurking in every corridor. Instead, she would have to pass through the bailey and then bribe the guards at the gate to look the other way while she left.

Joan moved as quickly as possible, traversing the courtyard with brisk steps, her heart eager at the thought of seeing her son. She was surprised—and dismayed—to see a sizable number of men congregating in front of open fires, their guttural laughter echoing through the still air. She had not anticipated that so many would be out here at this time of night.

Her resolve faltered, but thoughts of her son soon

revived it. Frowning, Joan pulled the hood of her cloak forward, hiding not only her golden hair, but her profile. She recognized several Fraser soldiers and needed to ensure they did not ascertain her identity, knowing her former husband would gleefully reward any of his men who humiliated her.

Joan kept one eye on the men and one eye on her destination, walking as swiftly as the uneven ground allowed. She felt a brief moment of ease when the castle gates came into view; then suddenly a menacing shadow loomed in front of her, overpowering and threatening.

She froze. A cold trickle of sweat ran down her spine at the sight of the battle-scarred forearm that reached for her. Joan shrieked with pain as a pair of beefy fingers captured her hand, then tightened around her delicate wrist in a viselike grip.

"Where are ye off to in such a hurry, lass?" the man leered.

*Iain!* She would know that voice anywhere. He was captain of the Fraser guard, a man lacking in honor and scruples and inordinately proud of his blind loyalty to Archibald. He leaned forward and she could smell the sour wine on his breath. Reflexively, her head snapped back at the foul odor, but thankfully, her hood stayed in place, guarding her identity.

For the moment.

She tamped down the waves of fear that washed over her, knowing if she allowed her panic to rule her, she wouldn't be able to think clearly. It would be impossible to physically overpower Iain, but she could outwit him. 'Twas her only hope of a quiet escape.

"Release me at once," she commanded, her tone cold and steady.

Iain paused, loosening his grip and cocking his head questionably. "Lady Joan?"

God save her, he had recognized her voice! Heart pounding, Joan twisted her hand free and stepped back, taking refuge in the shadows, praying that fate would be kind and allow her to get away. She backed off slowly, steadily, carefully over the rough ground, eyes darting nervously from Iain to the solid front door of the great hall.

*If I can reach it, I'll be safe from him.*

Iain followed her movements, his face glowering down at her. Eyes narrowed with suspicion, he reached out a thick hand and roughly pushed back her hood. His breath caught in chilling recognition, and then he reached for his dirk.

Joan stumbled, shrieking in terror as the point of his blade was pressed against her throat. Fighting back, she raised her knee and slammed it into Iain's groin. He moaned, bending low. She heard the dirk fall to the ground. Seizing the advantage, Joan turned to flee, but Iain grabbed her arm.

Pain exploded through her back and shoulder as her body was slammed against the wall of the building. She could feel the coldness of the stone seeping through her cloak and gown as he pressed harder.

"Ye bitch!" Iain shouted. "Laird Archibald always said ye were a she-wolf."

She looked up at him, keeping her gaze level. "And ye were always a drunk and a bully, Iain Fraser," Joan bit out. "Release me."

"Nay. I'll leave it to yer husband to decide what's to be done with ye."

"I have no husband." Joan's voice was strong, but the look in his eyes made her tremble. "Now once again, I demand that ye release me!"

Iain muttered a curse and tightened his grip. Determined not to go meekly, Joan managed to reach down and pull the knife from her belt. She brandished it in front of him, yet the weapon barely gave him pause.

Instead, it seemed to anger him. He raised his fist menacingly. Joan cringed, but the blow never struck.

"Ye heard the lady. Release her."

A broad-shouldered warrior materialized from the shadows. He had a solid grip on Iain's raised arm, preventing the punch from landing on Joan.

"Be gone!" Iain shouted. "This is none of yer concern."

"I disagree," the warrior insisted. "I cannae allow ye to strike a lady."

Suddenly, the warrior pulled down on Iain's arm. Hard. The distinct sound of a cracking bone echoed through the still night air. Iain howled, then dropped to the dirt, writhing in agony.

Swallowing down the bile of fear that rose from her gut, Joan looked up. Fragments of moonlight illuminated the face of her rescuer, and her heart skipped a beat when she recognized him.

*Malcolm McKenna. Bloody hell, of all the men in Christendom, why did he have to be the one to save me?*

"Are ye hurt?" Malcolm asked in a gentle voice.

Joan's breath caught as his eyes slowly traveled over her body. He wasn't leering, yet the scrutiny agitated her.

"I'm fine," she growled, distressed to hear her voice sound so harsh. The last thing she wanted was for him—or any man—to realize how affected she was by his presence. "I must hurry."

She turned without another word and scuttled away, wanting to be long gone before the other Fraser soldiers appeared to investigate why Iain was howling like a dying wolf.

Malcolm fell in step beside her. The gesture initially

annoyed her, but she quickly realized it was a comfort to have him—and his sword—by her side.

"Is it really so difficult fer ye to be gracious and provide me with a genuine word of thanks?" he asked.

Joan's cheeks grew warm as shame filled her. Her rudeness truly was uncalled for, given his noble actions this night. He had stepped in to aid her without knowing her identity, yet when he realized it, he had not hesitated. She had enough experience to know that there were few men who would have come so unquestionably to her aid, and fewer still who would have helped once they realized who she was.

She straightened. "Forgive me. I dinnae wish to be beholden to any man, though I do thank ye fer yer help."

"Yet ye would have preferred that I not interfere?"

"Did I say that?"

"Nay, but that furrow in yer brow speaks far louder than words."

Och, now he was goading her. She had offered her thanks—what more did the man want?

Joan exhaled impatiently. "Did ye not know? 'Tis against my nature to be deferential."

"Aye."

Joan shrugged. "Truth be told, I find it exhausting hiding the less than appealing aspects of my essence. Therefore, I no longer try."

"An enlightened, though perhaps dangerous view," he replied. "Ye'll never find another husband unless ye gentle yer ways."

Joan couldn't resist a small laugh. "Rest assured, the lack of a husband is not something that keeps me awake at night."

Malcolm frowned. "If ye were the wife of a strong warrior, ye would not have needed my help tonight."

She rested her palm on her stomach. "And who was there when I needed protection from my warrior husband when he acted like a beast anxious to devour his prey? Not my kin. Not any of the noble knights in his service. Not anyone at all. Nay, I'll take my chances on my own, though I shall heed yer warning and promise to be more careful in the future."

They had reached the threshold of the great hall. *Back to where I started.* The realization that she was no closer to being united with her son rankled, but Joan refused to accept defeat. She would try again the moment Malcolm departed.

She turned to him expectantly, hoping the unwelcoming scowl on her brow would send him on his way. But undeterred, he placed his sword hand on his hip and gazed down at her.

"Shall I escort ye to yer chamber?" he asked.

Joan's stomach churned with indecision. It would certainly be the quickest way to get rid of him, but precious time would be wasted.

"I'm fine on my own," she replied. "I've no wish to keep ye any longer. I bid ye good night, Malcolm."

Joan dismissed him with a flick of her wrist. He appeared startled by the gesture and for a moment remained exactly where he stood. "Good night, *Joan.*"

Taken aback by the familiar use of her name, she barely took notice of his exaggerated bow. It was only as she watched his retreating form that she realized he had answered her in kind—in her haste to have him take his leave, she had dropped the formality of his title.

She and Malcolm were somewhat distantly related, as her first cousin was married to his brother, so it was not entirely inappropriate. Still, it was an intimacy that she preferred to avoid. Joan felt her cheeks heat with embarrassment. This night was naught but a series of mishaps.

Yet this incident with Malcolm was hardly the worst of it. She leaned against the hard, cold wall, unable to free her mind of the ugly confrontation with Iain. The memory brought on a surge of panic and she surrendered to it, her body shaking and shivering. Once it passed, she let out a long breath and willed her heart to return to its normal cadence.

She glanced briefly toward the staircase, then turned away. She knew the sensible course would be to return to her chamber and hope for a chance to slip away on the morrow to see her son.

But that was impossible. She would be unable to sleep if she did not see Callum and assess with her own eyes that her child was safe and being well cared for by Mistress Claire. Though it was still dangerous, the unpleasant incident in the bailey had yielded important information; she now knew where the men were gathered and thus should be able to avoid them.

Ever practical, Joan reached into the pocket of her gown and pulled out a dirk. 'Twas a thin, almost dainty knife, but lethal nonetheless, with a long, sharp blade. Gripping it tightly in her fist, she hid the weapon in the folds of her cloak and once again stepped into the dark night.

She had promised Malcolm that she would be more careful, and that was a vow she was more than prepared to keep. For her sake, as well as her child's.

Malcolm watched Joan stumble through the door of the great hall, emerging into the darkness not ten minutes after he had left her. She appeared calm, in control, but instinct warned him that all was not as it appeared.

Was the woman daft? 'Twas madness to be out alone

at this hour, as her very recent encounter with that brutish Fraser soldier had proved. What was so important that she would risk her person again?

An assignation with a lover? The idea seemed ludicrous but it was hardly impossible. Joan was a stunningly beautiful woman. Many a man would happily look beyond her prickly nature to claim her.

Curious, Malcolm followed. He kept to the shadows, moving stealthily through the darkness, his mind puzzling over where she was going. He noted that she was very deliberate in her movements, turning her head frequently in all directions, obviously searching for potential danger. Fortunately, she found none—those gathered in the bailey barely gave her a second look.

Amazed, Malcolm watched her scuttle through the castle gate unchallenged. The guards had clearly been enjoying more than a healthy portion of ale, as they barely glanced in Joan's direction. He made a mental note to warn his father, brother, and their men to be on guard. For it was clear they could not count upon the Armstrong soldiers to keep the castle safe from intruders.

He followed her down the dirt path that led to the village. Here all was quiet—and very dark. No torches were lit and the moon was hidden by a thin layer of clouds. Malcolm concluded that she must know this route well; her feet never stumbled and she moved with increasing speed.

Suddenly she stopped and looked behind her. Assuming she must have sensed his presence, Malcolm quickly moved into the shadows. Cocking his head, he listened, trying to decide what he would say to her if he was discovered.

For a long moment all he heard was the deep sound of her breathing, then she once again began to walk—away from him. She turned down a small alley, stopping at a thatched-roof cottage set off from the others. She knocked once and the door opened.

Pressing himself against the outside wall of the structure, Malcolm looked between the gap allowed by the leather covering placed over a window and peered into the dwelling. The mystery deepened when he saw Joan speaking with a short, dark-haired woman. But his attention was soon drawn by the sound of running feet. A wee lad with blond hair entered the room. The moment he spied Joan, he ran toward her, joy and love lighting up his sweet face.

Malcolm watched in astonishment as Joan opened her arms and enfolded the child in a big hug. Lovingly, she ran her cheek back and forth across the top of his head, then pressed several kisses on his brow. Several other children of various ages spilled into the room, their voices raised with excitement.

The lad took her hand and pulled her toward the fire, obviously wanting to show her something. Laughing, she followed, taking a seat on the low stool. The child immediately climbed into her lap. He gestured toward the others, his mouth constantly moving as he babbled. Malcolm could hear the high pitch of his voice—along with the delight in his tone—but was unable to distinguish any of the words.

One of the older lasses handed the lad a crudely carved wooden horse. He lifted it eagerly to show Joan. She nodded and smiled, obviously admiring the toy, then tightened her grip on his shoulders. Though happy, she seemed unable to cease holding the child close to her. 'Twas almost as if she feared he would vanish if she wasn't touching him.

The dark-haired woman shooed the other children

away, leaving Joan and the lad alone. The child snuggled closer and Joan cradled him in her arms. He was a sturdy, well-built lad, but she held him securely, with an ease that bespoke of practice.

The light of the fire illuminated her face, giving her refined features an ethereal glow. Malcolm watched, transfixed, as she began rocking the child back and forth. Never in his wildest imaginings had he believed he would see such a tender, vulnerable expression on Joan Armstrong's face.

The love in her eyes was unmistakable. This had to be her child—hers and Archibald Fraser's. But why was he hidden away?

A twinge of longing pierced Malcolm's heart. He had been away from Lileas for over a week and hadn't realized how fiercely he missed his mischievous daughter until this moment.

Joan began to sing. 'Twas a song he immediately recognized as the same lullaby his mother had sung to her children. The simple tune reverberated through the room, surrounding everything with a calm peace.

Joan smiled down at the child as she sang, pausing now and again to rub her cheek against his. Slowly, the lad's eyes began to close, his body visibly relaxed. The wooden horse slipped from his fingers, but was nimbly caught by hers before it clattered to the floor.

She finished her song, but continued humming and rocking the child. After a time, the dark-haired woman reappeared. The two spoke briefly and then the dark-haired female extended her arms.

Joan's reluctance was obvious. She bowed her head and held the sleeping child close to her breast for a long moment, then grudgingly allowed the other woman to take him.

Malcolm drew his brows together as he watched Joan rise to her feet. She rubbed the back of her hands across her eyes, wiping away the tears. He moved closer, hoping to hear the final exchange between the two women, but Joan left before the dark-haired woman returned.

He stayed in the shadows, trailing Joan back to the castle, making certain she arrived unharmed. This time she nearly ran, slipping inside the great hall without incident. After Malcolm saw Joan close the door securely behind her, he released a deep breath, uncertain why her safety mattered so much to him.

He only knew that it did.

The next morning Malcolm sat with his father and brother in the great hall as the trio broke their fast. The brown oat bread was warm, the cheese sharp, the ale cold, yet Malcolm could barely taste any of it. The long awaited meeting with the MacPhearsons was scheduled to take place within the hour and his nerves were on edge.

"I've agreed to allow some of the Frasers and Kennedys to attend this meeting," the McKenna announced, signaling one of the pages to refill his tankard.

James ripped off a hunk of bread with his front teeth, chewed it heartily, then swallowed. "Are ye sure that's wise? MacPhearson will claim that Malcolm fathered his daughter's bairn, Malcolm will swear it isn't true, the MacPhearson lass will be shamed, and her father humiliated. The fewer who are privy to it, the better."

"We have come here seeking justice and truth," the McKenna insisted, his voice raised to a level that made it clear he didn't care who was listening. "'Tis not our intention to pass judgment on the character of others. We are all proud men of Scotland, loyal to the land and our true king. This is a serious matter, but it can be settled in a civil manner. Fighting among ourselves benefits no one—except the English."

A mutter of accord rippled through several of the men seated at the other tables. The McKenna nodded, clearly pleased his message had been heard.

However, disagreement flickered in James's eyes. "I still think it would have been prudent to make this a private matter."

"Nay." The McKenna reached for his tankard. He took a long sip, then lowered his voice as he spoke. "'Tis important that we have witnesses from more than one clan. This way, if the MacPhearsons are unhappy with the verdict and decide to attack us, they'll be in the wrong.

"I'll do all that I can to avoid a fight, but if it comes, we'll have the right to retaliate and our allies will have to support us."

"Ye seem overconfident at the outcome," Malcolm replied, stabbing his eating knife into a wedge of cheese.

"I am," the McKenna replied cheerfully. "Ye said ye'd know the truth once ye see the lass. If ye are the father of this babe, then ye'll do right by the mother and make her yer wife. And if ye're not, Laird MacPhearson will have no cause to demand yer head.

"He'll be forced to remove the bounty and declare he has no feud with ye or our clan. He'll have to keep to his word, too, since many other honorable men will have heard him speak. This way, ye won't have every fool in the land trying to hunt ye down in hopes of earning some ill-gotten coin."

A glint of doubt lingered in James's eyes. "I still think it's better not to air our dirty laundry in front of others."

"Fie, the truth cannae be any worse than the gossip that's being spread," Malcolm said glumly, shoving away his food.

"But what is the truth, Malcolm?" James asked. "Ye have no recollection of the event."

"As Father said, I'm hoping that once I see the lass, speak with her, I'll know," he replied, ashamed that his irresponsible actions had brought this upon them. No matter what the outcome, Malcolm was hard-pressed to believe it would not have far-reaching consequences.

He was grateful for his father's and brother's support, yet felt a fool for putting them all in this ridiculous situation in the first place. If only he had pushed away the wine at the fete, instead of calling for more, none of this would have occurred.

A few of the others began to stir and Malcolm realized the time of judgment had arrived. Walking tall beside his father and brother, he entered the solar that Laird Armstrong had chosen for this important meeting. They were the first to arrive, but the chamber soon filled.

Malcolm looked up as the murmurings of those huddled in the solar suddenly died. Surrounded by a ring of tall, burly warriors, Laird MacPhearson strode into the chamber. His hands were curled into fists as he scanned the features of the men.

When his eyes lit on Malcolm, his face broke into a thunderous expression. He lunged forward, reaching for the sword that wasn't at his side.

Though feeling naked without his own weapon, Malcolm was glad his father had demanded that no weapons be allowed for this meeting. If not, blood most likely would have been shed before the first words were spoken.

"Ye're a brazen one, Malcolm McKenna, to be staring at me so boldly after what ye've done," Laird MacPhearson shouted.

Malcolm stood tall in the face of Laird MacPhearson's

blustering wrath. "It has yet to be established exactly what I have done."

Laird Armstrong held up a hand for silence. Laird MacPhearson continued muttering under his breath, then finally heeded the command.

Ignoring the tension that was knotting his neck, Malcolm didn't flinch at the hard glares aimed at him from all the MacPhearson men. His steady demeanor earned him a slight grunt of respect from Laird Kennedy and a stoic look from the others.

"Where is the Lady Brienne?" Laird Armstrong asked. "She must give her account of what has occurred."

Laird MacPhearson shook his head adamantly. "Nay. I'll speak fer her. I refuse to have my daughter humiliated in such a fashion."

"'Twas ye who made this such a public matter when ye placed a price on Malcolm's head," the McKenna cried indignantly.

"I've every right to defend the honor of my daughter and my clan," MacPhearson answered hotly.

"And I've the same right." The McKenna turned away in disgust. "I wouldn't be here unless I hoped fer a fair and peaceful solution. Dinnae allow pride to guide ye, MacPhearson. Use yer common sense and summon the lass."

Laird MacPhearson's upper lip twitched. "Dinnae tell me what to do!"

"Fine! We'll let Armstrong decide," the McKenna replied.

All eyes turned to Laird Armstrong. He wiped the sweat from his brow and surveyed the crowded chamber, then cleared his throat. "The McKenna makes a fair point. Bring the lass."

Malcolm tapped his foot impatiently as they waited. After several long minutes there was a flurry of commotion at the doorway. His chest grew tight and every nerve in his body rose in alert. Would he recognize her when he saw her?

Five women entered the solar, their demeanor somber. Two of them hovered protectively over a third—Malcolm decided they had to be the MacPhearson lasses. Following close behind them were Lady Agnes and Joan. They stood a respectful distance behind the trio.

Malcolm's gaze focused intently on the woman in the center of the group. She was small and slender, with dainty, attractive features. Her hair was dark, her eyes the color of midnight. She held her sister's hand tightly and looked at no one in the chamber save her father.

A peaceful sense of relief fluttered through Malcolm's gut as he observed her. There was not a flicker of memory in his mind or his body. She was a comely lass, but far too young for him. No matter how drunk, he would not have flirted with, much less bedded her.

"Lady Brienne, what can ye tell us?" Laird Armstrong asked.

She paled. Her frightened eyes sought her father's, searching for assurance. The MacPhearson nodded.

"The man I lay with at the fete was Malcolm McKenna," she whispered, so low that many strained to hear her. "He's the father of my babe."

Though this accusation was known by all who stood in the chamber, her declaration brought a grumble of surprised chatter among the men.

"Did he force ye?" Laird Armstrong asked.

Brienne's cheeks flushed. "Nay, he was gentle and kind. He called me his sweet posset and promised that we would be wed as soon as the proper arrangements could be made. I hoped that would happen when the fete ended, but he said he needed more time. Though disappointed, I returned home, my heart filled with joy. When I discovered that I carried his child, I hid my condition from my family, believing that all would be put to rights, but he never came fer me."

Brienne sniffled and wiped her eyes. Malcolm could feel the bite of contempt aimed directly at him as several of the men made low sounds of disapproval.

"Malcolm?" The McKenna turned to him with questioning eyes.

Malcolm didn't flinch at the hard glares the others sent his way. "God's truth, Father, I've never seen the lass before today."

Laird MacPhearson slapped the tabletop in anger. "Och, well, isn't that convenient."

"There are plenty of witnesses that saw ye in yer cups more than most during the fete," Gordon Kennedy remarked. "'Tis understandable that yer memory of the lass fails ye. Many a man doesn't remember much after a night of strong drink."

"I'll not deny that I enjoyed my share of good wine and whiskey," Malcolm admitted. "But Lady Brienne is a pleasing and gentle maiden. She is not someone I would easily forget."

"Many of ye were also at the fete. Do any of ye recall seeing my brother and Lady Brienne together?" James asked.

The men exchanged looks, all shaking their heads. Feeling the tide of opinion turning his way, Malcolm let out a slow breath.

"He was too clever to be caught courting her openly when he never intended to marry her," MacPhearson cried. "Instead he used honeyed lies and trickery to seduce and dishonor her."

"I would never treat an innocent young lady so cruelly!" Malcolm exclaimed defensively.

"Ye express regret only because ye've been caught," MacPhearson said bitterly. "I wager if ye'd been captured and brought before me, ye'd be singing a far different tune."

James hissed out a warning. "And ye'd be facing an army of McKenna warriors out fer blood."

Malcolm reached out and grabbed his brother's arm. "Laird MacPhearson's anger is justified, however misplaced," he said. "I have a daughter. If any man were to treat my Lileas in such a disgraceful manner, I'd cut off his balls."

"A fitting punishment," Laird Kennedy interjected.

Malcolm lowered his voice, his tone sincere. "If I believed the child was mine, I would marry the fair Brienne willingly, but I dinnae see how it's possible."

"Och, so the word of a MacPhearson lass isn't good enough fer ye?" Laird MacPhearson shouted. "She made her confession to the priest the night she gave birth. My daughter isn't lying."

Lady Brienne sniffled again and for the first time turned her attention toward Malcolm. Her lips were quivering, her shoulders shuddering. She looked frightened to death, the dark circles under her eyes attesting to her lack of sleep.

Not knowing what else to do, Malcolm gave her a polite, respectful nod.

Her eyes widened and the last thread of her poise visibly crumbled. She let out a gasp, then clutched her heart. Without further warning, her legs gave way and she fell to the floor in a dead faint.

# Chapter Six

One of the MacPhearson men rushed forward, but it was Brienne's two sisters who managed to catch her before she hit the floor.

"Bloody hell, McKenna!" Laird MacPhearson shouted, his face reddening. "Ye've upset the poor lass so completely that she's fainted."

"Malcolm has done nothing but state the truth," the McKenna retorted.

"Nay, he's denied the truth and shamed my Brienne. I demand justice!"

The chamber quickly filled with the sound of angry male voices as they each shouted their opinions. Ignoring them, Joan moved forward to stand with the MacPhearson women. Agnes, she noted, chose instead to move closer to Laird Armstrong.

"I dinnae understand why ye are all so concerned," Archibald sneered. "Women are weak, flighty, emotional creatures. She'll recover quick enough if ye show her the back of yer hand."

Joan's temper flared at her former husband's cruelty. "By the saints, ye would be the one to advise striking her while she is down," Joan interjected bitterly.

Archibald's expression tightened. He turned angry eyes in her direction, and for an instant she cowered with fear. But pride rescued her. She sent him a withering glare, then reached down to help the MacPhearson sisters lift Brienne, who hung limply near their feet.

The lass was out cold. They patted her cheeks and fanned her brow and gradually Brienne's eyes opened. She blinked with confusion, her eyes widening when she realized what had occurred.

Horror edging her words, Brienne began muttering. Joan caught only one phrase, though it made little sense: *He said his name was Malcolm McKenna.* Brienne grew more restless, frantically clutching her sister's arm, her eyes wide and confused as she continued to mumble.

"Hush!" the taller sister commanded. "We will speak of this later, in private."

With Joan's assistance, the three women managed to steady Brienne on her feet. Her face was pale, her breathing shallow. She looked so lost and forlorn. 'Twas pitiful.

"She needs time to recover," Joan announced, moving toward the door.

All turned to Laird Armstrong for guidance, but he was glaring at Joan, his lips white from being pressed together so tightly. Joan knew her father was furious with her for interfering, but honestly, someone had to take charge.

Joan poked the taller MacPhearson sister in the ribs to get her attention. They exchanged a glance; Joan was relieved to see the other woman's eyes light with understanding—and gratitude. She nodded, indicating that she would follow Joan's lead. Together, the four women exited the chamber before any of the men had a chance to gather their wits and stop them.

"My bedchamber is the nearest," Joan said. "This way."

Joan shut the door the moment they were all inside, sliding the bar across for good measure. At the sound, Brienne began sobbing so hard that she choked and hiccupped. Her sisters guided her onto a chair as her wailing grew louder. Her raw pain affected all of them—even Joan.

One of her sisters stood beside her, stroking her back, trying to soothe her. It seemed to have little effect. Brienne's hands were shaking, her teeth chattering. She could barely sit upright in the chair.

Joan poured water into a wooden bowl and doused a cloth. Wringing it out, she handed it to one of the sisters, who ran the cloth over Brienne's brow.

"Dinnae fret so, Brienne," the other sister said. "All will be well."

"She needs a dram of whiskey to settle her nerves," the tall sister decided.

"Nay!" Brienne shook her head. "I need my babe. Where is my son? Where is my precious Liam? Bring him to me. Please."

"We cannae leave ye," the sisters said simultaneously.

"I'll fetch him," Joan volunteered.

She hurried down the hallway and up the stairs to the chamber assigned to the sisters. Once inside, she discovered the nurse they had brought along dozing by the bed, her soft snores filling the chamber. Joan approached unchallenged, staring with curiosity at the tightly wrapped bundle lying in the middle of the bed.

Someone had fashioned a cozy place for him by propping pillows on either side of his small body, so he wouldn't fall off if he rolled over. Joan leaned down, surprised to discover the quiet babe was awake.

His eyes were open and curious, and he seemed content chewing and suckling on his fist. Though she was a stranger, he looked at her trustingly when she leaned closer, kicking his legs in excitement and dislodging his bunting.

"Aren't ye a nice, plump lad," she cooed, rubbing his belly.

He cocked his head at the sound of her voice, released his fist, and favored her with a toothless grin. She cooed again and his smile widened, creating a dimple in the corner of his chubby cheek. Fascinated, Joan traced the indentation, marveling at the feel of his soft, smooth skin.

He was a handsome babe, with a sweet face, a button nose, and large, round eyes the color of spring grass. She leaned closer and caught a whiff of that special, magical scent that only babes could produce. It instantly filled her heart with memories of when Callum was an infant.

Those were dark days. Archibald was unreasonably jealous of any time she spent with their son and she feared he would turn his fists toward the helpless babe. Fear for her son made her realize that no matter what the cost, she had to escape Archibald, if not for her own safety, for her child's.

Joan picked up the babe, surprised at the hefty feel of him. He was heavier than he looked—a sturdy, solid little lad. He was a bairn any man would be proud to claim as his own.

"Yer mother will surely cease her crying when she holds ye close," Joan said as she rewrapped the bunting.

She shifted Liam in her arms and turned to leave just as the nurse awoke.

"What are ye doing?" the woman screeched. "Put the young master down at once!"

The loud noise caused the babe to start whimpering. Joan began bouncing him up and down and patting his back, all the while shooting daggers at the servant.

"Quiet!" Joan cried. "Or I'll tell yer mistress ye were sleeping instead of keeping a sharp eye on the child."

"He was asleep, too," the woman protested, reaching for Liam. "There was no danger."

Joan turned away, refusing to relinquish him. "His mother has need of him. I'll bring him to her."

Joan left the chamber with the huffing nurse trailing on her heels. All three women looked up anxiously when she entered the chamber. Brienne's sniffles turned into a relieved sigh of contentment when the child was placed in her arms. She kissed his head and nuzzled him close to her breast, which quickly produced a few whimpers.

"He smells yer milk and now wants another meal," the nurse warned. "Best give him to me."

"Och, I fed him barely two hours ago," Brienne replied with a small laugh.

"Ye mustn't spoil the greedy lad by giving him the teat anytime he wants," the nurse insisted, reaching to take the child.

Brienne's expression sobered as she protectively gathered the babe closer. He immediately started rooting anxiously, his tiny fist grabbing at his mother's breast. "A few sips will quiet him and comfort me."

"Nay," the nurse replied.

"Aye," Joan added, giving the nurse a commanding stare. "'Tis best fer mother and bairn."

With uncertain eyes, Brienne gazed first at Joan and then at her sisters, striking Joan anew at how young she appeared.

"Go on," the taller sister encouraged. "Feed him."

Brienne nodded. She unlaced the front of her gown, pushing it off one shoulder. The babe latched on the moment her nipple was bared. Brienne smiled again, her face visibly calm as the infant suckled.

The sight gave Joan a pang. She had wanted to feed Callum herself, but Archibald had refused her that maternal joy, insisting that only peasants nursed their babies. Without consulting her, he had installed a wet nurse, a slovenly creature, overly fond of men, ale, and wine. Joan had despised and resented her from the first.

Yet she had used the woman's vices to her advantage. Whenever the wet nurse had been preoccupied with men and spirits—which was often the case—Joan had secretly nursed Callum. Those precious stolen moments had forged an unbreakable maternal bond between mother and child and given her the courage she needed to flee Archibald's tyranny.

Joan's memories faded as she heard the sisters talking quietly among themselves. She stepped closer, hoping to learn more.

"He's such a sweet, innocent bairn," Brienne said softly. "He rarely fusses or cries, always smiles. Poor lamb, what's to become of him?"

"We must pray fer guidance," the shorter sister said.

The taller sister scoffed. "The Lord has forsaken Brienne these many months. We must rely on our wits and cunning to save her."

"Father will be furious," the shorter sister warned.

"He might take Liam from me," Brienne said woefully. "If he does, I know I shall die of grief."

"He's a strong, healthy bairn. Surely Laird MacPhearson is proud to have such a fine grandson," Joan suggested.

"He's a bastard," the taller sister said.

Brienne cringed. Her eyes filled with tears as she tenderly stroked the babe's head, the love she carried for him displayed on her face.

"He's a beautiful lad with such pretty eyes," Joan marveled. "I've never seen such a color."

"His green eyes are just like his father's," Brienne said proudly before bursting into another round of sobs.

Her two sisters gathered close, pushing Joan out of the way. She easily stepped aside, her mind playing and replaying Brienne's words. 'Twas yet another piece of a mysterious puzzle that continued to baffle.

*His green eyes are just like his father's.*

Joan had heard it clear as day. Yet how could that be? Malcolm McKenna's eyes were blue.

Joan sat at the window in the women's solar, a piece of embroidery resting idly in her lap. She had come here after leaving the MacPhearson sisters, wanting some time alone to ponder all that she had discovered. Again and again her mind twisted and turned as she tried to decipher the meaning of Brienne's words, tried to understand the implications of what she had overheard.

*He said his name was Malcolm McKenna. . . . His green eyes are just like his father's.*

By rights Joan knew that she should bring this information to the attention of her father. Or the McKennas. But she felt pity for Brienne and was not about to expose her until she was certain of the truth.

Experience had taught her that rash actions led to foolish behavior, and the lives of too many people could be affected if she acted rashly.

The door opened and Lady Agnes entered the solar. Joan's hopes for just a few more minutes of peace and quiet were shattered, but she dare not let her disappointment show on her face, knowing it would give Agnes great pleasure.

"Och, so this is where ye've been hiding," Agnes said shrilly.

Uninvited, she came closer, her feet crushing the dried rushes underfoot. The pleasant scent of herbs filled the air, but Joan's expression remained sour.

"What do ye want?" Joan asked.

"There's much to be done before the evening meal," Agnes said in an irritating, nasal tone.

"I'm confused, Agnes. One moment ye are crowing with delight and declaring yerself the chatelaine of this castle and the next ye are coming to me begging fer my help."

"I've never begged fer anything in my life!" Agnes retorted, her eyes blazing with indignation.

Joan wrinkled her nose as though she had stepped in a pile of horse dung. "I've neither the time nor the interest to discuss this, Agnes," Joan said, smiling coolly. "Be gone."

Agnes turned away in a righteous rage, but halted after taking a few steps. "Yer father willnae be pleased to learn that ye are neglecting yer duties. No matter what the reason."

"I am not neglecting my duties," Joan insisted.

"Ye are and I know why. Ye protest loudly about wanting to avoid Laird Fraser, yet 'tis obvious to me that ye pine fer his attention," Agnes declared snidely. "Though some might think yer plan clever, I'm uncertain it will work. The man is not a lackwit."

"What are ye babbling about, Agnes?" Joan asked wearily.

Agnes arched a mischievous brow. "No need to be coy with me. I see clearly what ye want and exactly how ye think to get it. And, since the end result would be yer leaving Armstrong Castle, I'm not entirely opposed to lending ye a hand."

Joan rubbed her temples vigorously. "I've neither the inclination nor the patience to unravel yer riddles. Speak plainly, or not at all."

Agnes's eyes darkened, but her temper held. "I am speaking, of course, of how ye are using yer son to capture his father's attention. I'm sure ye believe that if the lad somehow gains Archibald's affections, the laird will look more kindly upon ye. He might even welcome ye back to his castle, though I doubt he'll marry ye again. At least not right away."

Joan blinked. She had to be imagining the glee in Agnes's face. "What?"

Agnes smiled broadly, yet it was a decidedly unfriendly grin. "Some might think it unseemly to use yer child as bait, yet it is difficult to argue its affect. I'm sure by the end of the day Laird Fraser will be quite smitten with the lad."

Joan's heart filled with cold distrust. "Archibald has neither seen nor spoken to my son."

"Oh, but ye are mistaken," Agnes said lightly. "I saw the lad walking into the stables with Laird Fraser not more than ten minutes ago."

Joan's heart gave a hard tug of panic. "Ye're lying."

Agnes's eyes flashed. "Och, I understand. Ye wish to keep all this a secret. Well, I'll not say a word to anyone."

A muscle ticked in Joan's jaw. What game was Agnes playing now? Callum was safely hidden away with Mistress Claire. Joan had left strict instructions that he was not to return to the castle until all the visitors had departed.

Agnes angled her head and stared at Joan expectantly. Joan searched her face, desperate to know the truth. Was it possible that Callum had come back to the castle?

Worse still, was it possible that Archibald was with the child this very moment?

A muffled whimper fell from Joan's lips. She leapt to her feet and tossed her sewing on the chair. Then turning her back on the snickering Agnes, Joan hurried away, picking up speed with each step. She burst through the doors and into the bailey with a loud bang.

The wind was bitter and sharp, but Joan felt numb as naught but the vision of Callum in Archibald's clutches registered in her mind. Though it felt like hours, she reached the stables in but a few minutes, running as fast as her legs would carry her.

Breathlessly, she stood in the doorway, her eyes squinting in the dim light. "Callum! Callum!"

Silence.

Joan moved forward, her eyes darting frantically from one stall to the next. It took a moment for her vision to adjust to the dim light, but all she saw was horses crowded in their berths.

Joan swallowed hard, then closed her eyes. Callum was safe. *'Twas just another loathsome way fer Agnes to show her disdain and I fell fer it. Evil, conniving witch!*

Joan's relief at discovering Agnes's lie soon gave way to anger. The animosity between them was fast plummeting onto dangerous territory. She had thought the inevitable confrontation could wait until this matter with the McKennas and MacPhearsons was settled, but realized that this had put her at a disadvantage.

A dull flush rose on her throat as she conceded that Agnes was winning the battle between them. The other woman had clearly identified Joan's weaknesses and was pressing them to her full advantage.

Well, two could play at that game.

Joan had witnessed Agnes preening for the attention of

the younger soldiers. 'Twas in all likelihood an innocent flirtation, but Laird Armstrong was a very jealous man. He would not take kindly to a wife who openly admired the face and form of another, younger man. A pointed remark within her father's hearing would plant the seeds of jealousy. Then all she need do was wait for Agnes to cast her gaze at a few of the other Armstrong warriors and her father would quickly lose interest in the spiteful woman.

Joan was so lost in her thoughts of revenge that she didn't hear the approaching footsteps. Suddenly, the heavy stable door slammed behind her, trapping Joan inside. Startled, she turned and came face-to-face with the last man she wanted to set eyes upon.

"Joan." He inclined his head regally.

Warily, she did the same. "Archibald."

He stood unmoving, yet she was hardly fooled by his deceptive stillness. He could strike without warning, fast and hard. Joan's mouth grew dry as she glanced at the door he blocked. 'Twas the only means of escape. As he was well aware.

"I noticed ye running in here. Are ye waiting fer someone? Yer lover, perhaps?" he asked casually.

Dear Lord. His possessive nature was as strong as ever, the jealousy he seemed unable to control ruling his actions. Joan's wits scrambled. She couldn't tell him the truth, fearing if she mentioned her son, Archibald would demand to see him.

"I need to speak with Cook," she said. "I was told that he was in here, but apparently I was misinformed."

Archibald raised a skeptical brow. "Cook? Why would a cook come to the stables?"

Distressed at being caught in the lie, Joan lifted her

chin, determined to brazen it out. "'Tis no concern of yers, Archibald."

"Consorting with lower servants these days, Joan?" He chuckled. "I suppose I shouldn't be shocked by such appalling behavior, yet I confess that I am."

Archibald's tone was smooth, pleasant, the expression in his eyes curious. Joan marveled at how easily he fooled those who didn't know his true nature. On the surface he was a handsome, gallant knight; inside he was a monster.

Unexpectedly, she recalled the first time she had met him. The marriage contracts were drawn but unsigned. Fearing her parents might try to marry her off to an old man, she had refused to take her vows without first speaking with her intended.

Her father had shouted, her mother had pleaded, but as always, in the end Joan was granted her wish. Archibald had waited for her in her mother's solar and her first impression was of a tall, solid male, his body toned with muscles from years of wielding a heavy claymore.

His flinty blue eyes had lit with appreciation when they fell upon her, his stern mouth softened into a smile. He had bowed elegantly and presented her with a nosegay of fresh wildflowers, tied with a fine white satin ribbon.

She remembered preening under his obvious approval, coyly gazing up at him beneath her lashes as she accepted his gift. He had gently kissed her hand and she had blushed. His masterful presence intrigued her; his gallant manner delighted her. She had returned to her parents well pleased with the match, eager to become handsome Archibald's bride.

How very foolish and naive she had been.

Archibald moved closer. He reached out and caught a section of hair that had come loose from her braid. Joan's scalp stung painfully and her eyes welled with tears as he tried to use it to pull her toward him.

Yet she refused to budge. Refused, also, to allow any emotions to cloud her expression, since experience had taught her never to show fear in front of him.

"Let me pass. I am needed in the castle," Joan announced, yanking her head. Stars burst behind her eyes at the extreme pain, but she was free of his grasp, even though she knew it was only an illusion. She could see the golden strands dangling from his large hand, a tinge of red blood at the roots. "Someone will come looking fer me if I dinnae return right away."

"Let them look." Archibald shook his hand, tossing her hair onto the dirt floor. "We have much to discuss."

"It will have to wait fer another time."

"Nay." Archibald scowled. "Though I am glad to be rid of ye, Joan, I find that I dinnae like the idea of another man rutting between yer legs, claiming what once belonged to me. If ye were willing to lift yer skirts fer a servant, then ye can do the same fer the man ye once called husband."

*My God!*

Her stomach rolled and pitched and for a moment Joan thought she was going to be sick. Sunlight filtered through the gaps in the wall, slashing over his face, revealing the demonic gleam in Archibald's eyes. Yet she refused to stand there like a frightened, hunted rabbit, waiting to be attacked.

She darted to her left. Archibald reached for her, but she was too fast. Joan leapt for the door. She was nearly there when he grabbed her shoulder with a strong, rough hand and spun her toward him.

Frantic, Joan shoved against his chest. It made no difference. He tightened his grip, then bent his head and covered his mouth with hers. Joan heaved at the contact. He smelled of ale and sweat and danger.

She tore her lips away and turned her head, prepared to sink her teeth into his shoulder, but she knew it would only perversely arouse him. Instead, she raked her nails down the side of his face until she saw streaks of blood.

With a roar of pain, he thrust her away. She fell on her back, the breath knocked from her lungs. "Christ, ye've made me hard as a stone," he said, fumbling with the ties on his braies. "I'll take ye first, then beat ye after."

Joan shifted and crawled frantically across the dirt floor, scraping her hands and knees. Archibald reached for her, but she rolled away before he could pin her down. A scream built in her throat, but she held it back, knowing she would need every ounce of her strength.

The door opened. Ripples of relief crawled up Joan's spine at the distraction. Mayhap now she could escape.

"Get the hell out!" Archibald yelled at the intruder.

Not waiting to hear the stranger's reply, Joan pulled herself to the open doorway. Her body tensed and instinctively recoiled when she felt a pair of strong hands close around her waist. Her panic grew when she gazed upward, seeing only a shadowed figure and the broad shoulders of a tall man.

Was it friend or foe? Someone who would aid her or just as easily hand her over to Archibald?

A few desperate seconds passed. Joan braced her hands on the ground, her body trembling. Then with a most unladylike grunt, she pushed herself to her feet. The hands around her waist tightened, steadying her when she rose. The moment she was on her feet, she pulled away.

"What's going on?" the stranger asked, reaching for his sword.

"McKenna," Archibald growled. "This has naught to do with ye. I was having a word with my wife."

"It looks like ye were doing far more than talking." Malcolm looked toward Archibald, then back at her. "Are ye hurt?"

"She's fine," Archibald insisted. "She tripped on the uneven ground. Poor Joan, she always was a clumsy lass."

Joan stared at him in disbelief. Did he honestly think she was going to deny his brutality?

Archibald's eyes narrowed, as if daring her to dispute his account. She opened her mouth to protest, but a shiver ripped through her. 'Twas shameful to be treated with such savagery. It made her feel small and insignificant and inexplicably as though she was somehow to blame. The need to conceal crept over Joan, clouding her judgment.

"I was just leaving," she muttered. Clutching the torn sleeve of her gown tightly around her, she glanced at Malcolm. "Please let me pass."

"Are ye certain that ye are unharmed?" Malcolm asked.

"Aye."

Joan pulled in a deep breath, then another as she waited for his response. A part of her wanted him to ignore her denial and instead draw his sword and cut Archibald down, once and for all ending the possibility of torment from her former husband. Yet the shame of this mistreatment kept her silent.

Malcolm's hand remained on the hilt of his sword as his brow puckered in consternation. Archibald straightened his clothes, his stance deceptively casual. Joan knew he was skilled with both sword and dirk and not opposed to fighting dirty.

There was no guarantee that a battle between the two

warriors would result in the desired outcome of Archibald's death. In truth, it could make things considerably worse.

"Ye must allow me to accompany ye, Lady Joan," Malcolm finally said, holding out his arm.

For a moment she simply stared at it, unwilling to have physical contact with any male. But her choices were few. The easiest way to depart without a fuss was to accept Malcolm's help. Again.

She stiffened her back and allowed her hand to hover over Malcolm's outstretched arm. Archibald growled low in his throat, but made no other protest.

"We shall finish our discussion later, Joan," Archibald called out as they left the stable.

*Over my dead body,* Joan thought grimly. *Or better still, over yers, Archibald Fraser.*

# Chapter Seven

Malcolm increased the length of his stride to keep pace with Joan as she hurried across the bailey. Once she finally gripped it, her hand never left his arm—in truth she clutched it so tightly her fingernails dug into his flesh. She kept her back straight and her head high. Many eyes followed them, but she avoided looking directly at anyone they passed.

"I owe ye my thanks once again, Malcolm," she said as they drew near the entrance to the great hall. "Ye seem to be making a habit out of rescuing me."

Malcolm cleared his throat. Her hair was in disarray, her lips bruised, the sleeve of her gown torn. He believed he had reached her before the worst had occurred, but there was no way to know for certain without asking.

"Did Archibald . . . ?"

"Attack me," she answered. "Aye. But thanks to yer timely arrival he was unable to do any real harm." Her jaw clenched. "Though it would have been far more helpful if ye could have come a bit sooner."

She lifted her chin in a stubborn, haughty manner. Malcolm was momentarily speechless. Christ, was the woman ever gracious about anything?

He was just about to call her to task when he noticed she was biting her bottom lip so hard it drew blood.

"Joan?"

"I'm fine," she insisted.

"Ye're crying," he said softly.

"I'm not!" She swiped at her tears angrily with her sleeve.

Malcolm's gaze locked with hers.

"Why are ye always so kind to me?" she accused, fresh tears gathering in her eyes.

"I dinnae know. 'Tis one of my greater faults, I believe." He smiled gently.

"Aye." Her lovely eyes were now swimming in tears. "Ye must be sure to confess this grave sin the next time ye speak with a priest. I imagine ye'll have to do a substantial penance to save yer immortal soul."

She tried to smile, but a sob broke free. Joan's eyes widened in horror and she immediately put her fist in her mouth to stop it. Malcolm's heart softened as he watched her valiantly try to conquer her emotions.

She wore her fierceness and haughty manner like a suit of armor, showing the world a most formidable will. Yet beneath it he could see a frightened, vulnerable woman. Aye, there were times when she was arrogant and selfish, mayhap even manipulative, yet he realized there was far more to her character than his original opinion.

Her temper was driven by her passionate, uncompromising spirit. He had believed that her beauty hid a cold, dark heart, but after seeing her with her son, Malcolm knew there was love and kindness within her soul. And she was clever enough to realize that it made her vulnerable.

Her beauty blinded most men, her caustic tongue kept them at bay, and she used both to advantage, in order to survive. By what right could he find fault with that behavior? Nay, in truth, he was drawn to it, admired it.

As he looked closely, Malcolm could see that she was still shaking. No doubt from shock.

"Forgive me fer not arriving sooner," he said sincerely. "Though of the two of ye, I'd say that Archibald looked the worse fer wear."

She let out a brittle laugh, reached up, and touched the back of her head. "'Tis good to know the bald spot on my scalp isn't that noticeable."

Malcolm's eyes followed her long, slender fingers. He saw streaks of bright red blood among the golden strands of her hair, and a darker red scab forming on her scalp. Obviously, the hair had been painfully pulled out by the roots.

"Bloody hell! I should have drawn my sword and run it through his black heart."

"Nay. While nothing on earth would bring me a greater sense of peace than knowing Archibald had taken his last breath. And I've no doubt of yer fighting skills, but he's too clever to let himself be drawn into an honorable fight. Against those odds, ye might not have been victorious."

"I'm touched that ye would show such tender feelings of concern fer me, Joan." Malcolm grinned.

She scowled. "Dinnae be daft! I am, as always, thinking of myself. If Archibald had defeated ye, I would be forced to carry the burden of yer death. 'Tis far too heavy a weight fer my conscience to bear."

Her barb fell short, for Malcolm saw right through her attempt to once again paint herself as cold and uncaring. Gently, he covered his hand over hers. "Ye must have a care never to be alone with him."

"I can assure ye that this meeting was not my choice," Joan replied.

"Ye went willingly?"

"I was foolish, trapped by another's lies." She shook her head, making no effort to hide her disgust. "I'll not be so easily duped again."

"Aye, this could have ended very badly," Malcolm said, his mind swirling with various possibilities, all of them dire.

The color drained from her cheeks. "I confess fer a moment I feared that he might kill me. But then I remembered that I am far too stubborn and proud to die at the hands of such a lowly worm."

She tossed her head as she said the last, her eyes suddenly blazing with defiance. "I must find my maid at once. Though it's doubtful that Archibald has any interest in my son, Gertrude must go to Callum. I'll not feel any ease until I am certain the lad is safe."

*Her child. Of course.* It was probably how Archibald lured her into meeting him.

"I'll see to the lad," Malcolm volunteered.

Joan's face darkened. "What do ye know of my son?"

"I followed ye the other night. I know which house the child is being kept in. I assume ye are hiding him because of his father?"

She nodded sharply. "Archibald has no conscience and no heart. He disowned Callum when our marriage ended and has no care fer him, but I dinnae want to tempt the fates and put the lad anywhere that Archibald would see him."

"A wise precaution. I can easily locate the house and ensure that all is as it should be."

Joan's eyes filled with worry. "It will appear suspicious if ye are seen wandering the streets of the village. 'Tis best if Gertrude goes, but I thank ye sincerely fer the offer." She sighed. "It seems that I am constantly finding myself in yer debt."

Malcolm could tell by her tone that she was not pleased by that fact, but she was clever enough to realize she could ill afford to turn down any help. "I'm not a man who would take advantage of a woman," he said, trying to allay her fears.

"I know."

Her reply surprised him, and his heart lightened to hear her opinion, though he was confused as to why her feelings about him mattered so much. *Probably because of this mess with the MacPhearson lass,* he told himself. There were just so many times a man could hear himself called a dishonorable rogue without it having an effect.

"I would, however, be pleased to accept a small token of thanks from ye, Joan," he said.

"What sort of token?" she asked warily.

He let his gaze drop to her lips. She stared back at him in confusion, then realizing what he meant, favored him with a stern glance of consternation. "I beg ye, Malcolm, dinnae go spoiling my rising regard fer ye by asking fer a kiss. 'Tis unseemly."

"Ye misunderstand me." He laughed, a bit too loudly, cursing himself for making his desire so obvious. Cursing, too, that she seemed so opposed to the idea.

She raised a skeptical brow. "Do I?"

"Aye. I dinnae think of ye in that way."

"What way? Like a woman?"

"Och, ye're twisting my words, Joan."

"Ye dinnae find me desirable?"

Malcolm swallowed a groan. "We both know there's no possible way fer me to answer that question."

"Hmm . . . perhaps." Her eyes sparkled and he was pleased to be able to provide her with some amusement, even if it was at his expense.

"What would ye say if I asked fer a wee kiss?" he ventured, putting forth his most charming smile.

Joan tilted her head and considered him for a brief moment. "Honestly, I'd rather kiss my horse."

Inwardly, Malcolm winced, though he kept his smile in place. "Aye, I believe that ye'd both enjoy it more than kissing me."

Joan's eyes came alive as she broke into a giggle, but her laugh ended abruptly. "Bloody hell, here comes Archibald."

Malcolm whipped his head around and saw the Fraser laird stomping into the bailey, nearly spewing fire from his mouth. Archibald glanced at the faces of the men gathered in the courtyard, then snarled when his eyes lit upon Malcolm.

"Defend yerself, McKenna," Archibald shouted, pulling the claymore strapped to his back and raising it over his head.

Malcolm barely had time to shove Joan out of the way, pull his sword, and position himself to deflect the blow. The clang of steel rang loudly in his ears. 'Twas only due to his wide stance and strong legs that he was able to maintain his balance.

"Is there a particular reason ye want to fight or are ye just in the mood?" Malcolm asked, as the two of them crossed swords again.

"I dinnae like any man interfering with my wife," Archibald declared, swinging his sword with a loud grunt. "I willnae allow such an insult to go unpunished."

"She's not yer wife anymore," Malcolm replied, leaping back. Archibald swung again in a wide arc, coming so close to Malcolm's head that he felt the wind of the blade near his cheek. "Ye need to stay away from her."

Archibald beat his chest with his sword and roared. "No man orders me! I'll do exactly as I wish!"

Enraged, Archibald attacked with a flurry of sword strikes. Malcolm blocked them all, hardly believing his opponent's strength. Each time the blades struck, he could feel the vibrations run through his entire body.

Malcolm caught Archibald's blade high, then low, pressing forward too quickly across the uneven ground and losing his footing. From a distance he heard a female scream as he fell—*Joan*?

Blood pounding, Malcolm hit the dirt, rolled, and regained his feet just in time to block Archibald's next swing. The clang of metal exploded in his ear.

*Christ, the man is out to kill me!*

Their swords met again. Malcolm matched Archibald strike for strike, then suddenly spun around. Grasping his sword with both hands, he hit Archibald in his lower back with the flat of the sword, knocking him down.

Triumphant, Malcolm stepped forward to place his foot on Archibald's chest and end the fight, but Archibald moved too quickly, scrambling in the dirt, twisting, and sitting upright.

He reached for Malcolm's ankle. Malcolm sidestepped the hand, but stumbled, giving Archibald time to regain his footing. Breathing hard, both men faced each other. They circled slowly, methodically, each searching for a weakness.

Archibald suddenly lunged, and Malcolm spun to his right. Fortunately, Archibald's sharp blade glanced off his upper arm instead of piercing his chest. Emboldened by drawing first blood, Archibald's eyes flashed with confidence and he swung harder.

'Twas in that moment that Malcolm realized if he made his swings with less force, yet more precise, he could conserve his own strength and drain Archibald's. Swinging their swords in rhythmic arcs, the two men continued trading blows, each straining as they struggled for the advantage.

Swords crossed, they leaned into each other, their faces mere inches apart. Malcolm could see the sweat on his opponent's face, hear the bellows of his breathing. Archibald was tiring, thank the saints. All Malcolm need do was parry a few more thrusts and he should be able to toss him in the dirt.

'Twas difficult for Malcolm to be cautious in this fight, when every instinct bade him to deliver the appropriate justice to a man who abused and frightened women. Yet he held back. His patience was rewarded when he saw Archibald's confidence growing with each sword strike.

He allowed Archibald one final hard blow, but as he stepped forward, Malcolm stumbled over a rock. Flaying his arms to keep his balance, he lost his grip on the sword. The weapon clattered to the dirt with an ominous sound.

Menacingly, Archibald approached. Knowing he was fighting for his life, Malcolm clenched his fist and swung upward, landing a hard punch to Archibald's jaw. The sound was brutal, and while the blow stunned him, Archibald somehow remained on his feet.

Malcolm spun around again, this time aiming his foot at the back of Archibald's knee. Archibald screamed when Malcolm connected with the target. Cursing and yelping in pain, Archibald crumbled, a shower of dust filling the air when he landed.

There was a brief cheer when Archibald hit the ground. Malcolm looked up and realized a crowd had formed to watch the melee. Being Highlanders, the onlookers had naturally been wagering on the outcome, as he saw several men exchanging coins. Picking up his sword, he nodded at one of the McKenna soldiers, pleased he had been able to help the man gain a profit.

"Ye dinnae fight like an honorable knight," Archibald accused, clutching at his knee.

"Ye had no cause to attack me," Malcolm retorted.

"I had every cause," Archibald insisted, as he slowly stood.

"Malcolm!" a deep voice called, and he readied his sword, then slowly lowered it when he saw his father and brother approaching.

"Christ's wounds, what in the name of all that is holy are ye doing?" the McKenna bellowed.

"Laird Fraser and I had a difference of opinion," Malcolm answered. "We decided it was a matter best settled with swordplay."

"Swords and trickery," Archibald muttered bitterly, rubbing his jaw.

"'Tis how the knights on Crusade defend themselves," Malcolm said pleasantly. "My brother James taught me."

Archibald replied by spitting in the dirt.

James caught Malcolm's eye and smiled. "I could have beaten him in half the time," James proclaimed, never missing the opportunity to fan the flames of competition between himself and his older brother.

"Not bloody likely," Malcolm protested, gratefully accepting the shoulder James offered to lean upon.

The McKenna examined Malcolm with a critical eye, his expression softening when he realized Malcolm was not seriously injured.

"Out of respect fer Laird Armstrong and his generous hospitality, the two of ye will confine yer swordplay to the practice yard," the McKenna commanded.

"I shall abide by yer wisdom, Laird McKenna," Archibald said. Then waving his hand wildly toward

Malcolm, he added, "Make certain that yer son does the same or I'll not be held accountable fer the outcome of a second match."

Though he made a great show of cooperation, Malcolm knew inside Fraser must be seething. 'Twas galling to be defeated in front of a crowd that included men who served you. Strength and power were essential elements for survival in the Highlands. A laird could ill afford to lose either.

Archibald turned and stalked away, but Malcolm caught the flash of contempt lurking deep in his eyes. James must have seen it also—his body tensed and his hand inched toward the hilt of the sword sheathed at his side.

"Fraser is a treacherous man, lacking in honor and possessing a blood thirst that borders on madness," James declared. "Beware of him, brother."

Malcolm nodded grimly, agreeing completely with James's assessment.

"Ye're bleeding."

The voice was feminine; the tone decidedly displeased. *Joan.*

Malcolm glanced down at his arm and saw a nasty wound. "I hadn't realized the blade cut so deep," he said, surprised at how much it stung.

"It needs tending or else it will fester," Joan decided. "Come with me."

He hesitated. She huffed in annoyance, placing her hands on her hips. "'Tis best to do it right away. My offer to aid ye does not extend to cleaning a rotting, putrid wound."

"Och, ye've a rare talent fer painting a pretty picture, Joan," James said sarcastically.

"I merely speak the plain truth," she countered. "Are ye coming, Malcolm?"

Deciding he had had more than enough fighting for one day, Malcolm meekly followed Joan into the castle, through the great hall, and up a narrow, twisting stairway. They entered a large chamber with colorful pillows on the chairs, an intricately patterned rug on the floor, and fresh spring flowers in an urn on the table—the women's solar.

"Remove yer shirt," she commanded. Joan poured water into the bowl, wet a cloth, then paused and looked at him with narrowed eyes. "Wine, ale, or whiskey?"

"Whiskey," he replied without hesitation.

"Aye. I'll send fer it."

She left the chamber and stood on the landing, her voice bellowing an impatient command for a servant to attend her.

In due course a line of servants entered the solar. They brought more water, whiskey, bread, cheese, and a basket filled with instruments and medicine. Joan instructed them to set everything on the table, then dismissed them with a distracted wave of her hand.

Using a fresh wet cloth, she cleaned away the dried blood and bits of materials that clung to the wound. Malcolm flinched at her ministrations; the pain was sharp and deep.

"It will need to be stitched," she decided.

She poured him a whiskey, washed her hands, then began sorting through the contents of the basket. She selected a needle and thread, dumped the water from the wash bowl, filled it with whiskey, and dropped the thread and needle inside.

Malcolm groaned at the waste of such fine liquor. "Why are ye doing that?" he asked.

Joan shrugged. "I'm not sure. 'Tis what the healer

always does before she stitches a man's wounds and those rarely fester."

Swiping the whiskey bottle, Malcolm set it next to him, just in case Joan had any other foolish notions. Whiskey this fine belonged in a man's gut, not on his skin. He watched curiously as she tore strips of linen, set them in a neat row, then ran her fingers over them carefully. Frowning, she repositioned two of them, took a deep breath, then hastily made the sign of the cross.

Malcolm shot her an uneasy glance. "Have ye much experience as a healer?" he asked.

"Enough." Joan replied briskly, in her usual challenging manner.

She picked up the needle and thread and glared at him. Cursing beneath his breath, he drained his glass, refilled it, then nodded that he was ready.

As she brought the needle close to his flesh, Malcolm tensed. Joan placed her hand comfortingly on his shoulder and his heart lurched at the unexpected contact. Puzzled, he reached up and touched her cheek. She startled and their gazes met.

"Are ye in pain? Do ye need more whiskey before I start sewing?" she asked breathlessly.

"Nay, I . . ." Feeling foolish, he allowed his voice to trail off. Didn't she feel it, too? This maddening urge to embrace, this fierce need to brush their lips together. "Go on. Do yer worst."

She leaned closer and Malcolm's senses filled with the intoxicating fragrance of lemon mixed with spicy lavender. His gaze fixed on the perfection of her delicate, face—her soft, creamy complexion, her startling blue eyes, pert nose, and wide, sensual mouth.

She favored him with one of her sullen glances and astonishingly the need to kiss her intensified. Had the whiskey gone completely to his head—and then his cock? Malcolm took deep breaths, trying to calm himself.

"Yer squirming is making me nervous," Joan warned. "Would ye rather I call someone else to tend to ye?"

The sound of her voice reverberated somewhere low in his gut. It had a sensual quality that he had never noticed, a husky, almost breathless edge. Mesmerized, he imagined the throaty moans of pleasure she would make if he kissed and caressed her sweet, lovely flesh.

"'Tis ye I want, Joan."

Her swift intake of breath told him she was startled by his response. Yet she chose not to acknowledge the innuendo. Lifting her brow imperiously, she inquired in her most regal tone, "Shall I begin?"

"Aye." Malcolm's voice was husky with a desire he couldn't completely contain.

Slowly, carefully, Joan pierced his flesh with the needle. He had half expected her to jab him savagely in an effort to cool his ardor, but she was gentle and deliberate. Her brow furrowed in concentration as she stitched, leaving him with the ridiculous urge to caress the lines on her forehead.

Malcolm tightened his lips, hoping the pain would distract him. It did for a few minutes, but then his traitorous gaze landed once again on her exquisite mouth. He couldn't think straight staring at those plump lips. But where else was he to look—at her breasts?

The tightly fitted bodice of her gown emphasized their full, round, perfect shape. He imagined they would sport the same milky white flesh as her complexion, with the added enticement of dusky, pink nipples.

Bloody hell, that was even worse than staring at her mouth!

After what felt like an eternity, Joan finally tied off the

last stitch. She lifted his hand and placed it on the linen strip that covered his wound. "Keep that in place while I mix a paste."

"Will it smell as nasty as it looks?"

"Worse," she said cheerfully. "Be grateful that I was able to stitch the wound closed or else my father's healer would have insisted on using a hot blade to seal the jagged edges."

That graphic image should have doused his ardor like a cold bucket of water. It didn't. Malcolm shifted slightly, hoping she wouldn't glance down and see how his stiff cock was straining against his braies.

"I prefer the needle to the blade," he finally managed to utter, wondering if he sounded as half-witted as he felt.

Joan nodded. "The loss of blood will make ye feel light headed. Ye need to put something in yer belly besides whiskey."

She broke off a piece of bread, spread it with honey, then handed it to him. He stared at the offering, watching a drop of the golden nectar run onto her thumb. Unable to resist, Malcolm grabbed her wrist and licked the honey with the tip of his tongue.

Joan squealed and snatched her hand away. "Whatever are ye doing?"

"'Tis a sin to waste such fine food," he muttered innocently.

She narrowed her brows and stared at him in disbelief. Malcolm schooled his expression into angelic innocence, doubting he could fool her, but needing to try.

"If I dinnae know any better, I would swear that ye were trying to seduce me, Malcolm McKenna," she said, her expression taut.

"And if I were?"

She stiffened. Only slightly, but he was watching her so closely, he caught it. "Ye'd be sadly disappointed."

His fingers skimmed the length of her bare hand. "I beg to differ."

For an instant Joan gazed at him in sheer wonder, then she blinked, as though regaining her senses, and abruptly stood. "Ye've had too much whiskey," she declared.

Fingers trembling, Joan wound the unused strips of linen and placed them in the basket, along with the jars of herbs and salves. She refused to glance in his direction.

But he hadn't missed how her face had turned a brilliant shade of scarlet and her breath quickened. Though she might protest with her usual indignation, Joan was not unaffected by his touch.

The thought pleased Malcolm far more than he had a right to admit.

# Chapter Eight

Joan hated how her hands trembled, how vulnerable she felt, but she ignored those emotions and continued packing the medical supplies. Malcolm's words made her shake with the usual distaste she carried of men and their lust . . . and yet there was something else brewing inside her that she couldn't identify.

Everything seemed exaggerated—the stillness of the air, the sound of Malcolm's voice, the sensitivity of her flesh where he had touched her. The intoxicating scent of his skin surrounded her, scattering her wits; the blood roared in her ears, quickening through her veins.

She had the oddest sense of being swept away in something that was too powerful to resist. Desire? Passion? Nay, 'twas impossible!

Joan could feel his eyes continue to bore into her, searching for—what? Her acquiescence? She nearly burst into gales of nervous laughter. Och, he'd be sadly disappointed.

Clenching her jaw, she avoided his gaze. Her nerves were near to shattering and she could barely tolerate another moment of his scrutiny, yet she owed him a debt for protecting her from Iain and saving her from Archibald.

A debt she intended to repay.

'Twas hardly in her nature to put others above herself, but in this instance Joan never hesitated. She had given it a fair amount of thought and believed she had come upon a reasonable solution that would resolve the MacPhearson matter without bloodshed and enable both sides to walk away with their male pride intact.

No small feat, indeed.

"Have ye decided what ye are going to do about Brienne MacPhearson?" Joan asked.

Malcolm's brows drew together. "There is naught fer me to do. The child isn't mine."

"Dinnae delude yerself," Joan warned. "The meeting this morning resolved nothing in Laird MacPhearson's mind. He'll not allow the matter to be dropped until he is satisfied with the outcome."

Malcolm rotated his wounded arm cautiously. "I'll not marry the lass and I'm not about to let him pluck out my eyes or run me through with his sword just because he believes I am responsible."

"Aye, I agree that either of those punishments would please him greatly," Joan admitted, dismayed to see a small stain of red on Malcolm's bandage. "Brienne is an honest, God-fearing lass who loves her babe. I dinnae believe that she is lying."

Malcolm recoiled, his expression strained. "Ye think that I'm the one who is playing false?"

"Nay." Joan reached over and adjusted the linen strip on his arm. "I dinnae think that either of ye are lying."

"One of us has to be," Malcolm replied. "Or else we have all witnessed a miracle of conception."

"There might be another explanation," Joan ventured. Before he could open his mouth to ask, Joan raised her hand to stay his questions. "I need to speak with Brienne and her sisters first. Give me an hour; then meet me in the chapel."

"The chapel?"

"Aye. Though Father John tries his best, 'tis a seldom used building. 'Tis the only place that I can think of where we can speak openly without being overheard."

Malcolm nodded—reluctantly—and Joan was pleased to discover that he trusted her. Carrying her basket of medicines, she left, and after an enlightening discussion with the MacPhearson women, Joan arrived at the chapel an hour later.

The church was shrouded in gloomy light when she entered, though Joan soon noticed a hulking shadow near the altar. *Malcolm.* She hurried forward, then stiffened, her footsteps halting. He wasn't alone.

Her heart tripped in a fearful rhythm until she realized the two men huddled with him were his father and brother. Of course! Malcolm respected and honored his father and the McKenna always showed great concern over the welfare of his children. It stood to reason that he would be there.

Alas, her own experience was quite the opposite. The last person in the world she could turn to when faced with adversity would be her father.

All three men faced her as she approached; Malcolm with curious interest, James with mistrust, and the McKenna with a fierce scowl. Joan took a steadying breath, praying that she had not misjudged the McKennas. Powerful men were often looking for someone to blame and women were always a convenient target.

"Well, lass, we've gathered here like a group of docile sheep, just as ye ordered. What do ye have to tell us?" the McKenna inquired.

Despite his acid tone, Joan was rather impressed that the McKenna was able to hold on to his famous temper. "I've spoken with Brienne and her sisters. Though she fears her father's wrath, she's agreed to explain why she claims that Malcolm sired her child."

"She admitted to ye that she lied?" James asked.

"Brienne acted in good faith," Joan replied. "But there is more to the story and I've convinced her the only way to resolve this dilemma is to confess all."

The men were momentarily bewildered by her cryptic response. James narrowed his eyes; Malcolm cocked his head; the McKenna drew his scowling brows tighter.

"What did Brienne confess?" the McKenna asked impatiently.

Frowning, Joan peered up at him. "I'll tell ye what I've learned, but first ye must all swear an oath."

The McKenna furrowed his forehead suspiciously. "What sort of oath?"

Joan flushed. She was used to challenging strong-willed men and conceded that the McKenna's reputation for intimidation had been well-earned and was not in the least exaggerated. He was the most terrifying man she had ever met. However, she would not falter; she would keep her word to the MacPhearson women.

"Ye must pledge that no matter what I reveal to ye, ye'll not seek vengeance against the MacPhearsons," Joan insisted. "Ye must also pledge that ye will aid Brienne, if the need arises."

James's gasp was audible. "Aid Brienne? We shall do

no such thing! The lass started this feud with her lies and accusations."

"She dinnae lie," Joan declared.

"Are ye saying that Malcolm did?" James protested hotly.

"Nay. I'm saying 'twas an honest mistake."

"How could such a devious lie be an honest mistake?" the McKenna challenged.

"I'll explain it all after ye make yer pledge." Joan lifted her chin at their dubious glares. "Men thirst fer retribution, especially when they believe that their honor has been slighted. Shedding blood between yer clans will accomplish nothing and most likely lead to more bloodshed. Will ye swear not to seek vengeance?"

The McKenna shook his head slowly. "Ye tie my hands with this demand, lass."

Joan sighed. "Aye, 'tis indeed the point."

The McKenna men exchanged glances. Joan nearly stomped her foot in frustration at their suspicious expressions. She was offering them a solution that would save their honor and their hides. Pray God that they were smart enough to take it.

There was a bit of low grumbling between them and then Malcolm spoke. "I trust that Joan is doing all that she can to aid us," he said, breaking away. Standing directly in front of her, he ceremoniously dropped to one knee. "I give ye my pledge."

Something snapped inside Joan as she looked down at him—a coil of emotion that felt like pride. No one— especially no man—had ever valued her opinion so highly, had ever trusted her so unconditionally. Straightening her shoulders, she turned toward James and the McKenna.

They were both staring at Malcolm. James was clearly

puzzled by his brother's gesture; the McKenna seemed even more suspicious.

"There! Ye have yer pledge," the McKenna declared with a smug grin. "Now, tell us all."

Joan returned his grin with a haughty, accusing glare. "Aye, I have Malcolm's pledge, but not yers or James's."

"I dance to no one's tune except my own," the McKenna insisted, pounding his fist on the altar for emphasis.

Inwardly, Joan cringed, battling the instinct to shrink away from his fury. For just a moment she considered abandoning her promise to Brienne and telling them everything she had discovered.

In the past, Joan knew she would never have subjected herself to such a difficult task at the behest of another. And if she had gotten involved, she would have taken the easiest route, spoken her peace, and walked away. Or at the very least, bargained for something that would benefit *her*, and her alone.

But she had changed.

She knew the feeling of being a terrified, powerless woman, beholden to the whims of the men in her life. And she now knew the importance of helping another who suffered the same desperate turmoil. She had promised to aid Brienne and she intended to keep that promise, no matter how long or loud the McKenna shouted.

Beneath her woolen gown, Joan's knees trembled, but she raised her chin defiantly. "We've called fer another meeting between the McKennas and the MacPhearsons."

Disapproval framed the McKenna's face. "We'll not be there—we've naught left to say."

"I agree. But there's plenty that ye'll want to hear." Joan held her breath. "Do I have yer pledge? James?"

James looked to his brother, then nodded. "Aye."

"Laird McKenna?"

The McKenna squirmed. Clearly annoyed, he finally grumbled, "We pledge no vengeance upon the Mac-Phearsons. But I'll be damned if I make the same vow about the Armstrongs!"

Malcolm knew that it was wrong, nay, almost disloyal, to feel such delight watching Joan best his father. Yet it was so eerily similar to the disagreements he had witnessed through the years between his parents, he could not help but smile.

Joan was fearless in her attitude, passionate in her determination. Malcolm's admiration for her soared, along with his sincere thanks. He listened carefully to her explanation, impressed at how she had managed to decipher the truth.

He noted that James and their father were also intently engaged, though their expressions gave no clues to their thinking. 'Twas a great deal to take in and all were silent when Joan finished speaking.

"Does Laird MacPhearson know this?" Malcolm asked.

Joan shook her head. "Nay. Brienne feels great shame fer the disgrace she has brought upon the clan and fears her father's wrath will fall on her son once he learns the truth of the lad's parentage. 'Tis the reason why it was so important that ye vowed not to seek revenge."

"So he'll be hearing it all fer the first time at this meeting? Do ye think that's wise?" Malcolm questioned.

"There'll be no other men in the chamber except my father, a few MacPhearsons, and the three of ye when Brienne confesses. We thought that best."

"We?"

"Aye. Myself, Brienne, and her sisters."

"Och, so ye've got this all planned out, have ye?" the McKenna said.

Joan nodded.

James groaned. "God save us all from meddlesome females."

"This meddlesome female has most likely prevented a clan war," Malcolm said with a pleased grin. "We owe Joan our gratitude."

"I'll be saving my thanks until we witness the outcome of this meeting," the McKenna answered wryly. "When will it take place?"

Joan cleared her throat. "Now."

The McKenna raised his brows. "Ye were very sure of yerself, Joan Armstrong."

"I was hopeful, Laird McKenna. Nothing more."

The McKenna grunted in disbelief. Malcolm hid another grin and proffered Joan his arm. She accepted it with a nod and led them from the chapel.

All were grim faced as they entered Laird Armstrong's solar for the second time that day. Confident that he would be exonerated, Malcolm steadily returned the hard glares of the MacPhearson men without flinching.

Brienne sat in a chair, her sisters standing immobile beside her, each with a hand on one of her shoulders. She looked slightly lost and very young. Her body tensed every time another person entered the chamber. Fortunately, as Joan had promised, there were not many.

"Why have ye brought us here again, Armstrong?" Laird MacPhearson asked.

Laird Armstrong turned in surprise. "I was told that ye—"

"I sent word on my father's behalf," Joan interrupted smoothly. "Brienne has something she needs to tell all of ye."

All eyes swung in Brienne's direction. She paled, looking as though she would bolt if she could only reach the chamber door. Malcolm's heart softened at her distress and he wondered if she was going to faint again.

"All will be well," one of the MacPhearson sisters said, squeezing Brienne's shoulder in support. "Tell them."

Brienne shifted, running her hands up and down her arms as though to warm herself. Finally, she spoke. "The man who wooed me at the fete told me he was Malcolm McKenna."

"We've already heard these accusations," Laird Armstrong cried in a huff, rapping his knuckles impatiently on the table. "More than once."

"Ye might have heard it, but ye're not listening," Joan interrupted. "Brienne said the man *told* her his name was Malcolm McKenna. Yet once she set eyes upon the true Malcolm McKenna this morning, she realized that he was not the man that had taken her maidenhead."

"'Tis why she fainted," one of the MacPhearson sisters added.

"Is that true, Brienne?" Laird Armstrong asked.

"Aye." Brienne's reply was so low, 'twas barely audible.

Laird MacPhearson froze at the confirmation. "Why did ye not tell me, daughter?"

"I . . . I couldn't." Brienne bowed her head and scrubbed away the tears on her face with the heel of her palm. "All these months I told ye 'twas Malcolm McKenna who fathered my babe, because it was what I believed. When I realized my mistake, I knew I'd made a terrible mess of things. I dinnae know how to say that I was wrong. So very wrong."

Her voice strained with desperation, clearly heard by all in the chamber. The MacPhearson men shifted uneasily on their feet, refusing to meet Malcolm's eyes.

Laird MacPhearson's shoulders slumped as he abruptly sat, his soft sigh cutting the air. "What's to be done?"

"First, we must all agree that Lady Brienne is innocent of any wrongdoing," Malcolm insisted, glad to see the furrows of shame on Brienne's face ease a bit.

"Aye, she showed her true mettle by confessing her error and revealing the truth to one and all," the McKenna agreed. "We shall not condemn her."

"We dinnae want yer pity," Laird MacPhearson said proudly.

"I'm not offering it," Malcolm countered. "The lass is not at fault. 'Tis true that she was wrong in naming me as the father of her child, but she did so unintentionally and without guile. Ye should be proud of her. When faced with a dark realization, she chose to be honest and truthful."

"The real rogue is the shameful cur who played her false and impersonated my son," the McKenna declared. "What can ye tell us of him, Lady Brienne? Did he wear the McKenna plaid?"

"Aye, he wore the plaid. 'Twas how I noticed him that first morning." Brienne blushed. "He is tall, though not as tall as Sir Malcolm, and very handsome."

"That's hardly a unique description," Laird Armstrong said tartly.

"The man's eyes are green," Joan offered. "The same as the babe he fathered."

"'Tis not much to go on, but a help nonetheless," Malcolm said. "We shall start searching and hopefully flush the rogue out."

"Ye cannae be dragging every tall, handsome, green-eyed man in Scotland to McKenna Castle fer justice,"

Laird Armstrong jeered. "How will ye even know if ye catch the right one?"

"Lady Brienne will know him in an instant," the McKenna said. "Will ye help us, lass?"

Laird MacPhearson's lips curled in suspicion. "What are ye suggesting, McKenna?"

"'Twould behoove us both if Lady Brienne returned to McKenna Castle with us and resided there whilst we search fer this culprit," the McKenna answered.

"Nay." Laird MacPhearson shook his head.

"'Tis a sensible suggestion, Father," one of the Mac-Phearson daughters implored. "We all want this man caught."

"We would be in yer debt, and Lady Brienne's," Malcolm added.

Brienne reached up and fingered the gold cross that hung around her neck. She seemed intrigued, though her gaze was wary. "May I bring my child?"

"Of course!" the McKenna exclaimed. "My wife likes nothing more than to coddle an infant. She will be very pleased to have ye both beneath our roof and under our protection."

Laird MacPhearson drew back his shoulders. Malcolm could almost see the gears spinning in the man's head as he contemplated the proposal.

"Yer saintly wife will welcome her? A lass who has birthed a child without benefit of marriage?"

"She would." The McKenna nodded fiercely.

"Aye," Malcolm agreed. "We hold no malice toward the lass."

Laird MacPhearson's expression grew speculative. "'Twas my hope that when I left here, I'd see my Brienne either avenged or married."

"The vengeance will have to wait until we find the right man," Malcolm said evenly, tamping down the sudden, uneasy feeling churning in his gut.

"And the marriage?" Laird MacPhearson lifted a brow. "'Tis still possible to make a match between ye. Brienne's future would be assured if she carried the McKenna name."

All eyes shifted to Malcolm. He looked to his father for guidance, but the McKenna shrugged, letting him know the decision was entirely his own. The suggestion actually held some merit. An alliance through marriage with the MacPhearsons was a good way to bury this unpleasant incident and every man in the chamber knew it.

Malcolm studied Brienne, trying to open his mind to the notion. She was a comely lass, with a gentle bearing. He had spoken the truth when he said he held no malice against her, nor did he object to the fact that she had a child. But she was simply too young. He needed a woman with greater maturity and spirit.

Unbidden, his eyes traveled to Joan.

It was difficult for Malcolm to reject Brienne so publicly, especially when her confidence and reputation had been so newly restored. But taking her as his wife would be no favor to either of them.

As if sensing his hesitation, Laird MacPhearson pressed on. "Is Brienne not a fine lass, worthy of the McKenna name?" Laird MacPhearson's chin jutted out. "Ye just said that we should be proud of her honesty and courage, Sir Malcolm. Were ye lying?"

Malcolm favored them all with a congenial smile. He was not about to get snared in the trap that Laird Mac-Phearson had set—yet he knew he must extricate himself in a way that would cause no insult.

"Lady Brienne is indeed a fine woman, with many qualities to recommend her," Malcolm said, keeping his tone deliberately light. "Any Highlander would be proud to claim her as his wife."

"Including ye?" Laird MacPhearson asked.

"Aye." Malcolm turned his expression regretful, hoping he looked sincere. "Alas, 'tis an impossibility."

Laird MacPhearson's hand moved to the jeweled hilt of the dirk at his waist. "Why?"

Malcolm folded his arms over his chest. "I am already betrothed."

"What?" James cried.

"When?" the McKenna bellowed.

"To whom?" Laird MacPhearson sputtered.

The chamber grew silent as all awaited his answer. Malcolm felt but a slight hesitation before calmly uttering, "I am to marry Lady Joan."

Joan's mouth dropped open. She could feel the eyes of all those in the chamber trained upon her, could hear the grumbles and whispers. She closed her mouth to stop the swift denial that sprang to her lips, took a long breath, and counted to fifteen. She would have to tread carefully. They were so close to achieving a peaceful solution; any misstep now and it would all crumble to dust.

She found it impossible to look at Malcolm, fearing all would see the absurdity of his lie reflected in her expression. Instead, she dared to risk a glance at her father.

Laird Armstrong's lips were tight with displeasure. "Explain yerself," he demanded of her.

"'Tis only recently been decided," she said weakly.

"We are both of an age to make these decisions of our

own accord," Malcolm said, moving closer and placing a hand on Joan's shoulder. "Are ye displeased with the prospect of an alliance between our clans, Laird Armstrong?"

"We are already aligned through James and Davina," Laird Armstrong answered tersely.

"And now the bond shall be even stronger," Malcolm concluded.

Joan stiffened. She could see the hard spark of temper in her father's eyes. Desperate to avoid an outburst, she looked to the MacPhearson sisters. They all appeared in shock.

Needing to shift the attention away from herself and Malcolm's ridiculous announcement, Joan turned to Brienne.

"Will ye come to McKenna Castle, Lady Brienne?" she asked.

The abrupt change of subject brought on a rumbling of conversation from the men in the chamber, yet they quieted when Brienne spoke.

"If my father allows it, then I shall accept Laird McKenna's offer to travel there and do whatever he asks to aid him in finding the imposter." She favored Joan with a shy smile. "And I wish ye and Sir Malcolm much happiness in yer marriage."

Joan held her breath as she waited for Laird MacPhearson's answer. A visible sadness lined his weathered face as he gazed at his daughter. Finally, he nodded. "So be it."

Laird MacPhearson stood. He approached Malcolm, his arm outstretched. "I'm trusting ye to care fer her and the babe," he said, his jaw flexing with emotion. "Dinnae fail me in yer duty."

Malcolm clasped Laird MacPhearson by the arm. He held tightly for a moment, then nodded.

The low murmurs of discussion began again as those who had gathered filed out of the chamber. Joan kept her eyes downcast, refusing to meet Malcolm's gaze when he left. She hugged each of the MacPhearson women, stalling for time. When the room emptied, only she and her father remained.

"Ye made me look the fool in front of the MacPhearsons and the McKennas," Laird Armstrong roared with anger.

Joan bit her lip in frustration. Why was he always so prepared to be disapproving of her? She had done naught but work hard and try to ease his burdens since she returned home. Yet he never appreciated any of her efforts and instead looked to find fault in everything.

"I thought ye'd be pleased to settle the matter without bloodshed," Joan replied, making her voice deliberately calm.

"I was charged with resolving this feud, not ye!" He turned away from her and began pacing in agitation. "And yer betrothal to Malcolm McKenna. I'd not believe it unless I heard it with my own ears, directly from his lips. I've half a mind to refuse to allow it, but that would mean I'd lose the chance to be rid of ye."

Joan's breath stuck in her throat. Her father never made any attempt to hide his feelings for her, yet his words hurt more than she could have imagined. Still, Joan hid that hurt, unwilling to give him the satisfaction of seeing her pain, of letting him know he possessed the power to wound her.

She had intended to denounce the betrothal the moment the MacPhearsons departed, but hesitated at her father's angry expression. Her mind spun in circles as she tried to find the words to explain it all without raising his ire further, then realized now was not the time.

"We will speak of this later, when ye are not so angry," she said.

'Twas the wrong thing to say. Laird Armstrong's nostrils flared. He gripped her arm firmly, hard enough to be painful. A harsh look darkened his face. She could not help but compare it to the look of tenderness and regret Laird MacPhearson bestowed upon Brienne, and Joan felt another pang of sadness.

She pulled away, heading for the door. He followed. She turned.

"Dinnae *ever* tell me what to do," he snapped, his cheeks flushed.

His arm swung wide and backhanded Joan. The blow was so unexpected it caught her completely unaware, striking her jaw. She fell to the ground from the force of it, wiping the blood that trickled from her mouth with her fingers.

Joan slowly rose to her feet. Never before had her father struck her, even when she was a young lass. She stared at him in astonishment, speechless at his lack of control.

His eyes were remote and she realized no sense of family loyalty or connection existed between them. Whatever affection they might have shared when she was a child had long since vanished. She was an embarrassment and a burden to him and would remain so for as long as she drew breath.

With an unsteady gait, Joan walked away, her heart bruised, her pride wounded, but her spirit, as ever, unbroken.

# Chapter Nine

By the time the evening meal had started, Joan was calmer. Her father's anger would cool—eventually. Until then, she needed to make herself scarce and stay out of his sight, a task made easier by the number of visitors still at the castle. As long as she made certain there was plenty of hot food and drink for the guests, she would barely be missed.

After checking that all was as it should be with Cook, Joan wound her way through the halls toward her chamber. She would have Gertrude fetch a simple meal that she would eat in her room, then wait until complete darkness before venturing into the village to see Callum. Just the promise of her son's sweet face and exuberant hugs gave Joan a much needed sense of peace that she was desperate to embrace.

"I've been searching everywhere fer ye."

*Malcolm.* Joan's heart tripped when she spied him coming toward her. *Saints above, I'm not certain I've the strength to face him right now.*

Malcolm glanced down at the stained apron she wore over her gown and frowned. "Are ye going to change yer clothes before the meal? I'll be pleased to wait fer ye."

"Thanks to ye, I'll not be showing my face in the great hall until the clans have left," Joan replied with a huff.

She started up the staircase and he followed close behind.

"Why?" he asked innocently.

"Our betrothal." Joan took a deep breath and somehow resisted the urge to turn and box his ears.

They reached the landing and stood facing each other. Malcolm grinned, but then a flash of discomfort tightened his expression. "Aye, we need to discuss what occurred earlier."

"I'll warrant that ye were in an unenviable position when Laird MacPhearson pressed ye to wed Brienne, but was that truly the best excuse ye could devise—marrying me?" Joan asked.

He shrugged. "It seemed an inspired idea at the time."

"Och, well, not from my side of it." She thrust open the door to her chamber and he followed her inside. "Did ye not consider the consequences fer me? It will be mortifying when the betrothal is broken," she lamented. "Agnes will no doubt gloat fer days."

"The solution is obvious." Malcolm drew himself up confidently. "We should, in truth, marry."

"Each other?" The tension and exhaustion of the past few hours boiled over and Joan began to giggle.

"Aye." Malcolm folded his arms across his chest as Joan succumbed to another fit of laughter. "I dinnae know why ye find the notion so amusing, Joan."

She snorted, then shrugged, unrepentant at her reaction. "I willnae be teased so mercilessly, Malcolm, though I confess to enjoying the jest."

Arms still folded, Malcolm leaned toward her. "I dinnae seek to amuse ye, Joan. It will insult the MacPhearsons greatly if we dinnae marry. It might even start a clan war and that's the last thing any of us want. Ye need a husband to protect ye and yer son. I need a wife. A union between us is the best way to achieve a situation that will benefit us both."

He was serious! Another round of nervous giggles started, then quickly died on Joan's lips. Of all the unsettling things that had transpired these past few days, this was by far the most shocking. "I fail to see how taking me fer a wife will be advantageous to ye."

He assessed her for a moment, then his lips curved into a sensual grin. "It will be my greatest pleasure to show ye, lass."

Joan froze. Desire shimmered in Malcolm's eyes. Dark, provocative, intriguing, and strong enough to take her breath away. It frightened and repelled her and yet . . .

Her memory flickered back to the first few months of her marriage, when the feel of Archibald's hands upon her flesh had piqued her womanly curiosity. When she had foolishly told him of her feelings, he had declared her a wanton and the pleasant sensations had been replaced with brutality.

"*That* is hardly an enticement," she declared pointedly.

She waited for his outburst, certain she had caused offense. Waited, too, for him to step forward and attempt to intimidate her, to ridicule her, or worse, take what she had so adamantly rejected.

Instead, he remained calm, with a thoughtful expression on his features. "I know that yer marriage to Fraser wasn't a happy one," he said.

She let out a small, hollow laugh. "'Twas a nightmare. Archibald was cruel with both his words and his fists. My will is strong, my opinions difficult to keep to myself. He was determined to make me a meek, submissive wife and was greatly angered when he failed."

Malcolm unfolded his arms and moved closer. "Ye need never have a fear of speaking yer mind to me. I shall willingly make a solemn vow and pledge never to strike ye."

She raised her brow and leaned away from him. "No matter what the provocation?"

"Aye."

His words did not comfort. "Ye answered too swiftly. It gives me cause to doubt yer sincerity," she challenged.

Malcolm reached out and caught her fingers, lacing them between his own. "'Tis nigh impossible to prove something that I willnae do," he countered. "All that I can say is that the McKenna men dinnae beat their wives."

Joan shivered and wrestled her hand away. "Docile, obedient women dinnae anger their husbands."

Malcolm laughed. "'Tis clear that ye have never met my mother. My father tells her nearly every day that she is the boldest lass in all the Highlands. There's nary a thought or opinion that remains silent once it comes into her head. Truth be told, she rules my father far more than he rules her."

Joan shook her head in disbelief. "The McKenna's fierce temper is legendary."

"Aye, 'tis not an exaggeration either. The rafters shake when my father bellows. Yet my mother knows all his bluster and anger will never be turned toward her—or any other defenseless creature. 'Tis reserved for his enemies." Malcolm's expression gentled. "I understand yer reluctance to trust me, but I think there's more to yer objections. Do ye find me distasteful? Repulsive?"

Joan rested her hands on her hips. "I'll not be extolling yer manly virtues, fer fear that yer head will swell, but we both know there isn't a lass within a hundred miles who wouldn't call ye handsome."

He favored her with a soft smirk. "Only a hundred?"

Joan tried—and failed—to hold back another laugh. "Ye are a vain man, Malcolm McKenna. Perhaps even more so than I. Yet another reason that we would have a terrible marriage."

"Aye, we would bicker constantly over which one of us is the prettiest." He smiled again, but then the mirth faded from his face and his eyes grew serious. "There's more that ye're not saying, Joan."

She hesitated. She was not inclined to share her secrets with anyone, woman or man, and was loath to start now. Oddly enough though, she was tempted.

Did she dare tell him the truth? Speaking so frankly about the intimacy between a husband and wife was hardly proper. Yet she felt she owed him her honesty, even if her response shocked him.

"I deplore having physical relations with a man."

Malcolm hissed in a quick breath. She raised her chin, trying to decipher his thoughts, but his expression turned bland.

"Were there any others besides Fraser?"

"Nay! I'd never truly kissed a man until my wedding day."

"Was it that bad?" Malcolm asked quietly.

"Not at first. But later." She shuddered at the memory. "He took great delight in forcing me, claiming me. I hated it."

"It would be very different with me. I will honor and respect ye and show ye that great pleasure can be found between a husband and wife."

Malcolm's blue eyes darkened, tantalizing her with wondrous possibilities. She had heard other women talk about the joys and delights of the marriage bed, had seen the glow of love and devotion in their eyes.

Was it possible that she could feel the same? About

Malcolm? He was indeed a very handsome man, with a smile and a swagger that she could admire, if she allowed herself the luxury. Being near him wasn't horrid. Truth be told, his nearness had the power to send a spark of excitement to her belly, though she quickly suppressed it.

But what if she were wrong? Her eyes fell on his large, strong hands, then followed the muscles in his forearms up to his biceps. Clearly, he possessed the strength to hurt her—badly.

What if he proved as harsh a man as Archibald? She had barely escaped the nightmare once; it seemed impossible that God would be so merciful a second time.

"I cannae risk it," she said flatly.

His face fell and she felt a stab of regret at disappointing him. The emotion surprised and dismayed her, yet she was determined to ignore it—along with her fluttering pulse.

Malcolm blew out a breath of frustration. "Ye need to be practical. If ye believe nothing else, ye should have faith that I'll protect ye and yer son."

She knew that he was right. Her father would not provide the safety she and Callum needed, especially if he married Agnes. Joan would be forced to find another home for herself and her son. But marriage? To Malcolm?

Nay, if she ever married again, it would have to be to a much older man, one who lacked the interest or ability to share her bed. Only then would she consent. Marriage to a young, virile man was out of the question, unless . . .

Joan licked her dry lips. "I might consider becoming yer wife if we could reach some sort of understanding before we say our vows."

His body tensed warily. "What sort of understanding?"

She knew what she was about to propose would be

interpreted as an insult, but that didn't prevent her from saying it.

"I acknowledge that men have carnal needs and I know that I cannae fulfill them. If we married, I would not object if ye found yer pleasure with other, willing women." The lines between his brow deepened. "As long as ye agreed to stay out of my bed," she added hastily.

Malcolm's eyes darkened like thunderclouds and for a moment Joan feared she had gone too far. Men never liked being told nay, especially when it came to bed sport. They all believed they were irresistible to womankind.

"I'm sorry that he hurt ye so fiercely, Joan. No woman deserves such treatment." Malcolm stepped closer, capturing her wrist in a grip that was surprisingly gentle. "May ye take comfort in knowing that there is a special place in hell fer men of his ilk."

Malcolm's measured response was puzzling. A trick? Joan had been fully prepared for outrage, censure, even condemnation, and instead she received kindness and compassion. Had she misjudged him?

"Ye'll consider my request?" she asked, her voice quavering with hope.

He waited a long moment before slowly shaking his head. "Nay. The vows of marriage are sacred, including the pledge of fidelity. I dinnae take them lightly, nor toss them away when they are inconvenient. My wife will be the only woman that shares my bed, and if we are so blessed, will bear my children."

Her hopes plummeted and she let out a long sigh. She had not expected to feel such a crushing blow of disappointment. Joan turned her head, so he would not see. "Since ye refuse my condition, then the matter is settled."

"Is it settled?"

"Aye," she retorted, raising her chin. "There's naught

to say. That is, unless ye are going to spout a legion of flowery, empty promises in order to have yer way. Will ye promise to fill my days with happiness and my nights with bliss? Will ye see to my every comfort, grant my every wish, fulfill my secret longings? Will ye shower me with affection and devotion and vow to love me with yer whole heart and soul until ye die?"

"I might. If ye do the same fer me."

She felt her cheeks heat with embarrassment. Where had those ridiculous, girlish words come from? She had no idea nor could she fathom why she was unable to control the need to say them to him. 'Twas ludicrous.

"I'm speaking nonsense. Forgive me."

His expression softened. "All women want to be wooed. There'll be plenty of time fer it after we wed. I promise." He leaned closer. "I've seen ye with yer son, Joan. If we marry, there will be other children."

His words cut straight to her heart. Callum was the one bright spot in her otherwise dark life. Just the thought of having another child brought a sense of longing that reached deep into Joan's soul.

"What of my mother's madness?" she whispered, voicing a long held worry.

"'Twas her own, brought on by greed. I dinnae fear it in ye, nor in any child ye bring into this world."

Joan's heart wrenched. He had met each of her objections with calm acceptance, but the anxiety that dwelled inside her had too strong a hold.

"I cannae marry ye," she repeated. Her voice was determined, but reluctance had crept into her mind, causing her to feel an unsettled sense of confusion.

"Then I request a boon from ye before we part," he said solemnly. "A single kiss."

*Nay!* Without thought, the reply sprang to her lips. But

she didn't speak—yet—curious to see how far she could test him. "Why did ye ask, when ye simply could have taken what ye wanted?"

"'Tis far more pleasurable when we both participate," he answered.

"I warn ye, a kiss from me will not be very enjoyable," she cautioned.

"The only way to know fer certain is to try."

His thumb moved slowly across her cheek, leaving a trail of warmth. It piqued her curiosity, though she forbade herself to be fooled by the fluttering in her stomach.

"A single kiss," she agreed, deciding it was the least she owed him.

Malcolm smiled and his eyes gleamed down at her in a most disconcerting manner. Logic dictated that she fear him, and while part of her did, another part felt intrigued. Still, she faced him with her shoulders squared, unwilling to appear weak or cowed.

"'Tis a kiss, Joan, not a punishment."

"I'll be the judge of that," she snapped.

His fingers touched her chin, raising her face so their eyes met. Her belly tightened as she braced herself for his assault. He loomed above her—broad chested and muscular, with an unmistakable superior strength.

She nearly cried out in protest when he dipped his head, but his lips met hers gently, as though coaxing her to join him in their embrace. It was not the aggressive, rough treatment she'd expected, and the shock of it caused her to drop her vigilance.

He deepened the kiss and the scent of his skin drifted between them. She could feel the rasp of his beard, taste the remnants of the wine he had drunk earlier. She allowed herself to embrace this invasion of her senses, surprised to realize she found it oddly stimulating.

He cupped the back of her neck, slipping his hand into her hair to hold her steady as his tongue pushed between her lips. A frisson of heat seared her, yet her body shivered. 'Twas a most amazing puzzle, but one she left alone, to ponder and solve another day.

Instead, Joan closed her eyes and savored the feelings. The bold touch of his tongue sent her heart into a wild canter. For one brief instant, she joined him in this playful delight, sweeping her tongue against his. He responded with a low-throated moan, and she felt a deeper pleasure surround her senses.

But she feared surrendering completely. Tearing her lips away from Malcolm's mouth, Joan broke away from the sensual web he was spinning. She opened her eyes and found him staring. He looked at her for a long, thoughtful moment, seemingly as surprised by the kiss as she felt.

"Are ye certain ye dinnae want to be my wife?"

Her heart was beating fast and hard. She felt herself sway on her feet and was glad to be able to lean against his solid strength. Her mind struggled to make sense of these confusing thoughts and feelings. Surprisingly, the idea of marriage was not as repugnant as before, but Joan hit upon another, better notion.

"I would consider a handfasting," she ventured.

"What? Ye want to pledge to live together as man and wife for a year and a day? Then, if at the end of that time we agree to stay together, we'll make our marriage vows before a priest?"

"Aye. And if we choose not to marry, then we part," she added. It seemed a reasonable compromise, but Malcolm's expression told her that he would not be easily persuaded. The church frowned upon such arrangements, as did many nobles.

"There's not been a handfasting in the McKenna clan fer over a hundred years," he said. "I can find no good reason to have one now."

"Why do ye insist on a traditional marriage? Ye should feel relieved that ye'll have the chance to be rid of me. I'm prickly, selfish, strong willed, opinionated, and annoying."

His lips curved into a faint grin. "No one's perfect."

Joan threw up her hands in frustration. It seemed that no matter what she said or did, he was determined to follow this course.

Malcolm gently stroked her hair. "'Twas a cruel blow being wed to Archibald, but fate has seen fit to give ye a second chance. Take it."

The temptation was overwhelming. Confused over her conflicting emotions, Joan wanted to turn and run, but Malcolm embraced her, cradling her against his chest as though he would protect her from all the evils of the world. 'Twas an intoxicating feeling for a woman who had fought her own battles for so long. Despite her intention not to, Joan savored it.

The reality of her limited choices surfaced and she began to question her resolve to never again take a husband. In all likelihood her father would marry Agnes, which would make life unbearable for Joan and her child. Malcolm was offering her the chance to escape that fate—yet it came at a high cost.

"I need to think," she whispered.

"There isn't time. I've already announced our betrothal and I fear the repercussions fer both of us if I leave here without ye and yer son."

Joan's hand fluttered to her throat. A wife was the property of her husband. Did she dare trust that Malcolm would keep his word and treat her with honor and respect? She shut her eyes and prayed. Aye, it was a risk, but the promise of safety, security, and a home for her and Callum was simply too enticing to refuse.

Kissing Malcolm elicited many confusing emotions, but it didn't make her cringe. He was a man of honor. He'd proven it to her time and again. And truthfully, the thought of being left behind made her feel bereft in a manner she didn't fully understand.

Hardly believing what she was about to say, Joan inhaled deeply, dislodging the lump that had formed in her throat. It took every ounce of courage to fight off the sense of anxiety sweeping through her, but she knew she must remain calm.

"Aye, I shall marry ye, Malcolm McKenna, and I pray to God that it is a decision neither of us will live to regret."

Walking with a single-minded purpose, Malcolm strode toward the great hall in search of Laird Armstrong, replaying in his mind the kiss he had just shared with Joan.

The taste of her lips had sparked a flame of desire deep in his gut, nearly making his head spin. Yet he had held back his passion. She had given the kiss most reluctantly, convinced she would find it distasteful. Convinced, also, Malcolm believed, that he would not be satisfied with a mere kiss and demand more.

In truth his body was aching for things to go further, but Malcolm had only ever lain with willing, eager partners, and Joan hardly qualified. Thankfully, she was not unmoved by the kiss. He had felt a small ripple of pleasure move through her and it brought a rush of satisfaction surging through him.

She was not cold and dispassionate, as she claimed, as she believed. Their kiss had proven that she was capable of feeling passion and desire, if only she allowed herself to. But her fear was real and he respected that it came from a brutal past.

Malcolm was so caught up in his own thoughts that he took no notice of those around him until he was roughly jostled. Instinctively, he wrapped his hand around the hilt of his sword, then slowly eased his grip when he saw his brother's muscled frame blocking his path.

"James! Is anything amiss?"

"'Tis I who should be asking ye that question," James replied grimly. "I realized that ye were being backed into a corner, but what could have possibly possessed ye to tell Laird MacPhearson that ye were betrothed to Joan? His anger will increase tenfold when he discovers yer treachery."

"I wasn't lying, James."

His brother's eyes widened with shock. "Damnation, have ye taken leave of yer senses? Ye cannae marry her!"

Malcolm arched a brow. "I dinnae see how this is any business of yers."

"Of course it's my business! Ye're my brother. I know ye better than to think yer head has been turned by her beauty, but I cannae fathom why ye would do it. Marry Joan! She's a heartless, selfish shrew. 'Tis madness, I say, and nothing but misery will come of it."

Malcolm's ire heated at the passion in James's voice. He had expected some resistance from his family, but not such adamant objections. "Joan's not the devil incarnate."

"Are ye certain?" James muttered. "My memories of her are anything but pleasant."

Malcolm blew out a rough breath. "She's changed."

"I dinnae believe it," James retorted flatly.

"Why not? Ye've changed. Ye returned from the Crusades with a heart of ice, but Davina melted it. We've all heard the stories about Father and the kind of hard, unrepentant warrior he was before he married our mother. He changed."

"Father is still a hardened warrior," James interjected.

"Aye, but he has a heart that has made him a better, stronger, loyal man to his family and his clan."

James shook his head, clearly unconvinced. "I want the best fer ye, Malcolm. 'Tis what ye deserve. Joan willnae make ye happy."

"Ye're wrong. She'll bring the excitement and challenge into my life that I've been craving." Malcolm placed a hand on his brother's shoulder, imploring him to understand. "She's not the same woman that ye knew years ago. Aye, she has a stubborn pride and at times a haughty air, but she uses it to shield herself from disappointment and hurt. I've seen the quiet sadness in her eyes that she tries to hide from the world and the flashes of vulnerability on her face when she speaks of her son. She needs me, James, just as I need her."

"Bloody hell, dinnae tell me that ye've fallen in love with the woman," James cried.

Malcolm paused. He, too, had wondered the same thing. "I cannae say exactly what it is that I feel fer her. All I know is that it is strong. It beckons to me in a way I dinnae fully understand."

"Walk away," James urged. "Ye can always return in the fall or next year. I doubt any other man will make her an offer of marriage."

Malcolm wished he could explain, but he couldn't put into words what he didn't fully comprehend. "I'll not wait.

We shall be married in the morning, before departing fer home. Will ye be there?"

James let out a rough grunt. "Aye. But I willnae be happy."

'Twas not precisely what Malcolm had hoped to hear, but it was better than nothing. The mood between the brothers glimmered with unspoken disagreement, but each realized an open debate would yield nothing but an estrangement.

"Sir Malcolm, a word." Laird Armstrong stepped from the shadows and advanced. James favored his brother with a cryptic glance, then turned and swiftly departed.

"Laird Armstrong." Malcolm inclined his head respectfully. "I was hoping to speak with ye privately after the evening meal."

"I assumed as much. I could scarcely believe my ears when ye announced yer betrothal to Joan in front of the MacPhearsons. The vein throbbing on the laird's forehead looked near to bursting." Laird Armstrong chortled. "'Twas a clever move, though now ye'll need to be even bolder in order to find a way out of it."

Malcolm swore beneath his breath, yet held his temper. Why did everyone simply assume that he had lied and would now reject Joan? "Joan and I shall marry tomorrow morning."

Laird Armstrong stepped back in surprise. "Truly?"

"Aye." Malcolm tried to temper the harshness in his voice. Though he doubted that Laird Armstrong could prevent the marriage, since it would serve no purpose for him to openly oppose the match.

The shock deepened on Laird Armstrong's face. "She has no dowry," he proclaimed. "Fraser kept it after he cast her aside."

"Ye dinnae challenge him fer it?"

"Nay. It wasn't worth the effort. In spite of her beauty, I doubted any other man would be fool enough to take her in marriage."

Malcolm stiffened at the blunt words, yet let the insult pass. "No matter. I've more than enough to provide fer her."

Laird Armstrong stroked his chin thoughtfully. "What about the lad? Will ye allow her to keep him or will ye leave him behind?"

"A bairn so young needs his mother. 'Twould be cruel to separate them."

"Aye. The child is her greatest weakness and the best weapon to crush her willful, disobedient tongue. She might be brought to heel faster if ye threaten to take him away."

Malcolm was taken aback by such a harsh statement—from Joan's father no less. "I'd never resort to such brutality. I have a fondness fer a woman with spirit and shall relish the challenge of winning Joan's heart."

Laird Armstrong eyed Malcolm as though he spoke in jest. "Joan doesn't have a heart. She cares only fer herself."

'Twas impossible not to hear the certainty of judgment in the older man's tone. A shiver of anger trickled through Malcolm. "I disagree. Joan has a tender side along with many fine qualities that appeal to me. She will make a splendid wife."

"I dinnae think that ye were fool enough to be captivated by her looks. Beauty fades, Sir Malcolm, leaving misery in its wake." Laird Armstrong's jaw muscle twitched. "Be forewarned. If ye cast her off, I'll not take her back. Ye'll have to lock her away somewhere, that is, if ye can find a convent willing to take her."

Malcolm shook his head at Laird Armstrong's gruff

tone and attitude. Joan was hardly the easiest woman to abide, but she certainly deserved better from her own kin.

"When we wed, she becomes a McKenna," Malcolm said stiffly. "And the McKenna guard and care fer their own."

"Ye are welcome to her." Laird Armstrong turned away, paused, then turned back. "I wish ye luck—ye'll be needing it."

# Chapter Ten

Joan walked toward the chapel just after sunrise broke, with her maid, Gertrude, at her side. Despite the persistent mist of falling rain, the bailey was busy with its usual morning activity. Carts laden with food were pushed through the courtyard toward the kitchen, several soldiers were heading toward the practice yard with a group of squires following closely behind them, and servants hurried to the castle to begin their duties.

Joan could see pages fetching water from the well, smell the aroma of baking bread, hear the clang of the blacksmith's hammer. As she walked among them, few gave her more than a passing glance, though she was certain many members of the clan knew she was being married this morning.

Yet few cared. There would be no wedding feast, no drinking, no music or dancing to celebrate this union, leaving most disinterested in the event.

When she arrived, Joan counted no more than twenty people gathered outside the church doors, nearly all of them McKennas. 'Twas embarrassing to have such a poor showing of Armstrong support, but she was hardly surprised. She was not beloved by her people—nay, she was barely tolerated. Those few that were in attendance were most likely there out of morbid curiosity.

Head held high, Joan favored them all with her most haughty look, desperate to control the rising swell of sickness in her throat. *What am I doing?* A wife is ruled by her husband; he wields enormous power over her person. When she escaped from Archibald, she had vowed never to become the property of any man, yet here she stood, ready to place herself once again in such a helpless position.

Joan's knees began shaking and she grabbed Gertrude's arm for support. The enormity of what she was about to do fell upon her like a stone wall, sending her into a near state of panic.

As though he sensed her fear, Malcolm turned to her, his eyes calm, his expression steady. His confidence rattled her even more. She was incapable of being the wife he expected. The wife he deserved. She was not honorable and selfless, kind or loving.

Malcolm claimed to want a woman with spirit, but no man appreciated having his will thwarted, his orders questioned. She would most assuredly disappoint him in any number of ways, trampling any budding feelings of regard he might have for her.

The realization brought on a profound wave of sadness. She tore her gaze from Malcolm's, her heart pounding wildly. She must speak up now and put an end to this farce. For both their sakes.

Then what? Where would she go? What would she do? How would she provide for Callum, protect him, and most importantly, be assured that he had a worthy future? Was there another choice?

Her eyes darted frantically, instinctively searching for her father. He had dressed formally for the occasion, had even taken the time to shave. But Joan could see the cold calculation on his face. There would be no help from him.

Agnes stood at his side, a triumphant expression on her face. 'Twas clear they were each relishing the idea of being well rid of her.

Father John took his position in front of the chapel doors. Ignoring the rain that was now falling harder, he spread his arms wide and loudly proclaimed, "Is there anyone here who can show just cause why Lady Joan and Sir Malcolm cannae marry?"

No one spoke, yet Joan's mind raced with dozens of reasons. She wondered if a bride or a groom had ever had the nerve to make an objection, then decided if the bride had, she would have most assuredly been ignored. And then silenced.

"Shall we go inside?" Malcolm asked, as he held out his arm.

Asked. Not commanded. Joan's fear receded slightly. She summoned Callum's sweet face from her memory, straightened her back, and accepted Malcolm's arm.

One step, then another. In an almost dreamlike state, Joan took the journey to the altar. Dozens of thinly tapered beeswax candles twinkled through the dimness of the chapel. It added a warmth that was sorely needed and Joan was surprised that her father would have approved such an expense. More than likely he did it for the McKenna's benefit.

"Fer ye." Malcolm handed her a beautiful bouquet of early spring flowers, tied at the stems with a blue silk ribbon. "There was not time to get ye a proper wedding gift. I hope these will suffice fer now."

Joan was speechless. She adored flowers. How did he know? She caught a glimpse of a beaming Gertrude and surmised her maid must have told him.

"Thank ye," she finally managed to croak, amazed at the thoughtful gesture.

"Where is Callum?" Malcolm asked.

Startled, Joan stared at him wide eyed. "I knew he'd be unable to stay quiet fer any length of time, so Brienne agreed to care fer him."

"As ye wish, though I wouldn't have objected to his presence."

A jumble of emotion caught in Joan's throat, but there was no chance to ponder that revelation as the priest began the ceremony. She tried very hard to concentrate, yet her dreamlike state continued as she listened to Father John's voice in a strange, disjointed manner.

"Wilt thou love him, comfort him, honor and obey him, keep him in sickness and in health, and forsaking all others keep thee only unto him as long as ye both shall live?"

*Obey?* The word mocked her, giving rise to every fear she had struggled so hard to conquer.

The priest cleared his throat. Twice. "Lady Joan?"

They were all waiting. Waiting for her to take her vows, to say the words that would bind her to Malcolm forever. *Words, they are only words.*

Yet their meanings were clear. If she spoke them here and now, in good faith, she must abide by them. Nervously, she licked her lips, then peered at the chapel door. If she walked swiftly, she could escape to freedom in a mere minute.

As if somehow reading her thoughts, Malcolm placed his hand on her shoulder and gazed down at her. "Joan?"

"I beg yer forgiveness, Malcolm, but I dinnae . . ."

He reached down and took her hands in his. Squeezing them gently, he spoke in a low, clear tone. "In the name of God, and before these witnesses, I, Malcolm, take ye, Joan to be my wife, to have and to hold from this day forward, in sickness and health, to love and to cherish, to honor and to guard, forsaking all others until we are parted by death. This is my solemn vow."

He nodded, indicating it was her turn. Joan's pulse steadied. He had kept his word to treat her as an equal, giving her the opportunity to repeat exactly the same vow.

"In the name of God, I, Joan, take you, Malcolm to be my husband, to have and to hold from this day forward, in sickness and health, to love and to cherish, to honor and to guard, forsaking all others until we are parted by death. This is my solemn vow."

James handed the ring to the priest. After he blessed it, Father John placed it in Malcolm's outstretched palm. Smiling, Malcolm slid the solid gold band onto the fourth finger of Joan's left hand, where the vein went directly to her heart. The ring felt cold and heavy, yet oddly comforting, too.

"She dinnae say the proper vows," Agnes protested. "Are ye certain they are truly married?"

"Aye, they are indeed husband and wife," the McKenna insisted. "All they need now is the priest's final blessing."

Father John blustered for a moment, and Joan thought he might protest. Yet under the McKenna's withering glare the priest recited the traditional prayers as she and Malcolm knelt at the altar.

And then it was over. Joan held tightly to Malcolm's arm as she stood, hardly believing she was once again a wife.

"Aren't ye going to kiss her, Malcolm?" the McKenna bellowed.

There was a rumbling of nervous laughter at the question. 'Twas not the usual practice, but Joan knew that some considered kissing a legal bond that sealed all contracts, while others believed it was the best way to ward off evil spirits. For Joan, it seemed the most basic way for a man to assert his dominance over his newly wedded wife.

"Joan?"

Everyone was staring and she felt a rush of blood warm her cheeks. She shivered, remembering the strength of his arms, the rough scrape of his beard, the gentle caress of his lips, and realized she was not opposed to experiencing it again.

But in front of an audience?

She nodded, fully intending to accept the kiss with open eyes and closed lips. Malcolm reacted by slipping his arm around her waist and pulling her against his chest. Her heart started pounding as he lowered his head.

Joan's eyes closed as their lips brushed. She held herself stiffly at first, but then seemingly of their own accord, her lips softened, her body yielded, and she succumbed to his embrace. Malcolm slanted his mouth across hers and she felt herself lean into him, her breasts pressing against his chest.

The McKenna hooted in delight and Malcolm reluctantly ended the kiss. For a moment Joan couldn't catch her breath, nor slow the hammering of her heart. Malcolm smiled and ran the edge of his thumb across her cheek. Then he winked.

*Saints alive!* The gesture felt nearly as intimate as his kiss. Flustered, Joan looked down at her bouquet of flowers, busying herself by stroking the soft petals.

Arm in arm they left the chapel and found the MacPhearsons clustered outside. The laird and his daughters stood on the steps while most of their soldiers were loitering near the horses, waiting for the signal to leave.

Callum was there, holding tightly to Brienne's hand.

He broke free the moment he spied her, running as fast as his legs would carry him. Joan scooped him up in her arms and held him close, then reluctantly passed him over to Gertrude when the MacPhearson sisters came forward to offer their congratulations.

"We've many miles to cross to reach home. Are ye ready to depart, Joan?" Malcolm asked, scrutinizing the sky. The rain had ceased, but dark clouds remained on the horizon, an ever present threat.

"Gertrude and I packed last night." A twinge of shame stabbed at her pride and Joan lowered her eyes. "I shan't be bringing much."

"Good. It will make traveling easier." Malcolm continued to gaze upward. "The wind is fierce, the sky ominous. Be sure to dress warmly. We'll probably spend the better part of the day trying to stay ahead of the storm."

It took less than an hour for Joan and Gertrude to be seated on their mounts mingling with the rest of the McKenna party. Most brides traveled to their new homes with laden carts, but since Joan had none, 'twas decided that all would ride, including the women and children.

Brienne appeared excited at the prospect of the journey, though there were traces of the tears that she had shed earlier when bidding farewell to her sisters and father. In contrast, Joan's eyes were bone dry; Laird Armstrong had been brief and distracted when Joan said her good-byes and was already inside the great hall, breaking his fast.

The chains rattled noisily as the heavy iron portcullis was lifted. With the McKenna in the lead, the clan contingent passed beneath them, two abreast. Malcolm rode at Joan's side, with Callum seated securely in front of him. The lad was quiet and still for once, equally fascinated by the large horse he sat upon and the man who held him so protectively.

Somehow, they managed to avoid the worst of the rain, a miracle considering how often they stopped to allow the women a chance to stretch their legs and answer the call of nature. They made camp before nightfall in a sheltered valley, with a broad stream running beside them. A few of the men tried their hand at fishing and the fruits of their labor were being cooked over the fire.

Joan sat on a log near the blaze, with Callum on her lap and Gertrude and Brienne on either side of her. The latter held her sleeping babe in her arms, patiently allowing Callum to lean close and touch the babe's foot.

"He's going to wake that infant," Malcolm cautioned as he came to stand near them.

"Aye," Joan agreed. "Callum's full of mischief after spending the better part of the day sleeping in the saddle."

"He needs to run," Malcolm decided, motioning toward his men. Two of them obediently appeared at his side. "Take young Callum down to the riverbed. I'm sure there are many rocks he'd enjoy tossing in the water."

Joan stiffened. "I will see to my son's welfare."

"Our son," Malcolm corrected.

Joan looked at him in surprise. While pleased to have Callum so easily accepted, she balked at the notion of having someone else decide what was best for her child.

"Callum has a great fascination with water," she warned.

Malcolm nodded. "Guard the lad closely and have a care that he doesn't get wet," he instructed his men.

"I should like to go, too," Brienne announced, following after the trio.

"And me," Gertrude added, taking her place beside Brienne.

"Was it something I said?" Malcolm wrinkled his nose and sniffed his tunic. "Or do I need a bath?"

"Nay." Joan smiled. "They all have the misguided notion that the newly wed bride and groom wish to be alone."

"Aye. Women are ever the romantics."

She gazed at him, then bowed her head. "Not all women."

Malcolm reached for her hand and kissed the back of it. "Then it falls to me to be the gallant swain. Shall I recite a poem to yer beauty, praise yer talents, and extol yer numerous virtues?"

"Will it impress me?"

"Alas, I fear not. I'm a dreadful poet."

"And I have few virtues to extol," she added.

"Och, we are the perfect couple, lass. Let us toast to it."

Joan accepted the cup Malcolm offered, gasping as the fiery whiskey went down her throat.

"I thought it was wine," she choked.

"Ye looked as though ye could tolerate something stronger," Malcolm explained as he refilled her cup.

Joan wasn't certain what to make of that remark. She nearly handed the drink back to him, but the warm glow spreading through her empty stomach was pleasant and relaxing. Perhaps Malcolm was right. She took another few sips and realized the cup was empty.

She turned her head, almost screeching when she saw that Malcolm was closely watching her. His expression was intense, his eyes darkening with purpose. Something fluttered inside her at that look and she felt an odd anticipation sizzle in the air between them.

'Twas almost as though something was pulling her to

him. Joan had the most absurd notion to tip her chin toward his lips, wondering if he would kiss her.

A burst of male laughter on the other side of the camp broke the spell. *It must be the whiskey,* she decided before recklessly holding out her cup and asking, "Is there any more?"

He gave her a strange look, then filled her vessel.

Joan lowered her eyelids slowly and sipped her whiskey. It went down smoother now, with but a hint of burn. She finished it just as Gertrude, Brienne, and the children returned.

At Malcolm's urging, they all sat together in front of the large fire, partaking of the freshly cooked fish, brown crusty bread, and hard cheese. The mood was cheerful, the presence of the wee ones bringing smiles to even the most hardened of Highland warriors.

Though the food smelled tantalizing, Joan barely ate. Instead, she dangled her empty cup in her hand while staring at her food. Callum sat happily between her and Malcolm, chewing his meal with gusto. His appetite impressed the men, who encouraged him to put as much food into his small mouth as possible. They made a game of it with him, and while Joan supposed she ought to correct his horrendous table manners, she could not scold the lad when he was having so much fun.

The moon rose in the clearing sky, its silvery beams illuminating the campsite. Joan listened to the hoot of an owl and realized the hour had grown late. She cuddled Callum in her lap, wishing she could sleep beside him. But that was impossible—she had a husband now.

"'Tis time fer bed," Malcolm announced. "We've no tents, but my men have hung some blankets from the lower branches of several trees to afford us some privacy."

Joan's face heated as every detail of being bedded by

Archibald came flooding back to her. His wet kisses, groping hands, brutish possession of her body. 'Twas hardly an experience she was eager to repeat. The memories were disturbing, and though she tried, impossible to put from her mind.

"Good night, my brave little warrior," she whispered, hugging Callum tightly.

He snuggled against her, his eyes already half closed. Gertrude reached for him, but Malcolm was there first.

"He's too heavy a lad fer ye to carry," he said, picking the child up and handing him off to James.

Joan sat for a moment longer watching James carry her dear lad to a cozy spot near a group of warriors. Gertrude followed dutifully behind, settling Callum on his pallet, then placed herself protectively beside him.

Joan rose from the log, head held high, the skirts of her gown and cloak rustling around her. She walked ahead of Malcolm, having no difficulty locating the bridal bower he had described. She halted suddenly at the entrance and he bumped into her.

Joan jumped, her skin burning at the feel of his warm body. Instinct warned her to pull away and she reacted, stumbling. Malcolm caught her before she hit the ground, his strong arms enfolding her, his breath hot against her neck. "Are ye hurt?"

"Nay, I . . . please." Joan's heart thudded wildly in her chest. She shouldn't have drunk so much and eaten so little. Her head was spinning, her mind wrestling with warring thoughts.

*'Tis Malcolm*, she kept repeating silently to herself. *He will not harm me.* But the words could not penetrate her fear. She continued to struggle in the hope of freeing herself, her terror rising when he did not relinquish his hold.

Joan lifted her chin to hide her panic. "I give ye fair

warning. If ye ever beat me, Malcolm McKenna, I'll thrust a dirk between yer ribs the moment ye fall asleep."

He cocked a brow. "Sounds pleasant."

She slumped forward, the fight leaving her as quickly as it flared. "God forgive me. I am a sorrowful excuse fer a wife. I honestly dinnae understand why ye married me."

"A fair question, but one that is best answered after a restful night. Lay down, Joan. Things will seem far better in the morning."

"I'm not tired," she said peevishly.

"Well, I am."

Joan regarded him uncertainly in the moonlight. The tension between them grew and she could feel her heart starting to pound. "Which side should I take?"

"The left. My men will stand guard throughout the night, but I always keep my sword near my right hand, just in case." He placed his hands on his hips and sighed softly. "Ye need not look so afeared, Joan. I'll not ravage ye the moment ye lay down."

The stiffness in her mouth eased. "Ye are most considerate, husband."

"Aye, that I am. I'll be sure to wait a good ten minutes before I pounce."

Joan burst into nervous giggles. Was this how it could be in a marriage? Lighthearted teasing and smiles, instead of feelings of being powerless and out of control?

Slightly more at ease, she settled herself among the blankets. Malcolm joined her, lying back on his elbows, with his legs crossed at the ankles. Cocking his head, he favored her with a charming grin. "Go on, have yer wicked way with me, lass."

"I'd rather not," she whispered, almost with regret.

"Then we'll wait."

He leaned forward and kissed her gently on the lips.

Tensing, Joan held her breath. His mouth was warm and firm, yet true to his word, Malcolm moved away from her.

Her flesh tingled where his lips had touched. Joan brought her fingertips to her face and gently traced her mouth. The kiss had been affectionate and chaste—so why did she feel a flash of heat when their lips met?

Joan turned on her side, presenting him with her back. It felt rude somehow and she fretted as she lay there worrying that the gesture might have insulted him. Frowning, she stared into the darkness, trying to decide what to do. Her ears strained to hear any movement from him and then she realized the soft sounds of his even breath meant that he had fallen asleep.

Though they barely touched, she could feel his solid strength next to her and it brought her a sense of security that she had never known before. Malcolm would not hurt her; nay, he would protect her. Comforted by that thought, Joan closed her eyes and allowed herself to slowly drift off to sleep.

As the dawn broke, Malcolm awoke to the sight of Joan's lovely face lying beside him. Even in slumber it was perfection, the features delicate and feminine, the complexion unblemished and creamy white. Her head was on a small pillow one of his men had been able to find; her chin tilted upward as though begging for a kiss.

She had not removed her gown, but unlaced the bodice to allow herself more comfort while she slept. It hung loosely over the top half of her body, giving him a clear view of her breasts. They were perfection and Malcolm's body tightened with need at the appealing sight.

Though he longed to cup that round, ripe flesh, he instead traced her jawline with the tip of his finger. She stirred, yet didn't wake, her arms reaching instinctively to cradle the child that snuggled between them.

Aye, on top of spending his wedding night like a chaste monk, he now shared his bridal bed with her restless son. God help him if his brother ever discovered it. James would no doubt delight in teasing him about it for months.

Callum had woken in the night, crying for his mother. Joan had tossed at the sound of his whimpers, but exhaustion had put her in a deep, restful sleep. Malcolm had heard Gertrude trying to soothe the lad, but he wailed harder.

Knowing the easiest way to calm the lad was to bring him to his mother, Malcolm had retrieved the child. A frazzled looking Gertrude had been grateful for the assistance, surrendering Callum without question, though first warning the lad would need to empty his bladder.

That task completed, Malcolm had returned to a still-sleeping Joan. Once snuggled contently against his mother, Callum had smiled so sweetly Malcolm's heart had stirred.

He wondered briefly where the lad had inherited such a sunny disposition. Certainly not from either of his parents.

Malcolm debated rising when he suddenly felt Joan shift. She awoke with a start, her eyes bursting open wide, her nostrils flaring in confusion. 'Twas clear that she knew not where she was—but then her eyes met his and her shoulders relaxed. The gesture of trust warmed Malcolm's heart.

"Good morning, wife."

"Husband."

Her voice was husky with sleep, the sultry tone causing the throbbing between Malcolm's legs to twitch hopefully. He groaned and thrust his lust aside, knowing there was to be no relief this morning.

'Twas true that some men would not deny themselves in this situation and Malcolm almost regretted not being one of them. It would be so easy to push young Callum aside, roll Joan onto her back and bury his aching cock deeply in the sweet warmth between her thighs.

"Mama!"

Joan blinked away the glaze of sleep in her eyes and looked down in genuine surprise at her son. "Callum! How did ye get here?"

"He cried fer ye during the night," Malcolm explained. "I decided the easiest way to make him content was to bring him to ye."

"Ye dinnae mind?" she asked incredulously.

"Nay. Callum is a calm sleeper. Unlike his restless mother. My back is sore from all yer kicking. The lad saved me from further pain by lying between us."

Joan blinked, then met his gaze. "He might have wet the blankets," she added, clearly still trying to comprehend the situation.

"Fortunately, Gertrude warned me of that possibility, so I took the necessary steps to avoid an accident." Malcolm reached out and ruffled Callum's hair. The child giggled and rolled against him like a playful puppy.

Malcolm immediately began to tickle him. Callum shrieked loudly, his laughter so infectious that Malcolm found himself chuckling, too. So, amazingly, did Joan.

"What sort of mischief are ye getting yerself into, young master?" Gertrude called out.

Callum instantly stilled, jumping to his feet. "Baby?" he asked eagerly as Gertrude approached.

"Aye, ye can see the wee one if ye come with me." The maid held out her hand and Callum grasped it.

Malcolm began gathering the blankets and dismantling their bed. Joan joined him, a hint of gratitude shimmering on her face. They worked in companionable silence, accomplishing the task swiftly. When they were done, Malcolm turned to leave, but Joan stopped him, laying her hand gently on his arm.

"Thank ye."

A sliver of contentment crept through him. Their wedded life had been strange and unconventional from the start, yet he regretted none of it. Last night she had asked him why he had married her. Truth be told, Malcolm wasn't entirely sure. All he did know was that he was glad that he had.

# Chapter Eleven

By afternoon they had begun to climb into higher country. The weather continued to be damp and dreary, but no one complained. Malcolm once again held Callum snuggled in his arms as they rode, leading the contingent with his brother and father. The lad talked endlessly for the first hour—mostly gibberish that Malcolm failed to understand—then after greedily eating his noonday meal, promptly fell asleep.

As he slept, the child instinctively nestled closer to Malcolm's chest, and Malcolm was humbled at the innocent trust. Somehow the lad had seamlessly woven a spell of affection around him, and Malcolm was glad to feel it. Through no fault of his own, Callum had unfairly received little male regard in his short life.

Well, all that was about to change. Malcolm vowed he would protect and guide the lad, treating him the same as any of his natural children.

Of course, he would have to bed his new wife before there could be any more children to raise and love. That particular task was proving to be far more of a challenge than he'd anticipated, yet Malcolm refused to be discouraged.

Traveling with a large contingent in the damp spring rain was hardly the best circumstance to woo a reluctant woman. Once they arrived home, the opportunities would be abundant and he intended to take full advantage of each and every one.

Joan rode with the rest of the women in the center of the column, protected on all sides by the toughest McKenna warriors. Malcolm joined her for short periods, but mainly kept near the front of the column with his brother, their eyes constantly scanning the horizon for danger.

Riding a few lengths behind his brother, Malcolm suddenly became aware of the tension in James's posture. Moving his mount forward, Malcolm crested the hill and eyed the open valley below, immediately seeing why James was concerned.

"Reivers?" Malcolm questioned.

"Nay," James responded. "There's far too many of them to be a raiding party."

"Damn it, those are Fraser colors," Malcolm muttered.

"What are they doing this far north?" James asked.

"Causing trouble," Malcolm replied. His gut clenched and a cold chill invaded him. He looked to the men at his left and right, handing Callum off to the larger McKenna warrior. "Guard him with yer life."

The soldier nodded in understanding and melted into the background.

"Keep yer hands off yer sword hilts and dinnae allow yerself to be drawn into a fight," the McKenna warned his sons as he maneuvered his stallion between them. "If it's a test of wills Fraser is after, he'll not be disappointed."

"He will be when he loses," Malcolm muttered, his

leather clad fist tightening on the reins as the Frasers approached.

"Good day to ye." Archibald smiled as he moved closer, showing off even, white teeth.

"Ye seem to have gotten yerselves lost," Malcolm drawled. "Fraser land lies in the opposite direction."

"I had business to attend to with Laird MacPhie," Archibald replied. "Not that it's any concern of yers."

"The MacPhies have yet to pledge their loyalty to the Crown," the McKenna said, his brow furrowing. "Our young king needs us all."

"The boy king is in exile in France," Archibald said, his horse dancing in a nervous circle. "When—and if—he returns, those clans that are so inclined will support him."

Malcolm allowed the outrage he felt to show on his face. The McKenna clan had fought long and hard to help free them all from the yoke of English oppression and made no secret of their pledge to keep Scotland independent.

"Scotland needs unity if we are to stay free of the cursed English," James added.

Archibald shrugged. "I am no man's conscience. 'Tis up to each laird to decide fer himself what course he shall take." The annoying grin on Archibald's face faded and Malcolm realized he must have spied Joan among the men. "'Tis true then? Ye married the wench?"

"Aye, Lady Joan is my wife." Malcolm deliberately folded his arms across his chest, striking a casual pose, refusing to allow Fraser the satisfaction of thinking he believed him to be a threat.

Archibald pulled his gaze from Joan and allowed it to travel over the other riders. "And her whelp?"

"Are ye referring to my son?" Malcolm asked, his mood darkening.

"Ye've claimed him as one of yer own?"

"Aye, and proudly," Malcolm replied, his voice strong and steady.

Malcolm could tell by the narrowing of Archibald's eyes and the crispness of his tone that he was angry, though he feigned disinterest.

"I'm surprised that ye would be content with my leavings, McKenna," Archibald sneered.

Malcolm refused to be baited. Cutting his foe with a mocking look, he stated simply, "I know quality when I see it and I'm not so much of a pigheaded fool to let it slip between my fingers."

A wildness lit Archibald's eyes and Malcolm was glad to know his barb had drawn blood. He waited with conflicting emotions roiling his chest, almost wishing Fraser would reach for his sword so he could rid the world of his evil presence.

But alas, he was to be denied. Without another word, Archibald backed away, his soldiers falling in behind him. Malcolm watched them depart, Fraser's body tense with barely suppressed anger as he rode his mount hard and fast.

Concerned for his wife, Malcolm turned around and saw Joan was pale and tight lipped, clutching her horse's mane as though it was her only lifeline.

"As long as we've stopped, we'll take a moment to rest the horses and answer nature's call," the McKenna declared.

Malcolm nudged his stallion in Joan's direction. She waited for him to help her dismount, gripping his shoulders forcefully, her body pressed against his length as she slid down. She steadied herself when her feet touched the ground and surprised him utterly by flinging her arms around his waist and squeezing him tightly.

"I'm grateful, Malcolm, fer yer defense of Callum," she whispered. "Thank ye."

Pulling back, she threaded her fingers through his hair and cupped his neck before gently kissing his lips. Something primitive erupted deep inside Malcolm at her tender gesture of affection and he realized that he would have fought Archibald to the death to keep her at his side. The intensity of the emotion startled him, yet somehow it felt right.

"I dinnae think Archibald has any true interest in the lad," Malcolm declared. "More the fool he."

"Aye, he only ever used him as a weapon against me."

"Those days are over," Malcolm proclaimed, her tender smile giving him an enormous sense of satisfaction that nearly made up for his missed wedding night.

Nearly.

Five long, weary days later, they arrived at McKenna Castle. They took the most direct route, which unfortunately meant sleeping outside each night, as they passed no towns or villages. The initial sense of freedom Joan had experienced when the journey first began had faded, and though she was apprehensive over the kind of reception she would receive from Malcolm's mother, she was looking forward to being off the road and off her mount.

There was a murmur of excitement spreading through the riders when they crossed into McKenna land, but they had to ride for hours until the castle came into view. As she caught her first glimpse, Joan conceded there had been no exaggeration when others spoke of the size and grandeur of the place. It was by far the largest holding Joan had ever seen.

Equally majestic and foreboding, the castle was strategically situated on a hilltop covered in green spring grass. She judged the gray stone curtain wall surrounding the structure to be over six feet tall, stretching around the castle for what seemed like miles.

Joan counted six round towers, and two additional square guard towers that were set on each side of the gate. Even from a distance she could see the outline of the many men who walked the battlements, guarding the clan and its castle.

Cottages of wood and stone with thick thatched roofs surrounded the base of the castle, creating a thriving village. Large fields of freshly tilled soil on both the left and right side filled the horizon, seeming to disappear into the mountains at the end. Joan could hear the sound of livestock mingling with the voices of the farmers, shepherds, herders, and other workers. Many paused to wave, shout a greeting, or nod in respect as the laird and his traveling party rode by.

As they drew nearer, Joan was surprised not to see a glittering reflection in the wide moat, as it was free of water. Instead, 'twas lined with a methodically arranged assortment of lethal-looking spikes angled upward to prevent an enemy from gaining a close foothold.

The horses' hooves thundered loudly as they crossed a wide wooden bridge constructed over the moat. When they rode through the open gates, there were several people gathered in the bailey to meet them. A stately, middle-aged woman who Joan assumed was Lady Aileen stood on the steps leading to the great hall, and beside her was a younger female, who Joan guessed was Malcolm's sister, Lady Katherine.

There was no sign of Malcolm's daughter.

As they drew nearer a flicker of surprise crossed Lady Aileen's face when she saw there were women in the group. Joan tightened her grip on the reins until her knuckles whitened, anticipating a less than enthusiastic reaction from Malcolm's mother when she discovered that he had married her.

Suddenly, a lass darted out from behind a rain barrel and charged toward them. Shrieking with excitement, she ran directly at Malcolm. The action surprised him and startled his horse. The mount reared, kicking its legs frantically, almost striking the child in the head and unseating Malcolm.

Thankfully, he managed to get the animal under control before any serious damage occurred. Cursing beneath his breath, Malcolm vaulted from his mount.

"I've told ye time and again that ye mustn't squeal like that and alarm the horses," he yelled, catching the child by the arm.

Inwardly, Joan cringed at the thought of seeing him strike a child; then again, her actions could have resulted in grave injuries. 'Twas only by the grace of God—and Malcolm's superior horsemanship—that neither of them were seriously hurt.

The child burst into noisy sobs and flung herself at Malcolm, holding him tightly around the knees. He bent low and spoke with her for a moment. The lass lifted her head and Joan could see Malcolm's ire melting under the beseeching look she gave him.

Joan watched in astonishment as he lifted the lass in his arms and hugged her against his chest.

"God's teeth, who is that unruly child?" she asked, fearing she already knew, yet hoping that she was wrong.

"That, my dear Joan, is yer stepdaughter, Lileas," James answered with a gleam in his eye.

Joan could feel the knots of tension gathering in her shoulders. *What a brat!* How could such a sensible man like Malcolm allow his daughter to act so spoiled and willful? And why had no one else bothered to correct her? She glanced from one family member to the next; each carried an expression of concern along with some degree of indulgence.

Joan pressed her lips together and prayed for the patience to hold her tongue. Now was not the time to try and take the child in hand even though a part of her itched to take control.

Mind racing, Joan barely acknowledged the squire who took her horse's reins. He stood patiently waiting to assist her down. Flustered when she realized his intent, Joan accepted his help, then thanked him profusely once she was off her mount.

The McKennas gathered together greeting each other warmly, with smiles and hugs. Joan saw Laird McKenna sweep Lady Aileen into his arms and give her a hearty kiss. When it ended, she threaded her hand through his arm and leaned against him. He whispered in her ear and she smiled, blushing like a lass.

The escort of McKenna retainers dispersed, embracing the women and children who had spilled into the bailey. Looking a bit lost, Brienne came to stand beside Joan, the babe clutched in her arms. Joan turned to search for Callum and saw him holding Gertrude's hand, his eyes wide and curious.

Still holding tightly to her husband, Lady Aileen stepped forward, quirking a questioning eyebrow at Joan and Brienne. She examined them openly from head to toe, her expression stoic until her eyes came to rest upon the infant in Brienne's arms.

"Ye've married the MacPhearson lass, Malcolm,"

Lady Aileen said with a smile that seemed forced. "Well, then, let me see my grandchild."

"A baby! I want to see!" Lileas demanded, pushing herself between the two women.

"Not now, Lileas," Malcolm replied.

"Papa, please!"

He scratched his head sheepishly. "Well, maybe just a wee look at the lad, if ye promise to behave."

"I promise."

Brienne hesitated, then slowly lowered her arms so Lileas could catch a glimpse of her babe. Joan noticed the mischievous twinkle in Lileas's eyes as she stroked the infant's cheek. The lass knew perfectly well she should not have insisted, yet she persisted, knowing eventually she would get her way.

Joan pressed her lips together again.

"He's a fine-looking child," Lady Aileen said.

"Aye, that he is—but alas, he isn't my son." Malcolm cleared his throat. "Lady Brienne was mistaken when she named me as the infant's father. Well, not precisely mistaken . . ."

"'Tis a long story," the McKenna interrupted. "Best told in private."

"I'm anxious to hear it," Lady Aileen said brusquely. She once again turned her attention to Malcolm. "The babe isn't yers, yet ye have brought Lady Brienne home with ye?"

"All will be explained in due course," the McKenna said soothingly. He tried, unsuccessfully, to steer Lady Aileen through the large oak doors leading to the great hall, but she wouldn't budge.

A glimmer appeared in James's eyes as he stepped

toward his brother. "Malcolm, introduce yer wife to Mother."

"Yer wife?" Pivoting, Lady Aileen faced Malcolm. "Ye married her anyway?"

Malcolm blew out a frustrated breath. "I dinnae marry Lady Brienne. I married Lady Joan."

Lady Aileen's gaze shifted to Joan, her confusion obvious. "Laird Armstrong's daughter? Davina's cousin? *That* Lady Joan?"

Malcolm threw back his shoulders. "Aye."

His answer clearly startled his mother. "So 'tis true that she is no longer married to Archibald Fraser?"

Joan stepped forward, knowing her battered pride couldn't take another blow without her temper flaring. But she also knew she needed to avoid making an enemy of Malcolm's mother. Bowing her head, Joan bent her knee to Lady Aileen in a graceful curtsy. "My marriage to Laird Fraser was dissolved."

Lady Aileen gulped down a breath. "I've heard of such things, but never knew anyone who had actually done it."

A knot tightened in her stomach, yet Joan remained impassive at Lady Aileen's shocked expression. Joan suspected 'twas not only the annulment, but her son's choice of wife that the older woman had difficulty accepting.

The seeds of doubt as to Joan's suitability to marry Malcolm were most likely sowed years earlier, an inadvertent consequence of the friendship shared between Lady Aileen and Joan's cousin Davina.

The pair had formed a friendship through correspondence before Davina's marriage to James. Joan blushed at the thought of the stories Davina might have told Lady Aileen, ashamed of both the truth in them and the less than charitable behavior Joan had at times exhibited toward her cousin.

Thankfully, she had long since made peace with Davina, but the mistakes of her past could not be so easily dismissed. Especially by a mother as protective as Lady Aileen. Joan's only hope was that the damage to her character was not irreversible and she would have the opportunity to show Lady Aileen that she was not the same woman who had tormented Davina when they were younger.

As to whether or not she would be a good wife to Malcolm—well, that all depended on Lady Aileen's definition of "good."

While Lady Aileen continued to mull over this astonishing news, the young woman beside her moved forward, tilted her head, and smiled. "Welcome, Joan. I'm Malcolm's sister, Katherine. I wish ye much joy in yer marriage, though I'm selfish enough to admit part of my happiness stems from my delight at having a sister at long last. It isn't easy being a lass with overprotective brothers."

"Thank ye, Katherine," Joan answered sincerely.

"'Tis a pleasure to also make yer acquaintance, Lady Brienne," Katherine continued graciously. "We shall all endeavor to make certain yer stay with us is a pleasant one."

"Ye are very kind," Brienne replied, her cheeks flushing.

As though suddenly being reminded of her duties as chatelaine, Lady Aileen took a moment to visibly compose herself. Her steely glare softened and an edge of warmth entered her eyes. Was it a sign that she was accepting these sudden changes? Or had she merely gotten over the shock?

"Dinnae tug so hard on the bairn's blanket, Lileas," James admonished. "He might tumble down and get hurt."

"I want to hold him," Lileas declared, running her fingers along his side.

"Lileas! Leave that infant alone and come here," Lady Aileen ordered.

Joan braced for a tantrum, but surprisingly the child obeyed.

"Make yer curtsy to Lady Joan," Lady Aileen instructed. "She is to be yer new mother."

Lileas pulled back. She looked from Joan to Brienne, then back to Joan. "I dinnae want her to be my new mother. I want the lady who brought the babe."

Malcolm stepped forward and grasped Lileas's shoulders. "Make yer curtsy."

With a mulish frown, Lileas complied. Joan nodded her head regally in acknowledgment, yet it seemed as though both she and Lileas knew their gestures were insincere.

"Now can I hold the babe?" Lileas asked.

"Nay," Lady Aileen answered. "'Tis dangerous. Ye are too small and the babe too fragile. Ye might drop him."

"I won't!" A pout unfurled across Lileas's lips. "I'll hold him very tight," she insisted.

"Ye may hold him later, poppet." Malcolm affectionately patted the top of Lileas's head. "Lady Joan also has a son and he's old enough to play with ye. Would ye like to have a wee brother?"

"A brother?" Lileas's face shone with interest. "Fer me?"

"Aye, his name is Callum. Come meet him."

A bit of Joan's ire at Lileas's behavior melted at the tender way the young girl took Callum's hand and led him away. Always one to enjoy the company of other children, Callum followed her willingly.

"This is my new brother, Grandfather," Lileas proclaimed, standing before the McKenna. "His name is Callum."

The McKenna burst into laughter. "He's not a pet,

Lileas. He's a lad and he'll learn to pester ye soon enough. 'Tis what little brothers do best."

Lileas frowned at her grandfather, then proceeded to introduce Callum to the rest of the family. Her enthusiasm was contagious, bringing smiles to all.

"I shall have the servants bring in yer things," Lady Aileen said, casting her eyes at the packhorses.

Joan lifted her chin, hiding her embarrassment, yet saying nothing. There was time enough for her mother-in-law to discover that Joan had no dowry and the majority of those items weighing down the horses belonged to Brienne.

The babe began whimpering, then scrunched his face and broke into an earsplitting wail. "He's hungry," Brienne said apologetically, putting her finger in the babe's mouth to quiet him. He sucked greedily for a moment, then realizing there was no nourishment, burst into fresh sobs.

"Poor mite," Lady Aileen said, clucking her tongue. "How inconsiderate of us to keep him from his meal. I'll show ye where ye can tend to him in private."

Lady Aileen placed her arm around Brienne's shoulders, paused, then turned toward Joan as if suddenly remembering that as Malcolm's wife, 'twas Joan who should be receiving this sort of solicitous attention. The unspoken acknowledgment eased the tension in Joan, letting her know this slight was unintended.

"Perhaps Katherine can escort me to my chamber?" Joan suggested.

"I'd be honored," Katherine immediately answered.

The babe let out another hungry wail and the women scrambled. Joan followed Katherine through the great hall and up a winding stone staircase, glad the young woman was the one escorting her. There was a quiet steadiness to Katherine that made her far less intimidating than the rest of her family.

She carried enough of a resemblance to Malcolm and James to mark her as a sibling. Her pert nose suited her face, her fair complexion was one to be envied, and her hair a lovely shade of brown, shot through with vibrant streaks of amber.

She was a pretty girl, with almond-shaped eyes nearly the same shade of blue as Malcolm. But it was the intelligence lurking behind them that Joan believed gave Katherine her true beauty.

They crested the steps and Katherine led her down a short passageway. There was but one door at the end of it.

Upon entering the chamber the first thing Joan noticed was the large bed placed against the far wall. It was adorned with red velvet hangings and far more pillows than anyone needed to sleep on. Directly across were four arched windows, which provided a perfect view of the green valley below and the majestic mountains in the distance.

There were thick rugs on the floor, a small table with two chairs, and several trunks that Joan assumed contained Malcolm's clothing. The chamber was elegant and richly appointed yet felt welcoming.

*My new home.* Joan was surprised to feel her eyes moisten with tears as an unexpected tide of emotion overtook her.

"I'm sorry there willnae be enough time fer a proper bath, but I'll have the maids bring up hot water so that ye can wash off the dust of the road," Katherine said. "Let them know if ye require anything else."

"Thank ye, Katherine. Ye've been most kind."

Katherine's blue eyes sparkled as she smiled, transforming her from a pretty lass into a beautiful one. As

Katherine quit the room, Joan suspected that she had many suitors and wondered why she wasn't yet married.

Joan had just begun exploring the room when a sound at the door drew her attention.

"'Tis a fine chamber," Gertrude said as she stood in the open doorway. "I swear it's larger than the laird's room at Armstrong Castle."

"Where's Callum?"

"Sir Malcolm took him and his daughter to the stables to see some newly born kittens. When they are done, Lileas's nursemaid will take charge of both children." Gertrude's brows pulled together. "Lileas certainly is a high-spirited lass."

"Aye, she's a handful." Joan rubbed her temples. "Strong willed and far too perceptive fer her own good."

Gertrude clucked her tongue in agreement.

As promised, the hot water soon arrived, along with a stack of clean towels and a pot of soap that smelled of lemon and lavender. With Gertrude's help, Joan removed her travel garments and rinsed away the sweat and dirt. Feeling clean and refreshed, she stared critically at the garments Gertrude had laid out.

"Why do ye hesitate?" Gertrude asked. "The red velvet is yer best gown."

Joan fingered the gold embroidery on the sleeves. "Ye saw the way Lady Aileen reacted when she realized that I had married Malcolm. I fear appearing at her table dressed in all my finery will confirm her impression that her son's new wife is nothing but a vain, spoiled, pampered noblewoman."

Gertrude huffed. "Ye are a lady born and bred and need to make certain that everyone knows it. Now stop yer fussing and let me get ye properly dressed."

Joan gave her maid's hand a gentle squeeze. "Ye are ever my champion, Gertrude."

With efficiency that bespoke of years of practice, Gertrude helped her dress. After placing an airy white veil on Joan's head and securing it with a jewel-encrusted gold circlet, she held up a round hand mirror.

"Ye look ravishing, milady," Gertrude proclaimed.

"Aye, she most certainly does." Malcolm stepped into the chamber. "Ye steal my breath and wits with yer beauty, Joan. I shall feel like a king tonight walking into the great hall with ye on my arm."

"Ye look rather royal yerself," Joan commented, wondering where he had bathed and dressed, and aye, shaved, too.

"I bathed in the loch," he said, answering her unasked question. "I would have invited ye to join me, but the water was very, very cold."

Joan glanced at the closed trunks. If they did not contain his clothes, then what was inside them? "I thought this was yer chamber."

"Aye."

"But no one came to fetch fresh garments fer ye."

Malcolm smiled. "Plying her needle settles my mother's nerves. She stitched this shirt and tunic fer me while I was away."

"Och, so ye plan yer journeys when ye are in need of new clothes?"

His grin widened. "Sometimes."

"Shameful. Well, I give ye fair warning, husband, unlike yer mother, I brood and sulk when my mind fills with worries."

"Then I shall seek never to give ye cause." He offered her his arm. "Shall we?"

Joan's nerves fluttered, but she swallowed back her

trepidation and rested her fingers on his forearm. The warmth and strength she felt through the fine wool fabric gave her comfort, and she found herself uttering two words that she never believed she would ever say to any man: "Lead on."

Joan remained silent as they entered the great hall, but Malcolm could feel her grip tightening slightly at her first glimpse of the crowd. All in the clan were curious about his new bride, and it seemed as though every inch of space was filled, along with the tables and benches.

The assembly of people parted respectfully as they walked through, calling out greetings and congratulations. Malcolm answered them all, smiling and joking, genuinely enjoying the attention, though he knew 'twas really Joan who commanded every eye in the room.

She was a golden vision, radiant, poised, and beautiful. But it was her spirit that struck his heart. Joan had retained her composure and grace while meeting his mother earlier, an event that certainly must have been trying. Though not openly rude, 'twas obvious Lady Aileen had been shocked and a bit dismayed to discover their marriage.

Though he never doubted Joan's ability to hold her own against his strong-willed mother, a fierce protectiveness toward her had taken hold of him when witnessing his mother's reaction. It went well beyond the feelings of duty that a man normally had for his wife, and the intensity of the emotion had surprised him.

How ironic that he should feel this way even though their marriage was not yet consummated. Which begged the inevitable question—how strongly would he feel toward her after he had bedded her?

"Do ye sing?" Malcolm asked as he placed his hand in the small of Joan's back and led her to their seats on the dais.

"Not well enough that anyone would enjoy hearing me," she admitted. "Why do ye ask?"

"'Tis a McKenna tradition that the bride sings at her wedding feast."

She pulled back. "How can this be our wedding feast? We were married a week ago."

"But the McKennas dinnae have a chance to celebrate. In all likelihood the crowd will call fer a song from the bride, especially with the wine and ale flowing so freely."

"If it pleases ye, I shall try my best, but I warn ye, it willnae be pretty."

"Dinnae worry. I'll get Katherine to sing a duet with ye."

"Katherine? Why not my groom?"

Malcolm favored her with a grin. "I cannae carry a tune. I fear the clan might start pelting us with food if I start singing."

She smiled, as he hoped she would, and took her seat. "Then I shall make certain to duck if I see ye open yer mouth."

"I always said ye were a wise woman, Joan McKenna."

He leaned in and gave her a hearty kiss. Joan's lips parted in surprise and Malcolm took advantage of the chance to swipe his tongue sensually across her moist lips.

Sleeping chastely beside her these past six nights had been torturous. Lust coursed through Malcolm's veins, throbbing low in his gut, threatening to overtake his common sense. As a result, the kiss was far more passionate than he intended, especially in front of so many.

The distant sound of boisterous shouts and whistles reminded him of the audience witnessing this intimate display, giving him the fortitude to quell his physical desire. He ended the kiss while he still could, nuzzling Joan's neck before pulling away completely. Her cheeks flamed and he knew she had noticed the hungry, heated expression in his eyes.

Satisfied that he had successfully gained tight control of his desire, Malcolm favored Joan with a deliberately roguish grin. Her eyes widened and she suddenly became highly interested in the contents of the trencher they shared.

Deciding he had teased her more than he ought, Malcolm smiled and turned his attention to the meal, but his mind was on anything but the food.

# Chapter Twelve

Cheeks heated with embarrassment, Joan kept her gaze firmly locked on the trencher in front of her. Unlike the miserly hospitality of her father, the McKennas spared nothing for the wedding celebration meal. There was a seemingly endless stream of dishes, including a whole suckling pig, fresh and salted fish, stews of rabbit, beef, and venison, sausages and black pudding, braised cabbage, buttered peas, pastries made with dried apples, pears, and plums, and enough ale and wine to float a small ship.

'Twas a far cry from the oatcakes and dried meat they had eaten while traveling and all were savoring every bite. The distraction of food also provided Joan with the much needed opportunity to compose herself. Malcolm's kiss had been unexpected, but what was most surprising was the fluttering it produced inside her. Had they been alone, she might have been tempted to encourage him to give her another.

Of course that would come later tonight, when they finally consummated their marriage. Her heart began to race at the thought, but Joan firmly pushed it to the back of her mind. She could learn much about her new family and the clan during this meal if she kept her eyes open and her wits about her. Dwelling on getting into bed with Malcolm would only prove to be an unsettling diversion.

Joan nodded to the McKenna, who sat on her right, and Lady Aileen, who sat beside him, then casually glanced down the other side of the dais. She was glad to note that Brienne had also been given the honor of being seated at the dais, with James on her left and Katherine on her right.

Brienne appeared to be at ease, smiling often and eating her meal with obvious gusto. The biggest surprise, however, was the presence of young Lileas. She sat beside her father, in a long-legged chair clearly designed specifically for that purpose.

Servants scurried about the hall, arms laden with trays of food, pitchers of ale and wine. The guests also roamed the hall, stopping at the dais to speak with various members of the family and to offer Malcolm and Joan their best wishes.

Joan was introduced to so many clan members that she lost count, but she smiled graciously and made an effort to say something to each of them. Her reputation appeared to be unknown; this was her chance to establish herself as a friendly and benevolent lady and she seized upon it.

A new marriage, a fresh start, a new beginning. Joan had learned the hard lessons of her past mistakes and she was determined not to repeat them.

The McKenna stood, raised his wine goblet, and shouted for attention. The din of voices in the hall quieted. "Tonight, we celebrate the marriage of Malcolm and Joan. May they live a long and joyful life among us."

"And be blessed with a room full of bairns!" a male voice shouted.

The sounds of laughter, shouting, and fists banging on wooden tables filled the air. The McKenna smiled widely, raised his goblet higher, and drank. Stealing a glance around the room, Joan was glad to see everyone partaking in the good wishes, including James and Lady Aileen.

"Does Lileas always sit at the dais during meals, or is she being allowed a special treat tonight?" Joan asked when the McKenna resumed his seat.

"She usually eats here, with the rest of the family," he replied. "Malcolm had that special chair made when she turned three."

"'Tis highly unusual."

The McKenna shrugged. "Malcolm has always indulged the lass. Overindulged, most would say."

"Aye." Joan swallowed a bite of tasty beef. "Can ye tell me why no one stops him?"

"She's his daughter."

"Yet ye've all had to live with her."

The McKenna's eyes darkened and for a moment Joan feared she had gone too far. The laird was clearly protective of his family and she had all but insulted his granddaughter.

But instead of yelling in anger, the McKenna laughed in merriment. "Begging, tears, and pouting. She's accomplished at all three. Lileas likes to blame her behavior on being a poor, motherless child. Now that ye're here, she'll have to find another excuse. Or else be taught how to properly behave. Do ye have the courage to take on the task?"

"It appears that I must," Joan answered wryly, hardly relishing the notion.

Aye, she could take the spoiled Lileas in hand to the benefit of all—including the lass. But Joan suspected

Malcolm's feelings about disciplining his child would echo the way she felt about anyone interfering with her decisions about Callum. She could barely tolerate it.

Yet 'twas obvious to one and all that left to Malcolm, Lileas would only grow more impossible. Joan sighed. Another challenge to overcome.

Joan remained quiet through the remainder of the meal, silently observing Malcolm and his family. The ease with which they talked and joked among themselves spoke of a great affection between them. She was especially curious about his parents. She had heard the stories of how besotted the McKenna was with his wife, and it was clear Lady Aileen returned those feelings, for the love and devotion between the pair was evident in nearly every gesture.

They exchanged warm glances, shared private jokes, pressed their heads together like a pair of cooing doves. Lady Aileen needed only to place her hand on the McKenna's arm and he would immediately shift his attention toward her.

She made certain his trencher was filled with the choicest bits of food, his goblet filled with wine. He brushed a stray wisp of hair that had come loose from her cheek and insisted that one of the lasses sing a song he declared was Lady Aileen's favorite.

But it was the effortless, affectionate way they interacted that fascinated Joan the most. They communicated with more than words, seeming to be in a rhythm only they understood. They were, indeed, a rare and unusual couple.

"Hard to believe it was an arranged marriage," Malcolm said, noticing where her attention was captured.

Joan turned. "I've always heard the most scandalous tale—that yer mother chose yer father."

Malcolm laughed. "A rumor I believe was started by my mother. The truth is that she did have a choice. After a broken betrothal, her father gave her the power to refuse any offers fer her hand. And refuse them she did—until the McKenna came along.

"My grandfather—her father—did not prescribe to the notion that women don't have the strength of mind or character to choose their own husbands. 'Tis the reason that Katherine is not yet wed, as my mother has insisted that she be afforded the same right."

Joan took a small sip of wine. "'Tis highly unusual, but I am quickly learning that the McKennas do things their own way."

"'Tis what makes us all so charming—and strong." Malcolm smiled, then grimaced. "Och, they're calling fer the bride to sing."

Joan felt a rush of nerves, but true to his word, Malcolm brought Katherine to sit beside her. The musician began to strum his lyre and the crowd quieted. Joan cleared her throat and warbled a few notes and then Katherine's lovely voice joined hers.

The haunting ballad filled the great hall, rippling through the rafters in a gentle wave. Their joined voices created a unique, harmonious sound, beautiful and moving. As the final note faded away there was utter silence, and then the chamber erupted in cheers and applause.

They clamored for more and Joan and Katherine obliged with three more songs, their voices ringing out together pure and clear. Her throat parched, Joan drank several large sips of wine, surprised to see how late the hour had grown.

"I'm certain that he is asleep, but I should like to check on Callum before I retire," she said.

"Of course ye must see to Callum." Malcolm seized her hand and brought it to his lips. In a courtly gesture, he grazed a light kiss across her knuckles. "I shall join ye shortly in our chamber."

A red-cheeked squire escorted Joan to the nursery, eager to return to the festivities once she dismissed him. Joan entered the chamber quietly, surprised to discover that Callum was awake. He was seated at a child-sized table, a nearly empty bowl of porridge in front of him.

His precious face brightened with a smile when he saw her. Joan embraced him eagerly, holding him close even as he continued eating his food.

"Milady, good evening." A round, gray-haired woman with a kind smile bustled over. "I am Mistress Innes, the nursemaid. Master Callum awoke a few hours ago. He said that he was hungry and that he wanted porridge."

"'Twas kind of Cook to go to the trouble of preparing it fer him," Joan said, amazed that in the midst of serving such an elaborate feast the time was taken to grant Callum's request. "I must make certain to thank him in the morning."

"Her," Mistress Innes corrected. "Mary is the castle cook and a fine job she does of it, if ye dinnae mind me saying."

"She is skilled," Joan agreed. "This evening's meal was a veritable feast. Did ye have a chance to partake?"

"I did, thank ye fer asking. They brought up a tray with more food than I could eat, yet I finished every bite."

Mistress Innes's round face jiggled when she laughed and Joan decided she liked this woman.

"Have ye eaten all yer porridge?" Joan asked, bending low to kiss her son. He smiled and nodded. "Then it's time to sleep."

Joan helped Callum climb into bed, then pulled the

blankets around him. Leaning forward, she dropped a kiss on his cheek. She began to hum one of his favorite songs and his eyelids soon closed. Reaching out, Joan stroked his hand until his breaths were steady and even, his slumber deep.

"My bed is right there," Mistress Innes said, pointing to the corner. "I'll watch over him."

"Thank ye. But if there is a need, ye must send fer me," Joan instructed.

Following the nursemaid's directions, Joan was able to find her way back to the chamber she now shared with Malcolm. Thankfully, 'twas dim and quiet when she entered. As this was not officially her wedding night, they had been spared the traditional songs and crude jokes that most couples endured when they were brought to the marriage bed, an event she suspected the clan would have delighted in providing.

Gertrude arrived. Sensing her pensive mood, the maid remained quiet as she unbound Joan's intricate braid. Having her hair brushed always managed to soothe her and Joan made no protest when Gertrude continued gliding the comb through her golden tresses long after they were untangled.

"The hour grows late, milady."

The gentle sound of Gertrude's voice brought Joan out of her stupor. "Yet the celebration continues. I can still hear the music from the great hall."

"It willnae be long before Sir Malcolm arrives." The maid's words sent a cold wave down Joan's spine. "Shall I stay with ye until then?"

Joan patted her maid's hand reassuringly. "Nay. Ye should leave."

The reluctance to follow that order was clearly reflected in Gertrude's expression, but she did as she was bade.

Joan's chair scraped against the wooden floorboards as she dragged it closer to the fireplace. She sat in front of the hearth for a long time, staring into the dying flames. Every now and again she would take a sip from the goblet of wine she held, determined to keep her wits, no matter how frayed her nerves.

There was, of course, no true cause for such feelings of panic. She was hardly a virgin, knew precisely what happened when a husband crawled into bed with his wife. It was never particularly pleasant, even when she wasn't being abused by Archibald's tongue or fists, but she would manage.

*Manage.* Such was the lot of womankind.

Unexpectedly, a vision of Lady Aileen and the McKenna rose in Joan's mind. Clearly, those two did far more than manage, even after all these years. She couldn't account for it, but it made her wonder.

Malcolm was a very different sort of man than Archibald. His manner, his temperament, aye, even his kisses. Would lying with him be very different? Though a true Highland warrior who knew much of fighting and killing, there was a softer side to Malcolm.

Well, not exactly softer—kinder. Fair. Honorable. She had seen the affection he held for his parents and siblings, the unmistakable love and devotion he carried for his daughter. Was it possible that he one day might feel the same about her?

Was that something that she even wanted? Could she someday lay claim to Malcolm's heart? And what if by some miracle that happened? Those who loved expected it to be returned.

Could she allow herself to love him? Did she even know how? Ripples of unease traveled through her. 'Twas the question that frightened her the most. Her cousin Davina said that love was more than momentary desire and passion. It required respect, fondness, and affection.

*And trust. Dinnae forget trust. Fer me, that is above all the hardest thing to give anyone, especially a man.*

Joan shook her head vigorously. She must not think about these things right now. It clouded her already confused mind and heightened her nerves. She finished her wine, rose from the chair, and began restlessly wandering about the room. It seemed so odd seeing her things neatly placed within the chamber. They looked foreign and strange among Malcolm's manly possessions.

She blew away a wisp of hair that had fallen over her eyes, then picked up her comb. Though Gertrude had just finished brushing her hair, Joan needed the comfort it brought, so she began combing it again. It worked for a few minutes, but at the sound of approaching footsteps, her hands stiffened and the comb clattered to the floor.

Malcolm entered the chamber without knocking, his presence seeming to invade the space. "Has Gertrude left?"

"Aye." Joan cleared her throat, appalled at the squeak she heard in her own voice. "Will yer squire be in soon to assist ye?"

Malcolm leaned against the closed door, folding his arms across his chest. "Nay. I wear no battle gear and require no help in removing my clothing. Unless ye'd like to volunteer?"

"Ye just said that ye dinnae require assistance," she replied, hoping she didn't sound as breathless as she felt.

He reached down to remove his tunic. Nervously, Joan moved to gaze out the largest window. She could see bursts of stars twinkling brightly in the cloudless sky. How ironic that it was not until their journey's end that the weather cleared. She turned to share the joke with Malcolm but the words melted on her tongue when she saw him.

He had stripped down, and was clad in only a long white linen shirt and braies. The strings on the shirt were open, and she could see the swirls of dark hair curling on his chest. It continued down over the flat, muscular line of his stomach, vanishing into the materials of his braies.

Joan's mouth suddenly felt dry. He was a very attractive man. Perhaps that would make sharing his bed easier? She moistened her lips, her heart nearly leaping from her chest as she tried to imagine it.

"How's Callum?" Malcolm asked. "Was he asleep when ye went into the nursery?"

The deep baritone of Malcolm's voice made Joan shiver, but thoughts of her son pushed away her nerves. "Callum was stuffing his face with a bowl of porridge when I arrived, but took to his bed with no protest. Even after his earlier nap, he was tired."

"No doubt. It was a long journey."

"Mistress Innes seems a most kind and efficient woman," Joan offered.

"Aye, she has a good heart and a wealth of knowledge on the care of children."

*Yet despite all her knowledge and experience she is unable to control Lileas.* The thought came unbidden, but Joan held her tongue. Now was not the time to discuss Malcolm's unruly daughter.

He poured a goblet of wine for himself, then refilled hers and handed it to her. Once she was holding it, Malcolm pointedly raised his vessel. She did the same. He clinked his goblet against hers, then drank. She took a very small sip, since she had already drained one full glass before he arrived, in addition to the wine she had drunk at the evening meal.

He leaned back in his chair, crossing one leg over his knee. He leveled his gaze at her, his shadowed face filled with expectation. He grinned and Joan felt the breath catch in her throat. There was a hint of a dimple in the corner of his mouth she had never noticed.

*Saints above, he is a handsome devil.*

Joan glanced into her goblet, not liking the wide-eyed, uncertain woman she saw reflected on the shimmering surface. She raised her eyes and nearly gasped when she met Malcolm's dark, penetrating stare.

"Tell me, wife, are ye ready fer bed?"

Joan's eyes widened in shock and Malcolm cursed himself for being an overeager fool. She had made no secret of her distaste for the marriage bed. He needed to tread slowly, carefully, or else he'd ruin what he hoped would be a night of mutual passion.

"I am prepared to do my duty, Malcolm."

Her words were like a dose of cold water, yet astonishingly his ardor had not cooled. He had been grappling to control himself ever since he had entered their bedchamber earlier in the evening to bring her down for the evening meal.

Malcolm took Joan's hand and brought it to his lips. He kissed the top of her wrist, then turned it and gently caressed her palm. Her breath hitched. He moved his mouth higher, tracing the soft inner skin, and felt the rapid fluttering of her pulse.

Desire or fear? Impossible to tell, yet if he could hazard a guess, he suspected fear.

"I willnae bite," he murmured. "Well, only in a playful, pleasurable way. I promise."

He had hoped for an answering smile, but Joan's eyes were cool and watchful. So much for his irresistible manly charms.

"I've slept beside ye fer six long nights," he said. "There's no cause to fear me."

"Sleep?" She sniffed inelegantly. "Is that what we shall do when we are in that vast bed tonight, husband?"

Damnation! His new wife had an uncanny ability to take everything he said literally when it suited her. "Aye, we shall slumber in that bed. Eventually."

He cupped her cheek, then rubbed her lips gently with his thumb, hoping she'd be bold and grasp his finger with her teeth. She didn't. But she didn't turn away either.

Emboldened, Malcolm gallantly swept her into his arms. He carried her to the bed and laid her down. She attempted to crawl away to the far side, but Malcolm locked his arm around her small waist to prevent it.

His body was already hard. All it had taken was the sight of her in her sheer night rail and the memory of the few kisses he had shared with her to bring his desire to a nearly fevered pitch. But he would control it—somehow.

Malcolm turned so that they lay side by side, facing each other. He pulled her close and kissed her deeply, feeling her shiver when he claimed her lips. She pressed a shaking hand against his chest and he was uncertain if she meant to draw him close or push him away.

That worried him. He was not a man interested in a conquest. 'Twould be impossible for him to take from her what she did not give freely with at least some degree of passion. He wanted to convey that to her somehow, yet feared if given the choice, Joan would avoid his bed indefinitely.

Starting over, he lowered his head and nuzzled the delicate spot beneath her ear. She smelled delicious, more intoxicating and heady than the finest whiskey. He kissed her again, forcing himself to go slowly, allowing her to become accustomed to the feel and taste of him.

She met him haltingly and he felt his excitement flare. As gently as his fingers allowed, he pushed the fabric off her shoulder, exposing her breasts. Reverently, Malcolm cupped one luscious mound in his hand. She let out a throaty cry when he rolled her nipple between his thumb and finger, yet she didn't pull away.

Encouraged, Malcolm dipped his head, grazing his teeth sensually across the stiffening peak. Her breath hitched and he ravaged her with kisses, stimulating her with his mouth and tongue. He worked the garment off her other shoulder and down her body.

Her flesh was flawless; the feel of her skin was soft as silk. Impatiently, he tore off his shirt and braies, moaning with delight at the feel of flesh against flesh.

Continuing his seduction, Malcolm worked his hand over her stomach and down between her thighs. She flinched when he touched her. "Relax," he whispered. "Let me bring ye pleasure. I know that I can. I heard it starting in yer voice."

Her face grew red. "Malcolm, please."

He held back a sigh. He wanted her to feel desire, but he wanted more. He wanted to comfort her, make her feel safe and cherished, yet she continued to resist.

"Joan, ye are my woman, my wife. Ye need to trust that I willnae hurt ye."

"I'm trying. Truly."

He started again. This time he captured her lower lip with his teeth, biting her gently as he had promised. He continued to tease her mouth until she moved close enough to graze her breasts against his chest. Encouraged, his mouth sought hers in a hungry kiss, twining his tongue around hers until he heard soft moans coming from the back of her throat.

Yet they sounded oddly forced.

He lifted his head. "What are ye doing?"

Her throat moved visibly as she swallowed. "Kissing ye?"

"The noise, Joan."

"Ye said that ye wanted to hear my pleasure. But if ye'd rather I stay silent, then I shall."

With a groan, Malcolm rolled onto his back. Disappointment mingled with frustration. This was not going at all as he had hoped. He knew that some women enjoyed playing a game of refusal before surrendering, but this was different. "I want ye to do it because it makes ye feel good. Not because ye think it's what I want to hear."

She stayed silent and he could hear her breath coming in a long, deep rhythm. "Do ye desire me, Malcolm?"

"Och, Joan, I should think that is rather obvious." He cupped her chin and turned it toward him. Her eyes glittered in the candlelight, filled with emotions he could not fully decipher, but at least he saw no fear or revulsion.

"Will ye . . ." She hesitated, biting her lower lip.

"Tell me," he coaxed. "I want us to find pleasure together."

"Will ye indulge me?" she whispered.

"By leaving ye alone and sleeping on the floor?" he asked jokingly, half fearing that would be her request.

"Nay. By not asking fer the impossible tonight. I

believe that I can bring ye pleasure, if ye let me." Her thigh pressed into his as she moved closer.

"Joan, I'm not sure. . . ."

Her lips brushed his cheek, her warm breath fluttering on his skin. Then she angled her head and flicked her tongue across his ear.

His cock jumped and he nearly shot off the bed. Before he could catch his breath, Joan rolled herself on top of him. Her gaze locked with his as she settled herself between his thighs. Lacing her fingers through his, she stretched his arms over his head.

His interest was immediately captured by the sight of her breast, hanging low and heavy and oh, so close to his lips. Taking full advantage of this position, Malcolm lifted his head. His tongue darted out and first he licked, then he suckled the pink nipple.

Joan gripped his shoulders, her nails digging deep. Slowly, she eased herself down on his erect shaft. He could feel her body stretching, opening itself to him, accepting his length until he was buried deep inside her. She was tight, but wet. At least he had managed to do that for her.

Malcolm gave a ragged sigh, sliding his hands up to explore her body. Her narrow waist, soft hips, firm buttocks. Her skin was flawless, without a single blemish or mark. He let his eyes feast on that glorious sight before trailing his hands down her body. He brushed his fingers lightly against the back of her knees and heard her breath catch.

Malcolm froze. Had he finally found a magical spot? He caressed her again. She bowed into him, moving her hips tentatively. He could feel his penis swelling within her. Moaning, he thrust upward, pushing himself deeper.

"Do ye like it? Does it feel good?" he asked, unable to find the passion he felt reflected in her eyes.

Almost as if reading his thoughts, she closed her eyes. Tightening her knees against his side, she pulled herself up, then plunged back down, finding a rhythm that drove him mad with excitement. He could feel the smooth softness of her legs as they brushed against his, almost tickling the hair on his thighs. It drove him wild.

Joan twisted against him, and he groaned in pleasure. The heat was rising in his body, the pressure building. He tried to fit his hand between their bodies to stimulate her, but she denied him, thrusting her hips forward.

Suddenly, she reached down and pinched his nipple. Hard. 'Twas too much. With a shout, his body erupted, shuddering violently as his climax surged and pulsed through him. The pleasure was nearly blinding. Heaving in great gasps, Malcolm was amazed to feel Joan's arms tighten around his shoulders.

'Twas such an unexpected caring, intimate gesture, and for a moment he felt irrefutably bound to her. He strained upward, pouring the last of his seed deep inside her womb, and she gave a soft cry of pleasure.

Joan slumped over him, burying her face between his neck and shoulder. She lay there for a few moments, breathing hard. He ran his fingertips lazily along her spine and over her buttocks, enjoying his soft, female blanket.

After a few moments, Joan raised her head, then grimaced as she pulled herself away, separating their bodies.

Concerned, he asked, "Are ye all right?"

She tilted her chin and favored him with a small grin. "I'm fine. Relieved. 'Twas far less of an ordeal than I feared."

"Och, words to warm a man's heart and stroke his manly pride."

Her body went rigid. "Forgive me."

"Nay." He laid a soft kiss on her cheek. "Ye pleased me greatly. I only wish that ye had allowed me to do the same fer ye."

"'Tis better this way," she insisted.

"Shall I show ye how wrong ye are to say that, wife?" he quipped.

She paused, letting the night rail she had just grabbed slip through her fingers. "Is that an order?"

"Jesus, ye are my wife, Joan, not my squire."

Malcolm's heart ached as he tried to understand the type of marriage she must have had with Archibald and wondered how he could convince her that this time it would be different.

Eyes luminous, she stared back at him. "I am who I am, Malcolm," she whispered. "Not the woman ye think or wish me to be."

He gently caught her face between his hands. "Ye are far more than ye believe yerself to be, Joan. I know that in my heart."

He saw the doubt in her eyes and immediately wanted to ease it, yet held his tongue. 'Twould take time for Joan to change the way she thought of herself, to see herself as he saw her. To trust him enough to allow the passion he believed she held so tightly inside her to flow freely.

Joan rolled to her side and Malcolm followed, pressing himself tightly against her back. Nuzzling his nose against the tender nape of her neck, he inhaled her sweet, clean scent. Joan wiggled, inadvertently brushing her soft, round bottom against his groin.

His body tightened, the flames of desire so recently sated quickly rising again. Of their own accord, his hips thrust forward, poking against her softness. Joan sighed loudly, turned her shoulder, and tilted her head up to meet his eyes.

"Ye promised me sleep."

"I did."

"I trust ye, Malcolm. Ye are a man of honor, a man of yer word."

She spoke with a certainty that momentarily filled him with pride, until he realized it meant he would have to keep his word and allow her to sleep instead of coaxing her into another bout of lovemaking.

"Go on then, close yer eyes and start yer snoring," he grumbled.

Joan's triumphant expression fell and a look of horror crossed her face. "Do I truly snore?"

"Aye, like a burly blacksmith."

"I dinnae," she cried out.

"Ye do." He kissed her on the tip of her nose. "And I find that I like it. Very much."

# Chapter Thirteen

Joan woke the next morning alone in the large bed, feeling anything but refreshed. Unused to having such a large male sleeping beside her, she had tossed and turned well into the morning hours, all the while listening to Malcolm's deep breathing. The sound was a stark, unwelcome reminder of her own inability to slumber, worsening her mood.

Yet it wasn't only the feel and sound of her bed companion that kept her rest at bay. Her mind was racing with thoughts of Malcolm that continued to plague her, no matter how hard she tried to shut them out. His heady kisses, the touch of his lips and fingers on her body, the feel of him deep inside her.

Joan stretched, groaning at the soreness in her limbs and other places. She had tried to please him, as any good wife should, she was surprised to realize how important that was to her. Yet it paled in comparison to Malcolm's insistence that the pleasure they found in their marital bed be mutual.

The consummation of their marriage vows had been a contradiction of emotions for her. Malcolm had been patient and gentle and she was grateful for his consideration. But his insistence that she also find the act pleasurable had been puzzling and she truly had no idea why it was so important to him.

Was it a different form of male dominance and control? Was he hoping that her enjoyment of their passion would in turn create a need for him within her that could be used to bend her to his will?

Or was she simply being too suspicious? Malcolm had given her no cause to suspect him of such devious intent. Quite the opposite, in fact. He appeared sincere in his regard for her, honest in his emotions.

Yet her hesitancy persisted. Had her disastrous relationship with Archibald soured her to the extent that she was unfairly ascribing ulterior motives where none existed? Or was she merely determined to never again be held at the mercy of any man who claimed her as his wife? He might have the power to raise her passions, but she had the will to control them—and she was not about to relinquish it.

The intimacy that she had shared with Malcolm had brought forth very unexpected feelings of yearning and need deep within her. Joan didn't understand these emotions. Didn't trust them. And therefore wanted no part of them.

Yet her new husband had very different ideas.

Gathering her courage, Joan cautiously peered through the opening in the bed curtains, half expecting to catch a glimpse of a naked Malcolm. But the chamber was empty.

For a wee moment she considered succumbing to the temptation of pulling the covers up to her chin and seeking the sleep she so desperately needed. The bed was warm and cozy, the linen sheets finely woven and smelling pleasantly of rosemary.

But she could hardly spend the day abed, especially if Malcolm was not with her. All would believe her to be a slovenly woman, especially her new in-laws. Above all, Joan was determined to gain their respect.

Joan slid her night rail on before leaving the warmth of the bed and crossing the chamber to gaze out the window. A golden morning light bathed the land. In the distance she could see the glimmers of sunlight breaking through the mist, shimmering on the surface of the loch that sat at the base of the mountains. Surrounded by a tall green forest, it looked peaceful and calm.

There was a chill in the breeze that blew in through the window, but it was a welcoming blast of fresh, crisp air. The bailey was bustling with activity at this late hour of the morning. Wagons of food were arriving for the kitchen, livestock was being moved from the pens to the pastures, a band of carpenters was repairing the walls of two of the outbuildings, their hammers pounding rhythmically.

Joan dragged her hand through the tangles of her hair. She normally braided the long tresses at night, but had left them unbound at Gertrude's insistence. It took a while to comb through the knots this morning, but the familiar, simple task was soothing work. Gertrude arrived just as Joan finished, the maid's mouth creased into a smile. She carried a tray with fresh bread, dried fruit, cheese, and ale.

"Goodness, I'm not an invalid," Joan said, as Gertrude arranged the food on the table. "I can sit in the great hall and break my fast like the rest of the clan."

"Sir Malcolm ordered this repast fer ye," Gertrude declared. "He insisted that ye be allowed to sleep late. He also asked to be summoned when you woke, so that he may show ye about the castle."

"I'll need to visit the nursery first," Joan replied, a swirl of pleasure in her chest at her husband's thoughtful gestures. "I'll find Malcolm after I've seen Callum."

Joan stepped lightly as she entered the nursery, pleased that she had been able to find her way without asking for assistance. McKenna Castle was exceedingly large; it would take time for her to know her way through its many passages and it felt good to have already mastered one.

Callum ran forward for a hug and Joan swung him into her arms. Lileas hung back and Joan greeted her with a friendly smile. The lass dipped her chin and returned it with a shy grin of her own.

Mistress Innes was helping the children finish their morning meal. She cheerfully offered to find Malcolm's squire and send the lad to search for him.

Joan was glad to have the time alone with the children. She settled herself between them, but turned at the movement she heard in the doorway, expecting to see Malcolm. Her breath caught and her stomach clenched in fear when she instead beheld a large, ragged animal. It was filthy, covered in gray and white matted fur, with pieces of twigs and leaves clinging to its hide.

Its eyes were close-set and beady, its teeth long, sharp, and lethal. Part dog, part wolf, all danger, its large snout twitched as the beast lifted it in the air, sniffing in their direction.

*My God, how did it get in here?*

Holding her breath, she prayed that the creature would ignore their presence and move away, but it looked directly at them. Joan never hesitated. She snatched Callum under one arm and thrust Lileas behind her, placing herself between the children and the feral animal. It halted, appearing startled by her actions.

"But that's . . ."

"Lileas, keep silent," Joan demanded in a harsh tone, frantically searching for a weapon to defend herself and the children.

The table was filled with dirty bowls, cups, and spoons. In desperation, Joan lifted one of the bowls and hurled it toward the intruder. It crashed at the animal's feet, splintering into pieces and spraying shards of pottery in its path. The animal yelped and for a moment Joan thought she had succeeded in wounding it, yet saw no sign of blood.

Joan stepped back slowly, taking care to move carefully and keep her balance. If she fell, the beast would be on her in a moment, leaving the children unprotected.

As she drew near it, Joan noticed a small bench. She dropped Callum behind her, lifted the bench with both hands, and held it out in front of her. It was heavy and unwieldy, but the only barrier she could find.

The animal moved to the table. Not taking her eyes off the creature for a moment, Joan balanced the bench awkwardly in one arm and groped her way along the wall. It lifted its large head, sniffed again, and began licking the remnants of food from the bowls.

'Twas the distraction that Joan had hoped for, yet there was no route of escape. If they ran for the doorway, they would pass too close to it. She could feel her breath reduced to quick, short gasps as she realized they were trapped.

Her mind raced with a possible defense and then she heard the merciful sound of booted feet racing up the stairway. *Rescue!* Yet if it were one of the servants or a young page, he or she would be equally at risk.

"Have a care! We are cornered by a rabid beast. Summon Sir Malcolm at once!"

"Joan?"

"Malcolm, be careful!" Joan shouted.

"Oh, Papa, ye've come to save us!" Lileas stepped out from behind her, screwed up her face, then turned accusingly toward Joan. "Ye tried to hit Prince! With my bowl of porridge."

*Prince? Saints above, this foul creature has a name?*

Malcolm appeared in the doorway. He issued a stern command and the creature pulled itself away from the dirty bowls and obediently sat. A second command and the animal lay down on its belly.

Arms aching, Joan slowly lowered the bench she had been holding.

"Prince is Lileas's pet," Malcolm explained as he came into the nursery. "He would have been here yesterday to greet us, but he disappears from the castle sometimes."

"To terrorize the villagers?" Joan asked, raising a brow.

"Nay!" Lileas cried. "Everyone loves Prince. No one fears him. Sometimes the blacksmith's daughter cries when he goes near her, but she's not a brave lass, so it doesn't count."

"Well, it should matter," Joan snapped, her recent scare shortening her patience. "No child should be frightened inside these walls. What sort of animal is Prince?"

Malcolm's lips slowly curved. "A dog."

"Truly?" Joan eyed the beast suspiciously. "Are ye certain he isn't Cerberus?"

Lileas wrinkled her nose. "Cerb . . . who?"

"Cerberus," Joan repeated. "Also known as the hound of Hades. He is a monstrous, multiheaded dog who guards the gates of the underworld, preventing the dead from leaving."

Lileas's eyes rounded in horror. She flounced past Joan to stand at her father's side.

"I see that ye are acquainted with the Greek legends," Malcolm commented as he patted Lileas's shoulder.

"Only the gory ones, though I suppose they all have a somewhat gruesome ending," Joan replied.

"I understand yer fright, but I dinnae believe that Prince deserves to be likened to a beast with three heads, a serpent for a tail, and snakes protruding from various parts of his body," Malcolm said mildly.

Joan blushed. "Perhaps that is too harsh a comparison. But I believe that dogs belong in the kennels, or when the weather is very cold, they may be allowed to stay in a corner of the great hall. Not in the bedchambers or heaven forbid, the kitchens."

"Prince is Lileas's special companion," Malcolm said. "He has far more privileges than the other dogs."

Joan rolled her eyes. "Naturally."

Malcolm visibly chafed at her remark. "Prince is not a wild animal. If ye remember the full story, Cerberus was captured and tamed by Heracles."

"Aye, Heracles mastered him without the use of weapons, using his lion skin as a shield and squeezing the beast around the head until he submitted." Joan looked again at the dog. "But after accomplishing that great feat, he kept the animal in chains."

Lileas let out a cry of dismay. "Ye want to put Prince in chains! Nay! Papa, please, ye mustn't let her."

"Hush now, Lileas. Joan was merely retelling the legend of Heracles and Cerberus."

Lileas let out a loud sniffle, then rubbed her nose

energetically on her sleeve. "'Tis a horrid, awful, mean tale and I dinnae wish to hear any more of it."

Joan suffered a small pang of guilt at the child's obvious distress, but was soon distracted by her son as he toddled curiously near Prince.

"Doggie." Callum reached out eagerly, his hand dangerously close to the dog's sharp, angled teeth. "Nice doggie."

"Callum, nay!" Joan slapped her son's hand away, fearing Prince might chomp on his fingers.

Callum's lower lip quivered. Joan bit her own lip, contrition gnawing at her. He was only being curious. And brave. Not many would approach such a large, hairy beast with the hand of friendship.

"Och, what is that awful smell?" Mistress Innes appeared in the chamber, covering her nose with her hand.

Prince's tail began to thump in greeting and Lileas started giggling. "It's Prince." She turned to her father. "He needs a bath."

"I've no time for it now," Malcolm said. "Prince will have to stay in the barn and ye must promise that ye'll keep away from him, Lileas."

"But I've missed him so much," Lileas whined. "It willnae take ye long to get him clean, Papa. Please? Then Callum and I can play with him."

Joan tilted her head. "Ye are the one who bathes him?"

Malcolm cast her a sheepish glance. "Usually."

Joan swallowed what she wanted to say, then felt her color starting to rise as she tried not to laugh out loud, picturing her warrior husband bathing the hound. Yet all amusement vanished as she listened to Lileas continuing to plead with her father to bathe the dog.

Joan could tell by Malcolm's expression that he was weakening. 'Twas no wonder the child was impossible; her demands were seldom refused. Malcolm glanced Joan's way, his expression conflicted.

Joan's back stiffened and she folded her arms across her chest. She was not about to release him from his promise to show her about the castle this morning so he could further indulge his daughter.

"I'll do it," Mistress Innes volunteered. "The poor horses willnae be able to endure the stench if Prince is shut inside the stable with them. Come along, children. Ye can help me give Prince his bath."

"Me too!" Callum said.

"Aye, ye too, laddie. I'll keep him safe, milady, have no fear."

Mistress Innes grabbed Prince by the scruff of his neck and pulled him from the chamber. The children followed eagerly behind her. 'Twas on the tip of Joan's tongue to protest, but she held her words, not wanting to appear mean spirited in light of Mistress Innes's generosity.

"This was hardly how I imagined I would greet ye this morning," Malcolm said, breaking the awkward silence that had settled between them.

"I shouldn't have acted so foolishly over a dog," Joan replied, a blush of embarrassment forming on her cheeks.

"I understand. Prince can be somewhat terrifying upon first acquaintance." Malcolm's gaze traveled from Joan's head to her boots and back again. "Ye look most fetching this morning."

Joan momentarily lost her voice. Malcolm's tone was smooth, his eyes darkening with interest. Joan's stomach began to tingle and she felt her heart begin to race for an entirely different reason.

He looked especially handsome this morning. His jaw was freshly shaved and the deep blue of his tunic mirrored the blue of his eyes. Was it merely his looks or was it something else that drew her to him?

"Ye promised to show me about the castle," she blurted

out, needing to draw away his scrutiny. "Shouldn't we get started?"

"Aye, it would be my pleasure. But first, I expect a morning kiss from my bride."

Anxiety knotted the back of her throat at his predatory smile. His kisses had the power to fluster her senses and cloud her mind and she felt a great need to keep all her wits about her.

However, outward resistance could escalate the simple request into a contest of wills and she did not want to begin the day battling her husband. "Good morning, Malcolm."

Joan rose to the tips of her toes and brushed her lips fleetingly across his cheek. He reached for her, but she pivoted, managing to elude his embrace. She hurried to the door, not daring to glance in his direction until they reached the landing.

Malcolm's expression revealed what he thought of her kiss. She braced herself for his anger. Instead, he sighed heavily and offered her his arm, which confused her.

Mayhap that was his intent?

They descended to the lower levels of the castle, visiting the kitchens, storerooms, and stillroom. They climbed higher and she peeked inside his father's study and the women's solar, commenting on the lovely stained glass. On the upper levels were an impressive number of bedchambers, some large, most small, but all comfortably furnished.

After walking through what felt like miles of twisting corridors, they reached one of the towers and climbed to the battlements. As she stared down at the scattering of buildings in the bailey, Joan inhaled deeply, the bite of fresh air filling her lungs.

"'Tis a most impressive holding," she allowed. "Though I cannot help but wonder where my place will be in it."

"Ye are my wife," Malcolm said simply.

"Which means that I should be in charge of yer household. But this is yer mother's domain."

"I'm sure she would be glad to have yer help. I'll speak with her about it."

"Nay!" Joan grasped his arm. "I need no champion in this matter. When the time is right, I will approach yer mother myself."

Malcolm looked at her strangely. "My mother is hardly the easiest woman to persuade."

"I know. But this is something that I must do on my own."

"If ye are certain?"

Malcolm's voice trailed off and Joan was struck by how welcome his instinct to protect her felt. "'Tis best this way. Trust me."

Though he looked unconvinced, he nodded. She felt a twinge of pleasure at her victory. Perhaps, by some miracle, she would be able to find contentment in her marriage.

'Twas a hard idea for Joan to grasp.

Yet even harder to dismiss.


The morning was nearly over when Joan and Malcolm met Brienne in the courtyard. She appeared well rested and in good spirits, greeting them with a ready smile. She told them that she was taking advantage of this rare moment of freedom while her son was sleeping peacefully in her chamber, watched over by a McKenna nursemaid.

"My father would like ye to come to the practice yard

to have a look at the McKenna soldiers," Malcolm said. "'Tis possible the man who claimed to be me was one of our own."

"I should feel very awkward gaping at the men while they train," Brienne replied, looking beseechingly at Joan.

The last thing Joan wanted was to spend the remainder of the morning watching the men go through their training. The barely contained violence of their swordplay and the occasional sound of fist against flesh always made her uneasy. Yet she couldn't let Brienne face this on her own.

"We shall stay a discreet distance away, so as not to attract any attention," Joan decided.

Some of the young squires trained with wooden swords and all trained without armor or helmets, making it easy to view their features. Joan was impressed by the sheer number of soldiers and ceased counting when she passed two hundred.

Taking the request seriously, Brienne seemed to carefully study each man. Joan noticed her squinting, peering, and lowering her chin, but never once did a sign of recognition cross her features. As their training ended, the amount of men on the field gradually began to diminish until there were but a few left.

It was then that Joan observed Malcolm and his brother. They had moved into a readied stance opposite each other. They were laughing and joking with each other, but the moment James swung his sword, the brothers became deadly serious.

Their blades met, the clashing sound of steel shuddering through the air. Joan felt her own body tense when James lunged forward, the sharp edge of his blade only a breath away from Malcolm's throat.

With a grunt, Malcolm blocked the strike, then shoved his brother away. Feet planted, swords locked, they continued battling, each hoping to bring the other down, attacking and blocking until sweat poured over their brows. The few retainers who were left ceased their training and others gathered to watch, including the McKenna, Lady Aileen, and Katherine.

Excited by the display of skill and power, the crowd began shouting encouragements along with a few good-natured insults. Joan suspected wagers were also being made and she wondered which brother was favored. Each appeared equal in skill and stamina. Malcolm was the taller of the pair, yet James moved faster.

There was a sudden flurry of thrusts and James's sword went flying out of his hand. Placing the tip of his weapon at James's throat, Malcolm grunted in triumph, claiming victory. His eyes scanned the crowd and when they met hers, Malcolm smiled broadly.

James seized the opportunity, shifted away from the blade, bent at the waist, and rammed his shoulder into Malcolm's stomach. The surprise blow knocked Malcolm off his feet and he landed hard in the dirt, raising a cloud of dust.

The men cheered and started arguing over which brother had been the victor. The McKenna stepped forward, turned, and looked at the crowd. "Let that be a lesson to ye all. That's what happens when ye let yerself get distracted by a pretty lass."

James extended his hand to his brother and pulled Malcolm to his feet. Laughing, Malcolm slapped James on the back, but when he bent to retrieve his shield, Joan noticed that he winced. Lady Aileen must also have noticed. She approached Malcolm the moment he walked off the practice field, a mother's concern clearly on her face.

Malcolm shook his head repeatedly as she spoke, shrugging off her attempts to examine him. "'Tis nothing, Mother. But if ye insist, then I should like my wife to attend to me," he said in an exasperated tone.

All eyes turned to Joan. "I'll need some things from the stillroom," she answered, hoping that whatever ailed Malcolm was within her limited skills to cure. If not, she would be forced to ask for help, an embarrassment she wanted to avoid.

She would not allow her pride to jeopardize his health; however, she very much wanted to show his family that she had some redeeming qualities.

"I'll get what ye need," Katherine volunteered.

Joan sidled up to Malcolm, hoping he would lean on her, but he ignored the gesture. He moved slowly and deliberately, his lips pressed in a grim line as they entered the great hall. Joan was unsure if that was due to annoyance or pain.

At her insistence, he reluctantly sat on the stool near the fire as various family members gathered around him. Lileas wiggled her way between them, pulling Callum with her. Prince trotted happily behind the pair.

"What's wrong with Papa?" Lileas asked, her voice quivering. "Is he bleeding? Will there be stiches? I hate stitches."

"Nay, he just took a tumble in the dirt," Joan answered, not liking the labored way Malcolm was breathing. "He'll be fine, but it looks like Lady Brienne needs some help with the babe."

"She does?" Lileas raised her chin hopefully.

Joan exchanged a look with Brienne and the younger woman nodded in understanding. "Aye, 'tis time fer the wee one to take his nap and I need someone to rock his cradle. Could ye help me, Lileas?"

The little girl nodded eagerly, but then her brows knit together with concern and she turned her attention back to her father.

"Go on, the babe needs ye," Malcolm encouraged. "I'm fine."

Lileas leaned forward and kissed Malcolm on the cheek. Then she grabbed Brienne's hand and began pulling her toward the stairs. "Callum and Prince and Mistress Innes will come, too. But we must hurry before the babe starts crying."

After they left, most of the others departed. Lady Aileen and James stepped away, yet stayed close enough to observe. Self-consciously, Joan helped Malcolm remove his shirt. His muscled skin glistened with sweat and she could clearly see a dark bruise shadowing his left side.

She knelt, tentatively, running her fingertips over the bruised flesh. "Does it hurt a great deal?"

"Nay."

"How about here?" she asked, trailing her fingers over a reddened area.

"Nay."

Huffing out a breath, Joan leaned back on her heels. "Malcolm, clearly ye are injured. How can it not hurt?"

He shrugged. "I've had harder falls and deeper wounds. There's no need to make such a fuss." He reached for his shirt, but she stayed his hand.

"And there's no need to be so pigheaded," she proclaimed. "I'm certain yer ribs are bruised, if not cracked. Let me bind them."

His gaze dropped to her cleavage. "If ye'd really like to know where it aches, lass, ye'll have to go a bit lower," he said silkily, reaching for her hand.

The tightness eased in her chest. He couldn't be that badly bruised if he were able to flirt and leer at her.

"Malcolm McKenna, if ye pull my hand down between yer legs, I promise that ye will learn the true meaning of pain."

He started laughing, which brought on a fit of coughing and ended with a visible shudder. Joan looked anxiously toward the end of the hall. Where was Katherine with the medical supplies?

"Is it a trick of the light or is that worry I see on yer brow?" he asked.

"Of course I'm worried," Joan groused. "First ye deny that ye're injured, then ye lack the sense to allow me to properly tend to ye. We've only just married. 'Twould be inconvenient indeed if I were to become a widow so soon."

Katherine returned, clucking her tongue when she saw the bruises on Malcolm's torso. Together, they looked through the basket, selecting the longest strip of linen fabric. Though he grumbled again at her request, Malcolm raised his arms. Joan carefully wrapped the material around his ribs, hoping she was applying the correct amount of pressure.

Obediently lowering his arms when she commanded, Malcolm then took a deep breath. "It feels fine."

"Good." Joan removed a jar of salve, then repacked the basket of herbs and medicines.

"But I do require one last thing," Malcolm said. "A kiss to make me feel better."

Joan quirked an eyebrow. "A kiss?"

"Aye. To ease my pain and aid my healing."

"I'm not a witch. My kisses have no special power."

"They do fer me, lass."

Her heart quickened at his words. She pressed a hand to her breast to quell the sudden burst of delight. Reacting purely on the emotion, Joan stroked her fingers through his hair, then placed a soft, gentle kiss on his lips.

"There. Now, behave yerself."

# Chapter Fourteen

The hour was late. The dying flames from the fireplace in the great hall danced weakly across the table where Malcolm sat alone, a goblet in his hand, a bottle of whiskey at his elbow. The liquor aided in numbing the throbbing pain in his ribs, but did little to settle the thoughts in his head.

Thoughts of Joan, sleeping upstairs in their chamber. Thoughts of how he burned for her, how he longed to taste the pleasures of her delicious body. Thoughts that were insinuated in his head, impossible to dispel.

The injury to his ribs meant he wouldn't be making love to her tonight. Frustration burned like sour ale in his gut knowing that she was more than likely pleased about it.

He had been too long without the warm comfort of a wife in his bed. Yet now that he was once again married, it appeared he was still waiting for the comfort.

He was a man raised to set and achieve goals. Challenging goals, difficult goals, impossible goals. Success was his more oft than not and he was not about to let his wife be the first to hand him a resounding defeat.

With a sharp curse Malcolm rose to his feet. He might

not be able to make love to her, but he certainly could sleep beside her. He trudged up the stone steps slowly, quietly opened the door, and stepped inside the chamber.

A lone candle sputtered on the table near the bed, cutting through the darkness. Joan was curled in the center of the bed, turned on her side, clutching a pillow in her arms like a lover. The candlelight illuminated her skin, giving it the look of silk. His blood was roused by the sight, knowing it was as soft and sleek as it appeared.

He shrugged out of his clothes, blew out the candle, and peeled back the covers. Her even breathing skipped and she shivered at the sudden loss of warmth. The mattress ropes creaked as Malcolm knelt on the bed. He loomed over her a moment, hoping she'd wake so he could steal a kiss.

Joan sniffled and hugged her pillow tighter. Feeling an unreasonable bolt of jealousy toward her pillow, Malcolm slid in beside her, inching forward until his chest was pressed against her back. Nuzzling the nape of her neck, Malcolm breathed in her sweet-smelling scent.

She shifted again and sighed. "Malcolm?"

Her voice was a dreamy whisper, an indication that she hovered just beyond full alertness. With her defenses lowered, 'twas a moment ripe for seduction, yet his whiskey-clouded mind rippled with uncertainty.

His aching ribs meant the best he could manage would be a quick coupling. 'Twould ease the immediate ache, yet leave them both unfulfilled. He wanted more than only this night. He wanted the promise of tomorrow.

Malcolm kissed her nape softly, then sighed and said regretfully, "Sleep, Joan."

"Hmmm."

She snuggled closer, pressing her buttocks firmly against his cock. It rose and stiffened with great interest. Malcolm stifled a groan and tried to rein in his passion.

Admonishing himself for being a randy fool, Malcolm renewed his determination to wait for a more appropriate moment to begin his seduction.

Joan wiggled again, molding her body against his, and his cock jumped. God's truth, the woman was going to be the death of him. Grimacing inside, Malcolm kicked the covers off his body, hoping the cool air would drown his ardor.

It didn't.

He pressed his lips on her bare shoulder and nibbled a path up her neck to the tender spot behind her ear. She tasted like heaven. His body tightened with need, wracked by a spasm of lust. He wanted his hands and kisses to be everywhere. Malcolm took slow, deep breaths, attempting to tame and master his desire, fighting the raw male impulse to ravish her.

He struggled. Yet his will was strong, his determination complete. Somehow, he would keep himself from tumbling into the abyss.

*She's worth waiting fer*, he repeated to himself, pulling forth every ounce of patience he could muster. *I'm sure of it.*

Malcolm lifted his head and gazed down at Joan in the moonlight, a shudder going through him.

*Yet I pray the waiting doesn't kill me.*

Joan shifted the garments she held as she mounted the curved, narrow steps that led to the bedchamber she shared with Malcolm. The noise from the lower rooms faded as she climbed, bringing on a blissful quiet.

It had been a strange day. She had only seen her husband briefly. He had left the bedchamber by the time she awoke, but had gathered with the rest of the family after breaking their fast to bid farewell to James, who was very anxious to return home to Davina.

Malcolm then left with his father to attend to clan business. Joan in turn had spent the morning with Lady Aileen, Katherine, and Brienne in the women's solar, visiting and gossiping and getting to know each other.

Unused to the companionship of women, Joan felt slightly uncomfortable. She stayed silent most of the time, keeping her hands busy mending one of Malcolm's shirts.

Thanks to Katherine's and Brienne's cheerful chatter, Joan's lack of conversation was not glaringly obvious. After a simple midday meal, Joan walked the castle grounds holding Callum by the hand while Lileas pointed out every building, person, cart, and item in the bailey.

Her powers of observation were impressive for a child her age, lending further proof to Joan that the lass possessed the intelligence and understanding to behave correctly. What she lacked was the inclination.

Still, Joan felt it had proved to be a valuable afternoon. She had learned much about the castle and its workings and had managed to lessen Lileas's animosity toward her. Soon she should be able to begin correcting the child's spoiled behavior.

Joan smiled ironically as she reached the landing, knowing that was going to be a royal battle. Thankfully, she had never been a woman to run from a challenge. She nudged the bedchamber door open with her knee, relieved the latch had not been fully closed.

There was a meager fire burning in the grate and a distinct chill in the air. A strong wind ruffled the tapestries on the wall, revealing the source of the cold. Vexed, Joan moved to the far side of the chamber and pulled the heavy wooden shutters closed, dropping the bar across to hold them in place. The action cast the room into semidarkness, but she reasoned it was far better than enduring the cold.

"I appreciate yer concern, wife," a deep voice called. "Catching a chill while bathing would be a sorry demise fer a McKenna warrior."

Joan screeched and dropped the pile of mending she carried. "God's blood, Malcolm, ye nearly scared the life out of me."

"Did I? I beg yer pardon."

His apology startled her. She knew few men who admitted to uttering a thoughtless word and even fewer who would ask forgiveness for the deed. She turned toward the sound of Malcolm's voice and was astonished to see her burly husband seated in a large bathing tub near the meager fire.

Drat! The pile of clothes she had been carrying had obstructed her view of the chamber. If she had known that he was bathing, she would have quietly—and quickly—withdrawn.

"What are ye doing lazing about in a bath at this late hour?" she asked, bending to retrieve the garments.

"I took a few falls in the muck while training with my men," he explained. "I thought it would be a benefit to all if I removed the odor."

"'Tis most considerate of ye," Joan said, edging toward the door. He was staring at her with that intense, almost brooding look in his eyes that never failed to unsettle her. "If ye were once again on the practice field, I assume that yer ribs no longer pain ye?"

"They were never badly bruised," he insisted, neatly deflecting her question.

Joan's shoulders tightened. A man's pride was a foolish and fragile thing. While Malcolm might appreciate her concern, he was also mildly offended by it. "Still, ye need to be careful," she reminded him.

"Hmm. Did ye have a pleasant day?"

"Aye," Joan replied honestly. "I was with yer mother, sister, and Brienne this morning and the children in the afternoon."

"Since I've not heard anything, I assume that Brienne hasn't recognized any of the McKenna warriors."

Joan shook her head. "Isn't that good news? Knowing that whoever impersonated ye wasn't one of yer own?"

Malcolm shrugged. "It makes the task of capturing this man harder."

Joan's brows furrowed. "'Twas always going to be a very difficult undertaking. A nearly impossible one, most would agree."

"Dinnae let my father hear ye say it. He insists that a true Highlander faces his enemies squarely."

"Is this man truly an enemy?" Joan questioned. "I'll wager he's naught but a landless knight who used yer name to impress a young, vulnerable lass."

"Aye, and that left Brienne with a bastard child and nearly started a war between the McKennas and the Mac-Phearsons."

"What will happen to the fellow if he is caught?"

"At the very least, he'll spend time in the McKenna dungeon before being turned over to the MacPhearsons."

Joan winced. "Do ye think the MacPhearsons will show any charity to the man?"

"Who knows? Though she was badly deceived, Brienne once had tender feelings for the man. I doubt she'll want her father to run a sword through him. Although Laird MacPhearson might be tempted to cut out his tongue."

"Or cut off his bollocks," Joan murmured.

Now it was Malcolm's turn to wince. "And they say warriors are bloodthirsty. Let us speak of something far less barbaric. How are the children?"

"Napping."

Malcolm's jaw lowered. "Lileas is taking a nap?"

"Aye. She and Callum have been joined at the hip since we arrived. The overexcitement has led to some rather high-spirited behavior from both of them. A nice long nap seemed the perfect solution."

Malcolm leaned back against the tub. "How did ye manage to get Lileas to do it?"

"I told her a story."

A slow smile spread over Malcolm's face. "Were there dragons in it? She loves dragons."

"Aye. Dragons. Knights. Fairies. Princesses. And a loyal dog who saved them all."

"Sounds like quite the tale."

"'Twas epic."

They shared a quiet laugh and then silence fell between them. The crackle of the small fire echoed in the chamber, mingling with the sound of slopping water from Malcolm's bath. The intimacy of the moment suddenly struck her. Joan clenched her jaw and hurried to complete her original task, dumping the newly mended clothing into a chest and slamming it shut.

"I wouldn't refuse if ye wish to wash my back," Malcolm said, holding out a cake of soap.

"Ye appear to be doing a fine job on yer own," she said briskly, hoping her dismissive tone would dissuade him from the notion.

Being rude had always been the way she protected herself, yet a part of her felt guilty for acting this way. Malcolm didn't deserve such treatment.

His mouth thinned. "I cannae reach all the way around. It makes my ribs ache. Ye would do much better, I'm sure."

Joan swallowed the lump in her throat, trying her best to appear unaffected by the sight of so much solid male muscle. Truthfully, the very last thing she wanted was to get close to a naked Malcolm—in the middle of the day, no less. But he seemed quite determined to have his way and she could find no legitimate excuse for refusing such a wifely duty.

Sighing, Joan pushed her hair away from her face and rolled her long sleeves up to her elbows. Then keeping her eyes firmly trained on the wall tapestries, she slowly approached the tub.

"I've never bathed a grown man," she admitted.

"Truly? Did ye not assist yer mother when there were noble guests at Armstrong Castle?" Malcolm asked, watching her as she circled near the tub.

"Only once, when I was a young lass of fourteen. The Campbells were at the castle and my mother bade me to help her with the old laird's bath."

"What happened?"

"It all started out fine, but the maids had forgotten to bring clean towels, so my mother went to call the servants to bring some. The moment her back was turned, Laird Campbell reached up and pinched my breast."

"The dirty bugger!"

"Aye. I was shocked, yet I knew it would cause more problems if I complained. So I held my tongue. But I got my revenge. I picked up a bucket of cold rinsing water and poured it directly over his head."

Malcolm threw back his head and laughed. "He shouldn't have underestimated ye."

"Aye, 'twas a grave mistake." She smiled, remembering the old man's sputtering shouts of outrage and her mother's feeble attempts at an apology. All the while, Joan had stood there, an innocent expression on her face, feigning ignorance, claiming she thought the bucket was filled with warm water.

"I'm a man who learns quickly from the errors of others," Malcolm declared. "If I promise not to pinch yer breast, will ye wash my back?"

The instinctive refusal sprang to her lips, but she didn't utter it. The reaction sobered her. Perhaps she was starting to come around to Malcolm's notions of marriage. Or maybe her pride was merely insisting that she honor the bargain she had struck with him and try to be the kind of wife he deserved.

Joan drew in a shuddering breath and straightened her back. "Where's the cloth?"

Malcolm's head dropped back and he released a soft sigh. "It's sunk to the bottom of the tub. Ye'll have to fish it out."

Joan's eyes narrowed. "I'm not about to put my hands down there," she announced indignantly.

"Why not? Ye never know what ye'll discover."

Joan stared down at him, letting her gaze rest on his glistening chest, which was visible above the water. The hair on it was wet and matted, emphasizing his clearly defined muscles. His knees rose above the water, affording her a clear view of his powerful thighs and manhood. The sight made her belly flutter and her heart dance against her ribs.

She could see the steady throb of his pulse at his neck, beating as rapidly as her own heart. His bold challenge flustered her and his taunting grin told her that he knew it.

Joan didn't realize she had plunged her hand into the bathwater until she felt its wet warmth. The feel of it knocked out what little breath was left in her lungs. But she was not about to retreat from the path she had so impulsively taken until she achieved victory. She would conquer her nerves and her fears.

Her hand swirled rapidly through the water. Reaching down between Malcolm's knees, Joan's fingers closed triumphantly over the wet cloth. She snatched it from the tub before Malcolm had a chance to react.

Water droplets flew in all directions, wetting the front of her gown. A few landed on her face. Sputtering, she rung out the cloth. Then rubbing the soap a bit too hard into the wash rag, Joan knelt behind Malcolm and began scrubbing his back. She smoothed her fingers across the muscles of his broad shoulders, slowly running the soapy cloth over his skin, wondering if he could feel the tremors in her hands.

He shifted abruptly. Joan stared in fascination as rivers of water glided over his magnificent flesh, then splashed onto the floor. He shook his wet head, sending a spray of water whirling around him.

"Ye're getting my gown wet," she scolded, trying to master these odd feelings pulsing through her.

"Then take it off." His voice was sultry and coaxing. "Better still, take it off and join me in the tub. There's plenty of room."

"'Tis the middle of the day," Joan replied, astonished to realize her breathing had become strained. From the sheer perversity of it, she told herself. Not because she was becoming lost in the wicked gleam in his eyes.

"There's never a wrong time to indulge in a bit of passion." Malcolm caught her chin in his hand before she could move away, his strong fingers cradling her jaw. "Shall I show ye?"

The air filled with expectancy. Malcolm pulled her closer and put his mouth against hers. She could taste the richness of the ale he had drunk, could smell the warm spice of the soap on his skin.

It was heady, intoxicating. He moved his tongue along the curve of her bottom lip and Joan could feel herself trembling as she savored the sensations that coursed boldly through her.

A groan reverberated in Malcolm's throat. His hand moved to her nape, his fingers gently massaging the soft tendrils of hair. He deepened the kiss, slipping his tongue between her parted lips, freely exploring her mouth.

Joan closed her eyes and absorbed the feel of him. Her body felt strained and sensitive as her tongue entwined with his and she was filled with a sudden craving she couldn't identify. Unsteady, she broke away, her breath locked in her throat.

She stared down at him mutely, waiting. It had been . . . pleasant. Nay, more than pleasant, the kiss had brought on a restless, urgent longing that left her wanting. For what? She knew what came next. Joining with Malcolm wasn't nearly the trial it had been with Archibald, yet neither was it something that she was impatient to embrace.

Or so she had thought. Malcolm's kisses had managed to addle her, to muddle her thinking. Intrigue her. Make her believe that perhaps there was more to passion than she knew. Something shifted inside her and a shiver moved over her skin. Uncertain, Joan wrapped her arms across her stomach.

Malcolm tugged at her wrist, then pulled her hand to his lips and pressed a kiss against it. She shivered again. He extended his other hand, passing it over her breast. She flinched at the contact, yet didn't turn away. Her nipple hardened under his palm and she felt the excitement twist through her. Yet along with the passion, she felt a startling sense of vulnerability.

She looked into his eyes and saw that they were filled with possessiveness. The sight brought her back to the moment, back to her senses in a thrice. She let out a startled cry and stepped back.

"Dinnae pull away," he murmured. The deep timbre of his voice was hypnotic, but Joan's memories of the past were still too vivid. "Stay with me, Joan."

The nightmare of being Archibald's wife had left deep scars. Being forced to lie with him had left her feeling dirty and defiled. She had lost something enduring those years of humiliation—something precious, something essential, and there was no regaining it, no matter how gentle, considerate, or playful Malcolm acted.

"I must go. I promised yer mother and sister that I would help in the stillroom," she said, hearing the note of pleading in her voice and hating it. Weakness was something she deplored, especially in herself.

Frowning, Malcolm released her hand, but her flesh continued to tingle where he had touched it. Once unleashed, it appeared the overwhelming sensations he had the power to evoke in her could not be contained.

The thought should have terrified her, and she puzzled over why the emotions were not that dire. Somehow, the fear she carried of losing her wits and all sense of control with him no longer held such strong power over her.

Was she finally learning to accept it?

"Keep close to Katherine if ye wish to learn anything of value about healing," Malcolm said. "My mother enjoys concocting drams, tinctures, and salves, yet rarely finds anyone brave enough to use them. Even my father claims he is miraculously cured if she attempts to administer them."

"I thank ye fer the warning." Joan exhaled slowly. "If the weather holds, we might venture into the woods to replenish some of the medical herbs."

"Katherine can be reckless at times. Dinnae go beyond the gates without an escort," Malcolm cautioned. "I would never forgive myself if any harm befell ye."

Joan nodded, her heart hammering. Malcolm's voice was calm and controlled, but the glint in his eyes spoke volumes. He knew she was not unaffected by what had just occurred between them and that made her feel exposed.

She closed the door softly behind her and immediately felt a pang of loss and regret over what might have happened if she had accepted Malcolm's invitation and joined him in his bath. Would she experience the passion he was so determined to give her? Or would she be disappointed in the reality of being a wife?

Sniffling loudly, Joan rubbed the tip of her nose with the back of her hand. She would think upon it later. Obviously, her emotions were too overwrought to make any sense of it now.


The moment the chamber door closed, Malcolm dunked down in the water, submerging his head. His cock throbbed with unfulfilled desire, while his brain shouted that he had been a fool to allow Joan to escape.

The situation had been ripe for seduction. He could not have created a more perfect scene if he had planned every detail of it. Yet her reluctance told him that she was not yet ready and he was concerned over the repercussions if he pushed her too far, too soon.

She had been flustered, though—and a tad intrigued. That boded well for him.

With a frustrated sigh, Malcolm pushed the wet hair

off his forehead and vowed not to be defeated. Soon she would gaze at him with feelings unaffected by memory or fear. She would view him not as a man who wished to dominate or rule her, but a man who wanted to give and receive pleasure.

He would awaken the desire that dwelled deep within her and show her the wondrous emotions they could share. And together they would create the best memories of their lives.

# Chapter Fifteen

"Sir Malcolm has taken the children down to the stables," Mistress Innes told Joan. "He hinted at a surprise. 'Tis my guess he's gotten new ponies fer each of them."

Joan nearly stamped her foot in frustration. "Did ye tell him that Lileas was confined to the nursery for the remainder of the day?"

"Nay, I dinnae have to say a word. Lileas told him the moment he arrived. With a quivering lip and a few tears, she told him how sorry she was to have been a naughty lass. She promised to behave."

"Naturally," Joan answered, throwing her hands up in the air. "That's all she ever needs to say and my husband wilts like a flower in a hailstorm."

Mistress Innes's face reflected sincere sympathy. "It's always been thus, milady."

"Well, that's going to change."

Joan turned on her heel and flounced away, hurrying toward the stables. For the past two days she had tried to establish parental control over Lileas, with limited success. The lass seemed to thrive on willful disobedience, and no matter what punishment Lileas was given, she somehow managed to wheedle her way out of it—thanks to her father.

Earlier this morning, Lileas had taken Lady Aileen's embroidery scissors from her grandmother's sewing basket in the women's solar and cut Callum's hair. The soft curls were gone, replaced by tufts of short, uneven, spiky strands that stood on end. The poor lad resembled a demented rooster.

After learning this was not the first time Lileas had helped herself to her grandmother's scissors—and been expressly forbidden to do so again—Joan decreed that Lileas be confined to the nursery for the remainder of the day.

Yet once again Malcolm had rescinded the punishment, and even worse, rewarded his daughter with a new pony! Joan realized now that she had been a fool to think she could easily take control of her stepdaughter without a solemn promise from Malcolm that he would not interfere whenever she disciplined Lileas.

The stable was quiet when Joan entered. Malcolm, Lileas, and Callum were crowded around two sturdy-looking ponies, their tails swishing as they contentedly munched on a pile of hay. Joan cleared her throat loudly and they all turned.

"Mama! New pony!"

Callum ran to Joan and eagerly grabbed her hand, tugging her toward the others. Malcolm smiled in greeting. Lileas looked up, her eyes bright with guilt.

"Ye should not be here, Lileas, as ye well know," Joan said sternly. "And fer disobeying my orders, ye shall be confined to the nursery all day tomorrow."

"Papa?" Lileas's eyes swarmed with tears.

"I was the one who gave her permission to leave,"

Malcolm replied. "Lileas told me that she was very sorry and promises to be a good and obedient lass."

Joan raised an eyebrow. "Have ye seen Callum's hair?"

Malcolm grinned, ruffling the spiky strands atop the lad's head. "'Tis a bit short and uneven, but it will grow again."

"That's hardly the point."

Malcolm glanced hastily down at the children, who were both staring wide eyed at the adults. "We should discuss this in private."

"Aye. Away from the castle," Joan agreed. "I'll get my riding gloves."

By the time she returned to the stables, Joan's temper had cooled. Her mood lightened when they cleared the castle gates and she even managed a smile when Malcolm suggested a race. She pretended to consider it, then leaned low and kicked her horse's flanks.

The mare bolted, eager to run. Malcolm's shout of "unfair" made Joan snicker and she gave no quarter as she thundered through the valley. She could hear his stallion gaining ground and knew it would eventually overtake her, but for the moment she relished being in the lead.

The hills were covered in green and dotted with tight purple buds of heather. In a few weeks they would bloom, filling the air with a light, earthy scent.

Malcolm's steed soared passed her just as they reached the tree line. He turned, raising his brow smugly, and she saluted his victory. He guided his stallion onto the path that led through the forest and Joan followed, her sure-footed mare easily negotiating the large rocks and tree roots.

They stopped as they neared the loch. After securing his horse to the base of an oak tree, Malcolm came to her side. He reached up to aid her dismount, wrapping his hands around her waist. His touch was familiar, possessing the power to send a shiver up her spine.

Joan braced her hands on his wide shoulders, hoping to hide her reaction. But Malcolm must have known, for he seized the opportunity to hold her even closer, molding her softness against his thick, muscled chest.

The feelings of desire she believed she lacked reared and Joan surprised herself by admitting how much she liked it when he touched her. Kissed her. Folded her in his embrace and held her against his broad chest.

He had come to their bed very late these past two nights, long after she had fallen asleep, and taken his leave before she awoke. Joan had told herself she was pleased at his lack of sexual attention, for it put far less of a strain on their marriage.

He had made no romantic overtures since she had surprised him in his bath. By design? Mayhap he had lost interest in her? Or was that all part of his plan of seduction?

Biting the inside of her cheek, Joan pushed away those thoughts. They had come here to discuss Lileas, not their relationship. Given what she had to say, 'twas very possible that Malcolm would hardly be inclined to kiss her when she was finished.

Joan kept her eyes focused on the horizon, yet she felt Malcolm's gaze move over her. *What does he see when he looks at me so intently? A reminder of a foolish impulse that he now regrets?*

Joan expelled a slow breath. She wouldn't blame him. She was hardly the wife he desired. But damn it, she was the wife he had.

"If I am to be Lileas's mother, then ye must allow me to take charge of her," Joan declared, getting straight to the heart of the matter. "Ye must never interfere and especially never thwart my decisions once they have been made."

"What if I dinnae agree with ye?"

"We can discuss it, but in this instance my word must be the final one."

Malcolm tilted his head, his expression baffled. "She's my daughter."

"She is *our* daughter, just as Callum is *our* son," Joan insisted.

"I cannae bear to see her tears," Malcolm confessed. "They never fail to tug at my heart."

"They are often false, a rusc to get her own way."

"Guile at her tender age?" Malcolm shook his head adamantly. "Nay, 'tis impossible."

"Ye just refuse to see it because it makes ye look the fool."

Malcolm grew very still. "What did ye say?"

"I said that Lileas is making a fool out of ye and I will not allow her to do the same with me!" Joan struggled to modulate her tone, but her emotions were rising.

The transformation that came over Malcolm was swift and fearful. His lips contorted into a growl as he stared at her with open hostility. Joan shivered, feeling small beside him.

"I am not a fool fer loving my daughter! I wish only fer her to have a carefree, happy childhood."

Joan crossed to stand in front of him. "She must be taught to respect authority and to listen to her elders."

"She does!" Agitated, Malcolm began to pace. "Mostly."

"She does not. Ever!"

Malcolm's nostrils flared. "That's a lie."

"Ye're shouting," Joan accused.

"So are ye!"

"I'm trying to get ye to listen to me," Joan cried out desperately.

Malcolm swore under his breath. "It's not working. All it is doing is raising my ire. Rapidly."

He balled his fingers into a fist and she could see the anger coiling in his muscles, the unmistakable expression of rage on his face. She stared at him, breathing heavily, afraid to speak, afraid to move. The silence stretched between them, neither willing to give in, to lose the battle.

Joan braced herself, preparing to lunge if he raised his fist, though it was her heart that pained her most. It felt like a great weight was pressing down on her.

She knew full well that fury this strong could blind any man to reason. Even one who had vowed never to strike his wife. 'Twas a stab of disillusionment and foolishness to believe that Malcolm could in truth be different from other men.

With lightning speed, Malcolm hooked Joan's arm and swung her around. His features were twisted in anger, a snarl curling his lips, yet astonishingly she still thought him handsome. *Daft. Ye've gone daft.*

Joan screamed as he swept her into his arms. He kissed her hard, almost brutally. Her senses were overrun with emotions—surprise, fury, and most disturbingly, a flush of passion and desire. She didn't push him away as she ought, too stunned to react.

So rattled were her senses, she didn't realize he had walked to the edge of the loch until she felt a slight breeze. He extended his arms and then dropped her. There was no time to scream. Joan felt herself falling and then with a great splash she hit the water.

Her arms flayed wildly as the shock of cold water seeped into her bones. Her feet tangled in the folds of her gown as she kicked frantically, desperate to keep her head above water. She had never been a strong swimmer and the fear of being swept beneath the surface was very real.

"Ye bastard! Ye think to drown me!" Joan shrieked, slapping her hand against the surface of the water.

"I seek to cool yer temper," he answered calmly. "And my own."

Malcolm quickly shed his clothing and then to Joan's utter astonishment, jumped into the loch. He entered the water a few feet beyond her, turned, and started swimming the other way.

"Malcolm, please," she gurgled, as she felt herself sinking beneath the surface. Her arms felt leaden with the struggle to keep herself afloat and she further panicked when she realized how far she had drifted from the shore.

He ceased swimming and began floating on his back. "Stand up, Joan," he shouted. "The water isn't above yer head."

Feeling foolish, Joan harnessed her panic and calmed her movements. Straightening her legs, she sighed with relief when her booted feet touched the solid bottom of the loch.

She wheezed in a breath and coughed out a mouthful of brackish water. Malcolm's eyes were pinned on her as he continued to float lazily on his back.

Och, how she wished he was near enough so she could dunk his head beneath the surface and watch him sputter for breath!

Summoning her bruised dignity, Joan began dragging herself to the shore. Her water-soaked gown pulled at her, making it difficult to move. Joan floundered with each step, struggling to keep her balance so she would not fall back into the loch.

She had nearly reached the bank when Malcolm came up behind her. He swept her into his arms, cradling her against his chest. She resisted for a moment, then her arms reached up and encircled his neck. With a quiet sigh, Joan pressed her cheek against his wet flesh, tucking her head beneath his chin.

Once they reached the shore, he set her carefully on her feet, making sure she was steady before pulling away. Joan pushed a sodden mass of heavy hair off her face and stared at him with fresh eyes. His expression was earnest, his manner conciliatory.

His anger had been mastered by the cold temperature of the water and the physical exercise of his swim, making him far more approachable. Except that he was naked, his hard body and lean muscles on clear display. She swallowed.

"Ye'd best get out of those wet garments before ye catch a chill," he advised. "I'll build a fire to warm us and dry yer clothes."

Malcolm pulled on his braies, shrugged into his shirt, then handed her his tunic. Joan's fingers were clumsy as she struggled to untie the wet laces on the bodice of her gown. Turning her back, she removed her chemise and donned Malcolm's tunic.

It carried his scent, a heady mix of sandalwood and musk. Ignoring the tingle it gave her, Joan rubbed her arms, drawing a fortifying breath. She heard the crackle of burning logs. Stepping into the circle of firelight, she perched herself daintily on a log.

"A perfectly good pair of boots ruined," she complained, pulling off her waterlogged footgear and woolen hose.

"I would have given ye fair warning before I dropped ye, but I knew ye'd start to struggle and that might have led to an injury," he said.

"Fer ye or me?"

"Me most likely," he answered, amusement in his voice.

Yet Joan knew that she was the one who could have been hurt. At least he cared enough to prevent it.

"Why did ye kiss me?" she asked, extending her fingers toward the flames.

He grinned. "Because I couldn't resist. Yer color rises when yer angry, yer eyes sparkle like flame. 'Tis irresistible."

Malcolm produced a flask of whiskey from his pocket, took a long swig, then handed it to her. She imitated his action, taking nearly as large a gulp, managing not to grimace at the harsh taste. The liquid warmed its way through her body, easing the chill.

Malcolm watched her with hooded eyes while she tipped the flask and downed a second sip. "It will help improve my mood," she said, then ruined her regal bearing by hiccupping. Twice.

"Hmm, 'tis good to know that ye'll be a mellow drunk and not a belligerent one."

She tried to give him a frosty stare, but her mouth would not cooperate. It curved into a mischievous grin. Shaking her head, Joan slid her tongue over her teeth.

They sat in silence for a long while, the crackle of the fire and potent whiskey keeping them warm. Joan reached out, pleased to feel her gown was starting to dry. The sooner she put it back on, the better.

"Do ye think we can manage to discuss Lileas without shouting at each other?" she ventured.

"We can try."

Joan nodded, searching her mind for a simple way to make him understand. "If Lileas is my daughter, then ye must allow me to raise her. And that includes punishing her when she disobeys. She is a clever lass who has learned that she can have her way whenever she wants, as long as she pleads her case to ye."

He winced. "She's just a lass. I cannae believe she is that manipulative."

"Which is precisely how she gets away with it," Joan countered.

His eyes flickered away from hers and then back. "How can ye possibly know these things?"

Joan hesitated. "I was exactly the same when I was younger. Perhaps even more willful and spoiled."

Malcolm took a slow sip of whiskey. "Who spoiled ye?"

"My parents, especially my father."

Malcolm digested the words in silence, but Joan could see his doubt. 'Twas understandable. Malcolm had witnessed for himself how little her father cared for her. But when she was younger, it had been a far different story.

"My mother fell pregnant many times," Joan explained. "There were miscarriages and stillbirths and one poor mite who lived but a few weeks. I was my parents' only surviving child and they showered me with attention and allowed me all that I asked, anything I demanded.

"I grew to become a selfish, cunning woman and that led to a great deal of unhappiness in my life. I would spare Lileas that fate."

Joan lowered her chin. The bitter truth of those words could not be denied, yet 'twas difficult to admit them to herself, let alone speak them aloud to Malcolm.

*It must be the whiskey loosening my tongue.*

A muscle ticked in Malcolm's jaw. "I admire my daughter's spirit. I'll not have it taken from her."

"Of course. 'Tis a strength that will stand her in good stead as she matures and becomes a woman. But it must be harnessed. She must be taught that there are consequences when she disobeys and that she willnae be allowed to indulge every whim that comes into her head."

For a moment he appeared unaffected. Then Malcolm grumbled, his jaw working back and forth. Joan held her breath. Had she succeeded in making her point?

"So be it," Malcolm said grudgingly. "Ye shall tend to the raising of our children."

"Without interference," Joan pressed.

"The discord between us avails us naught. I willnae object to yer methods." Malcolm squared his shoulders. "As long as they yield results."

"All will benefit from this arrangement, Lileas most of all."

"Hmph."

She had won! Joan forced herself not to react with triumphant glee. "Dinnae look so contrite, Malcolm. Ye acted out of love. There is something rather endearing about a strong, capable warrior with a kind heart."

"Is there?" His lazy smile nearly blinded her. "Well then, ye best show me exactly what ye mean."

Joan eyed him dubiously, but Malcolm's smile never dimmed. By the saints, no woman alive could fire his blood as quickly or hotly as his wife. His desire for her pushed his self-control to its limits, even when she was shouting at him like a fishmonger.

She kept silent, electing not to answer his challenge, which only heightened his amusement. He stretched his frame with caution, ignoring the sharp twinge he felt in his side. The hard swim had not been the best exercise for his bruised ribs, but it had been essential for his temper.

He felt a stab of guilt, knowing he should have made certain Joan was not afraid of water before dumping her in the loch. He knew she would be safe even if she didn't know how to swim, but water need not be deep to prove fatal. He remembered well the tale often repeated to him when he was a lad about a clansman who had drowned after landing face first in a puddle of no more than a few inches.

Of course, being drunk at the time could have also contributed to the man's demise. At least Malcolm hadn't plied his wife with fine whiskey until after she emerged from the water.

She was in a mellow mood, thanks to the liquor, but Malcolm suspected getting her own way played a large part in putting that satisfied glint in her eye. It hadn't been easy for him to agree to let Joan take charge of Lileas, but deep down he knew it was for the best.

Joan leaned forward, passing the flask back to him. The front of his tunic gaped open and he caught a glimpse of her firm, full breasts. They were perfection. White, unblemished flesh and pert, rosy nipples.

He could feel the blood rushing to his groin and he felt himself swell and stiffen. The wicked temptation seemed to mock him; in any other circumstance he wouldn't hesitate to succumb to this desire. But he wanted more than a quick release. He wanted her to return his ardor with equal fire.

Thankfully, the easy, languid expression on her face was all the encouragement he needed to try a different approach. With a seductive smile, Malcolm reached for Joan's stockings, pleased to discover the warm flames had dried the soft wool. He deftly rolled one, then placed her foot in his lap.

He slid the stocking over her toes, yet made no move to pull it into place. Instead, he let his fingers glide up her naked calf. He continued caressing a path over her knee and up her thighs, feeling the goose bumps that prickled on her skin.

Joan stared at him, aghast, yet made no move to pull away.

"Ye have such lovely, dainty feet," he said, pressing his lips to the top of her ankle.

She trembled. Malcolm took a deep breath, then slipped his hand between her thighs, brushing his fingers gently over the springy curls that guarded her womanhood. Joan's eyes widened and she jumped, yet again made no move to pull away.

As gentle as a breeze, Malcolm's lips continued to caress her leg, slowly, tantalizingly moving upward. His flesh pulsed, ached. 'Twas almost impossible to believe that all it took was this simple touch to flood his body with warmth and desire.

A branch snapped behind him. Malcolm turned, yet saw no movement in the trees, no splash of color that did not belong. He stilled, tilting his head to listen better. Nothing.

"Malcolm?"

"Shhh."

Feeling uneasy without his sword beside him, Malcolm dropped Joan's foot and moved to retrieve his weapon. Suddenly, a flock of birds screeched from the treetops, flying in all directions. Malcolm craned his neck to look. Without warning, a pain ripped through his head and a shower of stars burst in front of his eyes.

And then there was only blackness.

Joan heard herself scream as Malcolm fell. She stared in astonishment at the mud-splattered men that suddenly appeared, their heavy footsteps crashing through the woods. A dirty-smelling hand covered her mouth, abruptly ending her cry. She bucked and wriggled against her captor, her head knocking his jaw.

The man cursed, digging his nails into her cheeks. "Cease yer struggles at once or I'll not hesitate to slit yer pretty throat," he growled, his foul breath wafting over her face.

Heart pounding, Joan swallowed her fear and forced her body to go limp. Her captor twisted one of her arms behind her back, hurting her shoulder, and she winced. No doubt a bruise would soon appear.

"Looks like we interrupted a tryst," the taller man announced.

"Aye, she's barely clothed," another agreed.

"But McKenna is still wearing some of his garments, so they must not have finished. Seems a shame to waste such a tasty morsel," the first man decided.

Two of the others laughed and leered, one of them crudely grabbing his crotch while the other stripped her naked with his eyes. Joan trembled with outrage and disgust. But the fourth man silenced them all with a sharp command.

"Unhand her. We've got no time to spare," he growled. "Take her mount, hoist McKenna on his horse, and let's begone from this place."

Joan could feel her anguish mingle with rising panic as she stared down at Malcolm's unnaturally still form. His eyes were closed, his face pale. His chest rose and fell in a shallow, uneven rhythm and there was a thick trickle of blood from his brow soaking into the grass.

The need to attend him was overpowering, tearing at her soul. Tears of frustration threatened, but Joan willfully held them back. Weeping wouldn't help him or her. *Think! I must think!*

There were four men. They were dressed as warriors, though none wore any clan colors. To a man their garments were of good quality, though well worn. Knights who had fallen upon hard times? Mercenaries for hire? 'Twas impossible to know.

If these ruffians were simple thieves, they would have stolen the horses and anything else they thought had value and ridden away. They wanted something else. But what?

They knew they were on McKenna land, had obviously intended to capture Malcolm. And hold him for ransom? It seemed unlikely. Only a very powerful clan would dare to threaten the McKennas.

"We cannae leave her," the one holding her argued. "She'll return to the castle and have the McKenna guard chasing us down in a thrice."

"Well, we cannae take her with us. 'Tis a long journey and we've barely enough supplies to sustain us," the other man insisted.

"Bind her to one of the trees," the man who held her suggested.

"And gag her, so she cannae scream fer help," another added. "The longer it takes fer her to be found, the better fer us."

"I've a better, quicker solution." The sharp sound of a sword being drawn turned Joan's blood cold. Overcome with horror, she closed her eyes and swayed.

"Nay." The fourth man held out a staying hand, keeping the sword away from Joan. "We'll not slay an innocent woman who had the misfortune of being in the wrong place at the wrong time."

The other man slowly lowered the weapon and Joan breathed a sigh of relief. The discussion continued as to what to do with her. Joan's initial impression that this man was the leader did not hold, for each man appeared to have an equal say in their actions. The argument became heated and two of the brigands cast her angry looks.

A low rattle of thunder abruptly ended the debate. The men looked to the sky and then to their horses. Was that it? Were they going to leave her behind? But what would happen to Malcolm? His chances of survival and escape would greatly increase if she were with him, tending to his wounds.

Seizing her one chance, Joan turned a pleading eye to the men.

"Please, I beg ye to take me with ye."

"What?"

Joan swallowed, frantically searching her mind for the right thing to say. *Think!* Her lie must be plausible, delivered with the cool aloofness of a lady, yet she must also appear vulnerable and helpless.

"Which way do ye travel?" she asked.

"North," one answered.

The others groaned; one of the brigands punched the arm of the man who had revealed that important bit of information. Joan's mind spun. She needed more time to plan this deception—but there was no time.

"I am Mistress Innes. My aunt is the prioress of Kilmarnock Abbey, which lies due north of here. She will reward ye handsomely if ye give me safe escort there," Joan said, speaking quickly before she lost her nerve.

"Ye want to be a nun?" one of them snorted in disbelief.

Joan skewered the man with a withering look, knowing none of them would have believed her if she told such a bold-faced lie. "I wish to leave McKenna land, but cannae do so on my own," she stated in her most desperate tone.

"Why not?"

Joan was at a loss for words. She could feel her heartbeat quicken and her palms grow damp. The men all stared at her, distrust evident in their faces. She had to say something—now!

"I need to escape the unwanted attentions of Sir Malcolm. He pursues me relentlessly, yet offers no honorable vows of marriage. Will ye help me? Please?"

Another rumble of thunder and a sudden crack of lightning decided her fate. It struck a nearby tree, splintering several branches. Tufts of smoke billowed into the air, and the scent of fresh cut lumber floated on the breeze.

"We can tarry no longer," the tallest man said. "Bind her hands and throw her on her mount. We'll sort this out later."

# Chapter Sixteen

Malcolm slowly drifted to consciousness, a nauseating pain filling his gut as he felt his body bouncing up and down. He opened his eyes, astonished to find himself looking at the slowly moving ground. 'Twas then that he discovered both his hands and feet were tied, his mouth gagged, and he was thrust, belly first, over his saddle. His horse was being led, though he could not clearly see by whom.

*Joan! Where is Joan!*

Malcolm turned his head and a searing pain shot through his temple. But his heart slowed when he recognized the rump of Joan's mare and the ramrod stiffness of her back. She was riding upright, though as they turned, he could see that her hands were bound and her mare's bridle was tied to the pommel of one of their captors.

Malcolm rubbed his wrists together, testing his bonds, disheartened to realize he was trussed up as tightly as a freshly killed buck. Why? Malcolm searched his mind, trying to remember all that occurred before they had been surprised and overtaken in the woods.

He was in the middle of trying to seduce his lovely wife when he heard a tree branch crack, alerting him to something moving through the bushes. There had been the distinct feeling of unease, the squawking flight of a flock of birds high in the treetops, and finally the blinding pain of darkness. He assumed he had been struck from behind. He had not gotten a good look at the men who attacked them, had not seen the color of their plaids nor even been able to count their numbers.

What did they want? If they were thieves they would have stolen the horses, mayhap even snatched his weapons. If they were reivers, they would have gone into the village, not the forest, and taken livestock or food stores.

There were no open hostilities with any of the neighboring clans. Yet whoever had surprised them preferred abduction over murder, and that gave Malcolm some advantage. For now.

His mount stumbled and Malcolm had to choke back a heave. The throbbing in his head intensified and he tried taking shallow breaths to manage the pain.

"He's awake."

The gruff male voice announcing that observation was unknown to him. Malcolm tried lifting his head, but his awkward position and bruised ribs made it impossible.

"That's good news fer ye, Robbie," a second voice proclaimed. "Ye struck him mighty hard with the hilt of yer sword."

"I needed to make certain he'd fall," the man called Robbie replied. "I've always heard the McKennas had hard heads."

"Och, ye have no idea," Joan interjected, and they all laughed.

Malcolm heard three, nay four, distinct male voices. Did Joan know these men? She seemed to have a congenial rapport with them. Malcolm shook his head in puzzlement. But her hands were also bound, an indication that they didn't fully trust her.

Desperate for answers, Malcolm tried pushing the gag aside with his tongue, but it wouldn't budge. His fingers curled into fists of frustration at his helpless predicament.

"Tell us, Mistress Innes, did ye have to suffer Sir Malcolm's unwanted attentions fer long?" one of the men asked.

"All winter," she answered promptly. "'Tis often the fate of a retainer's widow to be besieged by the laird or his sons."

"Especially when one is as bonnie as ye," the man replied.

Joan tossed her head, preening under the compliment. "Ye are too kind and noble, good sir. I dinnae know what I would have done if ye had not happened upon us when ye did. I refused the cur's advances and he threw me in the loch! Did ye see it?"

"Nay, but we heard yer screams."

"I nearly drowned, yet he cared not a wit." Joan turned and stared at Malcolm with fiery eyes of disgust, making certain that the other men saw her. "How fortunate that ye were near." She turned back to the man who rode beside her and fluttered her lashes. "Had ye been lurking long in the McKenna woods?"

"Only two nights. We had yet to decide upon a plan."

"Then it was a stroke of good luck fer all of us that ye came when ye did," Joan declared.

*Mistress Innes?* The puzzling exchange between his wife and these captors brought a searing pain to Malcolm's temple. Clearly, Joan had spun some sort of tale to save herself, deliberately hiding her true identity. Why?

"As a woman, I freely admit to knowing little about the important business of men," she said in a soft tone.

"However, I would venture to guess that the ransom Laird McKenna would pay fer Sir Malcolm's return would be as high, if not higher, than what Laird MacPhearson would give ye."

*Damn!* Malcolm closed his eyes and slowly let out a breath. The reason for his capture suddenly fell into place. These ruffians were unaware that the feud between the McKennas and the MacPhearsons had been settled.

They still believed they would be paid a handsome price if he were delivered to Laird MacPhearson. Malcolm shifted again, struggling against his bonds, knowing it was imperative that he and Joan escape well before these brigands discovered the reward no longer existed.

"We are too few to negotiate with the McKenna and live to tell the tale," Robbie replied. "Better to deliver our prize to Laird MacPhearson, where we shall be guaranteed payment."

"Aye, the McKenna would sooner run us through with his sword than part with his gold coin," another man added. "Even fer his son."

"Perhaps ye are right." Joan sighed, then sighed again. "Might I beg a kindness, and ask for a brief respite to see to my needs?"

If Malcolm had not been looking directly at her when she spoke, he would have been hard pressed to believe it was Joan who had spoken in such a meek and imploring voice. Beneath the filthy gag, his mouth curved into a slight grin. Never more had he appreciated her courage and audacity.

Though they grumbled over it, miraculously, the men agreed. Malcolm was once again in awe of his wife's clever mind. She seemed to know exactly how to manipulate their captors. His initial fear over her capture lessened.

Together, the odds of making an escape grew tenfold.

They stopped in a secluded glade. Joan prettily thanked the man who helped her dismount, then lowered her head and blushed when he sliced through the ropes around her wrists.

"What about McKenna?" the man called Robbie asked.

"Take him down," another answered. "We'll be able to ride faster if he's sitting on his mount."

Robbie removed Malcolm's gag, cut the bonds from his legs, and pulled him off his horse. Though his ribs ached, it felt wonderful to pull in a full breath of air. The lack of blood flowing through Malcolm's legs caused him to stagger unsteadily, but he pressed himself against his stallion's flanks and remained on his feet.

In the distance he could see the red of Joan's gown through the sparse bushes. At some point she had changed out of his tunic and donned her gown. He hoped it hadn't been too wet; wearing damp wool was hardly comfortable.

She brushed near him as she returned, her cheeks flushed, her expression aloof. She made a deliberate point of turning her back on him, yet stayed within range to conduct a whispered conversation.

"Are ye badly injured?" she hissed.

"Nay. Though I'm deliberately moving clumsily so they believe I pose no threat," Malcolm replied beneath his breath. "What of ye? Did they hurt ye?"

Joan shook her head. "They were far more interested in ye."

His heart raced at the sheer relief of knowing she truly was unharmed. More than anything he longed to close the distance between them and gather her in his arms. Malcolm stared at her, resisting the urge to stroke her cheek, knowing if any of the men witnessed their tender gesture, the ruse would be discovered.

"Ye told them yer name was Mistress Innes and that I

was trying to seduce ye?" he asked, wondering if he had correctly pieced together her tale.

"Aye, against my will. I begged fer their aid in escaping from yer evil clutches. 'Twas all I could think of to garner their sympathy and ensure our safety."

"'Twas a risky gamble," Malcolm sputtered, his voice unnaturally harsh. "They could have easily raped ye or slit yer throat."

"I know." Her fingers flexed nervously. "It took several casually asked questions to learn their plan. News travels slowly in these parts—they have kidnapped ye to collect the price on yer head from Laird MacPhearson."

Malcolm grimaced. "Och, they shall be gravely disappointed when they learn he is no longer asking fer it."

"Aye. Yer value to them ends the moment they find out MacPhearson willnae pay them."

"We shall be long gone before that happens," Malcolm declared.

"How?"

"I'll find a way fer us to escape," he vowed.

"I'll be ready." She turned her head. "I have complete faith in ye, Malcolm."

"What are the two of ye whispering about?" Robbie asked suspiciously.

"I was asking about the whiskey I assumed he'd have in his saddlebag," Joan replied airily. "He rarely goes anywhere without it."

She removed his flask and held it up in triumph. Malcolm regretted it was but a small container; four men deep in their cups would have given the couple an advantage in their attempt to escape.

Joan swished past him, looking aggrieved, as though he were nothing but a constant disappointment. Malcolm bit back his grin. A drunk and a seducer. His clever wife was doing her best to paint a debauched picture of his character to these fools.

He felt a surge of pride at her courage. Joan was a worthy partner, ready to fight with any means at her disposal.

The men shared the remainder of his whiskey, then returned to their horses. This time Malcolm was allowed to sit in his saddle. His feet were bound together beneath his stallion's belly and his hands tied behind his back.

Malcolm struggled to concentrate while riding in this unnatural state, pressing his knees and thighs tightly against his horse's flanks. 'Twas exhausting, especially when they started to climb the foothills. Several times he nearly slid off, but he gritted his teeth and bore it.

Several hours passed. Malcolm's head throbbed and his ribs ached. The noisy thunder and lightning had produced a brief shower and moved on. Now, the sun beat down on them. With nary a breeze, 'twas warm for a spring day.

The weather could, however, work in their favor. Water was scarce the higher they climbed. As the men and their horses became more heated and exhausted, they would need to stop again and search for fresh water.

When that happened, he would make his move.

The sun had emerged from behind the clouds and shards of late afternoon sunlight shone through the canopy of tree branches. Joan kept her expression blank, her gaze fixed forward as they climbed higher into the foothills. With each mile they traveled the tension inside her increased. It would be hours before anyone at the castle thought to search for them. By then the trail would be cold.

Somehow, she needed to slow their progress without being obvious. Earlier she had noticed Malcolm swaying in his saddle and the sight unsettled her greatly. The wound on his head had dried to a black scab, yet it still oozed fresh blood. He claimed that he was not badly injured, but she knew that he was hardly at full strength.

"May we please stop fer a brief moment? I must tend to my needs," Joan implored, hoping to inflect the correct mix of embarrassment and humility in her voice.

"Bloody hell, woman, how many times does a person need to piss in a day? Ye went not more than four hours ago," the tallest one grumbled.

Joan schooled her face into a pitiful, pleading expression. "My female constitution is weak and unused to such rigorous physical activity. Forgive me."

No one answered. The men exchanged glances, yet refused to stop. Helpless and frustrated, Joan stole a glance at the man who rode beside her, the one who had saved her from being assaulted, but there was no reading his expression. She ducked to avoid hitting a low branch and wiggled her wrists, but the ropes that bound them held tight.

She waited another half hour before making her request again, this time with greater urgency.

"Christ's bones, if ye pester us one more time, we'll tie ye to the nearest tree and ride on without ye," Robbie threatened.

"And forgo yer reward fer bringing me to the abbey?" Joan asked innocently. "I am my aunt's favorite niece. She will be more than generous in giving her thanks to ye, especially when I tell her of yer kindness and consideration."

Her reminder of a reward seemed to give them pause.

The man in the lead held up his hand when they reached a small clearing. He dismounted, yet the others remained on their horses. Joan struggled not to cringe when he lifted her off her horse.

Silently she held out her hands and he cut the ropes on her wrists. "Be quick," he commanded.

She nodded. Her hands shook and she hid them in the folds of her gown, not wanting to betray her unease. Joan walked away as far as she dared, then hunkered down next to a large oak to stall for time.

A few minutes would hardly make much difference, but she felt compelled to do *something*. She had every faith in Malcolm, but if their escape was to be successful, they must work together.

There was a noise, the sound of something scuttling through the bushes. Fearing one of the men had followed her, Joan curled her fingers around a small branch. 'Twas hardly an effective weapon, but hopefully it could inflict some damage.

She lifted the branch, but instead of a man, a large mass of dirty gray and white fur came crashing through the bushes. It launched itself at her. Unprepared for it, Joan fell onto her back.

"Prince!" Joan gasped in astonishment, hardly believing her eyes.

The beast stood happily over her, his pink tongue lolling as he panted with excitement. His long fur was tangled and full of snarls and brambles and he smelled atrocious. Ignoring the dirt and muck that clung to his long fur, Joan threw her arms around him.

"Ye found us! What a clever lad ye are, sweet Prince."

The dog fanned his tail rapidly, his entire hind quarters moving with delight. She continued petting him, then cocked her head and strained to listen, longing to hear the sound of approaching horses.

Joan's spirits sank at the ensuing silence and she struggled to compose herself. The slim hope that a band of McKenna warriors were following close behind Prince as he tracked them was nothing more than a fantasy. Joan surmised the animal must have been on one of his many jaunts through the McKenna forest and somehow picked up their scent.

Biting back a sob, Joan sat up and placed her head in her hands. Most likely, no one at the castle had yet realized they were missing. Attuned to her distress, Prince lay at Joan's feet. Whining, he nudged her hand, seeking to ease her fear and offer comfort. Grateful, Joan leaned over and hugged him again.

She held the dog as though she would never let go, releasing him only when she tasted the salt of her own tears. Her body shook with the vehemence of her emotions and then she straightened, steeling herself against any weakness, summoning calm in the midst of her panic.

Indulging in pity and despair would accomplish naught. There would be an opportunity for her and Malcolm to escape. She needed to constantly be on guard so that she would be ready to seize it. With an abrupt motion, Joan drew to her feet. Prince copied her actions, standing readily at her side.

Joan gazed down at him, wondering if there was a way to use the great beast to aid in their escape. Prince could be an intimidating creature, a formidable foe with his head lowered, hackles raised, and teeth bared as if he were ready to attack. Yet even if she could command Prince to do her bidding—which was not assured—she feared the brigands would raise a sword to the snarling hound.

She could not, in good conscience, put the faithful

animal in such peril. In fact, it would be best if the dog was unseen by their captors.

Joan patted his head affectionately one final time. "Home, Prince. Go home!"

Prince stared up at her, let out a loud yawn, and sat, placing his rump directly on her foot. Despite the gravity of the situation, a giggle rose up from Joan's throat and she began laughing.

"What use are ye to me?" she asked him, but then an idea dawned.

A preposterous, far-fetched idea, but one worth trying. Reaching under her gown, Joan tore a piece of her chemise and tied it around the dog's neck. 'Twas embroidered with her initials. Gertrude would recognize it immediately; Joan could only hope that its presence around Prince's neck would be noticed and raise the alarm.

That is, if she could get the daft beast to return to the castle. Time was running short. She had to get back before one of the men came looking for her.

"Where's Lileas, Prince? Where is she, laddie?" The dog's ears perked and his tail began to wag furiously. Hope burgeoned in Joan's chest. "That's right, Lileas. Find Lileas, Prince. Hurry."

On her command, the dog bolted away and disappeared in the woods. Joan was heartened by the sight—and the knowledge that the animal was at least running in the right direction.

She took her time walking back to the others, taking a winding route. Their impatient glares brought a tremor of warning up her spine. Heart thumping, Joan scrambled onto her horse without assistance. One of the men grunted in annoyance and they set out at a faster pace.

It took a few moments for Joan to realize that in their haste to continue the journey, they had neglected to bind her wrists. Holding tightly to the reins, she tucked her hands inside her sleeves, hiding the oversight.

They continued on a rough path that led through the forest, with the men frequently switching the duty of being in the lead and keeping watch of their surroundings. Joan thought it hardly a necessary precaution. The road seemed rarely used as it was rife with tree roots and overgrown brambles. It appeared highly unlikely they would chance upon anyone, more's the pity.

When they started up another foothill, Joan was surprised to feel a rumbling in her belly. Given the grave situation she found herself in, one would think the lack of a meal a trifling matter. Apparently her body did not agree. Embarrassed, Joan lowered her head, hoping no one heard the rude noises.

Unfortunately, it seemed that once begun, her stomach had decided to continue its protests over the lack of food. She pressed her hand firmly against her belly, hoping to somehow muffle the sounds, but that proved useless.

"Here. Have a bannock."

Joan's gaze slid to the man who rode beside her, the one she had mistaken for their leader. His arm was extended toward her and in his hand was a large oatcake. Most likely several days old and dry, it looked like ambrosia to Joan.

Mouth watering, she started to reach for it, then pulled back, remembering that her hands had been mistakenly left untied.

"Thank ye, but I find with all the excitement of today, I've no appetite," she replied, deliberately turning her head away from the tempting morsel.

His saddle creaked and she imagined him returning the food to his sack. Joan sighed with regret and her belly rumbled again, betraying her need.

"I know that yer wrists are unbound," he said, not

unkindly. "I also know what it feels like to go hungry. Now eat, before the others notice."

He flashed a brief, pensive smile that possessed the power to weaken a maiden's knees. Startled, Joan snatched the food out of his hand. Thoughtfully chewing her bannock, she took a moment to study him.

He was handsome, in a rugged, unpolished way, with curly hair that grazed his broad shoulders and framed his chiseled jaw. Surrounded by thick lashes, his eyes scrutinized her with an intelligent air. They were a striking shade of . . . *green.*

*Aye, they are as green as the new spring grass.*

Joan's breath caught and she began choking on a dry crumb. It lodged in her throat and she coughed until her eyes filled with tears. Each man turned to stare at her—Malcolm looking especially concerned—but she brushed them off with a toss of her head.

*Green eyes.*

Was it possible that this was the man who had impersonated Malcolm at the fete? The handsome man with the green eyes who had seduced Brienne MacPhearson and gifted her with a son who also possessed eyes of this color?

Joan's heart pounded with excitement. She swallowed, trying to clear the dryness from her throat. "Might I beg a boon of ye, kind sir, and ask fer a sip of water?"

He glanced at the other men, then lifted a pouch draped over his pommel and gave it to her. "Dinnae drink too much or else ye'll be pestering us to stop again," he cautioned.

Joan nodded agreeably and took but a small sip. "My thanks." When she handed it back, she glanced deliberately at the claymore that was strapped to his back. "'Tis a fine weapon. Do ye participate often in the tournaments and fetes? I hear tell there is good coin to be made for those who can fight."

His brows furrowed with suspicion. "Why do ye ask?"

"No particular reason," Joan replied airily. "'Tis only that ye have the look of a warrior about ye."

She summoned up her most curious, flirty smile, the one that had served her well when she was younger. It still had the power to dazzle, for it succeeded in erasing the suspicion from his face, yet he didn't answer her question. Instead, he spurred his horse forward and took his turn leading the group.

Biting the inside of her cheek, Joan glanced ahead, pretending great interest in a pair of chattering squirrels. They chased each other, leaping from branch to branch, wrestling and rolling together.

"No matter how far she runs, he always catches her," a rough male voice intoned with a snide chuckle.

The tall one had taken the warrior's place and now rode beside her. His eyes raked her from thigh to hip, coming to rest on her breasts. Joan lowered her chin to hide the anger and disgust that filled her.

"Aye, but if he gets too close, she bites him on the tail or the snout," Joan replied. "Hard."

The man let out a bellowing laugh. A cruel sneer twisted his features, making her feel vulnerable and exposed. Of all the men, this one seemed the most dangerous and unpredictable. She'd best be on guard whenever he was near.

When the light began to fade, they camped on a bluff at the edge of the forest. Joan wasn't entirely certain, but she believed they were no longer on McKenna land. The thought depressed her.

She tended to her horse, watching with wary eyes as the men set up camp. They had a fair amount of supplies, indicating they were well aware of the many days it would take to reach MacPhearson land.

"Joan!" Malcolm hissed. "Joan!"

Her heartbeat skipped as she glanced all around to make certain none of the men were watching. Assured she was being ignored, Joan sauntered casually in the opposite direction, then circled around toward Malcolm.

He was tied to a tree, his arms pulled behind him. Still, he was able to capture her hands in his the moment she was close, squeezing them reassuringly.

Joan breathed in the scent of his skin, reveling in the warmth of his flesh. For so many years she had feared and loathed a man's touch. How had Malcolm's caress suddenly come to mean so much to her?

Joan slipped a flat rock into his hand, then turned her back, pretending great interest in the flowers blooming at the base of the tree.

"There is some sharpness on one side of the stone. If ye are patient, ye might be able to cut through the bonds on yer wrists," she said.

"Aye. Though it will probably take me half the night," he joked.

She turned to face him. Malcolm's eyes locked with hers and didn't waver. Joan took comfort in his confidence, hope renewing in her heart that they would be safely delivered from this danger.

"I've news to share," she whispered. "Prince found me in the woods. He must have been near enough to pick up our scent. I tied a piece of my chemise around his neck, hoping if he returns to the castle, yer father will see it and set Prince along with the other dogs to track us."

"I know my father will already have men looking fer us. 'Twould be useful if Prince could at least point them in the right direction."

"Aye, instead of leading them through the forest to a warren filled with rabbits," Joan replied.

They shared a quiet smile. Suddenly, someone touched Joan's shoulder. Startled, she jerked around to look behind her. 'Twas the brigand they called Robbie.

"Ye spend far too much time in Sir Malcolm's company fer a woman who claims she is fleeing from him," Robbie said, his face dark with disapproval. "Ye wouldn't be playing us all fer fools, would ye, Mistress Innes?"

"Dinnae be ridiculous," Joan answered, defiance in her tone. "I can hardly avoid him in so small an encampment."

Robbie's eyes narrowed suspiciously. Joan twisted her face into an expression of pure innocence. Then with legs trembling beneath her gown, she stalked over to the small cooking fire and perched herself regally upon a boulder.

She lifted her chin to a scornful angle, daring him to challenge her. He stared back at her, seeming to consider it. Then with a shake of his head and a muttered curse, Robbie turned away.

# Chapter Seventeen

With her knees curled against her chest, Joan lay huddled beneath the thin blanket she had been given, unable to sleep. Three of the brigands were positioned near—too near—snoring loudly, while a fourth stood guard. The small fire they had built to roast the hares they had trapped was nearly extinguished, casting off a faint residual glow.

She was lying beneath the stars, yet felt stifled and confined. Every night sound startled her, every movement put her on edge. They had placed her on the other side of the encampment, away from Malcolm, and she missed the security of his warm strength.

He was sitting at the base of the tree, his hands and feet bound, his head lolling against the trunk. She could feel him watching her and his vigilance afforded her a bit of comfort. Sighing, she shifted on the uneven ground, trying to avoid the rock that was pressing into her side.

Joan hugged the blanket tighter, struggling to control the turmoil churning inside her. She knew that she would need all her wits about her as well as her physical strength when they made their escape. Still, sleep eluded her.

She closed her eyes and for a moment she was back at

McKenna Castle, languidly stretched out on the wide bed that dominated their chamber. Malcolm was leaning over her, his expression seductive in the candlelight, his hands tenderly reaching out to caress her.

Her skin caught fire when he touched her. Restless, she lifted herself closer. Soft and warm, his lips moved on hers, and Joan relished the taste and feel of his mouth as they kissed.

The fantasy was so real that for a moment she believed she could feel the pleasure they made together. But then the sound of thunder rumbled in the distance. Reality struck and she was once again shivering on the cold, hard ground—alone.

What a fool she had been to be so distrustful of Malcolm's amorous intentions! 'Twas true she didn't fully understand his ardor, but she should not have been so quick to dismiss him. Instead of exploring these inflamed feelings he evoked, she had fought against the desire, denying them both fulfillment.

Regrets tumbled over each other in her mind, distracting her and doing little to aid Joan in her quest for sleep. These thoughts continued to plague her, so intently that she lost all sense of her surroundings until she felt the surprising presence of someone moving behind her.

Joan tensed. A hand clamped over her mouth and an arm encircled her waist. Fear filled her throat. She bucked against her captor's hold, arching her back and struggling against him, trying to free herself. He tugged harder on her waist, and her stomach clenched in fear.

The need to break free increased and then he reached down with his other hand and lifted her skirts. She tried to kick him, but her legs tangled in the blanket.

"Now ye just stay quiet and calm, so we can have a bit of fun."

She recognized his voice. It was the tall one. Joan shuddered, repulsed by the feeling of his hot, moist breath on her neck. Fear choked through her and Joan increased her struggles, managing to open her mouth over the plump flesh of his palm.

The taste of dirt and salt invaded her tongue, yet she never hesitated. She bit him—hard—her mouth quickly filling with the coppery taste of blood.

He cried out, releasing his hold, then slapped her across the face. "Ye foolish bitch!"

Her head wrenched to the side. She rolled away, shaking her head to clear the blow. Joan clawed at the dirt, pulling herself away in a desperate bid for freedom. He scrambled after her, grasping her ankle, squeezing hard.

Despair welled up, nearly choking her, but she refused to relent without a fight. Joan's elbows struck him in the ribs and she heard his breath burst from his lungs in a loud howl.

The night erupted into chaos. There were cries of surprise and shouts of alarm. From the other side of the camp, Joan saw Malcolm rush forward. Somehow he had broken free of his bonds and not a moment too soon.

Malcolm grabbed her attacker by the shirt and threw him against the trunk of a tall tree. The brigand reached for the dirk at his belt and slashed out wildly, cutting Malcolm's forearm.

Malcolm pivoted, ducked low, and knocked the attacker off his feet. His head hit the ground hard. He let out a groan, then grew still and unmoving. If not for the shallow rise and fall of his chest, Joan would have thought him dead.

Sword drawn, a second man leapt at Malcolm from the shadows.

"Malcolm, watch out!" Joan's scream echoed through the night air, reverberating in her ears.

Malcolm lunged out of the sword's reach and picked up a sturdy branch. Steel struck wood with a crash that resonated through Joan's heart. The two men parried, yet each time their weapons clashed Joan could hear the splintering wood of Malcolm's branch. Soon it would be in pieces.

Malcolm fended off another blow, then brought his foot down hard on his opponent's instep. The man howled in pain. Malcolm hooked his branch on his opponent's sword and swung it upward. It came out of the brigand's hand and flew in a high arc. Malcolm caught the sword handle in midair, turned, and placed the tip of the blade over the brigand's heart.

Joan let out a cry of triumph, but her joy was short lived. Robbie lunged for her. He captured her arm, spun her around, and placed his dirk menacingly against her neck.

"Release him or I'll slit her throat," Robbie screamed.

Everyone froze.

Malcolm's chest heaved as he held the sword over the man's heart. He glanced frantically from his prisoner to the knife at Joan's throat and back again. A tendril of fear shivered up her spine; who knew what awaited them if Malcolm relinquished his advantage?

Joan's eyes sought the man she believed to be the imposter. He stood with his sword drawn, at the ready, surveying the action. The only way to shift the odds was to somehow bring him to their side.

"Brienne MacPhearson and her son reside at McKenna Castle," Joan cried. "If ye aid us, I will guarantee ye safe passage to see her."

The man turned to her sharply. "What?"

"Ye heard me." Joan swallowed hard. "Secure our release and ye'll be reunited with Brienne."

The man scoffed. "I've no interest in Brienne MacPhearson. Why would ye think such a thing?"

Joan closed her mind against her doubts and remembered the shadows of sadness she had seen lingering in his eyes. 'Twas unsteady ground, but she must take the risk to tread upon it.

"Brienne told me a great deal about the man who wooed her at the fete. She spoke of his courage and kindness and his pleasing features," Joan answered. "She said that he vowed his love fer her and promised to make her his wife."

"That has naught to do with me," he declared vehemently. "'Twas Malcolm McKenna."

"Was it?" Joan lifted a brow. "I, and many others, including Laird MacPhearson, know that is false. It was a man who claimed to be Malcolm McKenna."

The imposter turned his head. "Why do ye believe that I am that man?"

A surge of satisfaction shot through Joan. *I was right!*

"Ye might be able to run from the truth, but ye cannae deny it. Brienne's son has eyes as green as yers. He is a fine, healthy lad, sweet and innocent," Joan replied. "She calls him Liam."

In the light of the moon, Joan could see a series of emotions ripple across the imposter's handsome face. Disbelief, awe, joy, and finally frustration. "'Tis madness to trust ye," he finally replied. "If Brienne truly is at the castle, then McKenna must have married her."

"I dinnae marry the MacPhearson lass," Malcolm shouted.

The imposter's brows rose. "Even if I did believe ye, 'tis madness to trust ye," he said. "McKennas dinnae grant leniency to a man when they have been wronged by him."

Joan tipped her chin up. "They will if I ask."

"Ye are naught but a widow of the clan, fleeing the lecherous advances of Sir Malcolm," Robbie proclaimed in annoyance. "None will listen to ye."

"I'm Lady Joan McKenna, Malcolm's wife."

"She lies! About the MacPhearson lass, about her true identity," the man with Malcolm's sword at his chest shouted. "The bitch will say anything to gain her freedom."

"Nay, she speaks the truth," Malcolm said, moving the sword until the tip was pressed against the vulnerable pulse at his throat. "And dinnae refer to my lady wife as a *bitch!*"

A frown puckered the imposter's brow and shards of moonlight flickered over the rigid planes of his jaw. Then, slowly, deliberately, he swung his sword toward the man who held Joan. "Drop the dirk, Robbie."

There was a cry of outrage from the two others.

"Do it," Malcolm commanded.

Robbie swore, his reluctance obvious. His eyes darted from the imposter's sword to his face as though trying to judge his chances of fending off an attack.

"I willnae kill ye, but I'll wound ye badly," the imposter promised.

With a heavy sigh, Robbie lowered his arm, pulling the blade away from Joan's neck. A wave of dizzying relief swamped her. Shuddering, she moved away from him, bringing her hand over to massage the bruise on her side.

"Bring me a length of rope," Malcolm said.

Still rubbing her middle, Joan searched the saddlebags, quickly finding what was needed. Malcolm secured one man, while the imposter tied Robbie. As they rolled the third, unconscious man onto his back the insistent bark of a dog filled the air.

*Prince?* Joan exchanged a look of wonder with Malcolm. He smiled and shrugged and then a battle cry roared through the trees. Gasping, Joan looked up and saw a dozen McKenna retainers galloping into the camp, the McKenna leading the charge.

"Hold!" Malcolm shouted, rising to his feet. "Put yer swords away. I want these men kept alive."

Murmurs spread through the McKenna soldiers. There was a slight pause and then the sound of metal being sheathed in leather filled the night air. Joan was surprised to see that even the McKenna lowered his sword.

Prince burst through the bushes, wagging his tail madly. Joan braced herself for his greeting, but he managed to knock her down anyway. Laughing, she hugged the great beast, noticing immediately that the piece of chemise she had tied around his neck was missing.

"I can scarce believe this worked," Joan muttered, scratching behind the dog's ears.

"'Twas Magnus who first noticed the fabric tied around his neck," the McKenna explained. "We knew it must have been put there by a lady—our greatest hope was that it was ye."

With questioning eyes, Joan turned to the McKenna. "Prince first found me several hours ago. 'Tis too far fer him to have made his way to the castle and back in such a short time."

"He's an untrained, undisciplined beast, unfit fer proper hunting, but there's no hound in my kennels that's a better tracker," the McKenna answered. "He found our search party and made a nuisance of himself, refusing to cease his barking and pestering us until we followed him."

Joan petted Prince's head and he rolled on his back, looking so comical that she couldn't help but smile. Succumbing to the sweet plea in the animal's soulful eyes, she rubbed his soft belly vigorously, finding that certain spot that caused the dog's leg to shake.

"Ye've earned a reward," Joan said, smoothing her hand over his head. "As soon as we get home, I'm going to find the biggest, meatiest bone in the kitchen fer ye."

Tongue lolling, the dog nudged her hand repeatedly with his wet nose, begging for more. Joan obliged him, finding an odd sense of calm as she petted him.

"If I lie quietly on my back, will ye rub my belly, too?"

Joan lifted her gaze to find a smiling Malcolm kneeling beside her. Her heart quickened.

"Nay. I fear I'll catch fleas," she retorted, lowering her chin as she felt a blush spread across her face.

"Then I'll have to settle fer a kiss," he decided. Cupping her warm cheeks in his hands, he pressed his lips to hers.

His breath pulsed into her and Joan curled close, needing to feel his solid strength. Malcolm enveloped her in his embrace and she clung to him. When the kiss ended, she placed her cheek against his chest, calmed by the sound of his beating heart.

He moved his hand along her back in a slow caress. Relief surged through her and in that moment all felt right in Joan's world.

"If Joan needs to rest, we can wait until dawn breaks in a few hours to start the journey home," the McKenna said. "Though I must tell ye that yer mother is in a fine state of worry over the both of ye."

"Malcolm's arm was slashed," Joan said. "It needs tending."

"'Tis merely a scratch," he protested. "It's already stopped bleeding."

Joan crinkled her brow. "What if the wound opens when ye ride?"

"Then we'll stop and bandage it." Malcolm gave her a

final squeeze. "Let us be gone from this place as quickly as possible."

'Twas too dark to see clearly, so Joan poked her fingers through the tear in Malcolm's shirt. As he claimed, there was no wetness, only the slight roughness of a newly forming scab. Joan sighed, relieved her stoic husband was being truthful about his most recent wound.

Ignoring her bone-aching fatigue, Joan agreed it was best to start the journey home. The camp was easily dismantled and the three bound men hoisted and tied to their horses.

"What of him?" the McKenna asked, pointing at the imposter.

"Allow him his horse, but keep a close guard on him at all times," Malcolm replied.

"Ye dinnae want him tied like the others?" the McKenna questioned. "Why?"

"My reasons will become apparent in the light of day." The moonlight illuminated Malcolm's conspiring smile and Joan wondered how the McKenna would react when he saw the imposter's green eyes and discovered the truth.

Malcolm reached down to hold Joan's hand. "Ye'll ride with me," he whispered in her ear, and she nodded in agreement.

He lifted her onto his stallion and mounted behind her. Joan leaned her tired body back against Malcolm's chest. Encircled by his arms, she savored the feelings of strength and safety. Indulging in this blissful moment, Joan surrendered to her exhaustion.

The sound of cheering awoke Joan. Disoriented, she opened her eyes and realized that she was still atop Malcolm's horse, his arms holding her securely. As they rode through the portcullis of McKenna Castle and into the bailey the shouting grew louder.

The sky was filled with dark, low-hanging clouds, but there was a warmth and brightness surrounding her, thanks to the welcome they received.

A bittersweet ache tightened Joan's throat. Many were calling her by name, shouting their relief at her safe return. She knew some were cheering merely because she was Malcolm's wife, but the camaraderie of the McKenna clan called to her. She had been too afraid to hope for it, too hesitant to realize it, but here at last was her chance to belong, to shed the mantle of being an outsider.

She could abandon the aloof facade that had always protected her from the isolation of being an abused wife and an unwanted daughter. If she chose to embrace it, she would be welcomed into the clan, not relegated to watching and pretending that it didn't hurt to be distrusted, disliked, and excluded.

Malcolm broke away from the column and headed directly toward the steps where his family was gathered. Lileas leaned heavily against his mother, who was holding Callum in her arms. Joan fully expected her to break ranks and run to her father. Hopefully by this time she had learned to wait until he descended from his horse.

"'Tis a joy to set eyes upon ye both," Lady Aileen called out to them. "Are ye well?"

"We are," Malcolm replied. "And have quite an adventure to share."

He vaulted off his horse, then moved to assist Joan. Out of the corner of her eye she could see Lileas launch herself forward, but she ran past her father and instead threw her arms around Joan's legs.

"I'm so happy that ye are back," Lileas blurted out. "I cried fer hours and hours when ye dinnae come home.

I even said prayers and lit a candle in the chapel with Aunt Katherine."

Joan gazed down at the lass in shock. *Lileas pined fer me?*

"Dear Lileas was most inconsolable," Katherine said. "She missed Malcolm, of course, but she was more upset about ye being gone. I feared she would be plagued by nightmares, so I slept in the nursery with her and Callum last night."

Lileas tightened her grip on Joan. "I'm sorry. I know that ye went away because I was a bad lass and took Grandmother's scissors and cut Callum's hair and dinnae listen."

"Nay." Joan set her hand on the child's head and gently stroked her hair.

"I promise to be good. I promise I'll listen. I promise. Please say that ye'll stay and be my mother. I dinnae want to be a poor, motherless child anymore."

It seemed implausible, but the little girl's distress was clearly genuine.

"I'm not going anywhere," Joan said. "I missed you and Callum every minute that I was away," she added, realizing she spoke the truth. Despite all the difficulties, despite everything, she was indeed elated to be reunited with her family, including Lileas.

"What about me?" Malcolm asked, his voice filled with mock injury. "Isn't anyone celebrating my return?"

The females all cried out at once and immediately surrounded him. Joan reached for Callum, warmth pooling in her heart when he hugged her and placed a wet, sloppy kiss upon her cheek.

Malcolm swung Lileas up in his arms, then pulled Joan and Callum to his side. Together, they led the way into the great hall, with many of the clan following behind.

Despite the evening meal having been recently cleared away, the servants eagerly brought out more food and drink. Questions were asked and answered, though Malcolm and Joan glanced frequently at the children before carefully crafting a reply. Prince's role in their adventure was told several times, causing Lileas to preen with pride at her hound's accomplishments.

Joan was pleased to bestow her promised reward upon the dog. At her request, Cook produced a meaty soup bone and Prince lay contentedly in front of the hearth gnawing on his prize.

Lileas sat upon Joan's lap, reluctant to be parted from her. Every now and again Joan would rub her chin against the top of Lileas's head, surprised to find a gentle peace in her own heart when comforting the child.

After her initial assault of questions, Lileas turned silent. It took a while for Joan to notice, and when she did she was surprised to find the little girl had fallen asleep. She glanced down the dais and saw that Callum had done the same.

Joan motioned to Malcolm and he started to rise, but Katherine placed a staying hand on her brother's shoulder.

"Ye and Joan should stay and enjoy yer homecoming celebration. Mistress Innes and I will see the children safely abed," Katherine volunteered.

Joan nodded. Katherine lifted Lileas from Joan's lap while Mistress Innes carried Callum. A warm feeling filled Joan, knowing that she could trust her most precious gifts to the care of family who loved them wholeheartedly.

As the hour grew later, the noise grew louder. Music filled the great hall and there was singing and even a bit of dancing.

Yet all was not joyful. Joan's eyes darted frequently toward Brienne. She was calm and smiling, bringing Joan to the conclusion that Brienne had not yet set eyes upon the men who had planned Malcolm's abduction.

"Has Brienne seen any of the prisoners?" Joan whispered to Malcolm.

"Nay," Malcolm replied. "The McKenna got his first close look at them when we arrived home. Needless to say, he's gloating over capturing the imposter, but willnae pass judgment upon him and the others until tomorrow. Fer now, they are locked in the castle dungeons."

Joan heaved a sigh. "Do ye know what he plans to do with them?"

"I have a vague idea."

The wine on Joan's tongue suddenly tasted bitter. "That sounds ominous."

"We are alive and fer the most part unhurt. 'Tis the only reason those four men still draw breath." Malcolm gave her a considering look. "My father willnae be inclined to be lenient. Nor am I. One of them tried to rape ye."

Joan knew Malcolm was right. Highland justice was swift and oftentimes brutal. "What of the imposter? I gave him my word that if he helped us he would have safe passage to see Brienne."

"And so he has. He is unharmed from the journey." Malcolm gently eased a stray lock of hair off her brow. "Surely ye understand. The imposter cannae disgrace the McKenna name and honor and walk away unscathed. And once my father is finished with him, he'll be handed over to the MacPhearsons."

Joan took another sip of wine and slowly digested that news. She had assumed as much, but hearing it brought the harsh repercussions to bear. "We must warn Brienne that he is here."

"Are ye certain? I thought it a kindness to delay her distress," Malcolm replied.

Joan looked again toward Brienne, feeling only sympathy for her plight, wishing there was some way to ease her pain. "Perhaps it is best to wait, but not too long. We should tell her in the morning, so she will have time to prepare herself to face him."

Malcolm nodded. "The hour grows late. There's little chance she will hear about this from another. The McKenna will keep his own counsel on the matter until tomorrow."

"Except fer telling yer mother," Joan said with a knowing smile.

"Aye, they share everything, keeping no secrets from each other." Malcolm took her hand, his blue eyes warm with affection. "'Tis the kind of marriage that I hope we shall have one day."

His words gave her pause. Possibilities stirred inside Joan, doubts vanished and hope blossomed. She acknowledged that she was finished trying to fight to control the way her heart leapt whenever he touched her. To resist the wicked, sensual feelings he evoked.

It had taken her far too long to admit that she had nothing to lose and everything to gain by embracing the passion Malcolm created inside her.

It didn't matter that nearly half the clan was crowded into the hall watching them. Let them all see exactly how she felt about her husband! Joan's arms slid around Malcolm's neck and she joined her hands at his nape. She lifted her chin and caught her lips with his, pouring every emotion she had kept hidden into that single kiss.

Malcolm's arms tightened around her. She could feel his hardness pressing against her hip, confirming his desire. There were shouts and whistles from the men and bawdy giggles from the women.

Bracing his forehead against hers, Malcolm gazed down at her. "It pleases me greatly to know that ye share my wish."

"I do." She pressed her cheek to his, closed her eyes, and held him. "But there is more that I want, more that I crave from my virile husband."

"More?"

She favored him with a sultry glance. "I would like his undivided attention in our bedchamber."

Malcolm's gaze locked on hers with an intensity that made her tingle. "I believe that can be arranged."

"Splendid." Joan tilted her head coyly. She could tell that Malcolm was unsure what to make of her behavior, and that gave her the courage to entice him a wee bit more.

She slid her fingers through his hair, moving along his neck and shoulders and across his chest. "I've heard tell that when a man properly beds his woman the pleasure starts as a slow, sweet ache that builds to near madness before finally bringing relief. Is that true?"

His throat moved as he swallowed. "Aye."

"Show me."

# Chapter Eighteen

With each step they took together up the stairs, Joan became more and more aware of Malcolm. By the time they reached their bedchamber she was breathless with anticipation and trepidation.

What if she failed him?

Ever faithful, Gertrude was waiting in the chamber to assist Joan. She had lit candles, built up the fire, and brought warm water for washing.

"Leave us, Gertrude. I will act as Lady Joan's maid tonight," Malcolm declared in a deep voice.

Gertrude cast a surprised, suspicious eye toward him. Joan opened her mouth to reinforce her husband's command, but a sudden flush of embarrassment stole over her. Horrified that her emotions had gotten the better of her, Joan sent Gertrude what she hoped was a reassuring look.

The maid hesitated, glancing curiously between the two of them before breaking into a knowing grin. Joan's blush deepened. Gertrude dipped a quick curtsy and hurried from the chamber.

Pushing aside her fears and responding to the emotions brimming in her heart, Joan's feet padded across the bedchamber floor, closing the distance between them. Malcolm placed his hands on her waist and captured her in a tight embrace. She rested her hands on his chest, the solid muscle beneath her fingertips a stark reminder of his strength.

The scent of his skin filled her senses and she gave in to the temptation to raise her chin for a kiss. She tilted her head so they fit together easily, their breaths mingling, their tongues languidly twining and teasing. Gradually, the kisses turned demanding, deeper, more intense. Malcolm caught her lower lip between his teeth and tugged insistently.

Joan swayed unsteadily as the dizzying waves of sensation overwhelmed her. She felt a moment's hesitation, but turned away the doubts plaguing her mind and simply let herself feel the hunger between them. Within seconds, she was kissing Malcolm back, craving the excitement that tore through her, embracing the fire that scorched her from within.

She was struggling to catch her breath, delighted to hear Malcolm was doing the same. It gave her an odd sense of power and control to realize that she was able to evoke such a strong response in him.

Malcolm raised his head and their eyes met. His were dark with passion and full of a promise that lured Joan closer. She slid her hands up to the front of his tunic and clung to the edges. He bent her backward and they tumbled onto the bed.

Laughing, she held on tightly. He chuckled, too, and they sprawled together on the bed, half on, half off.

"Ye're a rather clumsy lover, husband," Joan teased.

"Aye, ye make me boneless, wife," he replied.

Joan's insides twisted as she gazed up at him, her heart pounding anew. The guard she had long ago placed around it began to quiver, breaking away in small pieces. 'Twas dangerous to trust so completely, yet she felt herself stirring with excitement as she allowed it to happen.

She knew she was on the verge of experiencing something wondrous, made all the more important because it was Malcolm who would be her partner.

With a warrior's yell, Malcolm lifted her into the center of the bed. He crawled after her, resting on his elbows above her. Despite the tingling in her body, the yearning in her blood, Joan felt exposed, even though she still wore all her clothing.

She swallowed, then smiled at him. A smile of encouragement. He kissed a trail from her neck down her collarbone to the top of her breasts. They strained against the soft wool of her bodice as his lips closed over her nipple.

He suckled hard, coaxing the bud to an even harder point through the wet fabric of her gown. Joan threaded her fingers through his hair, tugging on the strands. The sensations were heady, decadent, and she embraced them fully. He teased and aroused her until she felt on fire for more, his skillful hands and tongue robbing her of all control.

Joan heard the distinct sound of ripping cloth as Malcolm pulled the garments from her body, but she didn't care. Her blood ran faster, her body felt hotter than it ever had before. All she wanted was to feel his naked flesh pressed against hers.

He rewarded her newly bared skin with a trail of delicate wet kisses, leaving her quivering with excitement.

She felt as though she finally understood what he had been telling her about shared passion. The fierce possession and burning desire reflected in his eyes was not to be feared, but rejoiced in.

She allowed him to raise both her arms over her head. The action forced her back to arch and a surge of need filled her. She wanted to be closer, needed to be closer. She longed to experience fully the passion she had once feared.

With Malcolm. Only with Malcolm.

"What have ye done to me?" she whispered, her heart hammering against her rib cage.

"I've only just started," he said, moving his lips to her now naked breast. "I'm going to make ye faint with pleasure, lass, and taste every sweet morsel of ye."

True to his promise, Malcolm ran his fingers down to the juncture of her thighs, sliding them through the feminine folds. She trembled violently, closing her eyes, panting and squirming at his fiery touch. Joan could feel the vibrations of a moan lodge in her throat as his hand pressed deeper, teasing the spot that ached and throbbed again and again and again.

Time seemed to stand and hold. There was nothing beyond it except the two of them, entwined together on this bed.

"Ye know what happens when ye play with fire, don't ye, lass," he said, kissing small bites down her stomach. "Ye burn."

Joan moaned as the heat did indeed flood through her. She could feel the light touch of his lips as he alternated placing kisses and small bites lower and lower down her body. His tongue seared a path to the top of her thighs. She tensed, feeling the heat of his breath where his fingers had just been, having a vague inkling of what he was about to do.

Joan held her breath. *'Twas wicked.* His lips kissed the curls that guarded her feminine bud. *Sinful.* His tongue parted the moist folds and found her most vulnerable spot. *Oh, Lord!*

Joan's heart nearly stopped and she instinctively pulled herself away. "Saints above, is such a thing even decent?" she cried.

"'Tis better than decent, 'tis wondrous," he whispered wickedly. "That is, if ye agree to allow it."

Her eyes opened and Joan discovered Malcolm watching her. Waiting to see if she would accept what he was so intent on having her experience. She hesitated, the old fears emerging. She'd heard whispers of such things, but never had she imagined such a coupling.

"I would never hurt ye, Joan."

"I know."

"Or do anything that made ye feel uncomfortable."

"I know."

She did know. Her trust in him was complete. He had told her it was wondrous and what little she had experienced certainly intrigued her. With a timid sigh she allowed him to pull her forward. To her delight, the heavy warmth pooling between her legs started the moment his tongue found her again.

Clever tongue. Magic lips. Joan's vision blurred, the heat between her thighs increasing until it was almost painful. His tongue was moving in and out of her body, teasing her with short, sweet strokes. Her back arched up from the bed as she gave a low cry; her head thrashed back and forth as the tension continued to build.

The sensations he was provoking in her were indescribable. Joan bit her lip to hold back her scream and then suddenly her body seemed to crest and explode, coming apart in deep, convulsing tremors.

Malcolm continued to caress her, the stroke of his tongue light and erratic while her breathing returned to a more normal cadence. Languid and sated, Joan turned to look at him, shocked to realize he still wore his shirt and braies.

Smiling wantonly, she pressed her finger against his chest, then swirled it down his chest over his flat, taut stomach. The front of his braies rose and she could see his manhood thicken and stiffen beneath the fabric.

"Will ye remove yer clothing, Malcolm, or shall I tear it off?"

Joan smiled sweetly as she spoke, her grin widening when he crossed his arms and lifted his shirt, then pulled his braies off so quickly they nearly caught on his foot. His powerful body intrigued her; the wide shoulders, well-muscled chest and thighs, the springy hair that encircled his erect penis.

It seemed to grow even larger as she stared at it, forming a glistening drop of liquid at the tip. Curious, she touched it with the tips of her fingers, massaging it into his hard flesh. He groaned and rocked his hips forward. Grinning, she encircled her hand around his heavy shaft.

He was so hard.

"Will ye take me now?" she asked thickly.

"Show me what ye want."

Joan's nostrils flared. Her emotions spun, her desire spiraled. She swallowed, her body filling with a bold, brazen strength. Slowly, sensually, she sank back on the bed. Her heart beating erratically, she nudged her legs open in an act of trust and acceptance.

"My God, ye are beautiful," Malcolm cried out in a guttural moan, thrusting his hands beneath her buttocks and lifting her.

With one quick thrust, he sheathed himself inside her. Joan clutched his shoulders, her body opening to receive him. She lifted herself closer and he moved slowly, pumping against her with firm, deep strokes, letting her feel every inch of him.

The air was filled with the sound of their harsh breathing. Though he had brought her to climax only a few minutes earlier, her body once again grew tight with need. Shocking her. Delighting her.

Joan felt consumed by the fire he built between them. She arched her hips willingly, pulling him deeper inside. His thrusts were hard and steady, yet she wanted more, needed more.

She wanted to look into his eyes, gaze into his soul. She wanted to know that he felt the same intense emotions that were driving her to near madness.

"Look at me, Malcolm," she croaked.

His eyes opened. She saw the dark desire in them and it fired her blood to new heights. Their bodies were hot and slick with sweat, moving together in perfect harmony. It was not only the physical, for Joan felt herself drowning in a tide of feelings too strong to control.

This was how it was meant to be between a man and a woman. Passionate, primitive, pleasurable—a fever of hunger and need.

She squeezed her legs around him, drawing him closer. Faster, harder, deeper. She felt the tears on her cheeks and didn't know why she was crying. Her body started to crest again and Joan tightened her inner muscles, wanting to hold on to him for as long as possible.

Suddenly, Malcolm crushed her to his chest, burying his head in her shoulder while the spasms of release shuddered through him. She felt a warm wetness flood her womb and joyful thoughts of a child invaded her heart.

He lay sprawled on top of her for a moment, then rolled to his side, taking her with him. Floating on a cloud of sensation, Joan rested her head against Malcolm's shoulder. His hand stroked her back gently, soothingly, and she basked in the intimacy of the moment, in the joy of being in his arms and in his bed.

He hadn't lied to her, nay; making love with him was all that he had promised and more. She was glad that she had trusted him, was even happier that he had convinced her to marry him.

*We shall share this fer the rest of our lives!*

Sated and drowsy, Joan felt her eyelids start to close. She struggled against it until she realized there was no need. Malcolm would be here when she awoke, keeping her and their bed warm. The thought made her heart sing in anticipation.

Sleep soon claimed her, yet before she slipped away, Malcolm moved his lips to her ear. "I was right," he cooed. "Ye were worth waiting fer."

As the first light of dawn slowly crept into their bedchamber, Malcolm lay on his side, watching Joan. He could tell from the steady rhythm of her breathing that she was sleeping deeply. Her hand was resting on his chest, her nose was pressed against her pillow, and he had trapped one of her legs beneath his.

By rights he should be equally exhausted. He had woken her twice during the night to make love to her again, his body sated only until the cravings started anew. Never before had he felt such an intense need to possess a woman, never before had he allowed himself to be so completely enraptured.

It was an odd feeling to realize that he would never grow tired of the sight of her, the feel of her resting in his arms, the sound of her voice, raised in joy or even anger.

Men were enthralled by her beauty, but it was Joan's spirit and heart that had captured his.

Malcolm reached for her hand and held it, bringing it close to his lips. She mumbled in her sleep and snuggled closer. He breathed in the warm smell of her, the hint of lemon and lavender mingling with the musky scent of sex.

'Twas intoxicating.

Playfully, he blew at the wisps of hair that lay on her cheek. She sniffed and wrinkled her nose. Grinning mischievously, Malcolm did it again, and again, until he noticed her eyelids fluttered.

When they opened, Joan caught his eye and smiled. Malcolm's heart swelled. He smiled back.

"Ye're finally awake," he said.

"Not really," she replied, closing her eyes and snuggling back against her pillow.

"Ah, so ye intend to sleep the day away, ye lazy hussy," he teased.

"It seems only fair, since I got almost no sleep last night," she quipped.

"And whose fault is that, I ask ye?"

Joan opened one eye and stared at him. "Mine?"

"Aye. I'm a mortal man, not a saint, and ye are impossible to resist. Every bit of reason flies out of my head the moment I kiss ye and hold ye close."

She opened both eyes, then furrowed her brow. "I have come to understand precisely what that look in yer eye means, Malcolm."

"Och, 'tis a clever lass that I've married."

Malcolm ran his fingers down her arm and over her hips. Joan's eyes darkened with interest and it pleased him mightily to see how receptive she was to his caress.

"If ye take me again, husband, I'll not have the strength

to walk," she mumbled, though in truth she did not protest overmuch.

"Then I'll just have to carry ye," he whispered wickedly.

"Bring in the prisoners," the McKenna bellowed.

Joan stood beside a trembling Brienne as the four prisoners were brought into the great hall. They were a somber lot, sporting several scrapes and bruises. 'Twas obvious from their dirty clothes and gray, exhausted faces that they had spent an uncomfortable night locked in the dank, dark dungeon beneath the castle.

A few curious murmurs from the small crowd broke the silence. The McKenna turned to Brienne, waiting for her to answer his unasked question. Brienne grasped Joan's hand so tightly the knuckles turned white. Ignoring her own discomfort, Joan refused to pull away, knowing how much the younger woman needed her support.

Finally, Brienne lifted her chin. Joan saw the spark of emotion pass between her and the imposter when their eyes met, and she feared the younger woman would lose her nerve.

"Aye, Laird McKenna, that's him," Brienne finally croaked, her face as pale as snow.

The McKenna nodded in satisfaction. He gestured for the imposter to be separated from the others. The man stumbled as he was yanked to the side, while his three companions remained in the center of the room.

"I will have justice this day," the McKenna declared.

"Ye dinnae seek justice, but revenge," Robbie cried peevishly. "Ye've no right to hold us. We've committed no crime. Laird MacPhearson offered a bounty to any man who would bring him Sir Malcolm. We broke no laws by seeking to collect it."

"Ye ambushed and kidnapped my son," the McKenna shouted.

Robbie's eyes shifted. "Well, he wouldn't have come with us if we had asked him."

The other two men sneered. Joan's eyes widened at their foolish audacity. 'Twas like baiting an already angry bear. Clearly, these men had no idea what they were facing.

Their brief moment of joviality ended when the McKenna walked forward and began slowly circling around them. Though older by several decades, his powerful presence easily intimidated. After a long, tension-filled moment, he finally spoke. His voice was deceptively quiet, so low that all had to strain to hear him.

"Normally, I would offer a man the honor of trial by combat and let his sword speak fer his guilt or innocence. But ye three are not men—ye're worms."

The scowl that darkened the McKenna's features was terrifying. His hand moved to the hilt of his sword as he surveyed the three men in front of him. Any prior hint of grins on their faces vanished completely. Robbie licked his lips nervously and the other two blanched.

"If not fer the ladies present in the hall, I'd draw my blade and gut the lot of ye," the McKenna continued, his expression unforgiving. "But I'm a civilized man, not a barbarian."

He turned to Malcolm. "Is there anything ye want to say before I pass judgment?"

Malcolm shifted his black stare to the three prisoners, stalking over to them. He glared at each man in turn, stopping when he stood in front of the tall one. Without warning, Malcolm drew back his arm and slammed his fist into the man's jaw. He dropped like a stone, two teeth flying across the floor.

Joan thought Malcolm had knocked him unconscious until she heard him groan. The tall one rolled to his side, wiping the blood from his mouth with his sleeve.

Malcolm reached down, grabbed the fellow by his tunic, and hauled him to his feet. Blood seeping from his nose, the man started choking in Malcolm's iron grip. Eyes glowing with fury, Malcolm lifted his knee and rammed it between the man's legs. He howled in agony and once again fell to the floor, writhing in pain.

"By rights I should castrate ye fer trying to force yerself on my wife," Malcolm snarled, his face hardening into a scowl. "Lucky fer ye, I'm in a generous mood today."

A mixture of fear and sympathy rippled across the other prisoners' faces as they watched the tall one curl into a ball. There was a general rumble of approval from the crowd, though a few suggested a harsher punishment. The McKenna held up his hand and the great hall fell silent.

"Ye three shall pay fer yer crimes with the strength of yer backs and the sweat of yer brows," the McKenna decided. "The north side of our outer curtain wall needs repair. Ye three will fix it."

"I fear that might be too skilled a job fer this lot," Malcolm said. He cast a contrived look at his father and the McKenna smiled.

"Perhaps ye are right. Instead of rebuilding the wall, these men shall be sent to the quarry to extract the stone," the McKenna amended.

"'Tis backbreaking work," Malcolm added. "But if ye are diligent, and manage to stay alive, the job should be completed in a year."

"A year!" Robbie cried, a vein throbbing in his neck.

"Aye," Malcolm answered. "And if ye cause any trouble, any at all, the sentence will be extended to two years."

"Take them away," the McKenna said, slicing his hand through the air.

Two of the McKenna guards dragged the tall one to his feet. Robbie and the other brigand fell in step behind them, their shoulders slumped and expressions subdued. 'Twas a harsh sentence, yet Joan could see their undeniable quiver of relief; they fully realized they were lucky to leave with their lives.

"Bring the other one forward," the McKenna ordered. "I will hear from his own lips why this imposter perpetuated such an insult to the McKenna honor."

Noticing Brienne nervously moisten her lips, Joan was glad that the McKenna had agreed to make this a relatively small audience, with only the immediate family and a small group of clansmen in attendance. A larger crowd would have caused Brienne even greater anxiety.

The imposter took his place in front of the McKenna and Malcolm. His face was ragged and wary, but his bearing was proud, his head held high. His gaze traveled among them, resting upon Brienne. She, in turn, regarded him in stony silence.

This time, it was Malcolm who asked the questions. He folded his arms and looked sternly at the imposter. "Why did ye impersonate me at the fete?"

"'Twas an unplanned impulse," the imposter replied. "After the first melee, a McKenna plaid had been left behind on the battlefield. I picked it up, intending to return it, but that's when I first caught sight of Lady Brienne."

The imposter sighed, his eyes lighting with pleasure as he recalled the memory. "I thought she was the most beautiful woman I'd ever seen. She was surrounded by several other women and then suddenly she was alone. Seizing the moment, I boldly approached her. She noticed the plaid and assumed that I was a McKenna. When she asked my name, I said the only one that I knew—yers."

Malcolm's expression softened slightly. "I can well understand the power of a beautiful woman's allure. But that doesn't explain why ye kept up the charade."

The imposter's lips twisted. "I intended to tell her. I was going to tell her. But my affection fer her grew so quickly and I feared she would spurn my attentions if she knew that I was naught but a humble knight."

Malcolm peered down at him. "Is she so fickle a woman, so shallow a female that she would only bestow her regard on a wealthy noble?"

The imposter tensed, clenching his fists. "Say what ye will about me, but ye've no right to slander Lady Brienne. She is all that is good and decent in this world."

"Yet ye defiled her! Ye took her innocence and her honor!" Malcolm retorted.

"I loved her!" the imposter shouted, his voice straining with emotion.

Beside her, Joan heard Brienne gasp. She reached out a hand to comfort the young woman and realized that Brienne was shaking like a leaf in a strong wind.

"What did ye seek to gain by kidnapping my son and taking him to the MacPhearsons?" Lady Aileen asked. "Ye knew full well that he was not the one they sought. I cannae decide if ye were too bold or too witless believing ye could have collected the reward from Laird Mac-Phearson."

"'Twas never about the coin. I needed a way inside the castle walls and Sir Malcolm was the prize that assured me I could ride through the gates. I had tried to see Brienne months ago, but the holding was heavily guarded and the women's quarters impossible to breech."

"Ye tried to see her?" Joan asked.

The imposter nodded his head enthusiastically. "Aye. Several times. I even considered bribing one of the servants to deliver a note, but the whole clan was suspicious of any strangers in their midst. I had to find another way inside."

"What of the other men?" Malcolm wanted to know. "Did they know of yer plans when ye ambushed me?"

"Nay. They thought it an easy way to earn some coin. I assumed our arrival would cause a big commotion. 'Twas my intention to use that distraction to finally see Brienne."

"And then what?" Joan questioned.

"I hoped to explain it all. To throw myself on her mercy and beg her forgiveness." There was a flash of contrition shining in the imposter's eyes that was impossible to miss. "I am not worthy of her. I know it. But that doesn't lessen the love I feel fer her."

"Love?" Brienne slowly unfurled her hands and placed them at her sides. "Ye love me so much that ye lied to me, seduced me, made a fool of me. Is that what ye claim?"

"I do love ye," he insisted.

Brienne let out a low groan. "Saints preserve us, I dinnae even know yer true name."

"Alec. I'm Alec Ewing."

The McKenna frowned. "I dinnae think there were any Ewing men left alive after the battle of Bannockburn in 1314."

Alec grimaced. "Our clansmen fought bravely fer the Bruce, my father included, but most who returned from that victorious battle were gravely injured. There were too few to train the younger lads, like myself, and our skills were poor. We were no match fer the Douglas clan when they decided to take our lands and disband the clan."

"Ye carry a fine sword and fought at the fete," Joan pointed out. "Ye clearly had training at some point."

"Perhaps ye're only good fer mock battles, Alec Ewing," the McKenna taunted.

Alec bristled at the remark. "I've learned much in the years since the Douglas stole our land. Competing in tournaments is how I earn my living. Fer that, ye need skill to survive."

Joan noticed several of the men, including her husband, nodding their heads. Serious injury and death were common at these events.

"It seems that ye do far more than fight at the tournaments," Malcolm commented dryly. "Is the fair Brienne the only victim of yer treachery? Or are there other babes with startling green eyes populating the Highlands?"

"Nay!" Alec's eyes remained fixed on Brienne. "I have loved no other woman. Only Lady Brienne. And I shall continue to love her fer as long as I draw breath."

The McKenna made a rude noise. "God above, save us all from lovesick swains."

"Time will prove the truth of my love," Alec insisted, a spark of determination edging his voice.

"Yer betrayal has earned Brienne's disdain along with that of her father and her clan," Malcolm stated firmly. "They are all repulsed by yer behavior."

"If I had the chance, I would change much—"

"'Tis easy to see the folly of yer deeds once the consequences have been shown," Brienne said bitterly. "An honorable man acts to avoid them."

"Fer now I can do naught but beg yer forgiveness," Alec admitted.

"Thanks to yer lies, I participated willingly in my own downfall, disgraced myself and my clan. Ye have taught me the harsh lesson of how little a man values a woman,"

Brienne said tonelessly. "I suppose fer that I should be grateful."

"Nay!" Alec cried, lunging forward. He didn't get far. Two of the McKenna guards leapt forward and held him back.

"As punishment fer yer actions against me, ye will dig a long ditch at the edge of the south fields so water from the river can be directed there if the rains fail in the warm weather," Malcolm announced. "Once that is completed, ye will be sent north to Laird MacPhearson to await his judgment."

The guards started to haul Alec away, but he bucked and strained and struggled against them. "Wait! I aided ye in yer escape and in exchange I beg one small mercy."

Malcolm raised his hand. "Hold!"

The guards released Alec. He straightened, and Joan swore she could almost see the fierce emotions lodged in his chest. "I wish to see my son."

Malcolm tilted his head. "Ye ask fer something that I have no right to give. 'Tis up to his mother to give permission, not me."

Alec turned hopeful eyes toward Brienne. She looked away, pressing her lips together for a long moment.

Feeling the shudder that went through the younger woman, Joan leaned her head close to Brienne's. "I'm not surprised that he has asked to see the lad," Joan whispered. "In anticipation of this moment, I asked Gertrude to wait with Liam nearby."

Brienne anxiously chewed on her lower lip. "Does he think to manipulate me through my son?" she asked Joan.

Joan regarded Alec warily. "I'm uncertain, though his interest appears genuine. I see no harm in allowing it."

After another long, tense moment, Brienne nodded.

Rather than shout, Joan went herself to fetch her maid and the babe. Liam smiled the moment he saw her and began kicking his legs. He was such a sweet, innocent child.

Joan and Gertrude entered the great hall. Alec's face contorted in wonder and joy as he beheld his son for the first time. Liam stared at his sire solemnly, then favored him with one of his sweetest grins. Alec choked back a smile, his joy and pride evident. He gently placed his hand upon Liam's head, then bent forward and kissed his brow.

"I vow to make myself worthy of raising this child and becoming a father he can respect." Alec stared hard at Brienne. "And a husband ye can love."

There was a deep crease marking Brienne's brow, yet she said nothing. With the guards at his side, Alec strode silently from the hall. The only sound in the chamber was Liam's excited gurgles and coos. 'Twas almost as if he was trying to call his father back.

Joan was glad to see Brienne's chin go up a notch. She reached for Liam and he went eagerly to his mother's arms. Joan, Katherine, and Malcolm gathered around the pair.

"My chest hurts and my heart is pounding fiercely," Brienne confessed. "Yet so much of my worry is centered on Alec. After all that has passed between us, 'tis illogical to be so consumed with emotion over his well-being, but I seemed unable to control my perversity."

Joan ran her fingers over Brienne's forehead, trying to ease the worry from her brow. "He is Liam's father. Naturally, ye would have strong feelings fer him."

"My life has been altered by him, thrown into a direction I never would have imagined. By all rights I should hate him."

"Yet ye cannae," Katherine said sympathetically.

"Ye need time to take in all that ye have learned about Alec today," Malcolm said.

Brienne nodded. "I want to return home."

"Ye can return home whenever ye wish," Joan replied, patting Brienne's shoulder. "Malcolm will arrange fer an escort."

"If ye'd like, I will go with ye," Katherine volunteered.

"Thank ye, Katherine. I would be very glad of the company." With relief brimming in her watery eyes, Brienne squeezed Katherine's hand.

"These past few weeks have been a test of yer endurance," Malcolm said. "Ye handled yerself with courage and honor. I know yer father will be proud of ye."

"Are ye certain ye wish to leave?" Joan asked. "There is much unsettled between ye and Alec."

Sorrow filled Brienne's eyes. "Aye. 'Tis why I need to go. My emotions are in such turmoil that I cannae think straight. I need to get away from him."

"If ye stay here, ye can easily avoid setting eyes on him," Malcolm said reassuringly. "He'll be working very hard from sunrise to sunset, and when he isn't he'll be confined to the dungeon."

Brienne hung her head. "Just knowing he is so near will prey upon my weakness. I fear I might shame myself and seek him out. Nay, 'tis best if Liam and I return home. I am grateful fer all the kindness ye have shown me. But now I need the strength of my family and clan around me."

"We must keep our word to yer father and send Alec to him once he has served his punishment here," Malcolm warned.

Brienne took a harsh breath and hugged Liam close to her breast. "By then I shall be strong enough to bear the weight of whatever comes next."

* * *

"She still loves him," Joan observed.

Malcolm turned to his wife. They were alone, having stayed behind in the great hall after the others had left.

"Aye. She is hurt and mistrustful, yet I heard no venom in her tone." Joan's face softened. "Alec is not the black-hearted rogue we all believed him to be."

"Perhaps in time Brienne will remember what she first saw in Alec that made him worth loving."

"Why are ye smiling?" Joan asked.

"We had all ascribed such devious motivation to Alec's impersonation, yet it all started because a McKenna plaid had been left behind during a mock battle," Malcolm said, his voice filled with irony.

"If not fer that, then my father would never have been asked to negotiate a peace between the McKennas and the MacPhearsons. Ye never would have come to Armstrong Castle." She stepped forward, happily, into the circle of Malcolm's arms. "We never would have married."

He tilted his head. "Are ye saying that we owe Alec a debt of gratitude?"

Joan shrugged. "Well, I wouldn't go that far."

A wider grin appeared on Malcolm's face and his blue eyes twinkled. "I would."

# Chapter Nineteen

Joan sat on a stone bench under the pleasant warmth of the afternoon sun, watching Lileas carefully bend over the neat rows of delicate green sprouts. Having the lass weed the kitchen garden was the newest punishment Joan had devised to correct the child's mischievous behavior, and thus far Joan was uncertain of its impact, as Lileas seemed to almost be enjoying herself.

Callum was hunched nearby, his forearms resting on his knees, his expression earnest as he observed his older sister. Occasionally, he would reach out and run his fingers through the ever growing pile of weeds Lileas was making. She, in turn, would smile and pat his hand.

"Nay, not that one, Lileas," Joan called out. "'Tis a carrot top."

"Aye, Mother."

"Carrot," Callum repeated.

"Is this one a weed?" Lileas asked, pointing to a tall, thin shoot.

"Nay, that's a turnip." Joan noticed Lileas's fingers still hovering over the green top. "Move along, Lileas. Ye cannae pull it just because ye dinnae like turnips. They are yer grandfather's favorites."

"Turnips," Callum repeated.

Joan nodded. Her wee one was growing up. She was surprised at how many new words Callum had learned in the month since they had come to McKenna Castle. She knew that his expanded vocabulary was due in part to the lavish attention he received from all the members of his new family, especially Lileas.

The lass doted upon him and he worshipped her. A part of Joan was pleased they had formed a close sibling relationship, though her biggest fear was that her son would soon be joining his new sister in her escapades, and the pair would wreak havoc throughout the entire McKenna clan.

"I finished the row," Lileas announced.

"Start on the next one," Joan ordered.

With a loud sigh, Lileas complied, making Joan feel more assured over her choice of punishment. 'Twould not be an effective lesson if the lass did not find discomfort in the task.

A series of sharp barks from Prince drew Joan's attention away from Lileas. Relegated to the other side of the kitchen garden fence, the loyal hound had been dozing in the sunlight, but now he stood on guard.

The barking continued, along with a vigorous tail wagging, and in the distance, Joan saw Malcolm approaching. A smile came naturally to her lips at the sight of her handsome Highland warrior and a shiver of delight gripped her.

Powerfully built, tall, and well muscled, he was a formidable figure, but there was a boyish quality to his smile that bespoke of an inner peace and happiness.

A happiness they shared. Joan's lips curved higher. The love she felt for him seemed to grow stronger and deeper each day, until it had reached the very marrow of her bones. It surprised her, sometimes even frightened her.

She had never planned to feel this way about any man. Never expected it, never even wanted it. Yet now that she had experienced it, Joan could not imagine her life without it.

She had yet to say anything to Malcolm about it. She was waiting for the right moment to reveal her heart and gift him with thc words that she hoped would bring him joy.

"Papa!" Lileas jumped to her feet and hurried to greet Malcolm, crushing several rows of herbs in the process.

"Good day to ye, poppet," he replied, swinging her into his arms. "What are ye doing?"

Lilcas sighed dramatically and buried her face in his shoulder. "I'm pulling the weeds from the garden. I've been doing it fer hours and hours and I'm so tired. And look, I've got dirt on all of my fingers and under my nails."

Lileas waved her hands in Malcolm's face before continuing with her complaints. "Grandmother doesn't like it when I'm so untidy. Please, may I stop?"

Malcolm slowly set his daughter on her feet. "Why are ye pulling weeds?"

Lileas shrugged. "Mother is making me."

"Why?"

"She is angry with me."

"There must be a reason."

Lileas studied the ground a moment, then lifted her head. "I dinnae mean to open the sheep pen. 'Twas an accident."

"That's not what the shepherd told me," Joan interjected. "He said that he warned ye three times not to touch the gate."

"It's not a sturdy gate," Lileas countered, a distinct whine in her voice. "I only put my hand on it fer a second and it swung wide open."

"Sheep ran and ran and ran," Callum added excitedly. "Baa, baa, baa."

"Hello, laddie."

Malcolm ruffled Callum's hair—which had finally begun to grow in evenly—then lowered his chin. Joan could see he was making a valiant effort to hide his smile.

"I am so very sorry about the sheep," Lileas proclaimed. "I promise to be a good lass and do as I am told. May I go play with Callum now?"

Joan tensed. Malcolm had told her a few weeks ago that she would be in charge of disciplining Lileas, but this was the first true test of that arrangement.

"Nay, Lileas, ye are to do as yer mother says," Malcolm decided. "She will tell ye when yer punishment has ended."

Lileas crossed her arms over her chest and grumbled, but Malcolm ignored her. He came to sit beside Joan on the bench. Feeling a tad stunned, she wiggled to make room for him.

"Ye stood with me," Joan said slowly, her heart thumping with excitement. "I feared that the moment Lileas begged ye to release her, ye'd rebuke my orders and issue yer own, allowing her whatever she wanted."

Malcolm tilted his head. "I gave ye my word that I'd stand beside ye, lass. I might not always agree with ye— hell, I can say with certainty that I willnae—but I'll never forsake ye. Ye are my wife, my partner, and I value yer opinion, especially when it comes to raising our children."

A hesitant smile blossomed on Joan's face and she struggled with the unexpressed emotions that bubbled and brewed inside her. Then taking a deep breath, she spoke from her heart.

"I love ye, Malcolm," she whispered into his ear. "More than I ever believed possible."

He squeezed her waist in acknowledgment. Joan swallowed nervously, squirming in his arms. Did the declaration please him?

He nuzzled his lips against her ear and she held her breath, waiting to hear the words that she dared to hope he would utter.

"Finally," he muttered.

Joan's eyes widened as she pulled back. "What did ye say?"

"Ye heard me. I said 'finally.'"

The look of smug satisfaction on his face was exceptionally irritating, momentarily overshadowing her hurt. Yet as the silence stretched, Joan admitted that she had hoped for a far different reaction. She had hoped to hear a declaration from him, daring to admit to herself how desperately she longed to have his love.

Yet all she heard was silence. For a moment the maelstrom of her emotions made everything spin around her. He wasn't indifferent to her; she knew that he cared for her, even had some affection for her beyond his physical desire.

Joan set her hand on his cheek and Malcolm turned his face into her palm. *I shall make him love me!*

"Why do ye look so sad?"

Joan shook her head with a wistful smile. "'Tis nothing." Her eyes suddenly blurred and she blinked rapidly to clear them.

"Foolish woman." He pressed his lips to her moist cheek. "Ye must know that I return yer love. With every part of me, with every breath I take, I know that I shall love and honor ye all the days of my life and beyond."

*He loves me!* Her world tilted beneath her. Joan slid her hand to the back of his neck and brought her mouth to his, pressing herself into his embrace. It seemed impossible that she had been so fortunate to win the one thing she prized above all else, the one thing she never knew she craved and needed so desperately.

"Are ye certain?" she asked.

He reached for her hand, pressing it against his chest. "Ye hold my heart, Joan. In truth, ye are the other half of me."

His eyes swept over her face and she marveled at how she could feel the full force of his love shining from his eyes.

"Come, let's sneak away and leave Lileas to her weeding," Malcolm said, his voice husky with passion.

Joan bit her lip. The desire in his eyes started a flame deep within her. She imagined him sweeping her into his arms and carrying her to their bedchamber, then slowly stripping off her clothes, his hands and mouth ravaging her body with exquisite skill. The image caused her to shiver as if with fever and the urgency of her need climbed.

"If I dinnae supervise Lileas, she'll pull out the vegetable shoots as well as the weeds," Joan said thickly. "There will be nothing salvageable left. Cook will be very upset."

Malcolm's head lowered until his lips were pressed against the exposed flesh above the square-cut bodice of her gown. "I'll replant all the vegetables and herbs and anything else Lileas destroys."

"'Tis wasteful." Joan arched upward.

"We have more than enough seed. And I enjoy planting seeds, do I not, wife?"

His lips moved slowly, torturously to the valley between her breasts, leaving a streak of fire along her sensitive flesh. Joan could feel her nipples rise and harden as a tingling pleasure rippled through her. She swayed forward, biting her lip again to stifle a moan.

The air around them seemed to thicken. Malcolm caught her wrist and drew it down, pressing it between his thighs. Joan grasped his manhood firmly, feeling the length of his arousal. She moved her hand up and down; his penis stiffened and grew harder.

Their eyes met and held and Joan could see the intense desire she felt mirrored in the depths of his eyes.

"Lileas?" Joan croaked.

"Yes, Mother?"

"Have ye learned that ye must listen to the adults and do as ye are told?"

"Aye."

"And do ye promise not to go near the sheep or the chickens or the pigs unless ye've asked permission?"

"Aye."

"Good. Then ye may go."

"And take Callum with ye," Malcolm added in a husky voice.

"Can we go riding, Papa? My pony misses me."

Lileas's voice was very near. Joan jerked her hand away, fearing the child might have seen her lewd action, but Malcolm's body shielded her from view. He cleared his throat and turned his head, looking over his shoulder.

"I'll take ye riding later," he said hoarsely.

"When?"

"Later," Malcolm repeated sternly. "Now, run along. Cook was baking honey cakes earlier. Go to the kitchen with Callum and politely ask fer one."

"Can Prince come, too? He loves honey cakes."

"Aye, bring Prince," Malcolm replied in a strained voice. Mindful of her young audience, Joan held herself away from Malcolm until the children and Prince had disappeared from view. When they were finally alone, she wound her arms around his neck.

Malcolm lowered his head. His clever lips kissed her so thoroughly a frisson of heat shuddered up from her belly. Joan's entire being seemed to strain toward him, giving in wholly to the fierce, aching desire that threatened to consume her. There was no other man who could arouse her to such heights, could bring such fire and passion to her soul.

Malcolm. Only Malcolm. *And he loves me!*

"My knees are so weak I can barely stand," Joan marveled.

"Och, so if I am to have my wicked way with ye, lass, then I'll have to carry ye to our bedchamber," Malcolm growled in her ear.

"I dinnae think I can wait that long," she admitted breathlessly.

Malcolm swore, then placed his hands on her waist and lifted her. "Straddle me," he commanded.

Joan's eyes widened. "The children?"

"Are gone," Malcolm replied.

"But someone could happen by at any moment."

"Then we'd best hurry."

With an impatient groan, Malcolm pushed the fabric of her gown up to her thighs. Shivers raced through her as he caressed her most sensitive flesh with the tip of his finger. She could feel the moisture weeping from her body, eager for his possession.

Malcolm shifted, releasing himself from his braies. Soon, there was no barrier of fabric separating them. Joan's blood roared in her ears, her breathing coming hard and labored.

She did as he commanded and placed herself on his lap, her legs dangling on either side of his. Malcolm slid her gown from her shoulders, the soft fabric pooling at her waist. With a sensual growl, he tore away her chemise, baring her upper body. She shuddered as the cool air washed over her skin.

"By the saints ye are the most beautiful woman on earth."

"And I belong to ye."

He circled around her peaked nipples with lazy strokes of his tongue until the heat gathering in her body turned to a throbbing need. Bracing her hands on his shoulders, she lifted herself up.

"Guide me inside," he moaned.

Joan gasped as he parted her swollen flesh, placing himself at her entrance. Slowly, she moved her hips in a measured, sensual cadence, taking him deep into her moist warmth. Malcolm groaned and grabbed her buttocks, digging into her flesh. She held fast to his shoulders and increased the speed, glorying in the tandem rhythm they created.

Overwhelmed by the rising pleasure and the intensity of the emotions that followed, Joan clung to Malcolm as the pulsing heat of her release began. Her breath came in quick, shallow pants; her body shuddered and clenched around his.

He thrust faster and harder, coaxing her to blissful heights, then with a cry of pure male satisfaction, spilled his seed deep within her. Still trembling, Joan slumped against him. Malcolm tightened his hold around her waist to keep her from falling and she allowed herself to remain boneless.

After a few minutes, Joan reluctantly roused herself. Malcolm moved to lift her off his lap, but she stayed his hand. "Wait," she said softly. "I wish to savor the feelings a bit longer."

"God's teeth, Joan, ye are a wanton lass."

"'Tis all yer fault," she purred, brushing the damp hair from his forehead. "Ye made me this way."

"We are well suited," he said, nipping at the side of her neck.

"Aye," she replied, hardly believing she spoke the truth.

The passion she had long feared flowed naturally between them, but it was the aftermath that soothed her fragile soul. Being near Malcolm was all Joan needed for the contentment of her body and spirit.

How had that occurred? There was so much she didn't understand about her feelings for him, but it didn't matter. She savored them, believing in their power, realizing that somehow they made her stronger.

The sound of voices brought them both back to reality. Reluctantly, Joan moved off Malcolm's lap. He helped her lace her chemise and gown, she retrieved his braies, brushing off the dirt before handing them to him.

Smiling like a mischievous pair of youths, they righted their clothing and returned to the bench, sitting close enough so their thighs were touching.

"There was a reason I sought yer company this afternoon," Malcolm said.

"Aye, a glorious reason." She bit him playfully on the jaw.

He laughed. "Nay, another reason. Mother received a letter from Katherine today."

Sobering, Joan pulled herself away. "Is all well?"

"Aye. She will return home soon."

"Yer mother and I both miss her very much and are anxious to see her." Joan plucked a piece of twig from her gown and tried smoothing away the worst of the wrinkles, realizing how truly disheveled she must look. "What news of Brienne and Alec?"

"Alec's head still rests upon his shoulders. Fer now. When he arrived at the MacPhearson Keep, he spent the first three days and nights in the pillory. Katherine writes it rained much of that time, but certain clan members, especially the women, verbally expressed their displeasure of his treatment of Brienne with vigor—and rotten vegetables."

Joan winced. Prolonged exposure to the elements often resulted in serious illness and even death for those sentenced to the pillory. "Three days is a harsh punishment."

"Aye, but it hasn't broken Alec's spirit. He is determined to redeem himself and gain Laird MacPhearson's permission to marry Brienne. To atone fer his past sins, Alec toils in the fields with the farmers in the early morning, hunts fer food with the retainers in the afternoon, and practices with the soldiers before the evening meal."

Joan sniffed. "It sounds exhausting."

Malcolm shrugged. "Alec has much to prove, to both the laird and Brienne."

"Does she welcome his suit?"

"Alec has little time to woo her, but Katherine believes Brienne's anger has faded enough that she is starting to forgive him. He is devoted to Liam, which pleases her greatly."

Malcolm was quiet for a moment before continuing. "There's other news. About yer father."

Joan's heart skipped. "Has he fallen ill?"

"Nay. According to Katherine, he has taken a new wife."

Joan went very still. "Agnes?"

"Aye."

"How does Katherine know?"

"In exchange fer an evening's performance, a troupe of minstrels sought shelter with the MacPhearsons," Malcolm replied. "They had recently come from Armstrong Castle, where they had been hired to perform at yer father's wedding celebration."

"Minstrels? My goodness. It appears that he spared no expense. Agnes must have been preening like a peacock."

"They said the feasting lasted two days."

A strong wave of thoughts jumbled through Joan's mind, mixing and mingling with confused feelings. She was not entirely surprised to hear that her father had married Agnes. Not surprised either that he had not taken the time to write and tell her the news himself.

Or send a messenger.

Joan swallowed. "When did they wed?"

"At least a fortnight ago."

Her father and Agnes—a fitting pair. *May they both wallow in their shared misery together.*

Joan sighed. 'Twas an uncharitable thought and she swiftly made the sign of the cross in repentance.

"Are ye very disappointed?" Malcolm asked with concern.

"That Agnes is my new mother?" Joan blew out a loud breath, then broke into a grin. "Och, I shall take great delight in addressing her as such. If we ever see them again."

Malcolm took her hand and stroked it gently. "I know ye harbored great hopes that one day Callum might lead the Armstrong clan as their laird. But if Agnes has a son, her child will be the next laird."

It took a moment for Joan to comprehend the words, to accept the situation. Yet upon reflection, she was shocked to realize that it no longer mattered.

"Callum is a McKenna, just as I am," she said. "I have no worries fer his future. With ye to guide him, he shall find a place in this world that honors his name and makes his family proud. Of that I have no doubt."

"I love ye, Joan."

"And I love ye, Malcolm." She laughed, feeling a lightness deep within her soul. "Now take me to our bedchamber and prove it."

One month later Malcolm lumbered from the practice field, his arms and legs tired, his shoulder sore, his mood buoyant. His squire had bested all the other lads this afternoon, even those who were older and bigger in size. This feat was a credit to the training that Malcolm had tirelessly provided and he allowed himself a moment to bask in the feeling of pride and accomplishment.

In but a few years Callum would be old enough to start learning the skills of a warrior and Malcolm looked forward to teaching him. Naturally, Lileas would want to be included, and he wondered how the McKenna would react to having a lass being taught to wield a sword and use a dirk.

No matter what his father's reaction, Malcolm intended to teach his daughter, and Joan had agreed, insisting that all women should have the ability to defend themselves. Their smaller stature and size naturally put females at a physical disadvantage, but Malcolm's squire had proven there were ways to compensate and overcome it.

He turned past the stables and spied Joan walking with his mother and sister. Each was carrying lengths of fabric in their arms and he surmised they were heading to the chapel with the newly embroidered cloths for the altar.

His mother was very particular about her sewing and Joan had been excited when she was asked to help with this important undertaking. They had spent hours together deciding on the design, selecting the colors, and sharing in the work.

Joan had stayed up late for several nights, plying her needle by candlelight, determined to finish her section of the piece. Her efforts to please his mother had succeeded and the harmony between these two strong-willed women boded well for the future happiness of all the McKennas.

Feeling like an infatuated lad, Malcolm changed direction and followed his wife, waiting patiently on the chapel steps for the women to reemerge.

"Goodness, Malcolm, ye smell ripe." Lady Aileen waved her hand delicately in front of her nose. "I thought ye were on the practice field, not mucking about in the stables."

"I beg yer forgiveness, Mother. 'Twas a very rigorous afternoon. I was training several of the squires and we used the lower pasture."

"Where they graze the sheep?"

"Aye." He grinned wolfishly at Joan. "Apparently, I am in need of a bath. Will ye assist me, my love?"

Eyes wide, Joan nervously glanced at his mother. "There's plenty of water in the loch," she replied primly.

"It's freezing," he whined, sounding so much like Lileas they all laughed.

"The servants are too busy preparing fer our guests to spare the time to heat and haul water fer yer bath," Lady Aileen said. "Ye'll just have to freeze in the loch."

At the mention of guests, Katherine lowered her eyes and blushed. The Drummond and Fergusson clans were due to arrive within the week and the McKenna had made no secret of his interest in making a marriage alliance with either of these powerful clans.

Yet they all knew that the final decision on a bridegroom would rest with Katherine, thanks to their mother's insistence that her daughter be given the right to choose her own husband. 'Twas a promise that had the power to set the McKenna's teeth on edge, yet he had no choice but to honor it, since he had made that vow to his wife.

Malcolm could only hope that his sister would be as fortunate in her marriage as he and his brother, James, were in theirs.

Later that night, Malcolm was in a playful mood while he waited for Joan to join him in their bed. The moment she did, he rolled her over on her back, raised himself above her, and looked deeply into her eyes. "Fie, my love, yer beauty outshines the stars in the heavens."

Joan cocked an eyebrow. "I'm already in yer bed. Naked. Willing. Nay, eager. Ye've no need to shower me with pretty words."

"I like flattering my wife."

"Hmm." She wrapped her leg around his waist, pressing her heat close to him. "Just make certain that I'm the only woman ye favor with yer silver tongue."

"Are ye jealous?" he asked, secretly delighted at the thought.

"Nay," she replied, touching her hand to his cheek. "I know that ye would never betray yer vows to me. In thoughts or deeds."

Malcolm swallowed hard, humbled by her trust. She was a woman who could match wits with him as an equal and fire his blood like a courtesan. There were times he was astonished at his sense of fulfillment, hardly believing that he had been so lucky to win her love.

They belonged to each other for however long fate would allow. Holding Joan close, he knew that he had achieved his dream to marry a woman of spirit and courage. Their life together would never be dull or tepid, staid or ordinary, and that was exactly what he had always wanted.

He had earned Joan's trust and love and together they held what Malcolm desired most—the promise of tomorrow.

# Epilogue

*Six months later*

The great hall was slowly filling with hungry clan members gathering for the evening meal. The hum of pleasant conversation hovered in the room, mingling with the greetings Joan spoke as she walked among them.

The embers of the banked fire glowed while servants scuttled about, bringing out platters of hot food. One of the serving girls hurried past Joan with a tray of freshly baked bread, and Joan's stomach suddenly rebelled at the thick smell of hot yeast.

She turned and raced to the door, her breath coming in short, steady pants. She burst into the bailey, slumping against the wall as her belly rolled and pitched. Streaks of light from the setting sun painted the sky a brilliant mix of gold, orange, and red, and the brisk winds of late autumn howled around her.

Joan turned her face upward, closed her eyes, and let the breeze blow over her, glad of the refreshing cold.

Movement stirred around her, yet Joan did not have to open her eyes to know that Malcolm drew near. The fatigue and strain she felt disappeared the moment he placed a comforting hand upon her shoulder.

"Are ye all right?" he asked.

"I've managed to prevent myself from throwing up all over my boots," Joan replied. "A small victory."

Malcolm's eyes filled with worry. "The sickness still plagues ye? I thought by this time it would pass."

"So did I." Joan sighed. "This is far worse than when I carried Callum. That must mean the babe will be a lass."

Joan leaned against him, nestling close to his chest. Malcolm's hand slid off her shoulder to her stomach. He ran his hand soothingly over her slightly rounded belly. "Is there naught ye can take to ease the discomfort?"

Joan shook her head. "Nothing seems to help. I nibble on dry oatcakes, but they dinnae stay down fer long. I drink chamomile tea with a spoonful of honey and it soon reappears. I even tried one of yer mother's brews yesterday."

"Och, ye must be desperate to allow Mother to tend to ye." He placed a gentle kiss on her brow. "It pains me to watch ye suffer."

Laughter bubbled up her throat and she let out a chuckle. "This is easy compared to labor. And far more quiet."

His expression grew solemn. "I fear I shall go mad with worry when the time comes for ye to bring our bairn into the world."

Joan ran her fingers lightly over his furrowed brow. "Once my pains begin, I shall charge yer father with keeping ye drunk as a lord until our little one makes an appearance."

He smiled, as she intended. "I'm not the only one anxious for the babe to arrive," he said. "Lileas can barely contain her excitement."

"Aye. Ever since she heard, she asks me each morning

if today will be the day she gets to hold her new brother or sister."

"Och, 'tis going to be a long winter." Malcolm dragged his fingers through his hair. "I'll speak with her."

"Nay, I dinnae mind her questions. It shows how much she cares."

Malcolm groaned. "Lileas's passion over the things she cares about is going to be the death of me. Of us. She is still complaining about not being allowed to go with my mother when Davina gave birth to her son a few months ago. And I heard there was another incident in the stables this morning."

Joan waved her hand dismissively. "'Twas a minor mishap. I thought Mistress Innes was going to accompany the children to the stables for their morning ride and she thought I was going to do it."

"And when neither of you did, Lileas went on her own, taking Callum with her." Malcolm shook his head. "Will she ever learn to obey?"

"'Tis true that Lileas knows full well she should not have gone without me or Mistress Innes. However, she dinnae go near any of the other horses. She saddled both her pony and Callum's, but waited fer me to arrive before mounting. And she very proudly told me that she would never ride through the gates unless she had permission and a proper escort."

Malcolm sighed. "I suppose for Lileas that shows a great deal of restraint."

"It does. She is much improved," Joan insisted.

Malcolm's face creased into a puzzled frown. "Now I know the world has shifted when ye are the one defending Lileas's behavior."

"Lileas is learning the virtue of patience."

"Why does that not reassure me, wife?"

Their shared laughter filtered through the bailey. The merriment even helped to distract Joan from her queasy stomach. And the tenderness in Malcolm's eyes made her feel safe and cherished. She leaned against him for a moment and soaked in his strength.

Saints above, she loved this man. He had become the center of her world and in moments such as this she felt awash in happiness.

That he had chosen her was a gift of fate, that he had been so determined to win her trust and love, a miracle. One that she would be thankful for each and every day, for the rest of her life.

Despite the uncomfortable rumblings that persisted in her abdomen, Joan found herself smiling again. She tipped her chin and their mouths met in a deep, lingering kiss.

"The color is slowly returning to yer cheeks," Malcolm said, nipping playfully at the tip of her nose. "Do ye feel any better?"

She pulled back and looked up at him. "'Tis yer bold kisses warming me from the inside."

He grinned wolfishly and her heart melted anew. The emptiness that had dwelled inside her for so long was finally banished, replaced by the power of Malcolm's love.

Of the many blessings Joan was privileged to receive, that was by far the most miraculous, and she vowed to cherish it always.